D0961273

ALSO BY JUDY BLUNDELL

What I Saw and How I Lied

Strings Attached

The

High Season

The
High
Season

A NOVEL

JUDY BLUNDELL

RANDOM HOUSE

New York

The High Season is a work of fiction. Names, characters, places, and incidents are the products of the author's imagination or are used fictitiously. Any resemblance to actual events, locales, or persons, living or dead, is entirely coincidental.

Copyright © 2018 by Judy Blundell

All rights reserved.

Published in the United States by Random House, an imprint and division of Penguin Random House LLC, New York.

RANDOM HOUSE and the HOUSE colophon are registered trademarks of Penguin Random House LLC.

LIBRARY OF CONGRESS CATALOGING-IN-PUBLICATION DATA
Names: Blundell, Judy, author.
Title: The high season : a novel / Judy Blundell.
Description: New York : Random House, 2018.
Identifiers: LCCN 2017037646| ISBN 9780525508717 (hardback) |
ISBN 9780525508724 (ebook)
Subjects: | BISAC: FICTION / Contemporary Women. | FICTION / Family Life. |
FICTION / Literary.
Classification: LCC PS3602.L883 H54 2018 | DDC 813/.6—dc23 LC record available
at https://lccn.loc.gov/2017037646

International edition ISBN: 9780525511700

Printed in the United States of America on acid-free paper

randomhousebooks.com

2 4 6 8 9 7 5 3 1

First Edition

Book design by Debbie Glasserman

THIS BOOK IS DEDICATED TO NEIL WATSON

Life being what it is, one dreams of revenge.

—PAUL GAUGUIN

Memorial
Day

1

EVERY SUMMER RUTHIE gave away her house by the sea. During
the month of May, she packed and polished. Sneakers were
scooped up from their kicked-off positions. Earrings, loose
change, buttons were swept off the tops of bureaus. Post-its with
phone numbers marooned from their meaning had been thrown
away, anything threadbare or worn dumped into one of the summer boxes and sealed with squealing tape. T-shirts had been
whisked off the hooks on the backs of bathroom doors, and fra-
grant chunks of Provençal soaps nestled in blue-and-white bowls
by the sinks.

Ruthie knew how to create a house that looked lived-in, but
lightly. When her summer tenants walked through the door, they
breathed in peace and lemons. In this house no one ever had a
sleepless night. No child slammed a door, screaming of injustice.
No one was ever sick, or sorrowful, or more than pleasantly tired.
Summer was a forever season, and held no pain.

With a fistful of yesterday's news, she polished the picture window, spotless enough to slam into and raise a bruise. Now she had
a better view of her daughter slacking off. In the yard Jem was

doing what teenagers do, texting while doing a chore in a half-hearted fashion, loading gear into the truck bed with one hand while her thumb jitterbugged on a screen.

It was the first big weekend of summer, and winter's trap had sprung. All along the hundred miles of Long Island, from Manhattan to the East End, skeins of highway were traffic-snarled by eight in the morning. On the North Fork families were spilling out, stretching and inhaling after the dawn ride from Manhattan, parents having bawled at their children, still thickheaded with dreams, to pull on shorts and get the hell in the car. Barbecues were rolled out from the garage, convertible tops folded down, beach chairs snapped to.

High above the creeping cars, helicopter blades purled the air as they carried the rich and the lucky to the Hamptons on the South Fork. At the airport drivers waited by dark-windowed SUVs, patiently sipping coffee. Shopkeepers checked inventory on summer-weight cashmere. House managers reviewed details of schedules and flower deliveries to the vast homes behind the hedges.

Ruthie's renter would arrive at noon. Adeline Clay had paid like a rich person, taking the Beamish-Dutton house for the entire season, and the whopping check was sitting in the bank. By Thanksgiving the money would have disappeared, distributed to various wheezing accounts: the college fund, the taxes due, the unseen needed repairs. But right now Ruthie felt pleasantly, if temporarily, solvent, her feet on a wide-planked floor rubbed with beeswax, the sky bouncing light off the sea. There were a few details left to take care of: one more swipe of the counters, local honey and flowers from the garden to welcome the tenant, a final sweep, and then skedaddling off into their own summer in a rented guesthouse.

"The summer bummer," Jem called it, because giving up the house in the best months of the year was the only way to keep it.

Ruthie's phone vibrated in her pocket. A text from her board president, Mindy Flicker. Mindy had left her Park Avenue apartment earlier in the week to beat the traffic. Ruthie's phone had been pinging with texts for days. Mindy might not have known what she was talking about, but she was firmly committed to conveying it as often as possible.

> IDEA! A bouquet would be super to welcome Adeline Clay

> . . .

> W a card saying it's from the Belfry. Do you have a card? I could drop one off.

> I buy them in bulk.

Mike came up behind her as she texted *All taken care of.* As the director of the Belfry Museum, she knew that wealthy board ladies were part of the job. Cosseted as children, driven hard as young women, married off to suitably successful and politically like-minded men, tightly surgeried and whittled down to bone, they could be fierce and admirable or simply awful. Mindy was the latter. She had joined the board three years ago with an excess of sebum and verbiage, and with a combination of big money and a perfect attendance record at meetings, she'd taken over as board president only a year before. Since then, Ruthie's once pleasant and busy job had turned into a constant battle to deflect Mindy's more idiotic ideas while flattering her verve. It would be a summer of too many meetings, of texts and surprise visits and hair twirls accompanied by *Wouldn't it be interesting if we . . .*

"Mindy," she said to Mike.

"Can't you just ignore her?"

"Would you be able to ignore a hyena gnawing on a kidney?"

"Ow." He put his hands on her shoulders. Once, she would have leaned back against him. "Hey. You did it. The place looks great."

"World's perfect," Ruthie agreed. "Wait. The porch. Did you fix the second step?"

"Ruthie." The hands dropped.

Even in his weariness, in his mustard-colored T-shirt with the hole near the collar, he had allure. Forty-eight and he looked like a surfer. She was three years younger and looked like his grandmother. Teenage carelessness regarding sunscreen had taken its toll. Skin elasticity was beginning to break down. Middle age had settled into her laugh lines. Any moment now she'd be initiated into the feminine mysteries of the chin wax.

"Do we have time for coffee?"

"We can't make coffee. The kitchen is clean."

"She won't be here for three hours."

"Don't bother, Daddy," Jem said, stuffing shirts into a duffel as she walked. "God forbid we do some actual living in this house. For the past month I've had to eat my muffin on the porch."

"What say we finish loading the truck!" Ruthie suggested in what Jem called her "me-hearties" voice.

Jem settled the duffel on one shoulder and picked up a canvas tote stuffed with last-minute items—books, soap, sandals, a rolled-up pair of shorts, a box of linguine. She'd worn the same aggrieved expression all morning. It was an old fight; at fifteen, Jem had long passed the age where Mike and Ruthie could make a game out of packing up her room to make way for strangers who would eat off her plates and swim off her beach. It was no longer an adventure to stay in a borrowed trailer at a campground, or flop in a garage apartment. Jem was old enough now to realize that a sofa bed was no lark to sleep on.

They watched her go, blond braid swishing, flip-flops snapping a rebuke.

"We had a fight this morning over the bleach," Ruthie said as soon as the screen door banged. "She promised me she'd help me do the last-minute clean, and she tried to wriggle out of it. Meret wanted her to get a hot wax pedicure."

"What's that?"

"Seventy-five dollars."

"Meret," Mike muttered. "A fur cup of trouble."

"A fur cup with toenails." Jem's lovely best friend Olivia had moved away a year ago, and Ruthie still bemoaned the day Meret Bell had stopped by Jem's table in the cafeteria and said, "I like your hair that way."

"She'll be okay," Mike said, watching through the screen as Jem leaned against his pickup, texting furiously. Boxes and suitcases and a broken chair surrounded her in Joad-like fashion. "She's going through a girly stage."

"She's not going through a girly stage, she's a *girl*. She's a girl who thinks she's a woman."

"Didn't Gary Puckett and the Union Gap sing that?"

"You know, it would make me so happy if you'd worry with me."

Mike sock-skated across the wood floor, heading for his shoes on the porch.

"Sweetie, give me something worthy to worry about, and I can worry with the best of them. I can't worry about a pedicure. Whereas you like to exist in a fog of general anxiety. Probably why we're incompatible. Irreconcilable worry patterns."

"Reason number three hundred and thirty-seven," Ruthie said, following him to the door. It was an old joke. "Can you pick up Jem after work today? I've got Spork prep, and it's going to be crazy."

"Sure."

"And you're not allowed to call me sweetie, remember?"

"Ah, Rules for a Good Divorce. Thank God you remember them or we'd be in worse trouble."

"Hey. They were just suggestions."

"You emailed me a list. There were *asterisks*." Mike stood at the screen door. Dodge, the artist who lived down the road in the summers, honked and waved from his yellow convertible, yelling something as he went by, most likely "Cocktails!" All summer they would promise to have cocktails together and never do it. Dodge was the new breed of summer renter in Orient; he had a social calendar.

"Every year we watch them come back," Mike continued, waving at Dodge. "Every year we give up our house. How long can we do this, anyway?"

"Do what?"

"This," Mike said. "Live next to things we can never have. It gets worse every year. Did you see the house they're renovating over on Orchard? Dave said there's a home gym and a lap pool. A home gym! It's a death knell, I'm telling you."

He gazed out at the bay, a powdery blue today, with a scattering of white sails skittering toward Bug Light. A rainstorm the night before had failed to clear the humidity, and the world had summery blurred edges. "We wouldn't have to uproot Jem every summer if we sold it. And we'd have money. We've got to be at the top of the market right now."

When they'd sat down to discuss the divorce three years before, child custody had been decided in an exchange of less than ten words (*And Jem? We just have to . . . Of course.*)—but the house, ah, the house. Marital vows they could abandon, but a shingled house with a water view in an escalating market? They had put everything into the house, they had borrowed and scraped in order to renovate it. It was their version of a hedge fund, held against disaster and college tuition. If everything fell apart, they said, *they could sell the house.*

Divorce papers were inevitable, but it became an item on an ever-growing to-do list that could have been titled "Things to Ignore for Now." Divorce needed attorneys and turned amicable separations into expensive fights. They decided, for now, to treat divorce as a state of mind rather than polity. Yes, they were divorced. No, the state of New York didn't know it yet.

So Ruthie stayed in the house with Jem. Mike had moved into an apartment in the bigger village of Greenport, a few blocks from the hardware store, which was at least handy for a carpenter.

Her phone vibrated again. Mindy, no doubt. She ignored it.

"We should move to Vermont, or Nova Scotia," Mike said.

"To the real country. Where hot wax is on a candle where it belongs, not on your daughter's toes. Where people think Pilates is next to the Big Dipper. Where they've never heard of kale chips."

"Are we moving to Vermont or 1910?"

"Our town is a barnyard full of hammers and nails," Mike said. "You can't walk down a block without hearing a buzz saw. And the storms get worse every year—another Hurricane Sandy moves a degree to the east and we're finished. How can you time a last chance except by taking it? This could be the moment to cash out."

"We don't have enough equity yet," Ruthie said. "We're still paying off the loan for the master suite."

He pressed his lips together the way he always did when she brought up financial reality. He'd grown up as a Dutton, with streets named after his family in Connecticut towns. The fact that his father had run through the money by the time he was twenty should have made him practical, but it only made him less inclined to hear facts.

"She has two years of high school left," she said. "After that . . ." After that, what? The ellipsis defined the sentence. She didn't know.

The problem was, she thought they were lucky, and he did not. For Mike, losing the house for three months canceled out having it for nine. For her, it guaranteed it.

This was what she'd never had and what she always craved. *Home,* she thought. *This.* Even if she had to leave it in order to afford it, it was hers. This lovely, perfect village, neighbors who knew her, the bluest hydrangeas, the best view on the North Fork. *This!*

The only thing she missed, she thought, gazing at Mike's profile, was *that.*

"Now Jem's in that rotten crowd, with the pedicures and the purses and you have to wear pajama pants on Thursdays or you can't sit at the table at lunch . . ." Mike shook his head. "Remember that argument when you bought her the wrong slippers? Like you'd *stabbed* her. We're losing her."

"Of course we're losing her. She's a teenager. And we broke up. Don't you think it's sort of ludicrous for us to leave town together?"

Mike grinned. "Hey. We're divorced, but we're family."

A spark ignited in that tinderbox that was Ruthie's heart. It continually infuriated her that Mike was so adept at disarming her.

Which could be reason number two for why they were apart.

Reason number one? He'd decided that he wasn't in love anymore. ("I don't need a *pal*," he'd said to her. "I need a *destiny*.")

"We struggle so much just to keep it all going," Mike said. "We're still not happy."

"That's why you left, so that we'd all be happy. Remember?"

"Yeah," said Mike. "Look . . ."

A helicopter passed overhead, not loud enough to drown his voice, but he stopped.

So she obeyed him. She looked. The way he stood, half turned toward her, his hand flat against the screen door, ready to push. A man always half on his way out a door.

"Have dinner with me tomorrow? So we can talk?"

"Talk about . . ."

"I don't know, a rethink. Really talk."

The world shut down into quiet. There was something in his face she hadn't seen in a long time. He was really looking at her, for one thing. So much of the end of a marriage was exchanging information without eye contact. "I've got Spork tomorrow."

"It's over at five. After we can go to the Drift."

The Spindrift was the place they jokingly referred to as "the bad news bar," a local dive where once they had commiserated about disasters over drafts of beer and free hard-boiled eggs and peanuts. Sometimes that was dinner. Tim would slide the jar of mustard down the length of the bar and Mike would catch it in one hand. Outside light would be falling, Jem would be at a friend's, the twilight would last forever, their kisses would taste of hops and yolk.

"Sure." *The bar is not a signifier,* she told herself. *It's just a bar.*

Sound rushed in. Tires crunching over gravel. Adeline Clay swung down the driveway in her Range Rover, three hours early.

2

IF ONE END of Long Island was a fish mouth ready to chomp on the barb of Manhattan, the tail fin was the East End, split down the middle with Shelter Island between the two. Let the billionaires have the Hamptons on the South Fork, with the shops and restaurants and parties that re-created what made them so exquisitely comfy in Manhattan. The North Fork was two ferry rides away, and it showed. It was farm stands on actual farms. It was pies and parades and stony beaches that hurt your feet, banging screen doors and peaches eaten over the sink. Orient was the morsel at the end of the fork, the village clinging to the narrowest ribbon of land, where light bounced from bay to sound and the air was seasoned with salt.

Summer was the crucial season, when the population bloomed and the streets came to life with bikes and dogs and city cars. There were no famous faces in Orient, only famous résumés. There was one country store with world-class baked goods, the yacht club was a former potato shack on a wharf, the dress code was old sneakers. Transportation was bicycles, no helmets needed, just like the old days. But all that shabby hid a secret life of the moneyed, serious cultural class. In the summers there were writers and publishers, artists and gallerists; there was a sizable-for-a-hamlet lesbian population and a smattering of architects. When a lesbian architect rented their house for two weeks last August, Mike had called it the Orient Apotheosis.

Ruthie had been surprised last November when Dodge had called from the city, saying that Adeline Clay was looking to rent in Orient for the season. Usually they cobbled together summer rentals in two-week increments. It seemed a watershed kind of change, someone that glam leaving the Hamptons for the North Fork. Not only was Adeline rich, she was *visible,* well known as one of New York's most stylish older women, photographed at openings and benefits, all the places rich and famous people posed in front of logo-scattered backdrops together.

Ruthie and Mike had speculated endlessly about why Adeline would be interested in the amount of downscale their house represented—money problems? facelift recovery?—but in the end when the check came they celebrated with bottles of beer on the deck. Bundled up in down jackets and scarves, they clicked their Rolling Rock bottle necks to toast summer and another year of solvency. Inch by inch, they would pay back the bank loans and launch Jem into the world. Adeline Clay was the gateway to the now impossible American dream: a college education without debt, a comfortable retirement, an edge.

ADELINE WORE A delicate blue-and-white-striped shirt with rippling oversized ruffles down the front, white jeans, sandals, and enormous sunglasses. Impossibly thin, she resembled a well-tailored dragonfly. A purse the size of a small suitcase hung on her forearm. Her highlighted hair was short and cut cleverly around her head. Her outfit whispered, *I am rich, and this is appropriate summer attire, because this is as beachy as I am willing to get.*

From the passenger side a young man slithered out, one tennis-shoed foot at a time. He dislodged a paper napkin from the seat, and it pirouetted prettily on the breeze, fluttering like a heraldic flag. He did not stoop to pick it up.

Ruthie thought of two words she never used. The first was *lithe*. The second was *louche*. This must be Adeline's stepson, Lucas Clay. She'd last seen him when he was a toddler, when she'd worked for his father. He must be about twenty-two or -three now. And every inch beautiful: wheat-colored hair, broad chest, narrow waist. Even from here she could tell he'd inherited his father's startling light-blue eyes, the ones that photographed almost white.

Jem looked up from her phone, then down again quickly, her cheeks flushing, as Lucas shot her a tilted, lazy smile.

Ruthie noticed she was still clutching the bag of garbage. She dropped it off the side of the porch in what she hoped was a surreptitious move.

"I'm at the end of the world!" Adeline called.

Ruthie had met Adeline twenty years before, when Ruthie had been studio manager for the legendary artist Peter Clay, one of a few male painters whose work was often described by (mostly male) critics as "seminal." One night in Tribeca the studio assistants had all gone out for drinks with Peter and the blonde who had broken up his marriage. At first Ruthie hadn't thought Adeline was beautiful, but by the end of the evening she'd realized that none of them could stop staring at her face.

Adeline had been in her thirties then, Ruthie knew. Peter was in his sixties, into his second marriage, and with a toddler. As his studio assistant Ruthie knew firsthand that he'd never been faithful to his first wife, or his second—the breadth of his cheating had been legendary—but he had fallen hard for Adeline and they had stayed married until his death on 9/11. Not in the towers or on a plane, but in an emergency room, of cardiac arrest. For a famous person, it was not a good day to die. For the next year, people would say, "Oh, he's dead?" No one had time to mourn the passing of the merely famous on that day. It was the one day in America that only ordinary lives counted.

It could be said that Adeline Clay had been unlucky in marriage (if being married to a world-famous narcissistic genius could be classified as unlucky), but lucky in widowhood. Peter had left her wealthy, but as his reputation continued to increase (cited as one of the top five influences on young artists, even now) and her own management skills improved, she had grown even richer, forming the Peter Clay Foundation and becoming a powerful force in the art world.

Most people are awkward when approaching someone from a distance. They quicken their pace, or pretend to check their watch or their phone. Adeline took her time, her gaze roaming over the façade of the house, most likely noting every flaw.

Ruthie imagined how she would have handled the same maneuver. Most likely she would have waved when she got out of the car, then immediately regretted it and felt foolishly overeager. She would have quickened her step, then tripped on a flagstone. She would have made a funny face. By the time she'd reached the porch, she would have defined herself as an overly apologetic, frantic lunatic.

Ruthie knew that Adeline, like her, must have inhaled paint fumes in downtown lofts, drunk too much wine, gulped down truck exhaust on Canal Street. She was at least ten years older; how did she manage to look younger than Ruthie? As a museum director Ruthie spent most of her time knocking on the doors of the privileged, looking for funding. She was familiar with various forms of surgical help. But Adeline's face didn't look yanked and manipulated to approximate a younger human. The work had been done skillfully, as though with nail scissors. She resembled a twig-sized ballerina twirling in a jewelry box, lit by soft light and pink satin, breasts little plastic bumps.

"Sorry about arriving so early. We hitchhiked a ride on a bird to East Hampton with a friend. I had the car brought there, and I just hopped over on those two adorable little ferries. It reminded me of Greece!"

"It's not a problem," Ruthie lied. "We were just leaving." Summer renters usually didn't want the whiff of owner around, let alone coffee. A note explaining about garbage and recycling, beach chairs and parking permits, a drawer full of restaurant menus—that was all the greeting renters desired.

"Would you have time to show me the house before you go?" Adeline pushed her sunglasses up into her hair. Her eyes were an unclouded green, her eyebrows perfect. "Lucas, do you want to see the house?"

Texting, he waved a hand that must have meant, *No, go ahead,* because Adeline lifted her shoulders and started up the stairs. She tripped over the loose board on the second step, then frowned down at the chipped polish on a toenail. Ruthie felt the mood tilt into frost.

"Don't panic. Lucky for you, I'm a carpenter." Mike crouched down and inspected the board. "Needs to be fixed." Then he looked up and smiled.

"Ah," Adeline said, "so you're one of those astute carpenters I hear about."

"That's right," Mike said, standing. "And if you wait a sec, I'll identify a hammer and a nail."

They smiled at each other, and, just like that, Adeline's ice melted away. Mike had that effect on women. There might as well be a puddle on the floor, but Ruthie would be the one to clean it up.

"Won't take long," he said. "I can come out later today, or I can let you have the long weekend to settle in and come out on Tuesday."

She waved in the general direction of her Range Rover. "I was so happy to avoid the expressway. I get so nervous in traffic. I grew up in California, you'd think I wouldn't be intimidated by a few cars. But I've lived in New York so long I've forgotten how to drive."

That night in the bar—Peter had called Adeline *my farmer's daughter.* His arm slung around her neck, his face telegraphing the fact that he was besotted. Ruthie had been in her mid-twenties then, and had thought, *Ew.* She'd been repelled by the sight of

Peter's paint-stained, veiny hand on the smooth skin of Adeline's shoulder. She'd assumed that Adeline didn't love him, that she was playing the Manhattan game of advancement by seducing a rich and famous man. Adeline had been a waitress at Lucky Strike in SoHo, one of the beautiful young women who took your order in thin T-shirts with the sleeves rolled to reveal their tiny, tight biceps. That night Ruthie had wished Peter's morning breath on Adeline; she'd smelled it often enough.

But Adeline was talking, and Mike was listening. "All this week I've been dreaming of the Long Island Expressway. You know those landscaping trucks with a chain on the back that's supposed to hold all that lawn equipment in? I kept seeing a lawnmower crash through my windshield."

"I know how it is," Mike said, even though Ruthie knew he didn't. Only women were afraid of highways and lawnmowers. He stood like a doorman, holding the screen door ajar, and smiling at Adeline.

"I hate driving to Manhattan," Ruthie volunteered. "Once I ended up in New Jersey by mistake. Went right over the George Washington Bridge."

That was usually the signal for Mike to complete the story, how she'd called him in tears from Hackensack. It had been a dinner party staple for years. "Well, you made it," Mike said to Adeline.

"It feels like you're at the very edge of things here," Adeline said. She stopped short as they walked inside. "Yes," she murmured. She toured the room, trailing her hand on a sofa, stopping at the view. "You can't see another house. And the plantings!"

"Catnip," Mike said. "Yarrow."

"I knew when I saw the photos. I knew I could live here. I love your taste. It's just the right mix of sophistication and quirk."

Adeline Clay, whose Manhattan apartment had been showcased in *Architectural Digest*, was a fan of her quirk.

"The house was built in stages," Mike explained as they toured the kitchen with nods from Adeline and "Only four burners?"

when she saw the stove. "The original structure was built in, we think, the 1780s. That little office off the kitchen was once a birthing room."

"Really."

"I inherited it from my great-aunt Laurel."

Ruthie felt a slight sting. Mike had always said *we* inherited it. When did it become *I*? At this point, the house was so leveraged and mortgaged that it was joint property.

"Let's just say it was in a state of extravagant deterioration. We did most of the work ourselves. Put in the laundry room, all-new bathrooms, bumped out the back."

"You should see me with a sledgehammer," Ruthie said.

Adeline approved of the guest suite downstairs, perfect for Lucas, who had just graduated from Brown and was working at the Clay Foundation that summer. He'd be coming out on weekends. Upstairs she poked her head into the smaller of the guest bedrooms. "If you knocked down this wall, this could be a dressing room for the master."

"Terrific idea," Ruthie said, thinking, *A dressing room?*

Adeline stopped in front of one of Mike's paintings, hung in the hallway, a black-and-white abstract not typical of his work. Mike was a colorist. "Oh, I like this very much. Who's the artist?"

"That would be me," Mike said.

Adeline swiveled and regarded him, then looked at the painting again, as though comparing the two. "I'm sorry, I didn't realize you were a painter."

"Seems like the rest of the world feels the same," Mike said.

"Let me show you the laundry." Ruthie turned the corner into the stairwell. She waited for them on the stairs, trying to follow the murmured conversation, but the overheard word "transactional" propelled her the rest of the way downstairs to check her emails. It was going to be a long day. Spork was the first summer fundraiser for the museum, and she had a million details to take care of.

A text twinkled in from the vice president of the board, Carole Berlinger. *Can you come out later this afternoon? Deets for the house plus a chat. 3pm?* Carole would also be her landlord for the summer. She'd offered her guesthouse to Ruthie for a discounted rent. For once, Ruthie and Jem would have a luxe summer rental. The "plus a chat" was mildly worrying. Chats, for Carole, always seemed to involve the latest Mindy maneuver.

She texted back *Sure* just as Mike and Adeline came downstairs. "Lucas is a bit put out that I didn't take a place in the Hamptons," Adeline was saying. "That's where his crowd is. Orient is a little too slow for him."

"We pride ourselves on that particular quality," Mike said. "We take our time."

"Well, that's what I prefer, but . . . I think it will be good for him. He likes a scene. He's decided he wants to be an actor." Adeline gave a little laugh. "Don't they all."

"We can give you quiet if you want it," Ruthie said. "But there are some events you might enjoy. Lots of artists, dealers, architects . . . of course you know Dodge. He's right down the road. Everyone basically is right down the road. The Belfry picnic is tomorrow, everybody goes. The official name is Summer Fork, but we all just call it Spork."

"The Belfry . . ."

"The Belfry Museum—I'm the director. You drove by it on Main Road, right before the turnoff into the village. The white building with the barn in back."

"Oh! I think you told me, didn't you. Must be fun to run a little museum."

"We're small but scrappy."

"Frankly I came out here to avoid as much as I can," Adeline said.

"Well, if you change your mind, just drop in. I left a couple of tickets for you in the kitchen." As the director of a nonprofit, Ruthie knew how to go a half step beyond politesse without venturing into pushiness. "Is there anything else you'd like to know?" she asked. "My brain is a colander. I forget everything. I tell myself it's either hormones or a tumor."

Adeline didn't smile; she looked concerned, as though she were casting about for the name of a good specialist. *Please like me,* Ruthie thought desperately.

Adeline crossed to the window and looked out at the sea. "It's like I've stowed away on a ship. I can be myself here. In the Hamptons, *summer vacation* is an oxymoron."

Ruthie was confused for a moment. Her hesitation was part surprise that Adeline had made a joke, and part relief that Adeline had not just called her a moron. Then Ruthie was afraid that Adeline thought she didn't get her joke. She wondered how she could work *oxymoron* into a sentence again, just to prove she knew what it meant.

Adeline moved a bowl just a quarter inch to the right, then placed her hand on a chair in a proprietary way, her fingers stroking the back. Ruthie felt a sudden, sharp irritation. *Stop caressing my wood,* she wanted to say.

"It's just adorable," Adeline said. "This is such a delightful surprise."

"In my life, that's always an oxymoron," Ruthie said, and wanted to kick herself.

3

JEM'S PHONE

From: Jemma Dutton

To: Meret Bell, Saffy Rubner, Kate Summerhall

Momsta said no to pedicure r u still heading to spa? Meet up later?

Helloooooooooo, my day sucks

. . .

there is the hottest guy I've ever seen in my driveway right now no joke

. . .

He is amazing I think I can't breathe

. . .

OMG just looked him up on Instagram check it out @LucasClayNation

From: Lucas Clay
To: Jemma Dutton

Thx for your number landlord

From: Jemma Dutton
To: Lucas Clay

Technically I'm not your landlord my parents are

From: Lucas
To: Jem

But can I call you if there's a leak I might need help

From: Jem
To: Lucas

Try a plumber dude

From: Lucas
To: Jem

Harsh

What's there to do here anyway maybe you can show me where the action is

From: Jem
To: Lucas

No action Orient is all about the chill

From: Lucas
To: Jem

I don't do chill

4

FIRST, DOE POSTED the juiciest portion of the Gus Romany video on the Belfry Instagram account. Then she turned to her anonymous account *seekrit-hamptons* and posted the Daniel Mantis photograph (hashtag #justgoodfriends). Most important tasks of the day accomplished in ten seconds. Good omen. Then a bird flew into the sliding glass door. *Crack*. The small body lay on the concrete.

She took a moment to grip the edge of the table. Then she walked over and eased open the door. A tiny shudder went through the bird.

"Aw, fuckit," Doe said. "Really?"

She looked into its shark eye. Anger made her hands shake.

"You idiot bird," she told it. "Like you've never seen a window before?"

What kind of bird was it? If it were a seagull, she could enjoy its misery, considering how many fries she'd lost to them. But this bird was small and brown. Maybe a sparrow? What did she know about birds except they sang?

Doe could stand just about anything. Except the suffering of the stupid.

"Shit." Doe picked up one of the beach rocks that lined the path to the main house.

"I'm sorry," she said before she dropped the rock on the bird's head.

When she looked up, she saw her landlord's five-year-old twins, Shannon and Shawn, staring at her, their mouths open so far she could see half-chewed cereal. Fifteen-year-old Annie stood behind them, her eyes shining with female-role-model worship.

"You are such a badass!" Annie called.

"*Mom!*" the kids screamed.

THE DAY HAD kicked off with an early-morning walk with her boss. So right away, morning ruined. Catha Lugner had asked her to meet at 7:30 A.M., a really inappropriate request. When she was at work, she worked. Was she supposed to walk whenever Catha wanted her to? She spent eight hours a day at the museum with Catha leaning over her computer, breathing chai fumes and asking what she was working on, or leaving an article about social media from, like, a *newspaper* on her desk with a sticky note saying, *This is right in your swim lane; let's put a pin in it!* There was a reason everybody loved Ruthie and nobody liked Catha. A person who could put a semicolon on a Post-it was just advertising her smug self.

On the walk it all became clear. Catha had asked her to deliver a basket from Locavoracious in Greenport, leaving it on Ruthie's porch for Adeline Clay *that very morning,* as though it weren't Memorial Day weekend and as though you weren't supposed to order ahead. Catha had just said, "I totally trust in your ability to facilitate this."

Here was the thing: Doe had to make sure Ruthie wasn't there when she delivered it "because we don't want to bother Ruthie on move-out day." She had also asked her to post that Romany video to Instagram and told her not to ask Ruthie about it: "Just go ahead, initiative is part of your job description!" Then she told Doe that she was doing an excellent job and Catha had her eye on her. "I set a high bar with my compliments," she'd said, fixing Doe with her scary tiny eyes, the gaze that nailed itself to your spine. This was her way of letting Doe know that even a compliment was secretly about her own superior standards to the rest of the sorry world.

This would all be perfectly fine, because work sucked no matter where you worked, but Doe had a feeling that it was all bullshit. Catha was doing some down-and-dirty dancing around the board, trying to maneuver herself into Ruthie's job.

Doe had a work philosophy, and it was this: Don't shovel bullshit if you're not a farmer. It was actually a saying of her mother's. Which meant it was illogical and stupid, but sort of worked occasionally.

After the walk Doe had gone straight to Locavoracious and knocked hard on the door until the owner opened it. Doe had to basically beg her to assemble a basket, but it wasn't until she dropped Adeline Clay's name that the door opened wide. She was even offered coffee.

The basket now sat on her kitchen counter. She slipped out the note Catha had given her to tuck inside. Written across the top in puce block type was CATHA SHAND-LUGNER.

Welcome Adeline!

It's Catha Shand-Lugner, Deputy Director of the Belfry Museum. I just wanted to welcome you to Orient on behalf of the Belfry! Hope you enjoy the (organic) goodies!

CSL

PS. I'm enclosing an invite to our annual welcome-to-summer party, Spork. It's a fun event and a great way to meet fellow Orient-ers! Hope to see you there!

So much wrong in so little space. Just the word *goodies* alone . . .

She grabbed the basket and headed out to her car. Her landlord Tim was in the yard, balancing a mug of coffee and his keys. He frowned when he saw her, and her pulse did a little jump. She smiled and waved as she crossed to her car, giving him all the teeth she could.

"It was a mercy killing!" she called. "Promise!"

"Huh?"

Shit, he didn't know. "I'm heading out," she said. "Do you need me to pick up Annie at the farm stand later? I know it's her first day!"

Keep moving as you toss out the offer. Keep smiling. With every encounter she worried that Tim or Kim would start the ball rolling. *Doe, have you found a place, it's almost June, summer and all, and you're on winter rates . . .* so these days she had perfected the art of Conversing While Walking Away. Their garage apartment was the cheapest she'd been able to find, and if they kicked her out she'd need to answer "roommate wanted" ads, which was unthinkable, or live in her car, which she'd promised herself she would never, ever do again.

She could tell by the way Tim crinkled his eyes and rocked back on his heels that her question annoyed him as much as it tempted him. When she'd first moved into their rental, Kim and Tim Doyle had gladly taken all her offers to run errands, do chores, and babysit the twins. Kim had left the back door open so that Doe could come in without knocking. Soon Doe was doing things like emptying the dishwasher or setting hamburger meat out to defrost. Doe still remembered the dinner when Kim had taken the last brownie and said, "I know this is rude but you're family, so there."

She was *family*. She knew Kim hated her sister, she knew Annie was having a hard time at school, she knew where the green glass pickle dish went.

Since Easter, Kim had cooled. The back door stayed shut. She hadn't asked her to babysit in weeks. Doe knew how to sidle herself into friendship, how to be cheerful and available and helpful and see what the person or the family needed and supply it. The flaw was, she never knew when or why people started to turn.

"No, thanks, she has her bike. Doe, we really need to talk. I got your check, but . . . summer rates start in June. You know that."

She couldn't afford summer rates; she could barely afford winter. If she didn't supplement her income with occasional photo sales she wouldn't make it. Museums paid dick.

"I know. I thought maybe you'd give me a pass and I'd double up in August. Summer is when I pick up my extra income."

"Well, sure, Doe, we're not going to put you out on the street." Tim shifted his feet. "I mean . . . but we really need the money. Kim wants to put it on Airbnb."

Yeah. Here was the problem with her world. Everybody always needed the money.

"Oh," she said. "If you could give me another couple of weeks . . ."

"Sure. Anyway," he said, "I get the impression you'll always land on your feet."

Doe clicked her smile into place, but she felt the burn. Senior year of high school, when she'd practically moved into Jassy Chasen's house, tiptoeing barefoot past Mr. and Mrs. Chasen's bedroom and hearing, *Don't you get the sense that she's quite the little operator, though?*

It was weird how the things she did to make herself indispensable ended up making her dispensable. Like eventually she ended up highlighting some dividing line she was trying to cross. The pathetic truth was that she'd loved the Chasens and she loved the Doyles. Doe got crushes on happy families the way other girls got crushes on the bass player.

Tim backed out of the driveway in his truck. He didn't wave goodbye.

Shannon and Shawn appeared out of nowhere like spooky

ghost twins. They swayed side to side, in that creepy twin motion they had. "Mom said the bird was probably stunned," Shannon said.

"She said a bird gets knocked out but then they fly away again," Shawn said.

"There was no pulse," Doe said.

"Birds don't have a pulse."

"Yeah, they do," Doe said. "I know. I trained to be a vet."

This appeared to be something they couldn't fight, so they went away to ask Mom. Doe took the opportunity to get in her car.

She drove the short distance to Ruthie's. Mike's truck was in the driveway as well as a black Range Rover. Doe climbed out of the car and dumped the basket on the porch, but couldn't resist a peek into the window. From this angle she could see into the open kitchen. Adeline Clay leaned against a counter, laughing. Mike stood next to her, holding up a bunch of radishes. Jem cast a quick glance at a barefoot guy in shorts sitting in a chair, his back to Doe. His fingers tapped on a coffee cup. She could read his boredom.

Something about the scene was creepy, like a Gregory Crewdson staged photograph come to life. Almost like a family dynamic, all that emo pulsing around and under the waving radishes. She wished she could snap a photo. Not for Instagram, for herself. Instead she beat it back to her car.

She checked her phone. The Daniel Mantis photo already had thirty-six likes.

Doe had snapped this photograph two weeks before, on a rainy May weekend. Pure luck. She'd first recognized Stephanie Terrell, an anchorwoman on CNN, and then scrutinized the man she was with. He kept his head low, and was wearing a baseball cap. They were under an enormous red umbrella. She'd followed them for several blocks until they lowered the umbrella to duck into Ralph Lauren. Just as he opened the door she got the shot. The glinting silver rain, and Stephanie Terrell putting her hand over his as he held the door . . . Instagram-worthy, right there. Stephanie looked beautiful and windswept, and Daniel looked furtive. Doe had held the photograph until now, Memorial Day weekend, when it would make the biggest splash.

Mantis was known—discreetly—for having two girlfriends at a time. They were always serious women, journalists and UN attachés and businesswomen, and they all knew about one another. This year, one of those women was Adeline Clay.

Summer! When things got hot. Her season.

Mantis was a billionaire, an art collector, a financial raider who did yoga and wrote the bestseller *The Mindful Shark*. He was rumored to be thinking about political office, now that you didn't need experience to run. He was throwing a huge party on Sunday afternoon, which she was planning to crash. Traffic would be road-rage-worthy but it would totally be worth it. Rihanna might be there, and the cream of the Hamptons crowd.

She was sure she'd pick up at least one good shot. She was going for one million followers this summer, minimum.

Her ambition was simple: to become a thing.

She'd pissed off a lot of people last summer, but since the account was anonymous, she could just let it build. It only meant new followers (469,000 and counting!). Beautiful people on their fifth glass of rosé, celebrity couples looking glum for just a moment, the better for gossip blogs to speculate on their "last stages." Last summer the account had jumped by 23,000 after she'd posted the picture of supermodel Polina throwing up on a lawn in Montauk.

She wasn't just snarky. She made the beautiful more beautiful, too. She'd been a photography major, a useless degree unless you decided to treat pictures like nothing, free to the world. The pictures themselves didn't matter, only their ability to generate likes and regrams. She had an eye, and filters, and a killer photo app. Thanks to social media, you could build a whole career on people being judgy.

In the folder of wacky useless advice her mom had given her

there was one bit that spoke to her: *Make your living on the rich.* Other than that, it was *Wax your bush, A backpack is not a purse, Don't expect breakfast with a one-night stand.*

Thanks, Mom.

As if she'd summoned her by negative vibrations, her phone twinkled. It was Shari.

> Did you find out about that spa job got to get out of fla b4 a hurricane blows me away lol
>
> answer your mama doorangel pie you can't run from family
>
> . . . Dorie damn fuck this phone I'm driving
>
> . . .
>
> in other words you were right about everything you were right about Ron
>
> please can I live with you for a while

Live with her? Pinpricks of panic on her skin. She looked around, as if Shari were already there and she needed escape routes.

> Ron is out on bale he came by Ritas to see me. Bail! I hid in the bathroom Rita kicked him out she's brave as shit unlike me lol what a scene
>
> anyways if I could just crash with you until I'm on my feet
>
> . . .
>
> I looked up the word genuflect its just the same as truckle
>
> in case you don't get it I'm truckling
>
> keep on trucklin

This was followed by the happy face scrunched into a kiss.

5

Draft Folder

From: Jemma Dutton
To: Olivia Freeman
Subject: Ollie and Jem's Guide to Survivel

Porcupines MOVE SLOW. Use a stick to nudge it toward the sack. Throw a towel over its head then the sack. Then kill it with a LOG.

Remember? That notebook we kept? Fourth grade?

I know it's been a while. Okay, six months. But. I have a story. It's so long it requires ye olde email.

But first this. I was packing for the summer bummer. I cleaned for so long yesterday I smelled like beeswax and lemon, and not in a groovy Burt's Bees kinda way, like a Glade PlugIn kinda way. Anyway I found it wedged in the back of my pajama drawer.

Back when we read *The Hunger Games* in elementary school? We were totally going to rock dystopia. Teach everyone how to roast a porcupine. Build a solar still.

We turned it in for our English project, and we got sent to the school psychologist. Remember?

Well, guess what. I live in dystopia now. All your fault for moving to Iowa or Idaho or wherever. Meret surfaced. Jaws. Dun-dun. And I got dragged along for the ride. With teeth.

I wanted to say you were right.

Meret. Long story. It's a Tolkien, it's *Twilight,* it's *Game of Thrones* without the thrones just the games. This is why I'm resorting to that old-timey parental communication method, the EMAIL. If this summer continues to Suck So Bad, soon I'll be buying STAMPS, and you'll be checking that thing called a mailbox that your mom uses.

I know you said Meret would drop me because she always picked out a girl and groomed her like a pedophile (yes I totally remember you said that) and then dropped her after she blew up some teeny thing into a major betrayal.

I was so funny. She said. I was so pretty when I blew out my hair. She said. She was jealous of me. She said. Let's both work at the farm stand this summer so we can meet hot summer guys. She said.

She said

She said

She said

On and on. Until the voice in my head was Meret's voice. Creepy possession thing!

Get to the story, you are saying.

First I could tell that she must have realized that working at a farm stand would mean, you know, work. And she started talking about tennis academy, and how she didn't want to go but her mom totally wanted her to and she hoped the job wouldn't conflict with that if her mom made her go.

So I knew she was going to drop out of the working thing.

Which she did. Leaving me with farm stand job alone with Annie Doyle who now hates me because I dropped her for Meret. It's going to be a long summer.

So first this happened. We were hanging at Saffy's house. Remember Mrs. Rubner, who gave Saffy probiotics in kindergarten? You should see their pantry, it's a whole freaking cabinet of potions! So Saffy says, I had the sex talk with my mom. And we said, Well, that's kinda late, since Saffy and Nick had done the deed on New Year's Eve. Yeah, Saffy said, but here's the thing, she kept calling my vag a mayflower. And we just lost it. We were on the *floor*. Mayflower! We peed.

Saffy said the trouble with your first time is that even if you think you know what to expect, you kinda don't, because all of a sudden there's this thing coming at you and it's not *stopping*, and you're like, whoa. And Meret said, I hate surprises. She wants to lose it with someone she doesn't care about, someone experienced, like a college guy or even older, because if you pick someone you really like you can really make a loser of yourself (which was a dig at Saffy since she followed Nick around for a month and then he broke up with her) and he shows your sexts to his friends (yeah, another dig). And how are you going to be any good at it if every guy has been watching porn since he was eleven? Her point was, get it over with and get some experience. Right?

That's when Meret said to me, Let's do it. Let's lose our mayflowers this summer for sure. And I laughed, and she said, But of course everybody knows you're, like, frigid or something. The way Saffy and Kate laughed, I knew this was some kind of fun rumor. Who started it? One guess.

Now the second thing. Friday at school I stayed late for French Club and walked out past the outdoor courts, and there was Josh Frye, doing layups. I said hi, and he said hi, and that would have been that, but he tossed me the ball.

Does this ever happen to you, where you feel something in your hand, like a Polly Pocket or something, and then you're a kid again? Like Holden Caulfield with the skate key. (Yes, we had to ask our parents what a skate key was, and you hated that book, but *you will come around.*)

I hadn't played basketball in years. Not since I was on the team in sixth grade, remember? Josh and I played one serious game of HORSE. I really, really wanted to win, and I could tell he was pissed that it was so close. We were both on H O R S forever.

Skip to the interesting part you are saying.

So then I won, and I yelled "HORSE!" just as Meret was walking out the door all hair-flippy.

The *look* on her face.

Josh broke up with her last *Christmas*!

And we were just playing stupid HORSE!

She walked by, her face all screwed up into this tiny ragey fist, and didn't say hello or anything.

I've got a bad feeling in my stomach and two weeks of school left. I've texted Meret *four times,* all I get is crickets. I can *feel* it, I can feel being on the outside somehow.

This is the longest email in the world. Are you still awake.

Fellow Porcupine Slayer, I know I stopped answering your texts. Basically, I suck. But can you either send me a plane ticket to Indiana (ok, Iowa) or give me Survivel Guide tips?

Btw I'm not sending this

xojem

From: Saffy Rubner
To: Jemma Dutton

Meret said you called her a whore yesterday while you were
with Josh

From: Jemma Dutton
To: Saffy Rubner

Wtf?

From: Saffy
To: Jem

U yelled out WHORE right at her

From: Jem
To: Saffy

We were playing HORSE. I yelled HORSE.

. . .

I had a freaking BBALL in my hands!

From: Saffy
To: Jem

She says it's so obv cause u r frigid and jealous of her and Josh

From: Jem
To: Saffy

Wtf I don't like Josh

From: Saffy
To: Jem

Right that's why you called her a whore

From: Jem
To: Saffy

Joke? Because this is just stupid

From: Meret Bell
To: Jemma Dutton

so now I'm stupid, bitch?

6

TO GET TO Carole's you turned down a hidden gravel drive shaded by an allée of maples until you burst out into air and light and an expanse of bay. Ruthie couldn't see another house, just blue sea and the ferry lumbering its way to Connecticut. She pulled up close to the Berlinger house and shut off the car. She checked her phone. She hadn't heard from Mike all afternoon.

They'd always been best friends. *I married my best friend,* they'd say, trading fond glances. Three years ago when he first confessed his misery, his need to move out, what else could she do but hold his hand and keep a painful smile on her face, as if it were jerked upward with pliers and fastened to her face with safety pins?

For better, for worse, for richer, for poorer—everybody knew that drill. But what about bearable and unbearable? You notice *that's* not in the vows. Bearable is almost worse, somehow, than unbearable, when it comes to marriage. Unbearable makes choices easy. Bearable erodes.

Things happened and broke you, and you spent a lot of time putting yourself back together, and then it turned out you were the same old person, with sadness stitched in the seams. So for Ruthie, when Mike said things like *We should move away* or *We're family,* she remembered to remember that this was the way he'd always been, saying the thing but only meaning it for the moment. Mike had always been generous with his enthusiasms, and once, one of them had been her. Then slowly there had been this draining of life and loving, and their discourse consisted of reminders and confirmations like any married couple, except without the kissing.

It was surprising how long that could go on. You noticed it, maybe even thought about how to fix it, but days rushed on. You still bought the toothbrushes and he still took out the garbage. And your child grows older and suddenly she's not there between you, she's in her room or out with her friends. That's when you notice the silence and the space.

Late one night as he's sleeping you find yourself reaching out to grab the hem of his T-shirt and rub it between your fingers, just to have contact again. That's as close as you can get to your lover. Fabric.

CAROLE OPENED THE back door and waved. Behind her, the enormous shingled house loomed and rambled. One wing made a sharp turn, as if making a break for Canada. A rectangle of pool was crowned by a low, long pool house. Down a brick walkway lined with boxwood sat the converted barn that they'd be renting. Beyond it was a deer-fenced vegetable garden, nasturtiums waving a bright hello. Ruthie felt a sudden lift of her spirits. Maybe the incredible luck of having all this light and luxury would shift something, begin something, be the summer that summers always promised to be.

Unlike every other year they'd lived in Orient, this year Ruthie and Jem would have space. They'd be living like rich folks. Or at least guests of rich folks. Or, no, wait, the guests of children of rich folks, since the converted barn was "the playhouse," where the kids held sleepovers and parties. Carole was headed to Paris for the summer with her tribe of four children and her husband, Lewis, who was expected to solve some sort of financial crisis that could lead to the crash of global capital finance. Or something like that. Imminent disaster was an old song now, nobody paid attention to the details.

"Beware!" Carole called. "It's absolute chaos in here. Save yourself!"

Ruthie had been to the main house many times, for meetings and dinner parties and "come on over for a glass of wine" girl talk. Although every director of a museum could recite the warning "Board members are not your friends" in their sleep, Carole came as close as it got.

Carole and Lewis had hired an architectural firm in the city to build the house from scratch. The interior was so twinned that a second house could be built out of appliances alone. There were double sinks, double dishwashers, double ovens. There were double showerheads, double dressing rooms, and two laundry rooms, upstairs and down. There were two dining rooms, formal and informal, and two living rooms, same. The Paris flea markets had been scoured for lamps and tables; the showrooms of Milan for sofas and beds.

When Carole and Lewis spoke of the house, they would downplay its magnificence and speak earnestly about how it was a "family" house, all designed around the kids. Who would get older, Carole would say, and need a place they would *want* to visit. Most parents used hectoring to get kids to visit; apparently the privileged had more seductive lures. In twenty years, the now six-year-old Verity Berlinger would heed the siren call of a forty-thousand-dollar mattress and pick up the phone to call Mom.

Carole kissed Ruthie on the cheek ("Three times, I'm practicing for Paris!") and Ruthie followed her into the mudroom, as big as her bedroom, where blown-up photos of Berlingers hung on the walls. Berlingers dangled on Costa Rican zip lines and paddled on Peruvian lakes and glamped it up in Patagonia. Wellington boots were lined up on a copper tray and cubbies were stuffed with a rainbow array of Converses and Crocs.

Carole picked up a sheet of black poster board with rows of yellow Post-its stuck onto it. Ruthie saw directives like ANDREW: PACK INVISALIGN and VERITY: BLUE SWEATER WITH DUCK BUTTONS and DASHIELL: IPAD MINI CHARGER and ARDEN: NAVY CASHMERE CARDIGAN.

"Do you see this?" she asked, shaking it. A Post-it with DASH: CHOOSE BOOK FOR PLANE floated to the floor. "I saw it in *Oprah Magazine* at the dentist and had Margarita make it up for the kids. So they feel a part of the trip. They each have tasks, according to age. They are supposed to complete them and then rip off the Post-it. They've done *none* of them and we leave for the airport in *one hour.*"

"Can I help?"

"Yes. Make me a martini. Kidding!" Carole flung the poster board on the floor underneath a gigantic whiteboard calendar. May was crammed with Chinese lessons and tennis lessons and tutors—EXECUTIVE FUNCTION! FRENCH WITH JULIETTE!—concerts and cocktail parties and dinner reservations. A big line slashed through June and July and August trumpeting PARIS and SCOTLAND and ÎLE DE RÉ and LONDON and finally, HOME on August 31.

"And of course, Lew? He's meeting us at the airport. He spent the day at the office. You know how it is, leaving for France for the entire summer, there are a thousand details, and I can't find my Ambien!"

Ruthie put her hands on Carole's shoulders and felt bone. She'd once seen a photo of her in prep school, a hearty brunette kicking a soccer ball, but Manhattan and starvation had turned her into a tiny, taut-skinned blonde. "You are going to be fine. In only a few hours you will be on the plane, and a glass of champagne will be in your hand."

Carole shook her head. "You're always so positive," she said. "I love how you're always so nice. And it's *not* that you're *too* nice. You're just nice!"

Ruthie wished this particular compliment didn't sound like Carole was refuting a charge against her. "Have a seat, I have to yell at the kids," Carole said, gesturing at the matching sofas. "Then I'll walk you through the deets. The beds are all made up, ready to go. The gardener comes on Tuesdays and Thursdays and random days to harvest . . . help yourself to flowers and produce. Um . . . what else. Just keep an eye on things, that's all. And enjoy."

Carole walked to the stairs, trim in gray pants and a white long-sleeved tee. Not pants, *trousers,* Ruthie amended. Trousers tailored to Carole's body, not falling off her butt or too long or too short or slightly bagged at the knees. A paisley stole in muted colors was thrown on the back of an armchair next to a short, chic raincoat in the same gray as her trousers. On the floor sat a soft caramel-colored leather bag so delectable that Ruthie wanted to eat it like a goat.

"Margarita!" Carole shouted. "Are the kids getting ready?"

"Under control!" a voice came.

"Margarita is a love, but she has one fault," Carole confided. "Every time I yell her name, I desperately want a cocktail." A loud crash came from above, and Carole closed her eyes.

"Margarita!"

"No problem! Dashiell dropped his suitcase! My foot is okay!"

"Mommy! Arden borrowed your earrings without asking!"

"Shut up, Verity, you troll!"

"Oh, God," Carole said. "Come upstairs and talk, will you? I need to keep an eye on the mayhem."

Ruthie followed Carole as Carole followed the noise. A flash of pink careened toward them down the hallway. Verity wore a tutu over striped leggings, a sequined top, and a pretty necklace of silver beads wound around and around her neck that Ruthie instantly coveted. "Fancy!" she screamed at Ruthie.

"Sweetie, you're supposed to be in your going-away outfit," Carole said through her teeth.

Arden poked her head out of another bedroom. "She dumped her dress-up box all over her floor."

"Meanie!"

"Go clean it up right now, Verity Hazel," Carole warned. "Arden, are those my earrings? And say hello to Ruthie, you two."

"Hello, Ruthie," the two girls mumbled.

"I go to this incredible vintage store downtown for the dress-up clothes, I think it's where all the drag queens shop," Carole told Ruthie as she shooed Verity down the hall. "I can't stand the Disney crap, can you? I keep thinking of all those Chinese girls in factories keeping their eyes open with clothespins. So I buy vintage. Anything pink, I buy. Satin. Sequins. The girls at the shop save things for me. I send everything out to my fabulous cleaners, and dump it all in the dress-up box. And when I go to Brimfield with my designer or the Brooklyn Flea—have you been, it's divine!—I just buy tons of costume jewelry from the dealers, whole vats of it, or lots or whatever. Anyway I don't hear from Verity for hours. I'm going to write a book of mothering tips. How to keep your kids busy so you can drink. Kidding!"

"She's adorable," Ruthie said. "I think I want that necklace."

"Right? Once I found the most incredible beaded evening purse in there. I wore it on my head for the Man Ray party at MoMA. Such a headache but worth it." They came to the end of the hall and went up a few steps into another hallway. Carole opened the double doors and they walked into the master suite.

The room was all rose and gold, a toile bedspread with a golden cashmere throw tossed on the linen-upholstered armchair, rose-colored curtains that filtered the light, an acre of carpet. Three suitcases sat waiting in a corner.

Carole opened a door and sighed. Ruthie glimpsed T-shirts on an ottoman and a gold scarf trailing out of a plastic box. Closet rods and double-hangs and shelves and transparent boxes labeled LOUBOUTIN MULES CASUAL KITTEN HEEL SILVER and MANOLO PUMPS DRESSY 6 INCH BLACK. Linen shifts and silk blouses, jeans on hangers, what seemed to be six pairs of white pants. *Trousers.*

Carole had already packed for a summer away, Ruthie thought, agog. This was just the stuff she *left behind*.

Carole folded the scarf and touched a drawer, which glided toward them in silent majesty. Silk scarves were arranged by color.

"I sense an Arden attack," Carole said, replacing the scarf and the shirt. "She's only twelve, but she raids my closet *and* Lewis's. How do you deal with it?"

"Jem isn't my size," Ruthie said.

"Lucky you. You can hang on to your jeans."

Which meant that a twelve-year-old was Carole's size. Maybe she just shifted the *need a cookie* trigger to *need a pair of Louboutin mules casual kitten heel silver.*

"I know this is a bad time, but can we talk about Mindy?" Ruthie asked. "She called me three times today. What is this fixation on Adeline Clay? I can't control if the woman comes to Spork."

Ruthie had been lucky with her board from the moment she'd stepped into the job. Every director knew that a good board was a crucial part of the job, and you spent time shaping, nudging, and coddling them along. For nine years her board had written checks, applauded victories, formed committees, and stayed out of her hair. They were passionate about the Belfry but left the operation of it to Ruthie. Most of them were weekend people and lived in Manhattan. There were a few great professional women, but they didn't run it; they were too busy with jobs and families. That was left to the older members, the women who were primarily defined by their husbands, as in, *You know Jill, she's married to Jack, who used to be a big guy at [insert bank/law firm/hedge fund here].* The board as a whole did what great boards were supposed to do: raise money, follow Robert's Rules of Order, and show up at parties.

Then old guard Helen Gregorian (widow of Armand, former big guy at Deutsche Bank) had declined the presidency, saying she'd prefer to be secretary. No one wanted the job of president except Mindy Flicker, who lobbied Helen and Carole to propose her. Helen decided that the board needed an infusion of "the young," which meant, in Helen's eyes, the forty-somethings.

Ruthie had liked Mindy but not known her well, so she took Mindy on the recommendation of Helen and Carole, both of whom had taken Mindy on her own self-valuation. She was the right person for the job, Mindy assured them. She had the "energy," she said, forever putting Helen's nose out of joint for implying she was old. Could she start early?

The board was thrilled. Mindy came from serious money and had broken family tradition by choosing the North Fork over the Hamptons. She had a second home two towns away in Southold that she called "The Farm," three girls in varying stages of sulky young womanhood, and a clammy condescension that masqueraded as congeniality. Her attention to "action plans" was often mistaken for intelligence by the stupid. It hadn't taken long before Ruthie came to realize that Mindy operated around a fistula of privilege that choked off real human connection. Her first act as president was to suggest Ruthie fire her curator Tobie because she "never smiled" and had corrected her spelling of Jackson Pollock. Ruthie had laughed, then realized Mindy was serious. It had been downhill from there.

Likable and lovely Carole had assured her that Mindy was awful and that she would get no second term. Carole and Helen Gregorian, the biggest donors and the powerhouses on the board, would squeeze her out eventually. But until then Ruthie had to find "spaces of agreement." Those spaces had been narrowing to a vanishing point lately.

"One second." Carole shut the closet door and threw herself onto the pink love seat. She patted it, inviting Ruthie to sit. "I have five minutes of calm before things blow up again."

Ruthie sat. Carole pressed her hands together and leaned toward Ruthie. "Mindy wants to fire you," she said.

Ruthie shifted position and waited in vain for Carole to say, *Kidding!*

"Look, everyone knows you're doing a fabulous job, and you've taken the place from sleepy to woken up. I'm your biggest fan. I only came on the board because of you. I've tried to tell you that Mindy is pushing for all kind of changes—"

"Yes, irresponsible, stupid ones!"

"Absolutely. She's a pill!" Carole gave a reassuring pat to Ruthie's knee. It was not reassuring. "Look, I guess I'm not as Sun-Tzu-ish as I thought, or maybe it's because I have a life, but you know how we went on that big board drive, and then she formed an executive committee because the board was too big? Have you noticed that it's all new board members except for me, Gloria, and Helen?"

"But she hardly knows the new people."

Carole gave her a significant look. "She's been having lunches and coffees in the city for months. We never should have let Gloria be treasurer. Nobody likes her and so she was vulnerable. Mindy flattered her and now they're thick as thieves. Don't worry, you still have me and Helen! But. We need to switch tactics. Now it's time for you to stand up to her."

"You've been telling me to get along with her!"

"I know, but who can get along with her? She's saying that the gala is failing because you picked the wrong honoree."

"Gus Romany? First of all, I didn't pick him, the committee did, and it was a unanimous yes. He's done so much for the museum."

"He's not selling tables."

"We don't really start selling tables until July. Nobody's here yet. The locals can't afford tables. Only chairs."

"Well, she's using it. He's old, and outside of the North Fork nobody cares. You don't want to fall on your sword for this one."

"He's a great artist, and you know the locals will show up—everybody loves Gus."

"Sweetie, do you think Mindy cares about the *locals*? Gus isn't shiny enough to get support from the new summer crowd. She wants glam. It's ammunition for her argument."

"What *is* her argument?"

"That now that the North Fork is changing, now that we have some celebrities, some serious money here, the Belfry should have a bigger presence. Don't wince, I'm just *repeating*." Carole gave a surreptitious glance at her watch. "She wants us to be part of the Hamptons aesthetic—you know, like Robert Wilson, where we do a fundraiser and celebrities come, and we all wear white, and get photographed, and we're covered in the *Times* . . ."

"People come here to get *away* from glam. The point is, it's *not* the Hamptons."

"Helen and I have been working madly behind the scenes. We can't just stand up in a board meeting and say what we really think."

"Why not?"

"Sweetie, it would be better if you weren't defensive right now. I'm here to help you. It's not that you're not fabulous. It's just a question of style. You're kind of . . ."

Ruthie waited, internally wincing. This wasn't going to be good.

". . . um . . . how can I say this . . . you're not . . . business-y. Corporate," Carole said, pointing upward to illustrate her success at coming up with a word. "You know, the whole B-school thing. Mindy is married to that guy. *I'm* married to that guy. There's a certain way they talk. Just throw *metrics* into a conversation and you're good to go. Or *optics*. That's a good one. I can have Lewis recommend some books."

"This is unbelievable."

"I know!"

"Wait," Ruthie said. "How serious is this? Should I be looking for a job?"

"No! We can't lose you! Don't do anything while I'm in France. You have the summer to turn things around. Style, remember? It's not enough anymore to do a fabulous job. You have to do it on Twitter! *Everything* is about image now. Read the papers. Oh, wait, nobody reads a newspaper anymore." Carole ran a hand through her hair, and it reassembled itself into perfection. "Do you think I'd have all this if I hadn't lost twenty pounds and dyed my hair? Come *on*."

"So I should diet?"

"I'm not saying that, you're gorgeous. I'm saying it's not personal. Mindy and Gloria are dying to feel important. If they change the place, they get to talk about it at dinner parties. It doesn't matter if the Belfry is *better*. It just has to be *different*." Carole patted her knee again. Ruthie now wanted to bite her hand. Bite the hand that underfed her. The pat meant *Don't get hysterical, I have to catch a plane*. "Here's the good news. Because there's no there there, you can fight. Why don't you borrow an outfit from me for Spork?"

Ruthie frowned, puzzled. What was this, high school? Then she realized what this meant. "Because Mindy criticized my clothes?"

Carole looked uncomfortable.

"Tell me."

"She says you don't dress up enough. Gloria says you never wear heels."

"What?"

"Look, I'm just saying." Carole got up and began to rifle through the hangers. "Raid my closet! Please, I've had four pregnancies, I have a size that will fit you, double zero all the way up to *eight*. I was a *house* when I was pregnant with Verity. Here." Carole slipped a pair of white pants off the hanger and tossed them on the sofa. She waggled a hanger with a pink silk shirt on it. "This would look perfect on you. Or this, or this." She tossed more shirts on the pile, a sudden blizzard of pinks and creams and blues. "You're not going to win this dressed in Ann Taylor, sweetie. And you might want to rethink the ponytail. What size shoe are you?"

"Thank you for the warning," Ruthie said, standing. "And thank you for the offer."

"Oh, no, now you're offended!"

"I'm not offended," Ruthie lied. "But no. I can't change who I am."

"Of course you can!" Carole tossed another shirt on top of the trousers. "Listen, I'm not on Mars, just France! It's barely even a foreign country! We're friends. Which means I have your back." She cocked her head and studied Ruthie for a moment. "Just try to be . . . a little less you."

7

JEM'S PHONE

From: Lucas Clay
To: Jemma Dutton

I need to return a blueberry

From: Jemma Dutton
To: Lucas Clay

Get to the end of the line, sir

From: Lucas
To: Jem

Your rutabagas are delightful

From: Jem
To: Lucas

I have to stop texting u will get me fired

From: Lucas
To: Jem

how busy can u be, it's only May

. . .

When the corn comes in I'll leave u alone

From: Jem
To: Lucas

Shuck u

From: Lucas
To: Jem

Ya snap. I'm in so much trouble I can tell

but trouble w u could be worth it

8

A LITTLE LESS her.

Ruthie drove to the farm stand. Mike had texted, saying he was stuck on a job, his day was crazy, could she pick up Jem after all? Nothing about this morning. Nothing about tomorrow night.

Still. Summer, car windows down. If she blasted the radio she could grasp just a split second of feeling young despite an adulthood of airbags and disappointments.

Traffic was heavy. Travel writers undid themselves with headlines about the Un-Hamptons, with the predictable result that the North Fork was becoming more like the Hamptons every day. The locals were starting second jobs as bartenders and cashiers. They would do the shopping early, take the back roads, and curse the interlopers. Memorial Day weekend was only a taste of what was to come. August would be full of corn and cars.

Ruthie pulled into the parking lot next to a white Jeep. The sun was at an angle in the sky designed to bounce the accumulated heat straight at you like a punch and then scatter it skyward again.

Red-haired Annie Doyle was spraying escarole while Jem stood at the counter. Annie had spent many a Saturday night in her house before the triad of Jem/Olivia/Annie had been pitchforked by the alpha girls Meret, Saffy, and Kate. She missed the shrieks and the private jokes and watching whole casseroles of mac and cheese disappear. Instead she had glottal stops and nail care.

In her cutoffs and pigtails Jem looked adorable, but somehow . . . mature. This past year there had been times when Ruthie had seen her bicycling, or walking from afar, and not recognized her for a moment. Who was that Pre-Raphaelite with the legs?

Looking like a god in rumpled khaki shorts, Lucas sauntered toward her, carrying a bag with waving fronds of fennel poking out. He held a block of French butter in the other hand.

"You found the best farm stand," she called. "Good start!"

He stared at her blankly. Then he tossed the bag in the seat, got in the Jeep, and roared off.

Heat sprang to Ruthie's cheeks. Okay, the remark was inane, but, what? Had she offended him?

Then she replayed the blankness on his face. He had completely forgotten that he'd met her. That very morning. In her yard. She'd chatted with him for a bit before she drove off to work. They'd had a *conversation*. About the best times to avoid ferry lines to the Hamptons, her favorite restaurant in Greenport.

With cheeks that still glowed with humiliation, she stalked past the broccoli. "Hey, Annie, hello, summer!" she called.

"Hello, summer!" The back of Annie's pretty neck was sunburnt. She was about twenty pounds overweight and that meant that despite tilted green eyes and creamy skin she was not popular. She wore overalls and Doc Martens and kept her head down when she walked. No doubt boys walked by her in the halls and dismissed her. Someday she would be glorious. Someday she would flirt. Someday she would have sex and fall in love and betray someone and be betrayed and start all over again. And then, at forty-five, the iron gate of indifference would clang down and she would remember that overalled girl, and she would know she was stuck back exactly where she'd been in high school as if all that sex and attention had happened to someone else.

"Good luck, sweetie," Ruthie said, giving her shoulder a pat.

"If you're thinking salad, the red leaf is awesome," Jem said as she walked up.

"I just saw Lucas Clay," she said.

"Yeah, I'm happy he bought actual food," Jem said. "We helped Adeline unpack, and Dad totally mocked her groceries. It was hilarious, like, just . . . *berries*. Celery and radishes. He said she needed butter for the radishes. She said she hadn't eaten butter in twenty years. I actually think she was serious. Dad was like, oh boy, you need to *live*."

"Oh, God. He didn't give her his 'live while you're alive' speech, did he?"

"Yeah, well, a version. You know what I found out? She knows Roberta Verona! My favorite chef ever? She's, like, her best friend. Adeline said maybe I could meet her sometime, which would be amazing. She brought her own sheets and towels, by the way. Adeline, I mean. And she brought an espresso maker—one of the fancy ones—and a Vitamix. And cashmere throws, like, six of them in different colors. Dad said her car was like 'Bed Bath and Beyond Imagining.' "

Ruthie pictured six cashmere throws, flung on her couches, on her beds, ready for evening chill. Powder blue, sea green, seashell pink, lilac . . . did she need a Vitamix?

"I just have to prep the CSAs for tomorrow, then I can go," Jem said.

"I'll pick out some stuff for dinner. Carole said the kitchen was stocked."

"I put aside some beets. I can roast them."

Ruthie clasped her hands together. "My kid likes beets. I did something right!"

"Mom." Jem made a shooing motion with her hands.

Ruthie cruised the aisles, choosing lettuce and scallions and lemons and basil. Nonlocal blueberries. Maybe that was Adeline's secret, antioxidants?

A pickup truck barreled into the parking lot and her best

friend, Penny, raced out, her wife, Elena, following more slowly. "Hello, summer!" Penny cried, and waved at Jem. "Dude, please have garlic left!"

"On the left, dude," Jem called. Out of all Ruthie's friends, Jem was closest to Penny. They had bonded over pizza and *The Big Lebowski* and never looked back. Penny was a chef, and it was her extended tutorial on scrambled eggs—*Low heat! Tablespoon of butter per egg! Yes, I said American cheese!*—that had first sparked Jem's interest in cooking. It was a small, deep pleasure in Ruthie's life that her child and her best friend had a relationship outside of her.

"What are you cooking?" Penny asked as she peeked at Ruthie's basket.

"I don't know, maybe just a salad?"

"*Why* are you so boring?"

"I'm roasting beets!" Jem called. "And I have some fresh ricotta! And an orange!"

"Thank fucking God!" Penny yelled. She leaned over to fondle Ruthie's herbs. "That parsley is gorgeous. That reminds me, you need to come over soon. You can work for your supper and go clamming with us. We need to eat linguine and celebrate the beginning of traffic."

"So many needs with you," Ruthie said, handing her cash to Annie.

"All my wants are needs," Penny said. "Is this garlic from the farm or Stop and Shop?" she asked Jem.

"Farm," Jem said. "Promise."

"In that case, I will pay you. Linguine soon!"

"With lots of crushed red pepper." Jem and Penny fist-bumped, then waggled their fingers at each other.

"So how's your glamorous tenant?" Elena asked as they headed to their cars.

"Well tended," Ruthie said. "She's dazzling, if you stare too long you'll burn out your retinas. And she's got this gorgeous satellite stepson, who just saw me and didn't remember me, even though we had a conversation this morning."

Penny opened a bag of pistachios and offered them around. With tattoos and a CURSE YOUR SUDDEN AND INEVITABLE BETRAYAL T-shirt and not an ounce of fat, she almost looked like a teenager if you squinted. She cracked open a nut with her thumbs and put the shell in the pocket of her jeans. "Middle-aged-lady syndrome," Penny said. "You'll get used to it."

"I'm already used to it," Ruthie said. "Grocery clerks and waiters, sure. But we had a conversation!"

Penny shrugged. "Happens every day."

"That reminds me. How would you describe my style?"

"You have a style?" Penny asked. At Ruthie's look, she squinted amiably as she chewed. "I mean, okay, downtown slouch?"

"Downtown slouch?"

"Comfy stretchy things in mostly black? Like, today. You're wearing beige, and I'm like, whoa, she's breaking out."

"You're lovely," Elena said. "I always liked those beige pants."

"Just hearing the words 'beige pants' has cast me into despair," Ruthie said.

"Have a nut. Who cares, anyway?" Penny said. "You're presentable and dependable."

"At long last I've found my epitaph." Ruthie looked at her hands, with veins and freckles and one torn cuticle. She saw her mother's hands, and felt cast adrift toward a future wrinkled with sadness. "We're all dying, every day."

Penny and Elena exchanged a glance.

"Mindy doesn't like how I dress," she explained.

"Mindy? Belfry Mindy?" Penny asked. "Headband Mindy? *I never met a green polo I didn't like* Mindy? Mindy with the husband who is most likely right this minute relaxing at home in velour?"

"That would be the one."

"Why listen?" Elena asked in the sweet, rational tone with

which she faced the world. A copter flew overhead and she had to shout the rest. "Everyone loves you!"

"Except Mindy."

"Nobody likes her!" Penny exploded. "She's a pill! I was in a town meeting with her, my God! Hours of minutiae! She's like a walking game of Trivial Pursuit, and if I'm playing, there should be a cocktail in my hand." Penny tossed a shelled nut into the air and caught it in her mouth. "And speaking of minutiae, I saw your Catha this morning taking her *ass*-pirational walk."

"She's not my Catha, and what do you mean, aspirational?" Ruthie asked.

"First of all, she's an ass," Penny said. "You know that, right? Second, she goes on these woman walks."

Ruthie nodded. "She leans in deep."

"Please. Her route goes right by our house. I'm always there in the window with my tea. I started to notice. She only walks *up*. With women who can help her or her kids. You know, who's married to the guy who runs something, or who can give her kid an internship. It's so obvious. This morning she was walking with Doe, that tasty assistant person of yours who's always looking at her phone."

"Tasty?" Elena asked. "That's gross, sweetie. She's a kid."

"I'm not leering, just characterizing. She's adorable. My point is, Catha walked *down*. Odd."

"Catha is Doe's supervisor," Ruthie said. "Maybe they were having a walking meeting."

"What is this, California?"

"You don't like Catha," Ruthie said. "Everybody likes Catha. Why didn't I know this?"

"You never asked. I don't gossip unless you ask."

"You just did, honey," Elena said. "I like her okay. She's on the Save the Wetlands committee with me. And she's chair of the No Helipad on the North Fork committee. She drives a hybrid!"

Penny snorted. "And she'll drive right over you in it. You think anybody who cares about the planet is a good person. The only things she stands for are herself and the Pledge of Allegiance." She swiveled back to Ruthie. "Let's get to the important stuff. How is Casa Berlinger? In other words, how's the kitchen?"

"Miele dishwasher. Aga stove!"

"Whoa, after clamming let's go to your house," Penny said. "It might be the only place I'll be cooking this summer."

"What?"

Elena and Penny exchanged a glance. Penny looked away, which allowed Ruthie to notice for the first time that she was upset. No wonder she was cracking nuts as though they were the bones of an enemy.

"The restaurant closed yesterday," Elena said. "I mean, we knew it was dicey when the landlord raised the rent so high. In the end Aaron decided he just couldn't make it through the summer. It's not his fault."

"It *is* his fault," Penny objected. "He was a total shit for waiting for Memorial Day weekend to tell the staff. We're all left flat. All the restaurants have hired already."

"Someone will quit," Ruthie said. "You know chefs. So volatile."

"What the fuck do you mean, volatile? Elena thinks if I don't manage to get a gig, we should sell the rental property and open our own restaurant," she said. "Elena said I have to follow my dream or she'll divorce me."

"Please don't talk about me in front of me, love," Elena said.

"We went to this place last night in Greenport. Tiny! All this guy—Joe Somebody—serves is oysters and chowder. One fucking good wine list. He closes at eight. Is that genius? I was so happy, the oysters were so cold and briny, the place was packed, I loved the owner. Then I got home and was immediately depressed. What am I doing with my un-wild and precious life, anyway? I wish people would just stop quoting that fucking poem at me."

"It's all a sign you need to do something," Elena said.

"Apparently I've been so miserable I've been impossible," Penny said, opening the car door and tossing the bag of nuts inside. "I know I can't be like you and Mike. I can't be a happy divorced person. Remember that first year after you broke up? Horrible."

"I thought I was magnificent."

"I'd need you all to hate Elena as much as I did, and it would be exhausting for everyone," Penny went on. "My father keeps saying I shouldn't rely on his will to support us. I'm fifty-five years old, and he still thinks I'm on the edge of financial disaster."

"You *are* on the edge of financial disaster, sweetie," Ruthie said, leaning against her. "We all are. And you're fifty-seven."

"Mike was so supportive," Elena said. "I mean about the restaurant dream. We just ran into him in town."

"I could have killed him, actually," Penny said. "It was such an Oprah moment, I swear he and Elena both had tears in their eyes. Go for the dream, he said."

"He did not. He did not say go for the dream," Ruthie said.

"Well, okay, not exactly. He said if you're trapped in a life that's not your life, it's the worst thing in the world."

There came a pause. Ruthie distinctly saw Elena step on Penny's foot.

"I'm sure he didn't mean that personally," Elena said.

"Mmm," Ruthie said.

"He said not to give a rat's ass what anyone else thought," Penny added.

"And he's seen a rat's ass, so I'd believe him," said Ruthie.

9

RUTHIE AND JEM unpacked the car, shouldering the totes, cases, boxes, and suitcases into the playhouse, colliding in doorways, calling out from different rooms ("This room is a shriek of pink!" Jem shrieked, when she saw her room. "It's an intestine!"), bouncing on beds, turning on faucets, and exulting in a well-stocked open kitchen. Outside they dipped their feet into the pool and examined the pool house.

"Stacks and stacks of towels," Jem said. "And really good shampoo. My hair is going to smell like a meadow."

"It's a compound," Ruthie said as they surveyed the view. "We have secured the compound, Captain. And we have a vista." She swung her arms wide. *"Ich bein ein Berlinger!"*

"Mom, please. You are so beyond me-hearties right now."

Ruthie knew she was pumping up enthusiasm when the truth was she just felt beleaguered by the day. She'd met a goddess and been ignored by her stepson. Trouble at work that had seemed manageable now loomed, serious. Mike had leaned against the door and suggested a dinner "to talk." He'd told Penny and Elena that he was trapped in a life that wasn't his life. She'd been called presentable and dependable.

Maybe Carole was right. Had the disappointments of middle age, the sorrow of a failed marriage, drained something out of her, what her father used to call her *pep*? Had she lost so much vitality that a young man could see right through her?

She'd once been blessed with cherubic cheeks and good skin. Her thirties had been almost indistinguishable from her radiant twenties. Although slightly drier. Not beautiful but pretty, she knew how to talk to men, how to flirt and keep them abuzz. Of course now she knew that her currency had been mostly youth, because now nobody was looking. She saved the sass and crackle for her girlfriends.

She'd shut all that off because *men* had shut it off. On the north side of forty, they weren't leaning closer, weren't watching her mouth or her ass. They didn't give a shit if she tossed her hair or cocked an eyebrow. If she was witty they no longer wondered how she'd be in bed, they merely laughed. And it would be a surprised laugh, as though it was impossible for her, at this age, to give them even momentary pleasure.

Post-divorce you had to buy a good bra and inject things into your laugh lines, and she wasn't in the mood. Who was she going to flirt with, Lloyd Handleman, the local realtor who kept suggesting they have a martini so she could "take the edge off"?

Now she was rounding the corner toward fifty. She thought of Adeline Clay, her face taut, her skin glowing, her waist like a twenty-year-old's (no butter!), her body as supple as if she'd just stepped off the shiatsu table.

If Ruthie was going to carve a new person out of the old one, she needed more than drugstore moisturizer and outlet shopping.

She needed Carole's size eight fat pants.

"Come on," she said to Jem. "Let's invade the big house. I'll get the key."

. . .

"THERE ARE EIGHT pairs of Wellington boots," Jem said. "I counted. And two dishwashers."

"I know."

"There's a climbing wall in the boy's room."

"Really?"

"Are you sure we're allowed to be here?"

"Carole said it was fine." Ruthie regarded herself in the full-length mirror. She looked drawn. Was the mirror too used to reflecting the better-looking?

"Plus this dressing room is the size of my bedroom." Jem touched a drawer and it slid open silently, revealing triangularly folded silk panties in an array of colors, a line of matching bras in a column next to them.

"Whoa," Jem said.

"Honey, please don't ogle Carole's underwear, I feel spooky enough as it is."

"Rich people *match*," Jem said. "I bet if they lose a sock, they just throw the other sucker out. They don't even wait for a couple of laundry cycles to be sure."

They stared down at the drawer for a moment. Was this the secret that rich people knew? The things most people bought in batches, hurriedly, shaking them out of Gap and Target bags— T-shirts, underwear, socks—were, for the rich, silky secret fabrics that lay against their skin like talismans, reminding them that they did not have to worry about the costs of the ordinary: dry cleaning, orthodontics, lunch. They had the worries of a pleasant life with equally pleasant choices—London for theater this winter, or Turks and Caicos?—so maybe their base level of dopamine was higher than everyone else's.

Ruthie closed the drawer.

"How come I can't raid Verity's closet?" Jem asked.

"Because she's six."

"Oh. The other one."

"Arden. Because you weren't invited. Besides, she's twelve."

Jem sighed. "I bet she has better clothes than I do already."

"Are you okay?" Ruthie asked. "You seem off. Crabby."

"I've got finals and stuff. And the playhouse . . ."

"You don't like it? How can you not like it? You saw the kitchen!"

"Everything is so . . . I don't know . . . *done.*"

"Are you kidding me? For years you've been complaining about sofa beds and now you've got a European mattress and it's too done?"

"I know," Jem said. "I'm reverse spoiled."

"Nah. You're just spoiled. My fault. I only want you to be happy, and it's exhausting."

Jem leaned against Ruthie. Ruthie slipped an arm around her. She breathed her daughter in, feeling the humidity-swollen texture of her hair against her cheek. Jem stirred and she hugged her tighter. "Just another second. One day you'll love me again. But by then osteoporosis will have set in and I won't be able to hug you without fracturing a bone."

"You are a serious weirdo," Jem said, but she smiled as she pushed her away.

"So what is it?" Ruthie asked. "This is our best summer squat ever. Why the gloom?"

"I hate leaving my house. I'm going to spend an entire summer afraid I'll spill something."

"We need the money."

"Maybe if all those years you didn't buy me organic milk and stuff, you would have been able to save money and we'd still have the house in the summers."

Ruthie started to laugh, but then got momentarily lost in speculating if all those things they had always spent money on to protect Jem—from growth hormones in cows, from pesticides, from trans fats, from PCBs in plastic (all those expensive wooden toys!)—would add up to enough extra cash to give Jem exactly what she wanted, could keep her in Apple products and purses and vacations for years.

"Remember when we used to talk about fun things, like Death Eaters?"

"Mom!"

"I'm sorry about the pedicure, you can save up for one this summer."

"It's not the pedicure. Sometimes it just seems like . . . like everybody has money but us." Jem's finger trailed along a row of folded sweaters.

"Well, lots of people do. And lots of people are suffering."

"If you mention refugees I'm walking."

"That's exactly what they have to do, walk away from a life—"

Jem took a step and Ruthie pulled her back. She stroked her hair. Lightly. Held her like a moth, felt her fluttering wings. "Look, aside from cashmere throw envy, we have it pretty good," she said. "We're going to have a great summer. Speaking of which, I bumped into Meret's mom today. Doe's been doing this teen outreach thing, and Mrs. Bell is bringing Meret and a whole gang to Spork. So you can hang with friends instead of working the kids' table, okay?"

"I don't know if I can come. I'm working tomorrow."

"Only until three. You can come after work, with Daddy."

Jem set her jaw. "I can choose what I want to do with my time."

"Well, sure." Ruthie peered into her face. "Did something happen at school? Or with Meret?"

"Why did something have to happen at *school*?" Jem flung herself away. "I have to pee."

"Check out the toilet! It's Japanese!"

Ruthie found the pink shirt and white pants. She tossed aside her T-shirt and slipped on the shirt. Silk slipped over her arms and floated around her waist and fit her shoulders and cast a light on her skin as though she was carrying around Carole Lombard's cinematographer.

She never wore pink. But this pink was luscious. Inside it she would feel as though she'd burrowed into the heart of a rose.

She pulled on the white pants, satiny cotton sliding across her skin. She twisted in the mirror. Was that an actual *ass*?

"Whoa, Mom." Jem walked back in. "You look like a whole different person."

Ruthie slipped into her flats. "That's the idea."

"Okay, no." Jem perused the shoes and came up with MANOLO MULE KITTEN HEEL. "Here."

Ruthie slipped into the shoes. "Better," Jem said.

It was like resolving a painting. If you change a corner, the composition is thrown off. Couture had thrown the rest of her middle-aged self into relief. The bracelet she'd had since college, a plain silver band she'd bought at a flea market in NoHo. And her *hair*! Carole was right. Everything was wrong.

"My hair," she said.

"You just need product," Jem said. "And maybe a necklace or a bracelet?"

"I can't borrow Carole's jewelry. Wait, hold on."

She dashed to Verity's bedroom. She found the dress-up trunk and pawed through it, looking for that pretty silver necklace. The trunk was heaped with sequined tutus and costume jewelry, most of it too glittery for a Memorial Day picnic. Feathers flew as she tossed boas and hats aside. Something caught her eye, the dull shine of metal against all that sparkle. She pulled out a man's watch with a nickel case, one of those knockoffs that looked real if you didn't look twice. She wound it, and the second hand ticked forward crisply.

It was a little clunky and she liked the weight of it. She went back to the full-length mirror and posed. The tailored pants said *Jackie O on a Greek island,* the pink said *summer fun*. The heels winked *flirty*. Yet the man's watch made her look like a kickass Amelia Earhart—grounded, maybe doomed—but with an action plan.

"Nailed it," said Jem, and they were friends again.

From: Ruth Beamish
To: Michael Dutton

Jem said you boned with Adeline

From: Michael Dutton
To: Ruth Beamish

WHAT?

From: Ruthie
To: Mike

I meant bonded! BONDED

. . .

oops! Ha ha. Anyway do you think if you r still fixing step etc you could encourage her to come to Spork? I need her. Will tell you why. Fire up that Dutton charm offensive.

From: Mike
To: Ruthie

The Dutton charm is tattered at the edges these days, but ok.

10

SPORK HAD ALWAYS been Ruthie's favorite event of the summer, unlike the gala, which was always fraught with tension as the board ladies made their thrust-knee poses for the photographer, tucking their wineglasses behind their silk tunics. Spork was food held in fingers, people in shorts and hats, and the fizzy kickoff to summer pleasures.

The Belfry Museum was a hybrid of a place. It was named not for an architectural feature, but for a person, Vivian Clarke Belfry, who in 1972 left three million dollars and her house and barn to her son with the directive to create a "significant museum" to highlight "both local history and visual art" and, incidentally, kick Hampton ass. The historical collection, referred to in official publications as "choice" and by villagers as "dinky," was housed in a small side gallery. It was built around a few artifacts of Benedict Arnold, who had set up headquarters in Orient during the Revolutionary War. The Belfry family was descended from Arnold's secretary, who had served the general, been pardoned, and stayed to farm. It was a small collection, including the buttons of a coat reportedly worn by Arnold.

As in small towns all over the nation, a few dusty relics were enough for a start. An endowment was born, more money raised, staff was hired, a renovation completed by an architect who summered in Orient, and the buttons, tankards, musket balls, and a flintlock rifle displayed to busloads of yawning schoolkids. The Belfry lurched along for decades, open half the year, sleepy and striving, exhibiting watercolors and duck decoy collections, nudged by a succession of devoted board members who did much of the administrative work. When Ruthie moved to Orient she applied for a job in education and talked herself into creating a new position as chief curator. Three years later the director, an amiable scholar with a tendency to drunkenly topple into bushes at openings, retired. Ruthie took over temporarily and then permanently, after a cursory meeting with a board grateful to have her.

Since then she'd turned the barn into a modern open space for big projects by contemporary artists, the most notable being when Dodge filled it with vellum cut in undulating shapes that blew in the wind of a hundred or so vintage fans hung on wires, all lit by a ravishing blue light. Titled *Heaven*, it was ecstatically reviewed by the *Times* and put the Belfry on the map.

The trick, as director of a small regional museum, was to be scrappy, to find time to squeeze in some thoughts about Art while you brooded about Money. "Let's do it frisky, and let's do it cheap" was her motto, and over the years she'd managed to beg, borrow, steal, recruit, entice, shame, and flatter enough people to increase the small endowment, triple membership, quadruple school visits, start art camp and art classes, and, along with her curator Tobie, mount frisky and cheap shows that got them noticed. She'd hired smartly, fired kindly, and occasionally even kicked Hampton ass.

Ten years ago the summer picnic had been a desultory affair decorated with potluck pasta salads brought by the board ladies and a large crystal bowl full of lemonade with a few cartons of blueberries dumped in. Ruthie had changed the name to Spork, gotten the local farms and wineries to donate food, and introduced fun to the party equation. She'd ordered Spork T-shirts that became more prized as they grew faded from sun and salt. Now it was one of the main summer kickoff events on the North Fork.

Ruthie parked next to Gloria's and Mindy's SUVs, nestled in Teutonic twinship, but she didn't see them among the early arrivals. She inspected the tent, joked with the cooks in the food trucks, thanked the purveyors she had charmed into donating wine and beer, and cast an uneasy glance at the sky. It had been a changeable morning, banks of heavy clouds blowing past with occasional pockets of blue, and she hoped the showers would hold off. She greeted a few guests as she made her way into the coolness of the museum and climbed the stairs to the offices.

In the hallway outside her office Mindy stood, planted like a tuber on the carpet. Her thick blond hair was held off her face with a patterned green-and-yellow headband, chosen, Ruthie surmised, to match the Spork invitation. Mindy was the type of person who would plan this. Tiny Gloria leaned in, Mindy's pocket-sized factotum. In her early seventies, Gloria still projected a clenched vitality. Her hair was a spun-sugar cage of platinum privilege, and although the summer had just begun, she was already deeply tanned. Today she was dressed all in white, and Ruthie had a sudden image of the ghost dolls Jem used to make at Halloween out of tissues and a walnut.

They hadn't seen her yet. They were listening intently to Catha, who was speaking rapidly. There was a glittering excitement on her face that sent a trickle of foreboding through Ruthie.

Catha dressed like Hollywood's idea of an executive assistant, pencil skirts and jewel-necked tops and shoes with pointed toes that just might conceal a shiv. Her small dark eyes were bright with birdlike attention, and she accentuated the association by moving her head forward like a pigeon after she made an especially trenchant point.

Ruthie had offered the job of deputy director to Catha five years ago, when she was drowning in overwork and needed help.

She had known Catha slightly, the way one vaguely knew almost everyone in a small town, and she knew Catha had once been a marketing person (Ruthie had only a vague idea of what a marketing person did, exactly) at a cable network. One day she'd spotted her weeping in the produce section in the Southold grocery store. Ruthie had approached her tentatively to see if she could help. Catha had clutched endive to her bosom and confided the problem. Bobbing her head down and forward, she'd announced that her oldest daughter, Whitney, had decided to go to Wesleyan instead of Smith. Ruthie waited for a distressing anecdote to follow this news, but that appeared to be the tragedy. "I always confused Wesleyan with Wellesley," she'd told Catha, revealing her plebeian origins, and Catha had shaken her head, button eyes bright with tears, and said, "Wellesley would have been *excellent*. But this . . ." She cast the endive into her cart in despair.

Rather than dismissing Catha as a crashing snob, Ruthie had decided on the spot that any woman who possessed that amount of rabid attention to status could come in handy at a museum. So, even though Catha had no museum experience, Ruthie had hired her. She had always considered Catha her best hire, except for her tendency to avoid responsibility for missteps and take credit for every success. In the job evaluation in her head (and only in her head; Ruthie eschewed job evaluations) Ruthie would have checked off the Not a Team Player box.

Yet Catha was her friend. Had been her friend? It wasn't clear, suddenly. Once, they'd gone for drinks after work together. They'd confided in each other about kids and husbands. Ruthie knew the intimate details of the six-month period when Catha was thinking of leaving her husband, Larry. One evening she and Jem and Catha and Emerson had gone to Shelter Island for a dinner to celebrate Emerson's graduation from college (Wellesley!), and it had been a magical night. On the way back on the ferry they'd gotten out of their cars and watched the lights moving on the dark water. "I just know we'll be friends forever," Catha had said, slipping her arm through Ruthie's. That had been only a year ago. When had that feeling stopped? How many cues had she missed?

Clearly she was interrupting some kind of conspiracy, but whether it was about her or the color of the tablecloths she couldn't say for sure. Board ladies could be fierce about tablecloths. She tamped down her unease and walked toward them.

Three faces turned toward her. She had a sudden vision of her father's fish store, the fish laid out on ice, staring eyes liquid and opaque.

"I didn't realize we had a meeting," Ruthie said.

"It's not a meeting, we're just chatting," Catha said with a sunny smile.

She had hardly advanced a step when Mindy said, "Did you know that Daniel Mantis is Adeline Clay's boyfriend?"

"I would think that you would know about Daniel Mantis," Gloria said. She blinked rapidly. "Catha says his art collection is world-class."

"Of course I know who he is," Ruthie said. "He summers in East Hampton."

"He has a fabulous estate," Mindy said. "It was in *Architectural Digest*. We were talking about Gus Romany just now. I've been researching his artwork. Nobody ever accused me of not being prepared! Have you seen his killing chickens series?"

"He strangles a chicken!" Gloria interrupted. She mimicked whirling a chicken in the air.

Ruthie winced. "That doesn't sound like his work. When was this?"

"It's all over the Internet," Catha said. "Nineteen seventy."

"Oh, that makes sense."

"Strangling a chicken makes sense?" Gloria asked.

"I mean, it was over forty years ago. Shock art was part of a whole—"

"So graphic." Mindy shuddered. "Do we really want to sponsor that sort of content?"

"How are we sponsoring it?" Ruthie asked. "We're not show-ing the work. We're honoring him for his service to the museum."

"It's a video and it's on our Instagram account," Catha said. She held out the phone, but it was impossible to see it and she kept it out of Ruthie's reach.

"Doe posted it?" she asked.

"You mean you don't supervise Instagram posts?" Mindy asked.

"Well, technically, Catha is her supervisor."

"Arnie always says, if you're the boss, don't pass the buck," Gloria said.

"Don't you check the museum Instagram every morning?" Mindy asked.

"I really think the psychographic of our core members is in opposition to this," Catha said. "Come on, we're getting solar panels next year."

"Did you tell her to take it down?" Ruthie asked. "Never mind the psychographic, it's gross."

"I'm a pescatarian," Gloria said.

"I spoke to Doe immediately," Catha said. "I'm a believer in proactivity."

"We should be doing exciting things, like tie-ins with *Hamil-ton*," Gloria said. "I mean, we have Benedict Arnold's *buttons*. Have you explored this?" she asked Ruthie.

"Explored . . . *Hamilton*?" Ruthie asked. "Who can get a ticket?"

"You should write down every suggestion and have a time line to accomplish it," Mindy said. "Remember, we discussed this at your performance review?" She smiled widely, as if she were about to floss out some gristle. "Is Adeline Clay coming to Spork?"

Ruthie still hadn't heard from Mike, though she'd texted him that morning. "I invited her. She said she came here for privacy, so . . ."

"I sent Adeline a basket from Locavoracious," Catha said.

"So proactive, Catha!" Gloria applauded. Literally. Her hands came together in a clap. "They do wonderful baskets. And the name. So clever!"

Ruthie's stomach began to churn. The rapid peppering of accusations felt rehearsed. It was like she was one of those baby penguins being force-fed material already masticated.

"And *everybody* says they come to the North Fork for the laid-back vibe," Catha went on. "I said the same thing to Larry when we decided to move out here. Look at me now, I don't have a free day in the week! Larry curates *The New Yorker* for me, you know—he cuts out the articles I should read? Anyway, they are piling up in my home office, let me tell you. He had to scold me at dinner last night! But you know, work is so consuming."

"Oh, Catha, you do so much," Gloria said.

"Who knows, we could honor her at the gala!" Mindy cried.

"Adeline? But we're committed to Gus Romany," Ruthie said, smiling so hard she felt a muscle jump in her cheek. "We can't shove out someone just because someone richer comes along."

"I think we need to dream big, don't you?" Gloria asked. "And as treasurer, I'm always looking at the bottom line."

"But it would be wrong," Ruthie said, and they all swiveled to stare at her, startled at hearing such an unfamiliar word.

"Oh, my God!" Catha pointed out the window. "She's here!"

Mindy and Gloria craned their necks. Out on the back terrace of the museum, Adeline entered the party, surveying the guests with a chin-lifted interest. Behind her trailed Mike and Jem, who were stopped by Tina Childers, their summer neighbor from across the street. The architect Robert Sample touched Adeline's elbow and Adeline greeted him with a small cry and lifted her face to be kissed on both cheeks.

As if a bell had rung, the three women clattered across the hardwood toward the stairs. In seconds they burst out the front door. She watched Catha, in the lead, eagerly feint and scurry her way to Adeline's side, Uriah Heep in red pumps.

The three women had never stopped smiling. Yet underneath what they said, glinting like vein through rock, was something she recognized, from landlords in her childhood to Peter Clay: contempt. A man might feel anger right now. As a woman, she felt only shame.

11

LATER SHE WOULD remember the party's perfection, and give herself that, at least. The food, the music, the kids running to the craft tables, the conviviality, the pleasure of it. Neighbors and friends under a clearing sky: Dodge and his boyfriend, Hank; the Hellers; the Beavers; Dave Sandman and his daughter Cielo, who won the junior sailing race that year; the art dealer Alex Wilcox, whom everyone later learned was having a secret affair with Dodge that summer; Tracy Field before her stroke; Lionel Partridge telling a magnificent joke; so many pretty women dressed in white; Melissa Fein in a hat with flowers; Clark Fund in shorts so tight he was called "Quads" for the following month.

She saw Jem sticking close to Mike, who was talking to Adeline now. She saw Meret and Saffy wearing cropped T-shirts and tiny shorts, all thrust pelvises and boredom, sucking on lemonades. Catha made a beeline for Ben Farnley, who had just bought that huge spec house off Narrow River Road.

Ruthie stopped every few feet for kisses and hugs and hellos. She had the same conversations she had every summer, *Looks like a hot one* and *Have you seen* and *Have you heard* and, this year,

Did you hear about the whole helipad idea, it will never pass and *Did you hear Adeline Clay is here?*

Ruthie searched the crowd for the board secretary, Helen Gregorian. She needed a touchstone. Helen was a magisterial presence on the board and the owner of one of the most beautiful houses on Village Lane. She lived there most of the year, spending the coldest months in Palm Beach. Ruthie spotted her with Samantha Wiggins, a younger member of the board.

"Ruthie!" Samantha leaned in for an air kiss. "So terrific that Catha got Adeline Clay to come! I heard she sent a basket. Hey, what's all this about Gus killing chickens?"

She forced a chuckle. "It's nothing, an art film he did a long time ago."

Helen put her hand on Ruthie's arm. Ruthie loved her, but Helen tended to deliver information as though the world had been waiting for her to weigh in, on everything from weather to the current state of Syria. "Gloria thinks we should reexamine."

"Well, you know Gloria." Helen had once, in a moment of exasperation, referred to Gloria as a mummified ass.

"We don't want to court controversy unless it's the good kind. Progressive things like farms and sustainable energy," Helen said. "I thought Gus was a vegetarian. When I had him over for dinner, he didn't touch the pot roast. Ruthie, I love your blouse."

Helen cast her gaze around the party. "I don't recognize some of these people. Such a new, vibrant look about them! We do need to reach them. We should have initiatives."

"We do have initiatives," Ruthie said. She swallowed. "Helen, is there something going on I should know about?"

"You really made this party what it is today," Helen said. "I love your sense of fun, Ruthie."

Helen wasn't quite meeting Ruthie's gaze. Blood beat in her ears.

RUTHIE WAS WAYLAID by Mindy's parents. She'd met them several times, and she knew Mindy's husband, Carl, well. She liked him. He didn't do small talk. Often he told her about a dream that had made him sad, or theorized about the invention of things like perforated paper towels. Sometimes he would tell her an intimate anecdote about Mindy—usually something funny, like the time Mindy had farted in front of his father—things that Ruthie knew Mindy would not want her to know.

Mindy's mother was blond and pretty, with delicate bones that Ruthie was sure Mindy wished she'd inherited. Mindy took after her father, stiff and a bit stout, with the same air of someone who had been teased in middle school and had decided to take their revenge on the world at large.

Carl wore white bucks and a yellow-and-green madras jacket that matched Mindy's headband. He kissed her warmly on both cheeks and Mindy reintroduced her to Philip and Nan.

Doe drifted by, phone in hand. "Can I get a shot?"

They moved closer and smiled their public smiles. Doe was such a small lovely creature, her hair cropped short, her acorn-brown eyes lively. Ruthie rarely saw her without her phone in her hand, and she seemed to exist on a diet of pop culture and green juice. She needed to ask her about the Gus Romany Instagram, but not here. Doe waved and strolled off, with Philip trying and failing to avoid watching her walk away.

"Such a lovely day for a fete," Nan said. "I love your blouse. I can't wear pink. Mindy either. She has that florid complexion."

"Florid?" Mindy asked with a rush of heat to her cheeks that rendered her, well, florid.

"Mindy says this is really the event to kick off the season here on the North Fork, if you actually have a season," Philip said with a chuckle.

"It really is," Mindy said. She touched her headband. "I matched my outfit to the invitation. It's the kind of detail people appreciate. It's so funny how everyone notices!"

"We've always been South Fork people," Philip continued. "Have a place in Quogue."

"Summer is my favorite season," Nan said. "It's just delicious.

I love everything about it except corn on the cob. I'm with the French, it's for the pigs. Everything else, I adore. Sunshine, ocean swimming, peonies, pedicures . . ."

"There's a new pedicure place in Southold, Mom," Mindy said, chirping like a middle-schooler instead of a forty-three-year-old woman with three children. "We could go tomorrow."

"I don't know about staying over," Nan said. "I think we should just drive back."

"In Sunday traffic? It will take hours," Carl said. "All the day-trippers are out."

"Amateurs," Philip said, and Carl laughed.

"But I had Carmen make up your room! And the girls really want to see you at breakfast," Mindy said. "I was going to make that blueberry crisp recipe from the *Times*. Then we could all get pedicures together. The place looks cute. You can get hot wax and great massages—"

"Is it clean?" Nan asked. "It has to be clean."

"Of course it's clean, Mom."

Philip turned to Ruthie. "I understand you're a local. You grew up out here?"

"No, I grew up in Queens," Ruthie said.

"Really." He shoved his hands in his pockets and rocked back on his heels. "My farrier lives in Queens."

"I don't know why you'd want a pedicure, you only wear closed-toe shoes," Nan said.

Ruthie had the feeling she was the unwanted guest at the family dinner table. She tried to excuse herself, but Carl turned to her.

"It's the family trait," Carl said. "We call it the—"

"Peasant toe," Nan and Carl said together.

Mindy's father rolled his eyes. "Stop it, you two. Every summer I have to hear this."

"Sorry, Ruthie, family joke," Nan said. "Mindy inherited my mother's thick feet. The big toe is smaller than the second toe. So many of Mindy's cousins have it, too. When we're all on holiday together . . . oh, we laugh!"

"On our honeymoon in Umbria, I called it *paesano*," Carl said, and he and Mindy's mother giggled.

Ruthie felt a rush of sympathy for her nemesis, florid, thick-toed Mindy. Maybe that was the source of her sourness, that she didn't quite fit in with her crowd, right down to her toes. She could see that Mindy's armpits were damp, and she could smell her skin cream, a scent that Ruthie had always disliked. Mike used to say she smelled like a Rite Aid, which was unkind but rather spot-on. She didn't like this glimpse into an unhappy childhood, maybe even an unhappy marriage, because should your husband goad your mother into laughing at your big toe?

"I hear the pedicure place is great," Ruthie said.

Mindy shot her an incandescent look of rage.

"Mindy tells us that Adeline Clay is renting your house," Nan said.

"Let me have Catha introduce you, Mom," Mindy said, turning her back on Ruthie.

Oh, hell, thought Ruthie, *I'm losing my job.*

12

"WHAT A SHITSTORM!" Gus Romany said. Taco breath bathed her ear in heat as he kissed her. "What can I say? My father was a chicken farmer. Beat the shit out of me. It was my big Freudian fuck you. I can't believe those bastards found it!" For the first time since she'd known him, Gus looked old. His Hawaiian shirt was speckled with salsa.

"What bastards?"

"The bastards who find things and put them on the Internet! Ask the bastards if they ever ate a chicken! What I can't figure out is who got hold of it."

"Don't worry about it, Gus," Ruthie said. His face had gone red. His thick fingers picked restlessly at the buttons on his shirt, dislodging a small bit of tomato.

"Somebody told me I'm trending on Twitter," he said. "Some pretty young person who then patiently explained what Twitter was, like I was already dead. I'm sorry about the damn chicken, okay?"

"I know."

"Come and see me, Ruthie, I'm doing new work."

"I'll text you."

"Fuck you, text me, pick up the fucking phone and speak like a human."

"Okay, I'll pick up the fucking phone."

"You won't. You think my best days are behind me."

"Gus—"

"It doesn't matter. I like you anyway. I'm going to get myself another taco. I think there's part of this shirt that hasn't been stained yet."

MIKE STOOD APART, nursing a beer. It was his party stance, amiable, ready to chat, but you had to come to him. Why did that suddenly bother her? Or maybe it always had.

Ruthie walked up in her silk and heels, tossing her newly tousled hair just a little bit.

"You look tired," he said.

"That's because I've just lived through a work saga. Thanks for bringing Adeline."

"Wasn't easy," he said. "Catha freaked her out with cheese and exclamation points. Adeline asked why someone she didn't know sent her such a *haunch* of manchego. And she has another party to go to. But she came."

"Did you fix the step?"

"Yeah, but she found a couple of other things so I'll be there next week. Don't worry, nothing major, let me handle it, okay?"

"Catha took the credit for Adeline coming."

"Shocker."

"You don't like Catha, either?"

"This is a thing with you. I never liked Catha and you always made us have dinner with her and Larry."

"Oh, come on, just because she said she strives to live counterintuitively that *one time,* you decided she was an ass."

"All that cultural omnivorousness. Did I hear the latest Moth podcast? Did I read the article on Gober in *The New Yorker*? Art passes through her like an enema. She doesn't absorb anything. She's a cultural high colonic."

"Hey, watch what you say around a taco truck."

"And don't get me started on Larry," Mike continued. "What a misanthrope. It physically pains him to be pleasant. Every word is a turd he has to strain to squeeze out."

"He's married to a cultural laxative. There you go. Jack Sprat." Ruthie hesitated. "The thing is, I think she might be after my job."

"What? That's crazy. She's your friend. And everybody loves you."

"Not everybody. They're really leaning on me. I'll tell you about it at dinner."

"Dinner?"

"Tonight. The Drift?"

"Oh, shit."

"You forgot?"

"I didn't forget, I just . . . Adeline invited us to this party. I was just going to tell you. It's in the Hamptons. Roberta Verona is going to be there, and Jem's dying to meet her."

"Oh."

Jem ran up, her face alight. "Did Daddy tell you? Can I go? Adeline said she'd introduce me to Roberta Verona! Is it okay what I'm wearing? Adeline said it was fine."

Smiling, Adeline walked up behind Jem. She put a casual hand on Jem's shoulder. "Ruthie, I'm not kidnapping your daughter. You should come, too. It's my friend Daniel, he's sending a launch so we don't have to take the ferry."

"It sounds great, but I can't leave Spork until it's over."

"Well, think about it. You can come when you're done here. I'll text you the address and leave word at the gate."

A party in the Hamptons. With a gate. And could "Daniel" be Daniel Mantis?

"I might be able to get away," she said.

"Marvelous," said Adeline.

13

DOE CRUISED DOWN the side street in Greenport and pulled into the ferry line. It was long, stretching into a residential neighborhood, but she'd expected it. You couldn't make reservations, and locals knew better than to cross on a holiday weekend. She had no choice, and she had patience.

Her gaze drifted to the side, to a tall, narrow shingled house in the middle of a renovation. The house reminded her of a New England that scared her, the one with narrow stairs and attics and cellars and ghosts. She'd grown up in Florida in a concrete block house with no surprises, just an occasional gecko in your shoe. This house was peaked, narrow, gray, with windows on the side that resembled the eyes and mouth of a human face. She hated being scrutinized, even by a house. Today a red towel hung outside a windowsill, a wagging tongue of a taunt.

Guilty.

Gus was a nice old guy, and she'd helped him out a few times with his computer. She'd been the one to organize his digital files, and she found the film. Weird, interesting, some art critic would call it transgressive. She made the mistake of showing a few minutes of it to Catha. Just a snippet, like a cat video on a dull day. She didn't expect her to use it against Ruthie.

It was a slow-motion train wreck, and Ruthie didn't deserve it, but Doe knew that money ran over conscience like a semi ran over a skunk. Only the stink was left. Money like Mindy's was the real deal. There was no board lady alive who would follow her conscience in the face of Mindy's parents, who lived on Park Avenue and were on the boards of Lincoln Center and the Met.

So Ruthie, who was excellent at her job and kept staff on the boil without even seeming to be in the kitchen, would be gone soon. Catha would make a terrible boss, but if Doe could monetize *seekrit-hamptons* by the end of the summer, she could achieve her dream of freelance freedom. She'd never make money working at a nonprofit. She believed in profit, all the way.

She moved up on the line. She'd make the next crossing. There was a tiny stain on her Marc Jacobs seersucker sundress from the taco she had at Spork. She dumped water on it. The only straightforward advice Shari had ever given her? *Blot, don't rub.* It beat *Never buy a white bra* by a mile.

Doe had perfected the art of buying off-season. In the Hamptons the summer people gave to their housekeepers after Labor Day, and the housekeepers loaded up their Subarus and took the haul to the secondhand shops. That took care of clothes and shoes. She knew a Prius wouldn't mark her as a plebe, just someone with a social conscience. She wore no jewelry except fake diamond studs—not even a Muffie could tell if studs were real—and she knew better than to wear a watch. She kept her hair short because no one would notice her lack of a blowout. She had a Tory Burch cover for her phone, and she had scored a Marni canvas and leather bucket bag for two hundred dollars, a price that she could not afford and was why she couldn't afford to pay summer rates to the Doyles.

Drive across Shelter Island, second ferry to Sag Harbor. On

that ten-minute ferry ride she browsed through her bookmarks to calm herself down. She could do this. It could possibly be the biggest party she'd ever crashed, but she knew the neighborhood. She just had to skip out before Adeline showed up. Not that Adeline would recognize her, she was just the girl who took the pictures.

Who was in the Hamptons this early besides the usual crew? She flipped through gossip columns and blogs. She was up on actors and models but she had trouble with athletes and moguls. The rich kids were the hardest, the ones with jobs like "app codesigner" or "style consultant." They all looked the same to her, as though cloned from the same cells, and she had to work at it. She tossed the phone in the passenger seat as they bumped against the pier. She'd have her pick of the hedgie crowd, the media elite. Artists, too. Mantis's daughter, Lark, was some kind of entrepreneur in something Doe couldn't remember, financed by her father, Doe was sure.

She found a space in town, which was lucky. Lift folding bike out of trunk, pedal toward the house, already researched.

Doe had grown up in South Florida with no money, a mother with terrible taste in boyfriends, and a succession of dogs with names like Boo and Moon who escaped regularly and got run over. Her older sister got wise at the age of sixteen and moved in with her boyfriend. Her little brother had drowned in a pool. As soon as she could, Doe got out, working during high school as a towel girl at hotels for tips, making her way toward the glitter and swank of South Beach, where men had slipped hundred-dollar bills in her hand along with notes and numbers. She had come to understand how the hotel service industry had certain kinds of opportunities for advancement. Not one-night stands just for a handful of bills on a dresser, an occupation she felt, considering her background, she was destined for. But an honest living as a tipster. She got to know the bloggers, the photographers, and she tipped them off to the routines of celebrities—who went to which clubs, who would be at what restaurant when. Money was a constantly flowing river, from doorman to manicurist to pool girl to concierge. You got to know who was on the take and the make pretty early, and who you could almost-trust until you couldn't trust them anymore. Most of the celebrities didn't care; they actually wanted the photographers to dog them. Doe had financed a college education and a car on the proceeds. She had been making a decent living before she got mixed up with Ron.

When she got fired from the hotel, she put on a black dress and found the international art crowd. She became one of the art girls who roamed Art Basel, and she met a dealer who gave her a job and entrée to the right parties. He never knew that she took covert photos of celebrities. With just an iPhone, it was amazing what she could do. Sometimes she'd use a camera and just pretend to have press credentials. People rarely asked.

When she had to leave Miami, she needed to go far and fast. She took off with a surfer boyfriend to the Hamptons. He left for Costa Rica but she stayed, broke and freezing in Montauk in November. She walked the streets of East Hampton, took a look at the houses, some visible now, behind the wind-burned twenty-foot hedges. She saw a place to launch herself again. She found her way to the cheaper apartments on the North Fork and lucked into Tim and Kim's garage apartment.

Turned out she liked it here. She liked the quiet cold winters and the summers of opportunity. She had come to ground, she was digging in for a while, catching her breath and making plans. She invented a prep school past and a degree from Reed College— elite, but small and far away enough that she most likely wouldn't run into any alumni—and talked herself into a part-time job at the Belfry. She knew after ten minutes that Ruthie would check her references but not her degree.

When she first got to the North Fork she spent most of her time on tedious ferry rides to the Hamptons. She cultivated tipsters because she knew how to find them, just by hanging at bars in the off-season, making friends, and sleeping around: a manicurist, a waiter for the biggest society caterer, a dog walker, a party planner, some willing to part with information. If she read the local rags and tabloids and stayed alert, she could get lucky at least a few times a weekend with a good shot. There were so many outlets now on the Web, most not offering much, but *seekrit-hamptons* kept doubling and tripling followers.

She folded up the bike and stashed it, pushing it into a thick hedge. Then she took the usual route to get to the beach, racing across a lawn and gardens of a house that she'd heard was tied up in some sort of litigation. No security and no one was ever there. In minutes she was off down the beach, swinging her sandals. She'd learned how to walk like she belonged.

Nobody ever noticed her in the Hamptons. There were legions of tall blondes to ogle. She was small and could be mistaken for a twelve-year-old if you didn't look very hard, and people at these parties rarely did.

There would be security guys, but you could always count on a few people leaving the party to drink on the beach. That's why she always arrived late. The house was behind the dunes, blindingly white with enormous squares of glass. She could glimpse the serene flat plane of the pool in the middle of green grass. The patio was crowded, and people had spilled out onto the lawn. Some people had already walked down onto the beach, but she could see the muscular boys in white pants and tight white Lacoste shirts keeping an eye out.

She stopped to take a wineglass out of her purse. She swung it by its stem and walked toward the people on the beach. When she was a few yards away she waved.

A small clot of young people turned to look at her as she strode toward them.

"Hey, great party," she said, ignoring the eye-roll of one of the girls, clearly not happy at being interrupted. "I came out here with Spencer and I lost my earring! Can you believe it?"

"It happens," one of the blondes said. She turned her back on Doe.

But the gym rat security boys had seen her talking to the group by now, so she stepped back and trilled, "See you up there!"

She climbed up the steps to the patio. A long bench had been set up with a galvanized steel trench full of ice in which pitchers of water and lemon were continually replenished. For feet. She poured the cool water on her feet and an attendant handed her a fluffy white hand towel. Doe dried her toes and slipped back into her sandals. After that Sultan-of-Brunei-ish operation, she simply walked into the party.

She picked a virgin mojito off a tray and wandered across the lawn, scanning for celebs. It never failed to amaze her how uniformly fit and good-looking the people at these parties were. Good genes plus good doctors. Ugly men made sure to marry beautiful women, and their daughters turned out fine. Orthodontia and Botox, a twice-weekly hair appointment, clothes tailored to your body. They owned the world, and they looked that way. Sometimes she took the Long Island Rail Road to the city, and in just the walk from the train track to the subway in Penn Station she saw a variety of features—misshapen noses, shades of skin, moles, crooked teeth—that marked plainness or ugliness or hotness, didn't matter, but it added up to something coarse and alive. Maybe that was why she had to work so hard to navigate this pretty world—there were no obvious physical clues. Character had been smoothed out. The codes were all word choices and accessories.

The gigantic white house rising next to her looked barely tethered and ready to sail. A wall of glass faced her, and a cloud moved behind the sun. She could just see inside. In an almost empty room, a man sat with his back to her, cross-legged on a white leather bench. He wore a sweatshirt with the hood up. Now that she'd noticed him she couldn't look at anything else.

"You're blocking my view."

Doe turned. A tall, bony girl a little older than she was stood looking at her. The sun was behind her, sparking her blond highlights. Doe recognized her immediately. Lark Mantis, Daniel's daughter. Pretty, not beautiful, but dude, those legs. That style.

"Sorry." Doe didn't move out of the way.

"His hood is up," Lark said. She gestured with a hand holding her cocktail glass. The other hand held a silver flask.

"Yeah."

"When the hood is up, no one can interrupt him. It's his Bat-Signal."

"So why does he sit where everyone can see him?"

"That's the whole *point*? He's meditating or whatever?" She tilted her head and stumbled a bit. Doe realized she was half drunk.

"Hey, I don't know you."

"Doe Callender."

"Doe. As in 'a deer'? Wow, we both have parents who are seriously bad namers. I'm Lark."

"Lark is cool."

"Well, it helps when you're an apothecary to have a spirit guide." Doe could tell that this was a line she'd used many times.

"Apothecary?"

"I make potions. Like a witch."

"A good witch or a bad witch?"

"Which would you prefer?"

Doe hesitated. So they were flirting. "Bad. Definitely."

"Then I'll be bad, just for you." Lark smirked and poured liquid into Doe's glass. "Boring virgin mojitos." She leaned in close to Doe and took a sniff. "Nice. I'm going to guess."

"Guess . . ."

"What you're wearing. Your soap or lotion or perfume or whatever. I'm going to guess the dominant note. Can I . . . ?" Lark didn't wait for an answer but leaned in, and this time her nose touched Doe's hair and the heat of her breath hit Doe's earlobe.

"Lemongrass. Am I right?"

"Amazing." Doe decided not to mention she used soap from

the supermarket, soap she chose because it had no scent. "So you make . . ."

"Essential oils. Lotions. I had a farm in Vermont where I grew flowers and herbs. My dad was totally *not* into it. Didn't get it, whatever. Yale MFA, internship at MoMA, why am I picking daisies? Not daisies, I told him, *calendula.* For years he tells me to follow my bliss. Now it's, Get a job. You have no idea."

Lark stared out at the ocean. She had all the money in the world and the eyes of a broken person. For Doe, always an irresistible combination. She took a tiny sip of her drink. She had a rule about no alcohol at parties.

"So. Truth or dare?" Lark asked.

"Dare."

"I totally knew you'd say that!" She leaned in closer, lime and rum on her breath.

"Go in and interrupt him? Just get him to drop the hood. I need to talk to him. If you win, you get . . . you get . . . uh, me!" Lark clinked her glass against Doe's. "Dinner at Sant Ambroeus. Here or the city. My treat. Obviously. Or," she added, reconsidering, "lunch."

Doe felt the rum hit her almost empty stomach. She bit her bottom lip and squinted. "All I have to do is go in there?"

"And get him to take off the hood."

Her first rule was *No alcohol,* and her second rule was *Never attract too much attention.* But she'd get inside the house. She could get a shot of Daniel Mantis, another one, or maybe a guest in the inner circle, intimate enough to be in the house instead of on the lawn. She didn't believe for one second that this girl would ever follow through on a lunch date.

Lark grinned and grabbed her hand. She felt a jolt of dangerous attraction at the feel of Lark's fingers. She allowed herself to be tugged to the side of the house.

What Doe had thought was a floor-to-ceiling window was actually a door. Lark flipped a chrome panel and punched in a number.

"The white door on the right. Go, Doe."

Doe heard the hard g and the imprint of tongue on palate on the d. An erotic charge distracted her. For a moment, only a moment, only a flash, she pictured them in bed, Lark whispering.

Go, Doe.

She went.

14

RUTHIE SAT ON the ferry line for forty-five minutes, much of it facing a house that looked like a face with a tongue. She thought of Adeline and Mike and Jem on the launch. Who called a boat a launch? It seemed such a 1920s notion, something that Scott and Zelda would do, take a launch to a party.

She had left Spork as soon as she could, and she knew there would be a ferry line, but it had been a long time (never?) since she'd tried to get to the South Fork on a holiday weekend. There was no way, however, she would miss a Daniel Mantis party. It had been worth it just for the look on Catha's face when she'd told her she was leaving to go there. Catha had almost swallowed her wineglass.

She knew that the chances of meeting anyone she could woo to the museum were slight. Hamptons were Hamptons, and Daniel Mantis was a shark too big for her net. But she'd parlay this as far as she could, and she would beat back Mindy and her lieutenant Gloria. The problem was, what to do about Catha, who was clearly conspiring for her job? She'd watched Catha work the party, seen her scurry and smile. She had actually *scampered* to keep up with the interior designer who had that cable show. Usually at events they were partners, making sure things went smoothly. They would meet up, exchange information or a joke, move on.

This afternoon Catha had never caught her eye. Not once. Her avoidance had been striking. If she was the nail in Ruthie's coffin, Ruthie wasn't going to hand her the hammer.

They'd worked closely together for years, their skills congruent. She couldn't conceive of a person who would put ambition over decency, which meant she'd learned absolutely nothing from working for Peter Clay.

THE PARTY WAS crowded. She couldn't find Mike and Jem. Ruthie grabbed a drink and wandered over to the pool, where enormous hot-pink pool toys floated, three swans with surprisingly evil faces.

"I'm having fun with it."

She turned. Dodge was standing, smiling at her. He waved his glass at the pool toys. "The Whitney is interested. We're stalled, though. I want them to put a pool on one of the outdoor spaces. Liability is a bitch."

Oh, they were his. "I hadn't seen your new work. It's fun. Scary."

"Yeah, basically my favorite combo," he said. "Kitsch plus aggression. Listen, Ruthie, I just want you to know I'm with you."

"With me?"

"I get your vision. You turned on the gas over there. They're lucky to have you."

Once again, people were talking to her as if she'd been accused of something. "Um. Thank you."

"Hey, have you seen Joe? He's here somewhere," Dodge said, waving his glass. "You two must know each other. He was Peter's dealer, you worked for Peter . . . same time, right?"

"Joe?"

"Joe Bloom."

"Joe Bloom?"

Stop repeating his name, she told herself as the word *bloom* unfurled inside her. More than twenty years ago. Her summer fling that flung her straight into a wall.

She'd heard years ago that Joe Bloom had left the art world and moved out west. She had stuck a stupid cowboy hat on his head whenever he popped into her memory, and turned him into a cartoon.

"Yeah, he moved out here. He owns a restaurant in Greenport."

Penny and Elena. The oyster place. *Joe Somebody.* She could not reconcile Joseph Bloom, slim in his Hugo Boss suits, with a guy opening oysters at an old bait shack.

"Hang on. Joe!" Dodge yelled, and Ruthie closed her eyes, glad she had this instant, at least, to collect herself.

She turned. He was slightly heavier, dressed in khakis, bare feet in sneakers. He was older. So was she. He looked better. Men.

He smiled and walked toward her. "Ruthie?"

"Joe!" She managed to release the word, but it sounded like an accusation.

He leaned over to kiss her cheek. Impression of stubble and soap and underneath it the scent she remembered, an instant hit. "It's been so long. You look . . . different."

"You're not supposed to say that to a woman," Ruthie said. "You're supposed to say, You look exactly the same."

"I meant it as a compliment, actually."

"Oh, because I used to look so much worse than this?"

"Can we start over?"

"Hi, Joe," Ruthie said. "So great to see you again after all these long years. You look exactly the same!"

"You too!" He stepped back, and she felt herself scrutinized, the better version of her, the Carole version.

"Seriously, though," Joe said. "I remember you in a ponytail, some old T-shirt, splattered with paint. Overalls, even."

Maybe Ruthie should have worn her own clothes after all; Joe was used to seeing her stained. "I hear you have a restaurant in Greenport."

"It's fantastic," Dodge said. "Best oysters around."

"Not a restaurant. I can't handle a restaurant, but a shack with two items, I can do. It's sort of an early retirement." He tilted his head, and she saw the gray in his hair. He had a way of lowering his eyelids, as though he was thinking of either sex or a nap. She'd forgotten that.

"I'll let you two catch up," Dodge said. "I'm party-hopping today."

Dodge wandered off, and they just looked at each other for a moment.

"So," Joe said.

"So," she answered, the way people who had hurt each other a long time ago do.

He had been Peter's dealer, so they'd been on the phone often, since she ran the studio. Details of images to be sent, exhibitions to prepare for. They'd sat at the same expensive restaurant tables celebrating openings, only she would be at the far, far end, or else at the separate table with the nobodies.

Then she'd run into him outside Peter's studio one hot July afternoon. Peter was out in Sag Harbor; everyone in New York, it seemed, was away.

It's so hot. Shall we have a beer? Sure. Maybe it was his use of that slightly formal "shall" that had been the first seduction. She had walked into that bar not knowing what would happen, just feeling the current of sudden interest between them. An art dealer, a rich man, a slightly older man, way out of her league.

After the beers she'd brought him to her place to show him what she was working on. At the time she'd had an illegal sublet in Tribeca, five hundred square feet of loft carved out of a larger one in front. She had her own entrance, reaching it by a back staircase down an alley with an active rat population. She'd had to stamp her way down, making them scatter and dive. Sometimes she turned it into a dance. She was an artist with a loft in New York. Just that fact alone kept her level.

Joe had looked at everything, her books, her bedspread, her sketches pinned to the wall. He'd twirled a mobile made of fishing line and painted paper fish. At last he'd stood in front of the painting. He had pointed to an area where color met color.

"There," he said. "That's why you're good."

Edges were something that artists knew, how they were a test to resolving a painting. When Joe had turned around he'd reached for her, and even now when Ruthie thought of this she knew it had been some sort of peak in her life, Joe's approval and desire, all in the same moment.

Was he thinking of it now, that summer evening? That first kiss? Or was he thinking of the breakup, when she dumped her glass of wine in his lap, then reached over the table, grabbed his glass, and repeated the gesture? She'd almost forgotten that, how there had been a time in her life when she had acknowledged her anger. The Italian waiter had hurried over to bring her another glass and wipe down the table, ignoring Joe completely. Joe had sat, looking down, not even attempting to blot his pants. She had downed the glass the waiter had replenished in two long swallows and walked out. It was the last time she'd seen him except for Google. He'd married the woman he'd left her for.

A tall, pretty girl suddenly floated out of the background. "Hello! Joe, I didn't see you!"

"Lark." An exchange of cheek kisses, and Joe turned to Ruthie. "Ruthie, do you know Lark Mantis? Lark, Ruthie Beamish. Ruthie is the director of the Belfry Museum in Orient."

"The North Fork! I love it. So chill."

"Ruthie and I knew each other long ago and far away in a land called SoHo," Joe said. "Back when there were still artists there. Ruthie managed Peter's studio. We are the survivors of the great war. Peter Clay's ego against the world."

"Wow, every time I hear you talk about Peter Clay, I go all fan-girl spazzy," Lark said. "I can't really ask Adeline about him. Tell me one thing I don't know."

Ruthie exchanged a glance with Joe. What could they say? He liked figs and cheese? He never spoke to his assistants before noon? He sank her grant applications for years without her knowing? He would agree to be her reference, and then tell the foundation or the gallery or whoever it was that her work wasn't up to their standards.

Furious, she had confronted him. He had said that she needed to face her mediocrity. Her paintings were good but would never be great. However, she was the best studio assistant because she was a magpie, a mimic. To ask for genius was folly. He was doing her a favor.

His words were cruel, but better than when he was drunk and yelled across the studio, "Cunts can't paint!" While she was painting his canvases.

"Hmm," Joe said. "When he left my gallery, he let me find out by reading it in the art trades. Then he sent me a basket of fruit."

"Seriously?" Ruthie asked.

Joe laughed. "Apples from some orchard upstate. Clearly a re-gift. I took them down to his studio and just started throwing them at the windows. I learned that you can't break a window with an apple, you just look like an idiot. And that was the end of me and Peter."

"He couldn't handle guilt, so he gave parting gifts," Ruthie said. "They always missed the mark. A few months after I left and he screamed that he'd get revenge, I got a delivery. A whole shipment of art supplies, some of them used. It was like he'd just dumped the contents of a corner of the studio into a box. I think there was a half sandwich in there. Random CDs. Paints half squeezed. A pencil." She decided not to mention the blank canvases, one with C U N T scrawled on it in Peter's signature blue.

"A Peter Clay apology," Joe said.

"Or a taunt," she said. "I was never sure."

"Wow, this is awesome," Lark said. "I feel all insidery. Ruthie, Daddy has a killer Peter Clay. You should take a look at it. Just walk in the front door." She drifted off.

Joe smiled at Ruthie. "Now here we are again. Two insidery people, out here in the bucolic country."

"I never understood that word," Ruthie said. "It isn't nearly pretty enough to describe a landscape. It sounds like a stomach condition, or one of those old-fashioned medicines, like castor oil."

"Dress the wound with bucolic and call me in the morning?"

"Tums neutralize bucolic acid three times faster than milk."

"So tell me," Joe said. "Are you married now?"

"Separated. Divorced, really. We just haven't made it legal."

"Oh. Sorry."

"It's okay," Ruthie assured him. "We're still good friends. We parted amicably, as they say."

"How does one manage that, exactly?"

"Carefully."

"Wow," Joe said. "I had to move to Brooklyn when I broke up with my ex. We could barely share Manhattan. Now I'm as far east as I can go, in Orient. But don't go thinking I'm bitter. In my better moments, I know that it wasn't meant to work out for us, and I wish her well."

"How many better moments do you have?"

"I'm having one right now," Joe said, tilting his head back. "As a matter of fact I'm going all fangirl spazzy just seeing you again."

Ah, so this was why Cupid had a bow and arrow. *Thwack.* "How are you liking Orient?"

"Love it. It's beachy yet verdant."

"Now, there's a word that sounds like what it means. Verdant."

"Not like that nasty upstart, bucolic."

He smiled again, and Ruthie decided it was time to go. She was out of practice at repartee, and she felt winded. "This is nice. But

I'm sorry, I have to find my daughter," she said. "I'll see you around."

"That's what small towns are for, I hear. Seeing people around."

Ruthie turned and walked away, profoundly grateful that she now had an ass.

15

THE HOUSE ARRANGED itself around Doe as she walked in, the way perfect houses do. She'd been in a few in Miami where the space unfolded, the sight lines planned for the view. Floor, blue slate. An enormous freestanding gray stone fireplace in the middle of the room. The visual shock of just blue—ocean and sky—through enormous windows that were walls. She could happily move in here tomorrow and discover she had a soul.

Through an open archway (though it was square of course, no round forms in this house) she could glimpse the formal dining room. A long, long table she wouldn't want to have to polish. Uncomfortable-looking chairs. Her ass wouldn't last through the soup course. A scratchy abstract on the wall.

Facing her, an amazing Rothko, floating color, blue and that deep sad black. One of her art teachers had loved Rothko and talked about the depth of that black, of how spiritual Rothko was. *He paints the abyss,* he would say, *but he gives us hope.* Doe still felt impatient, remembering. Rothko was a master, sure, but spiritual? Overreach. His paintings were physical, color and form.

Art wasn't about feelings. If you want feelings, go to the movies. If you want God, go to a church.

On the opposite wall the predictable big Ed Ruscha. Every great house in Miami had one. Just yellow letters against blue. HAPPY MESS. Did it refer to Lark? That would require a sense of humor. Doe had yet to meet a super-wealthy person who would make fun of themselves.

It could be the most beautiful room she'd ever been in or it could be designed to make her feel flimsy.

What *the fuck* was she doing?

Doe turned away from her rumpled reflection in a mirrored sculpture that looked like a Louise Bourgeois. With a jolting heartbeat, she heard footsteps approaching. Nowhere to hide in a minimalist house, that was the trouble. Doe backed up, flattening herself next to the gray wall of the fireplace.

Footsteps clattered into the space. A woman in heels. How the hell did Adeline Clay get here so fast?

Adeline was too angry to see Doe. She went right to the door of the room where Daniel Mantis sat meditating and crashed it open.

"For God's sake, Daniel. Take off the hood."

Too good to miss. Doe slipped out of her sandals and tiptoed across the floor. By tilting her head toward the sculpture she could see the fractured reflected image of Adeline standing in the room, Daniel sitting cross-legged facing her. "I've been here for twenty minutes."

No answer.

"This is ridiculous, Daniel! Take off the hood!"

"I don't like scenes."

"This isn't a scene, this is me talking to you. You are being rude."

"This isn't ego-driven. Isn't everyone enjoying themselves?"

"We can all *see you* in here! I realize that's the point, but it's *comical*."

"Comical is this event that Lark talked me into. More farms

on the South Fork? As if these people are going to knock down their houses."

"Do we have to talk about this right here?"

"What is it with this girl and farms? She grew up on Park Avenue. I'm seriously worried. She just keeps . . . *flitting*. People ask about her and I have to lie. I don't enjoy that."

"She needs your attention."

"Thirty thousand dollars to throw a party isn't enough? Adeline, you're my hostess. You can greet the guests for a few minutes."

"I'm not the hostess. These people aren't my guests."

"Apparently one is. The guy in the Gap pants."

"It's Michael Dutton, he owns the house I'm staying in. I invited him with his family. It seemed like the nice thing to do. Am I not allowed to invite guests?"

"Is it just Lark who needs more of my attention?"

"Don't be ridiculous."

"Just so we're clear. This was your choice. We had an agreement. You were to live here this summer. You were the one who went ahead and rented a house without telling me. In a place I can't get to."

"There's this thing called a ferry."

"I had to send you a *launch*. A launch and a car. Now who is being manipulative? It's a *journey* to get there. You *removed* yourself from our plans. Without telling me beforehand, I recall. Didn't we say from the beginning, *Let's have honesty between us*."

"All right. I rented the house. I didn't want to be in the Hamptons, I didn't want to go to parties like this all the time. I wanted a place to retreat to if I had to. If we don't have an exclusive relationship, why should I give up myself for you?"

"I never asked you to give up yourself. I'm trying to teach you how to *be* yourself within the context of a committed relationship."

Doe had to muffle her snort.

"Committed relationship? When you have another woman and a third in the wings?"

"I have other committed relationships, yes. You accepted that. Have things changed?"

"I don't know. Yes. Maybe."

Adeline's voice skittered around, but Daniel never lost his soft monotone. Doe had to strain every muscle to hear him.

"I see."

"I did agree to your terms. Yes. But I didn't think that your latest mistress would be at the same parties, either! I don't care too much about Samantha's existence, but I do care that she's in my face. Our agreement was New York was my territory."

"She's staying in Amagansett, I could hardly not invite her. I thought you two could be friends. You have a lot in—"

"If you complete that sentence, that hoodie is in the ocean."

Oh, please, let me get that shot, Doe thought. Us Weekly, *here I come!*

She moved to the right of the door, hoping to get a photo at an angle.

"I can't talk to you about this now," Daniel said. "It is extremely unprofessional for you to bring it up—"

"Excuse me?"

"I didn't mean to say unprofessional. I meant to say unmannerly."

"Oh, really? Well, I meant to say fuck you."

Doe heard the footsteps and was around the fireplace before Adeline had clattered back into the room, moving fast. Doe flattened against the stone but the two were intent only on each other.

Daniel reached Adeline and grabbed her arm. It was a hard grab. Doe felt sweat spring along her spine. They were in profile, their faces and bodies in perfect tense lines of fury. She snapped the shot.

His voice was so clear. Doe knew that low pitch of threat. Her stomach turned over.

"You don't want to start this. Not with me."

"What is that supposed to mean?"

"It means I create the narrative. Not you."

Adeline threw off his arm. She stalked out of the room. Daniel let out a breath. She watched his shoulders move. He waited until he heard the front door slam. Then he walked out into the hall.

Doe backed up and slipped out the door. It closed behind her with a soft click. *Damn, shoes.* She'd left them behind.

"EXCUSE ME. CINDERELLA?"

Her sandals dangled from his fingers. He was about her age, twenty-two or -three. A face to take your breath away. She felt his ticking assessment, up, down, all around. Blond hair, blue eyes the color of Miami ocean when the sky was white.

She chose not to smile. This one was too used to the smiles of girls.

"Prince Charming—I knew you'd show up eventually. How did you find me?"

"You're the only barefoot girl." He held the shoes out of her reach. "How come I don't know you?"

"Do you know everyone?"

"I know all the beautiful girls in the Hamptons."

"I could have sworn you took in more territory than that."

"*Sabrina*!" He shook his head. "I've had about six girlfriends who were obsessed with that movie. I don't get it. She ends up with the boring old guy?"

"Who controls the family fortune. Is that so dumb? Anyway, it's all about the clothes."

"I knew that. So, I found these inside the house."

"I'm a friend of Lark's."

"Coincidence. Me too. Yet I don't know you."

"I had to tiptoe out. Daniel was wearing his hoodie," she said. "Apparently you're not supposed to interrupt him."

He shrugged. "Stupid house rule, right? But at least it's out in the open. It's those hidden ones that catch you. Anyway, I'd put up with it if I got to live in that house, wouldn't you?"

"I don't put up with anything," she said. She meant it to sound careless, but it came out hard and fast.

He tilted his head. She saw she'd snagged him. Before it was just play. "Lucas," he said.

"Doe," she said.

He didn't make the "a deer" comment, like everyone did. "I think I like you."

"The jury's out on you, though," Doe countered. "Just so you know."

"That's okay," he said. "I don't need to be liked. Just appreciated."

Lark suddenly careened into view, a full glass in her hand. She grabbed onto Doe and kissed her on the mouth. "You did it!" she cried. "Now I owe you me!"

Just like that, standing between the two of them, her summer shook itself out like a sail.

16

DANIEL STUCK OUT his hand. "Daniel Mantis."

"Ruth Beamish," Ruthie said, shaking his hand and trying to cover her embarrassment. "I'm sorry, you caught me admiring your Rothko. Your daughter told me to take a peek at the Peter Clay, and I got waylaid."

"You like Peter's work?"

"I worked for him back in the nineties."

"Then you must see the painting. But first, the Rothko. Come on, you need a closer look."

She followed him farther into the house. "It's a lovely party, thank you. I'm sort of crashing. Adeline Clay invited me."

He swiveled. "You know Adeline?"

"She's renting my house."

"Ah. You're the one with the nice husband."

"Ex-husband."

"I see."

A blue slate floor, and out the back, the sudden shock of ethereal blue of sea and sky through the enormous wall of glass.

White and blue everywhere. She tried to tiptoe. This was a space in which even a footfall felt unseemly.

"The house is extraordinary," she said. "It's like heaven, if God had taste."

"Ha. I like that. It's a sacred space, isn't it," Daniel agreed. "The volumes are so carefully articulated, yet you get no sense of effort. I look at this and I can't see schematics or blueprints. Just inspiration. It's as though it was always here, isn't it? Yet the modernity grounds you in the now."

His stump speech, she could tell. He recited it as though someone else had written it for him.

"Come, I want to show you something. I can tell you'll appreciate it." He moved farther into the vast cathedral of the house.

She could glimpse the formal dining room. A long table that could seat twenty or more, the wood polished and rich. A stunning Cy Twombly on the wall. "The chairs are beautiful."

"Jacques Adnet." He stopped. "Sometimes I just stand here for twenty minutes at a time. It's the exact center of the house. And of course the Rothko right in your center sight."

That Rothko, floating blue and anchoring black.

"The Richter abstract to your left." A knockout-punch Richter, skeins of bright paint over navy. Ruthie estimated maybe forty million. It was a guess; it could be worth more.

"Now look down."

She looked down at a tiny square of golden tile in the middle of the stone floor.

"I had the architect put in that square. The guy argued with me, like he was the boss. Look up."

She looked up into a blue sky through a skylight.

"I think of this space, right here, as art. Just here. Do you feel it? It's like my own Turrell. I walk in every Friday, and I stop. This is where I center. This is where serenity kicks in."

Could serenity actually kick?

"Do you feel it? Like you're at the center of a turning world?"

What does one say to a billionaire except "Yes."?

"Let's exhale."

Obediently she blew out a breath.

"I like to come here right after meditating, before espresso, without any chemical buzz. And now, the Rothko again. Do you see it now through a different lens?"

Ruthie struggled for the right thing to say, something that wasn't a hearty *Bullshit*. A riff. "When I first saw it I was struck by how well it reflects the elements of the house. Repeated forms, that deep blue. Now I'm seeing something *within* the painting, maybe back to the intent of the artist himself. I'm seeing that Rothko didn't suck out light, he infused the painting with it. Even the black."

"Exactly. It's a spiritual exercise, standing here." Daniel beamed at her.

He didn't command her to exhale, but she did.

"And now, the dialogue with the Clay."

"From the Dowager Series. A good picture."

They walked closer. On the opposite wall from the Rothko hung a signature Peter Clay portrait, a piece Ruthie was intricately familiar with, being that she had been the one to paint it. Peter had become bored with the actual process of painting later in his career, spending all of his time thinking about art rather than doing it. That was for his studio assistants. She'd gone from mixing colors to underpainting to painting under Peter's direction as he sat in the red upholstered armchair, drink in hand, and yelled instructions across the studio. She had a sudden plunge backward, remembering the smell of the studio, the blare of the music—the Allman Brothers, Pink Floyd, Fairport Convention.

In the beginning, just being in the studio with Peter was thrilling—she'd started when she was still a student. There were long stretches of boredom while he sat in a chair, talking to his dealer or collectors, and then sudden, brilliant bursts of talk and, occasionally, sketching. Peter could draw a line on a page and she could identify it as his mark, and probably still had the muscle memory to replicate it. She had been in the presence of something that ordinary people didn't have, maybe even couldn't comprehend, and she'd felt privileged to see it.

For a while.

She wasn't surprised that Daniel had a Dowager painting. Society portraits, Peter had called them, most of them commissions. Peter hadn't thought much of them but now those portraits turned out to be the ones that survived to influence contemporary artists, with their thin washes of paint and simple lines, close to cartoons. The subject matter made art critics foam and lather. He painted daring young socialites as dowagers, their older selves, and dowagers as ingénues, vacuous or rapacious. Some of them awkwardly, splendidly nude. They all loved the recognition but no doubt hated the portraits. "What a hoot," they had said, "how marvelous." They were rarely flattering, and most of the subjects had sold them.

"A dialogue? I'm not sure," she said. "More like a standoff. Rothko liked a raw, rough canvas, and Peter of course was the opposite, a very tight weave. He was all about precision, that sort of eggshell Renaissance quality. It's like Peter is saying, *You think you know blue, Mark, my friend? Now, this is a blue.*"

"Arrogant bastard," Daniel said, grinning. "That's why I love him. Didn't he always say he was a misanthrope rather than a misogynist? And people couldn't tell the bloody difference?"

"Actually he said people couldn't tell the *fucking* difference, but yes."

"Ha. I think it's brutal in all good ways," Daniel said. "The life force unleashed."

"Yes, he captured spirit, didn't he." She gestured at the painting. "But I have to confess I still see the misogyny."

"I don't believe in misogyny," he said. "It's too limiting. I believe in tribalism."

He reached over and touched her wrist, then lifted it. For a panicked moment she thought he was about to make a pass. But he only looked at the watch. "May I?" There was a detail on it, a slender piece of metal that she realized could slide as Daniel touched it.

Fairy sounds. *Ding ding ding* and then a higher *ping ping ping ping* . . . coming from the watch itself. Some kind of alarm?

"Lucky you," he said. "I almost bought one once. Just for that minute repeater music. The vintage ones are hard to find."

He gave her a look that indicated she was undergoing a re-evaluation. "I'll have to check out the Belfry sometime."

"That would be great. I'm always there."

"Dedication. I like it."

A woman appeared at the end of the hall, dressed in a white polo shirt and black pants. A housekeeper. She stood still, and Ruthie had a feeling it was a signal. Nothing so crass as a raised hand, or a nod.

"If you'll excuse me," Daniel said. "Party details. My daughter always tells me she'll handle everything and then halfway through she's dancing on the beach. Take your time, explore a bit, enjoy the art."

The two disappeared behind a white wall.

Ruthie peeked down a hallway and found another room, this one with a fireplace and an Ed Ruscha. She jumped when she saw herself reflected in a mirrored sculpture that looked vaguely like Louise Bourgeois but wasn't, and then into another room, this one with glass walls that faced the activity on the lawn and four white leather Mies benches placed in a perfect square. One exquisite curved steel hook in the wall with a gray hoodie hanging on it. That was it, no other furniture. No art, but she sat down anyway.

Ruthie lifted her arm. The watch slid like a bracelet, or a handcuff. She had barely looked at the watch this morning, just strapped it on. She noticed, maybe for the first time, how beautiful it was. She examined the smooth moony texture of the dial, the elegance of the numerals.

The hair on her neck prickled.

She reached for her phone and plugged in Patek Philippe. Scrolling and searching. AUCTION PRICES . . . IMPORTANT WATCHES . . . IMAGES . . .

What the heck was a minute repeater?

Holy crap. She pinched the glass on her phone, and the image bloomed. She looked from her wrist to the screen.

If it were real, it wouldn't be nickel or steel, it would be platinum.

With shaking fingers she unbuckled it, then looked at the transparent back. She pushed the metal slide again. *Ding ding ding ding ding ping ping tring tring tring tring tring tring tring* . . .

It was five thirty-seven. It had just told her the time.

Which meant she was holding at least a quarter of a million dollars in her hand.

How could it be real, tossed in a box for a six-year-old? But who could make a fake this beautiful, this intricate? Surely someone could. People faked everything.

What had Carole said? Vintage stores and Canal Street and the Brooklyn Flea. Canal Street vendors ran whole businesses on fakes.

Was it possible that it was real, and Carole didn't know? She'd bought a box full of junk for dress-up. A jumble of jewelry, of glitter and glass. A little girl pawing through it, ignoring the utilitarian, going for the bangles. A fortune tossed aside.

But if it was real . . . The cost of the watch would be so little to Carole and Lewis, a fraction of an annual bonus. For her . . . she could pay off the mortgage. They could own the house clear.

How many of her fights with Mike had centered on money? Where to spend it, how to save it. Unlike her, he hadn't grown up without it.

Mike wasn't used to the scramble for rent, let alone the fear. The shock of his parents' death in a car accident was followed by the shock of discovering that they weren't just New England parsimonious, they were in debt. They had been running on the fumes of the Dutton family inheritance, and it had petered out years before. They'd sold the family house and were renting from the new owners. The erosion of his dreams, for Mike, had resulted in an aggrieved battle with a world that had cheated him.

In one of their most spectacular fights, Mike had called her on the big lie of their marriage: that they got the best of the house. They said it at Thanksgiving, as they sat around the fire. They said it at Christmas, they said it on snowy February afternoons, they said it when the forsythia bloomed. Oh, the spectacular fall! The fairyland winter! The explosive spring! Bullshit! Mike had cried, brandishing a spatula in the air. They lived in a summer town, they had never had it between Memorial Day and Labor Day, not after the first year, when the house was still crap and they were broke. *We never made a home, we made an investment. Admit it!*

They had been doing the dishes, and Ruthie had gone on primly rinsing a cup, resisting the urge to throw it against the wall. She did not believe in hurling crockery during arguments. She didn't believe in arguments. Mike had never raised his voice to her before. When he was angry, he just accented his consonants. He called her by her name and hit the R hard, his lips forming an angry rosebud. *RRU-thie.*

"It's all such a compromise," Mike said. "Can't hang my paintings because they aren't neutral enough, have to have only white sheets and towels so that we can bleach them, only white paint, white plates, white cups, white fucking slipcovers." He shook a white plate at her. *This is our life!* he'd shouted. *This crummy white plate!*

What are you talking about, crummy? It's Williams Sonoma!

The plate had been Frisbeed against the wall, and shattered. Crockery had been thrown. Ruthie had stared at the shards and thought, *Well, it's only a salad plate. How bad could this be?*

Within six months, he'd moved out.

She rose and went to the window. How funny life was. She had stood with a billionaire admiring his fifty-million-dollar painting (How much were Rothkos now, worth unimaginable for one person to afford, yet they did, mere museums could no longer afford to buy these paintings . . . sixty million? Eighty?) while wearing couture and (possibly) a quarter of a million dollars on her wrist. Had Daniel's notice of the watch changed her in his eyes, was that the meaning of the warmer look, the reevaluation of her importance?

There was a whole world around her in this blessed landscape, with these beautiful people, that took these exquisite things as a given. Something painted out of anguish could sit on a wall and be worth fifty times her house, something purchased for ornament on a wrist could change a life. This was the stuff of revolutions, she supposed. But that never worked. This was the way of things. Money was the golden square. The fulcrum of the turning world.

If you held the thing that could change everything, if it could ease your anguish, repair what had been broken . . . if it could give you exactly what you wanted . . . would you just toss it back in a box?

She pushed the slider again. *Ding ding ding* . . . She heard the music of time marked, and even as she listened, she felt it pass.

Out the wide window, she finally spotted her family. Finally, there they were, her people. They stood talking to Adeline on the lawn. Strange how she'd been to two parties with Adeline and had yet to have a conversation. Ruthie was always on the opposite side of the gathering. Mike slung an arm around Jem as he laughed at something Adeline said. Sunlight on blond heads, a sky like a vault, a shimmering sea. Gold and blue.

Ruthie felt a wave of displacement take her over, and she placed her hands on the glass. She had a sudden urge to beat against it. The connectors to Mike, to Jem, already stretched (divorce, adolescence), now vibrated in her chest, close to a snap. *Heart strings,* she thought. She felt as fragile as paper, the fishmonger's daughter gazing down at royalty so fine it could only be envied, not overthrown.

It was only a moment, only a trick of the eye. It was this dappled buttery light, this ravishment, this ridiculous overripe Renoir in a rich man's garden, everything a stroke of pure pigment. It was not a premonition, she thought at that moment, though later, of course, she knew it was. Poor Ruthie! That pretty summer afternoon, she thought it could be happiness.

Independence
Day

17

ALL JUNE, RUTHIE heard about Adeline. Adeline was enchanted by the yacht club and wanted to join, even though she didn't sail. Adeline had bought an old bike and was spotted cycling down Narrow River Road. Adeline had asked when scallop season started and was startled to hear it was fall.

She read about her, too. Everyone did. They all clicked on the links. Her split with Daniel Mantis—that dramatic photograph of her holding up a hand, as if to hold him off, and Mantis looking like a thug—was splattered among the tabloids, but it was counted as a mark in her favor. She'd split with a billionaire!

They caught glimpses of her, driving into town, or her arms full of lavender walking down Village Lane. They liked her baggy shorts and Chucks. They liked how she made an effort to be just folks, even if she didn't socialize with more than a wave.

Ruthie was always struck by how Adeline moved radiantly through the world as if it were arranging itself around her. It was either Botox or inner peace. She never got close enough to tell.

. . .

THE VILLAGE WAS filling when Ruthie arrived for the Heritage Day parade. People streamed out of their houses, holding coffee mugs and dog leashes, everyone dressed in various combinations of red, white, and blue. The parade was forming at the end of the street, beribboned tractors and wagons and kerchiefed dogs and children on bikes trailing streamers. It was a day when bunting had its moment. The annual reading of the Declaration of Independence would be followed by hot dogs in Poquatuck Park. Today no one cranked about politics; they were happy to celebrate America.

As Ruthie walked and waved, she pondered. An ominous email had slithered into her inbox that morning, and Ruthie was still anxious about its significance. It was the Fourth of July weekend. It was time to call in the French.

Ducking down a side street, she dialed the phone, and relief flooded her when Carole answered. She hit her with the information in a sputtering barrage like a faulty artillery gun—Mindy had asked for a meeting with Gloria and Helen to discuss "the next phase," what the hell. She had a bad feeling. Did Carole know about this?

"*Merde,*" Carole said. "No idea. Things were going so well. Let me call her and I'll call you back. Or maybe I should call Gloria. Oh, God, don't make me call Gloria. Never mind. I'll call *someone* and call you back."

Ruthie walked back to watch the parade. She listened to the Declaration of Independence and petted dogs and spoke to neighbors and ate a muffin, all the while waiting for the hum in the pocket of her shorts that would signal Carole's call. When it finally arrived, she almost missed it. She said hello while ducking down a driveway.

"Okay," Carole said. "Here's the thing. Mindy and Gloria have a majority on the exec committee as it stands right now."

"*What?*"

"She got to Helen."

"Helen?" This was bad.

"After some hand-wringing she admitted that Mindy has her

totally confused but she's going to vote her way. Mindy keeps blabbing about 'making the Belfry the MoMA of the East End' and 'strong new leadership.' There's an emergency meeting of the executive committee on Monday. Which usually means some kind of vote. I can't call in, I'll be in the Hebrides. We leave in—oh my God, an hour."

"What?"

"I'm going on this tour with the kids, and it's a totally screen-free vacation, so I won't have my phone. Or email. Insane, right? But Dash and Arden are *addicted*, so I promised I'd do it if they'd do it."

"But you're an adult. You can cheat."

"I *promised* them I wouldn't."

"But, Carole. You could be the tie-breaking vote! Or talk them out of it."

"I never break a promise with my kids. It would undermine our whole relationship! I'm a mother before I'm a person. Did I tell you about this? We're taking a boat to this island and sleeping in tents and they bring cots and stoves and everything . . . it's fabulous. It's roughing it, but, you know, with mattresses and a chef. Think *Out of Africa* except in the North Sea. Dash is just obsessed with anything Neolithic. Look, just go tomorrow and see what they say."

SHE WOULD HAVE called Mike for advice, but there was a coolness between them. They'd argued about Jem a week ago and hadn't talked since. His June had been busy and she'd barely seen him. Whatever current had been stirred up between them the day Adeline arrived had been absorbed into the daily activity of staying afloat. One day he'd come by to pick up Jem; Adeline had offered to bring Jem to Roberta Verona's Sagaponack house to help her test recipes. Jem was a gifted and intuitive cook, and she had come back (two hours late) with a new energy that had resulted in some amazing dinners, so how could Ruthie complain? Something had happened, some separation from Meret and her crowd, but Jem wasn't talking, content to bake a variety of breads in the early morning and head off to her shifts at the farm stand.

Then a week ago Ruthie had received a call from Roberta's office asking for Jem's Social Security number. Apparently she had been hired by Roberta as a kitchen helper.

"Imagine my surprise," she said to Mike when she called him.

"Roberta was really impressed with her, and she needs some extra help. She's working on a new cookbook."

"Adeline should have checked with us."

"She did. I mean, she mentioned it to me while I was fixing that leak by the French doors. I might have said we could work it out, I guess. My schedule is pretty light right now, and we could alternate—"

"But you said yes without checking with me first."

"Adeline was trying to do a good thing. I thought it was generous. As long as we're talking about it, what do you have against it?"

"She made a commitment to the farm stand. It's a small operation. She could really mess them up if she walks out. Penny got her the job."

"Oh, come on, there's plenty of kids who can ring up corn."

"That's not all she does, she oversees the whole CSA program!"

Mike sighed, as if this point was drearily practical. "This could be good for her," he said. "Have you noticed how shut down she's been since school let out?"

"She needs a little time. Meret dumped her, apparently."

"She needs a bigger world. This could be that thing."

"It's *hours* away! Two ferries. Traffic. Or is Roberta going to send a *launch*?"

"Why do you always bring up obstacles right out of the gate?"

"Because they exist, and they have to be dealt with."

"If you'd just . . . just . . ."

He hadn't finished the sentence, but he didn't have to. *If you'd just be . . . not you* was implied. Should she just wear the pink shirt everywhere, to convince everyone she was a more fun version of herself?

"Look," she said, "I want her to be happy and have a glamorous job, but this is kind of crazy."

"Well, who would want to be *crazy*," Mike said, and a tidal wave of rage carried her up and over the wall. She wanted to say everything that had rushed up like blood to the head, hammer him like a prosecutor. She said nothing.

> From: Jemma Dutton
> To: Mom
>
> I called Adeline to thank her for help w the job w Roberta and she said you said no why

> From: Mom
> To: Jemma Dutton
>
> It's impractical. I have no idea how we'd get you there and back. It's at least ninety minutes coming and going. Plus ferry lines. etc

> From: Jem
> To: Mom
>
> Lucas said he could take me sometimes

> From: Mom
> To: Jem
>
> We hardly know him. So no.

> From: Jem
> To: Mom
>
> This is unbelievable

From: Mom
To: Jem

Maybe you could do it sometimes on your day off. Most important you made a commitment to the farm stand and to Penny who got you the job.

From: Jem
To: Mom

Dad said yes

From: Mom
To: Jem

I say no.

From: Jem
To: Mom

I AM NEVER SPEAKING TO YOU AGAIN

FOR A MONTH she'd used product in her hair, worn new shoes, borrowed linen and crisp cottons from Carole's closet, taken notes in meetings, gently prevented Catha from utilizing her usual habit of taking credit for things she had little to do with. Carole had sent her messages of encouragement: *Heard you did a fabulous job at the board meeting! The Garden Club loves you! I really think you've got this.*

In the afternoons she would look out into the humming hive of the office, Tobie at the computer, Vivian getting a cup of coffee, Mark hurrying by with supplies for the art camp. She looked beyond them out the window to the trees outside, to the road to the village, and her neighborhood, and her friends, and her daughter, and the boards and nails and walls and windows of her house. That's what kept pounding in her brain, in her heart. *I can't lose this.*

18

From: Annie Doyle
To: Jemma Dutton

Mr McManPants looking for you

From: Jemma Dutton
To: Annie Doyle

He's amazing right

From: Annie
To: Jem

Yeah but. Sorta skeeves me the way he keeps buying fruit from us. Actually you. He never gets on my line

. . .

btw sorry about group chat drama going on w Meret just so you know. what is this #mayflower thing

From: Jem
To: Annie

Dropped out of group chats canceled my Snapchat so I don't know and don't care tra effing la

I've got bigger things than high school on my mind

But she is bitch queen, no lie

From: Annie
To: Jem

seriously if this was "The Lottery" she'd be the kid w the rock

19

THE THING ABOUT dating Lucas was, you were never alone. Parties, groups, restaurants, phone. Even during sex Doe felt a crowd. At a certain point he would stop kissing her, considering the job done. His tongue would lie like a slab of Spam in his mouth, and she knew, on top of him, that she'd lost him to the porn in his head.

Despite that, the sex was good. A workout. Didn't matter anyway, because her head was full of Lark.

There had been long lunches at Sant Ambroeus in Southampton, there had been a beach walk, and there had been a kiss that Doe still thought about while Lucas was thinking about porn. It fizzed inside her. Snap crackle pop. Lucas had spent most of June in the city, except for weekends and Mondays. Daniel Mantis flew out on the weekends, so Lark was always unavailable then, which made Doe suspect that Daniel didn't know that Lark preferred women.

Doe had rules. After three weeks, she knew if it was going to last six. After six weeks, she knew it would be three-months-worthy. After three months she didn't know, because past that was an unknown country. She always had a backup, someone in the wings. She never went exclusive until someone asked her if she would. That was fine, but they had to ask. Simple rules. She should write a book. Only problem was, success depended on the possession of instinct and cunning. Most people were like Shari, they went into a relationship with hope and amnesia. Every fucking time.

"Good philosophy," Lucas told her when she explained why it didn't bother her that he was constantly texting other girls. "That's why you're my favorite."

She did not add that she knew he asked her out because of proximity and laziness, because he was stuck at Adeline's and needed company on the ferry. Not so much for the ride over but the ride home. He was always disappointed on the way home. The party was never what he thought it would be. It always sucked.

Yet he never said no, and he was invited to everything. Doe no longer needed to put a wineglass in her purse, or jam her bike in a hedge. She'd been boosted to the top-tier parties. She herself could be spotted in various Instagram accounts thanks to Lucas, along with comments like "hawt!" and "yesss deedy" and "omg-gdamn."

In only a month she'd been able to sell enough of her own pictures to float her through July at the Doyles', and at summer rates. *Seekrit-hamptons* was up to 678,000 followers, and there was an online buzz about who could possibly be behind it. It had been mentioned in *Hamptons Magazine* right next to "Trendy Workouts You Need Right Now," and a lively speculation about who was running it had taken up a column in *Dan's Papers*. Who had that much access and style? Rumor flitted from models to bloggers to famous wives, and Jessica Seinfeld was trending.

Adeline had leased Lucas a white Jeep for the summer. He rarely stayed on the North Fork; all of their dates had been in the Hamptons. They'd just been to a brunch party for two hundred in

Montauk to celebrate the opening of a sunglass pop-up shop, and Doe was tired and wanted to go home. For the last hour they'd played "if you were an emoji what would you be" with a table of at least twenty people, all drunk, and when Doe had said "an exploding star of sorry to be here," Lucas had laughed and jingled his car keys.

"Mind if we run an errand before we go back?" Lucas asked her. "It's on the way."

To Doe, an errand meant picking up toothpaste or dry cleaning, but Lucas drove to a semi-industrial section north of the highway and pulled into the parking lot of a storage unit company.

He sat behind the wheel, not getting out.

"What is it?" she asked.

"It's a big fucking pain in the ass," he said. "My nightmare dead mother."

"That sounds like something I'd stream with popcorn."

"It's beyond."

Simone Fischer Clay. Doe had looked her up. A poet. Beautiful. Peter's second wife. An alcoholic who moved to Italy and drowned. Maybe suicide. Lucas had gone to boarding school—more than one—and had bounced among Simone and Peter and Adeline during his childhood. In the summers he'd been on European bicycle trips and sailing trips and pre-college programs at fancy universities. It was sad in that way that the childhood of a rich kid can seem lonely, but you still have to think, Wow, I wish I had that.

"She packed up the Sag Harbor house and left stuff here," he said. "Just a couple of boxes I think. She sold everything else. I just want to stop getting the fucking bill."

He rubbed his eyes and kept his hand there. Fantastic. The guy was about to cry like a . . . well, like a guy who can't help crying even with a girl in the car. How many cocktails had he had? She didn't know him well enough to go through this kind of drama.

Not in her job description. But when he took his hand away she was relieved to see his eyes weren't all misty. They were as sharp and pale as ever.

"You can wait in the car," he said, opening the door.

"That's okay. I'll give you a hand."

She followed him while he checked in and borrowed a hand truck. He led her down a hallway of blue doors. He hesitated again, holding the key in the lock. And just like that, looking at his hand on the knob, not turning, she wanted to leave. Nausea twisted her stomach. She tried to catch her breath, like she'd been knocked off a stool and had hit the ground hard.

She was back in that hot hallway, her hand on the knob, counting breaths, afraid to turn it.

She had to do it when Shane died. Shari couldn't deal. Clean out his room, his pajamas still with his smell, his Finding Nemo sheets. *It's your fault so you have to do it I'm his mother nobody can expect me to do it you do it and don't let me see anything*

She'd been eleven.

"Hey," she said. "I know this is rough." It was the first real thing she'd said to him. She knew how to order his coffee— *cortado,* extra hot—but she didn't know anything about what he felt until now.

"You have no fucking idea," he said, and pushed open the door.

The room was the size of Doe's garage apartment, pretty much, but there were only three boxes sitting on the ground. The tape was loose, and Lucas opened one, then another, cursing steadily.

He held up a frying pan, then a pale-peach silk nightgown. "Can you believe this shit? It's full of crap. Dish towels. *Poetry books.* Jesus. What was she thinking?" He balled up the nightgown and tossed it back in the box, then kicked it. "Thanks, Mom. You fucking cunt."

Doe hovered by the door. She did not interrupt if a man was in a rage. She'd learned that the hard way, like most women. She let Lucas stack the three boxes on the hand truck by himself.

It started to sprinkle rain as they emerged. "Great," Lucas snarled. "Now it's fucking raining." He shoved the boxes into the back of the Jeep. She waited in the car while he returned the hand truck and the key, still scowling like a little boy.

Which he was. A little boy with car keys.

He got back in the car and reached under the seat. He took a swig from a flask.

"Let me drive," she said.

He didn't answer, just took another long swallow, his throat working.

"Look, you're upset, you want a drink, fine," she said. "But let me drive."

"I'm not fucking upset, okay?"

"I'm getting out, then," she said. "I'll get an Uber." But she didn't know if they had Uber out here, or even where she was.

He stepped on the gas. Driving fast, driving like an idiot in afternoon traffic, passing people on the Sag Harbor Turnpike, driving on the shoulder, hitting the brakes like a jerk.

"My parents," he said. "What a fucking pair. My father, most famous artist of his generation, right? Guess what he left me? Shit nada squat. My mother gets half of what he had, and she spends every fucking dime in ten years. He leaves me nothing until I'm thirty, like I'm a kid. I get an *allowance* from Adeline. And a fucking American car."

Oh, poor you, she wanted to say. *You went to Brown, your stepmom bought you an apartment and gave you a job.* "It's only eight years away," she said.

"But it's *mine*!" he screamed. "Not Adeline's!" He slammed the steering wheel. "I'm not a fucking *child*!"

Arguable, but. "Lucas, cut this the fuck out," Doe said. "I mean it. You just passed a Ferrari, for crap's sake." She knew she was scared, because she was talking in her Florida voice.

Suddenly he swerved, cutting across the traffic, and made a sharp turn toward a housing development under construction, a string of McMansions. He pulled up sharp in the dirt, jerking Doe forward. Relieved, she held her hand out for the keys.

But he just opened his door and disappeared. Doe got out. Lucas lifted one box at a time out of the back and shook out the contents. Items flew in the light rain, the quickening breeze, slender books, a lace tablecloth, a small embroidered pillow, a set of silver spoons tied with a ribbon. The nightgown was tossed by the wind, pirouetted, and landed in mud. Lucas turned the boxes over, shaking out every last thing. He was right. It was mostly crap. Just household stuff, nice stuff, but stuff.

"Fuck you, Mom!" he screamed to the gulls.

He was crying. Really crying, with heaving sobs. What to do. He didn't want her comfort. He didn't want her here at all.

Turning and angling her body, Doe checked her texts.

> From: Shari Callender
> To: Doe Callender
>
> I know u said u were working stuff out but im bad off here can you call?
>
> if u can it wld be yahoo
>
> if u cant it would be no sadder than today
>
> u r breaking every heart in my body

Lark twinkled in.

> i miss you wanna sleep over

Lucas's back was to her, his shoulders heaving. How long did she have to wait until she told him she had to go?

20

HELEN BROUGHT COOKIES to the meeting in Ruthie's office. Gloria came with her own thermal mug of iced coffee. Mindy arrived late. All three women were dressed in variants of red, white, and blue, an All-American firing line that would shortly be aiming their muskets right at her.

"You brought us where we needed to go," Helen said. She tucked her gray hair behind her ears and leaned forward. "There is no question of that. We're all so fond of you, Ruthie. But when things change, we have to change or die. Even old ladies like me. There's a new world out there—I don't understand it, but Mindy is talking about rebranding and the cyber media. Tapping the new people who are coming to the North Fork."

Mindy, her eyes on Helen, nodded through this speech, keeping time like a proud parent at a piano recital.

"We're all agreed," Gloria said. She looked as happy as Ruthie had ever seen her. Maybe it was delight at being part of a cabal. Ruthie felt a tiny spurt of compassion. She'd known Gloria for so many years of meetings and lunches and dinner parties. Gloria always showed up, her shoes shined and her jewels in her ears, and there had never been a person in the room who greeted her with joy. That must curdle a person.

Gloria was speaking, and she'd missed the beginning. ". . . was lovely, but the old North Fork is over. I'm not sure that this No Helipad movement is right. I mean, the journey here from Manhattan is ridiculous, and it gets worse every year."

"The Belfry has built a reputation that we can capitalize on if we think outside the box," Mindy said. "What do you think is outside the box, Ruthie?"

"Well, it's summer," Ruthie said. "Hot air?"

"Rebranding in a thoughtful, active way that will maximize our impact," Mindy supplied.

"Our membership grows every year."

"Oh, Ruthie," Gloria said, "you *tried*."

"No, I succeeded," Ruthie said. "Since I took over, membership has grown by fifty percent."

"But who comprises that membership?" Mindy asked, placing her hands on a closed Moleskine. "It's wonderful how you connected to the community here. To the local people, and children, and schools, and the retirees. But in the end, what did it get us?"

"A well-loved institution with award-winning programming that connects with the community?"

"Well. Now we have different needs. Financial needs if we're going to grow."

"There is something to be said for how perfectly we do what we do," Ruthie said.

The women exchanged a glance.

"This is the problem," Gloria said. "Vision."

"I *have* a vision," Ruthie said. "It's just not yours."

"Exactly!" Mindy glowed. "You need to share my—our vision! We need to professionalize our best practices to be impactful in a transformational way."

"Well said," Gloria said.

"But I *am* a professional," Ruthie said.

Mindy flushed deeply, grew *florid*. She snapped the band of her Moleskine and opened it. She fished out a piece of paper and pushed it across the desk. "You'll receive a three-month evaluation in September."

Ruthie's head buzzed as she read. "What do you mean by 'find and develop new revenue streams'?"

"Revenue streams are income, but in this case, novel, new ways—"

"I know what they *are,* I'm just asking specifically considering the realities of a small nonprofit."

"Well, admittedly you've raised money, but it's not a continuing source of revenue."

"Revenue streams for museums mean a café, or an online store, or annuities . . ."

"We were thinking of a café," Gloria said. "Light fare. Salads."

"We have town restrictions, first of all," Ruthie said. "Second, we don't have the attendance numbers to justify it."

"Well, that's not my job to figure out, is it," Mindy snapped. She had lost her sound of joyous authority and was suddenly petulant.

Ruthie consulted the list again, barely able to read it through a film of rage. "I outlined all the reasons the budget target wasn't hit, including the insurance hike and your fundraiser in the city that went over budget—"

Mindy grew sulky. "It was a fabulous party, everyone said so."

"Fabulous," Gloria said.

"I loved those little crab cakes," Helen said. "Let's focus on the positive."

"Is the positive on this list, Mindy?"

"This isn't how we want this meeting to go," Helen said with sudden firmness. "Mindy wants to do more regular check-ins with you, that's all. We've always done things so informally here. She wants to put some basic structures in place. It's like an engine check! If you wait too long, you run into problems. The light goes on while you're on the expressway!"

"I'm not a Toyota," Ruthie said. "You want to fire me, and you're setting up a case. Do you think I'm an idiot? I refuse."

Mindy was now bright red, having gone beyond florid into maroon. "You can't refuse. You serve at the pleasure of the board. The board has a right to set the parameters of your employment."

"Does the *full* board know about this?" Ruthie asked.

"The executive committee reports to the full board," Mindy said.

"I'm aware of how the executive committee functions. But it's not an answer to my question."

"Well, that's not an appropriate question to ask."

Helen stirred nervously. "This isn't the Spanish Inquisition. We're all friends here."

"Helen, does Mindy have a plan to fire me?" Ruthie turned and looked Helen in the eye. Helen looked away.

Ruthie pushed the paper back toward Mindy with such force that it knocked the Moleskine to the floor. A piece of paper fluttered out. Ruthie put her foot on it.

LEADERSHIP TRANSITION PLAN
By Catha Shand-Lugner

Step One. Stabilize staff. Ensure smooth transition by reaching out to local publications outlining my position as new cultural leader of the North Fork.

Step Two. Set up coffee meetings with board members in descending order of annual donations.

Slowly, Ruthie picked it up.

"That's mine!" Mindy cried. She snatched it out of Ruthie's hand. "It's a confidential document!"

"You're secretly grooming my subordinate to take over my position!"

"It would be irresponsible not to have plans in place if, in fact—"

"It is irresponsible and unethical to maneuver a director to re-sign while you secretly conspire with her subordinate! Who, by the way, has no museum experience outside of the Belfry."

"She has good ideas," Gloria said. "And a master's degree. She went to Cornell!"

Ruthie stood. "Are you asking for my resignation?"

"Ruthie, nobody said that." Helen reached out to her, a cookie in her hand. Ruthie was tempted to bite it. "Please sit down."

"This is not on the timetable," Mindy said, flustered. "We're not absolutely prepared to negotiate your departure right now in a way that—"

"When the game is rigged, only a chump stays at the table," Ruthie said. It was a saying of her father's and possibly the first time she'd quoted him in her life, aside from *Slice it paper-thin and thank you sir.* "I can stay through the gala and leave in Au-gust."

Mindy smoothed the Leadership Transition paper. "I don't like to make a decision quickly, but I think it's better if you leave and clean out your desk this weekend. Why prolong it?"

Ruthie came back to herself and realized that she was standing and that nobody was urging her to reconsider. She had fully ex-pected Helen to smooth it all over so that eventually she could sit down and eat a cookie.

"Mindy, that's crazy. Do you know what will happen?" Ruthie asked. "I've been here for ten years. People will talk. There will be pushback. Gossip. We're in the middle of our season right now. Let's do this in a way that's best for the institution."

Mindy raised her chin. "I'll decide what is best for the institu-tion. We'll pay out for the rest of the summer. I'll have my father's attorney draw up an NDA."

"A nondisclosure?" Ruthie's head spun. "For what? This isn't the CIA."

"Is this really necessary, Mindy?" Helen asked. "This is going so fast."

Mindy turned to Helen. "This is standard best practices."

"Of course," Gloria said. "Mindy is so thorough."

"But we aren't this way," Helen said, giving the two women a sharp glance. "We've never been this way. We should give Ruthie time. This should be done right."

"We can discuss the details in private," Mindy said. "I consulted my father's attorney. This is standard."

"You already consulted an attorney?" Ruthie turned to Helen. "Helen, you brought me aboard. My last review with you and Carole was excellent. You said I was doing a magnificent job. You used the word *magnificent*, Helen! That was less than two years ago! How can you support this?"

"They didn't use the right metrics," Mindy said. "The review was not pro forma. Legally we're in the clear."

"I don't know how this turned so acrimonious," Helen said. "I brought such delicious cookies."

21

HELEN FOLLOWED HER out to her car. She wore a chunky necklace made of resin blocks strung on colorful coated wire, and it rattled against her clasped hands.

"I feel terrible about that meeting," she said.

Ruthie fished for her keys. She couldn't make sense of her purse; it was like she was sucked into space and her hand was in a black hole. "I'm sorry you feel terrible, Helen. I'm the one out of a job, though."

"I know how it must rankle, but—"

"Rankle? *Rankle?*"

Helen took a step back. "We're in the heat of the moment right now. But Ruthie, you're so good. People recognize that. We both love the Belfry and it will have a life beyond both of us, after all. It will continue to serve the committee—I mean, the community! Isn't that the most important thing? That we meet the future with confidence?"

Ruthie looked at Helen, amazed. Her life was in tatters and Helen was giving her a chamber-of-commerce speech? She'd actually heard Helen say that last bit at the Spring Festive Fling a few months before. Helen looked supremely comfortable, or as comfortable as a person can be with three tons of resin strung around her neck.

Behind Helen's head rose the pure white form of the Belfry. Ruthie felt her throat constrict. She knew everything there was to know about the building. She knew the condition report. She knew she had to fix the air handler next year. She knew how the voices of the children echoed up from the education wing to the offices. She knew how cooling the breeze could be in late September. She knew that when she brought in food the platter could be cleared in fifteen minutes flat. She knew her employees, how Vivian needed to be encouraged, how Tobie was dealing with a husband with chemo, how Mark needed just a little room to spin before he came up with a brilliant idea.

There had been jobs that she'd liked, jobs she'd tolerated, jobs she'd loathed. She'd never had a job she'd loved. Standing here now, it felt as though something had moved through her and scoured out her insides.

Her hand found the keys. She clicked the lock open and swung behind the wheel. The car was a furnace. She started the engine and opened the window. To her dismay Helen didn't step away. She leaned into the open window, her necklace clanking against the car.

"I tried to protect you," Helen said. "But nobody says no to Mindy."

Ruthie's head swiveled. "What?"

"My doctor said, 'You have to stop the oppositional stress. Give in or be dragged!'" Helen fingered her resin. "Anyway, there's no use looking back. We have to move forward."

"But I'm the one under the wheels, Helen!"

"And just for the record, I was very much against holding that meeting with Catha."

"There was a meeting?"

"I thought it was . . . unseemly. We can do better."

The air-conditioning blew in her face, and she welcomed the blast. "Helen, please step away from the car."

Helen hung on to the car door. "We are still friends. I am going to continue to be a part of your life because I want to. You're so gifted. I can see you taking your skills to the next level, maybe working with artists?"

"Where?" Ruthie asked.

Helen waved a hand, and cookie crumbs went flying. Some of them stuck to her shirt. "So many wonderful nonprofits in the area," she said.

"Yes, I know all of them, and I know all of their directors. Most of the ones on the North Fork are *cutting* staff. I will have to *move*, Helen. Sell the house. Leave my community, my friends, take Jem out of school . . ." Ruthie fought against the thickness in her voice. "Do you *realize* that? When directors lose their jobs, they have to move!"

Helen looked down and adjusted the ring on her third finger so that the stone, pale yellow, slid to the exact center. "Catha thinks we should drop the 'the.' We might change the name to just Belfry. Or BM."

"That is a terrific idea," Ruthie said. "Do that!"

"I'm on the naming committee."

Ruthie gripped the steering wheel, afraid she'd push the pedal to the floor. She remembered how when Jem was a toddler, she had to force herself to speak softly when she was thick with frustration and sticky with spilled juice. The titanic rage of mothering a toddler was nothing compared with this.

What could she say to Helen, a woman who had told her over the course of years that they were "family"? *You are being a colossal shit. Your cowardice disgusts me.*

When she'd decided to apply for this job, her first directorship, she'd called her old boss. What are the pitfalls, she'd asked him. "If you want to be a director of a museum, just know you're going to get fired at some point in your career," he'd said. "It won't have anything to do with your job performance. It's usually one person who wants to make a mark. They rope in a few others who want power. If they're rich and nasty enough, they win. Boards are basically ovine in nature. One sheep says leap over the cliff, and next thing you know you've got a whole lot of haggis."

"Naturally I'll be a reference for you," Helen said. "You were the best director we ever had."

"Well, thanks for that," Ruthie said. "You just lost me."

"I know, and I'm so sorry about that. I feel terrible. Let me tell you something. I've lived a long time, and I know that you can't hold back change. The good news is, you're fabulous."

Ruthie stepped on the gas.

She couldn't fight this. She'd been in the museum business long enough to know that starting a board fight would be disastrous. Helen wouldn't stand up for her, none of them would, because there was no reason to act on principle when social comfort was involved. The women on the board bumped into one another all summer; they served on other boards together, they went to the same restaurants, the same shops, the same parties. They exchanged the same recommendations of the same Parisian bistros. They ran into one another all over the world, or at least the parts sanctioned by their travel agents. Why would they risk unpleasantness? Just for her? They were used to listening to authority. They were trained that way, the last generation of gentlewomen (Ruthie prayed!) who were passed down from father to husband and told to dress well, set a good table, and shut the fuck up.

22

SHE EMAILED CAROLE—*Meeting a disaster, please call me!*—but the email bounced back.

> Hello darlings, I am off the grid (yes, me, can you believe it?) roughing it in the fabulous Hebrides with my kids! I'll be back online by July 14 if we don't get kidnapped by the Loch Ness Monster. Love and kisses, Carole

Probably not a good idea to write Carole at this particular moment, anyway. One should fulminate with the trusted, not the trustee. She drove to Mike's apartment. She texted him as she parked, starting to hiccup panic now.

No answer. The man always forgot to charge his phone. She knocked on the door. No answer.

CALL ME, she texted. And then, the absurd *CHARGE YOUR PHONE!*

She drove back to Orient and turned down Village Lane. She glided past the store, past the pie shop, the yacht club, past the cottages. Her town. Her beloved town. Her house. Her beloved house. Without the job at the Belfry, how could they keep it? The second mortgage, the taxes . . .

Adeline's Range Rover was in her driveway. Plus a flash of yellow through the bushes. She pulled over and got out. Screened by the bush, Mike's truck was parked awkwardly to the side, its wheels halfway on the lawn, almost smack into the dwarf lilac tree that Helen had given her when she'd taken the job.

She thought he'd fixed the step, the leak, the window, the chores that had eaten up his June. It was almost six o'clock now, and he would be heading home.

As she approached the house she heard voices from the rear, and then the sound of Mike laughing.

"Hello?" she called, and heard the scrape of a chair.

"We're out back!" Adeline called.

When she rounded the side of the house, Adeline was half out of her chair, turning toward her with a smile of welcome that faltered when she saw Ruthie. Mike was sitting back, his ankle propped on a knee. There were two glasses of white wine on the table and a bottle sitting in the thermal cooler she'd bought for summer guests. Two bottles of water sat, politely condensing. A tray of empty glasses stood next to it. A bowl of olives. Mike's olives, the ones he made with Pernod and orange peel and fennel seed. She could smell it from here, licorice and citrus and garlic.

"Ruthie! I thought you were Roberta," Adeline said. "I'm expecting a caravan, actually. Lucas is meeting everyone at the ferry and leading them here. The McGreevys, a few others. You know the McGreevys, right?"

"A little," Ruthie said. Tom McGreevy was a blue-chip artist who lived on Shelter Island, which meant he was Hamptons, not North Fork. She'd been trying to get him to the Belfry for years.

Adeline was wearing saffron-colored capri pants and a fuchsia silk T-shirt, making Ruthie feel like a bundle of dry newsprint in her now wrinkled black shift. The breeze brought Ruthie a scent of Adeline's perfume.

Mike stood. His hair was brushed, and his shirt was pressed. It took Ruthie several long seconds to realize that he wasn't just having a drink before leaving, he was a guest at the party.

"I should go," she said, just as car doors slammed and they heard voices.

"Stay for a drink," Adeline urged. "We're out back!" she called, and started toward the side of the house.

"We have to talk," Ruthie said to Mike.

"I know." Mike looked miserable, as if he'd already heard. You couldn't quit a job in this town without the news going out in five minutes.

The group suddenly swirled around the side of the house, the tall, stylish McGreevys, Lucas, and a heavyset woman with flyaway gray hair to her shoulders who had to be Roberta. She had expected a woman like Adeline, thin, supple, and expensively dressed. But this woman was tall and twice the size of Lucas. Her dress was loose fitting and the color of red clay. She should be selling her own honey in a farmers market, not attending a chic dinner party.

Then Joe rounded the corner, nicely dressed in jeans and a blue shirt, and holding a bottle of wine. He looked surprised, then pleased, to see her.

"You're right, this is a spectacular view," Roberta said in a booming voice. "I'm dying for a drink. Tom and Lilah gave me *nothing*. I'm parched."

"We had to make the ferry," Lilah said. "The line gets so long on weekends." The bottom three buttons of her linen blouse were open, revealing a flat, taut stomach. She was wearing a watch without hands, just the words WHO CARES.

"Michael, will you pour Roberta some wine?" Adeline asked. "Or else she'll be a complete grump."

"I'm already a complete grump," Roberta said, popping an olive. "Michael, I hear you're a very good cook. I've been trying to get Adeline to eat for ten years."

"Adeline doesn't do anything she doesn't want to do," Lucas said. "You should know that by now."

He doesn't like her, Ruthie thought.

Mike looked rattled; cooking for this group, and especially Roberta, probably unnerved him. He wouldn't start to relax until people were midway through their entrées. Ruthie tried to puzzle this out. Had Adeline hired him to cook and then invited him to stay? Had he offered to help as a favor?

He disappeared into the house to do something with the food, and Adeline led her around for introductions. *Of course you know Tom. This is Lilah—you must see their place on Shelter Island. Roberta was so impressed with Jem. Of course you know her books. And of course you know Joe.*

Adeline headed into the house. Ruthie wished Mike would return. She wanted to ask him what they were doing here. These were summer people. These weren't their people. What were they doing on their patio?

"So this is Orient," Roberta said. "I had to live through one long dinner conversation with Adeline in the city about what sneakers to buy for this."

"Sneakers are signifiers for sure," Lilah said.

"Especially for Adeline," Roberta said. "She has to get the details right. Remember when she lived in London and had to buy a raincoat?" They laughed, but with affection.

The glass was sweating in her hand, and she took a sip. She would drink one glass, and then go. Adeline and Mike returned, Mike carrying a plate of something. Adeline carried two glasses of wine. Roberta took the plate from Mike and popped something in her mouth before starting to pass it around. Adeline touched Mike's shoulder and handed him his glass.

Ruthie had the sensation of something dropping inside her. Was it a penny? She could taste it in her mouth, sharp and coppery.

She hadn't seen much. A woman handing a glass to a man. But as Ruthie watched them move toward the McGreevys, she suddenly saw what any idiot would have seen long before.

Mike was sleeping with Adeline.

They were not touching, they weren't even speaking to each other, but she saw it as plainly as she saw the trees and the grass. She saw it in the way Mike stood, the way he held his glass, the way his fucking *hair* was combed.

They were freshly showered, those two. Sitting out at the table earlier, having a glass of wine before the guests arrived. The *domesticity* of it. The postcoital contentment.

They all knew, too. Roberta—*I hear you're a great cook, Michael.*

When had it begun? *And if you wait a sec I'll identify a hammer and a nail.*

Dad totally mocked her groceries.

And Mike . . . scrutinizing him, she finally realized how nervous he was. Not to be here, in this company, not because of the meal, but to be here *with her.*

Joe came up next to her with the wine bottle, and she realized her glass was empty. "I didn't know you'd be here. It's lovely to see you."

She held out her glass.

"This is a gorgeous Sancerre," he said.

She stared at him, trying to make sense of his words. Instinct was stronger than cognition right now; she didn't think she could speak. She drained the glass and held it out again.

"Bad day?"

She nodded. "The worst. Plus, I'm at a party where people say things like 'This is a gorgeous Sancerre.'"

Joe looked startled. Maybe she shouldn't alienate the only person at the party who had been pleased to see her.

Behind her she heard, "And we can never seem to get you over to dinner," from Lilah McGreevy.

"How cozy this all is," she said to Joe. "And how kind of me to supply the venue."

"Are you all right?"

She wanted to pick up speed and plow right into Mike, knock him down on the stones of their terrace. *Their* terrace! Look at the way Adeline was standing there, her expensively shod feet standing on Ruthie's very own slate! Standing there as if this was *her* house! Her husband, her house!

The group was talking the New York talk, restaurants, theater, books, music, Lincoln Center, MoMA, Met. But it was not the talk of those who went to the shows or read the books, or even those who read the reviews of the shows and the books, but those who dined with the producers, had been schoolmates with the editors, sat on the boards.

"No, he's actually working on a book about transparency, I don't know what he's thinking, but then again, he has a Pulitzer."

"The new restaurant with three letters. Ion?"

". . . the Ernst and Duchamp show . . ."

". . . bone broth . . ."

"Have you seen it? We went last week, it was brilliant. Henry Higgins is played by Cherry Jones as a closeted lesbian in love with Eliza, it's all about the self-hatred of the oppressed, it's amazing. She was totally singing from her uterus . . ."

"No, you mean Air."

"No, Eon."

And then Mike was saying, "No, it only looks like the Wall Street guys are running things. Isn't culture what really matters now? Well, that and shopping. No, I'm serious. Isn't that our biggest export? The creative class is really ruling the world, we just aren't interested in power. Yet. Can you imagine if all the artists and designers went on strike? The next war could be between the suits and the talent, I'm telling you."

She'd heard this theory before, at other dinner parties. These people were smiling. Tom McGreevy chuckled. Adeline had the glowing look of a woman delighted that her lover was pleasing her friends.

He suddenly looked so *at home* here, among these people.

Of course, he was at home. So was Ruthie. Except she wasn't. Ruthie had drunk a glass of wine very, very fast, but this much unsteadiness didn't come from the gorgeous Sancerre.

"I get what you're saying," Tom said.

"Clearly we need to organize," Lilah said.

"Do you want to leave?" Joe asked her in a low tone. Maybe she was weaving? Or steaming? Or stamping? She didn't know. Something new seemed to be in charge of her body. Some wild energy, an untamed, bucking mare.

"No," Ruthie said, and she realized that she'd shouted it.

The heads turned. Mike looked scared. How nice.

"No," Ruthie said, "I haven't dined at Eon, or was it Air . . . or was it *Id*? And I haven't seen anybody sing from their uterus, that's a treat I'll look forward to, along with the galleys of the next DeLillo, the intimate tour of Matisse, that divine private concert with Joshua Bell—talk about a cultural high colonic! Right, Mike, I mean Michael?"

Did she just shout that, too?

Everyone was half turned, looking at her.

"Ruthie . . ." Adeline said, and stopped.

"I'm sorry, allergies," Ruthie said. "You know. 'Tis the season. I'm allergic to entitlement. The air is just so thick with it."

They all faced her, frozen, drinks held, Roberta mechanically spitting out an olive pit in her hand, her eyes on Ruthie. Lucas, laughing.

"Let me take you home," Joe murmured.

"I am home," she said. "That's the funny thing."

23

MIKE'S FACE WAS the last one she registered—comically horrified, his mouth open—before she ran. She rounded the corner of
the house, stumbling as though she had her shoes on the wrong
feet. She struck out across the lawn. She realized she was still
holding the wineglass, and she turned and hurled it at the porch.
She heard the smash of it breaking. What a pleasant sound! Like
tiny bells. Like the striking seconds of a quarter-million-dollar
watch.

Joe hurried toward her but stopped a few feet away. "I'm sorry,"
he said. "That was a hell of a way to find out."

"Does everyone know except for me?"

He shook his head. "I don't know who knows. I'll give you a
ride home."

"I don't need a ride. I'm not drunk. I'm sorry to spoil the party.
But go back. Enjoy my view!" Why was she furious at Joe? She
didn't know. "I'm sorry. I really, really want to be alone," she
added.

"Ruthie—"

"Please. Please go."

She walked down the path, past the rocks that edged the lawn, beach stones that she and Jem had collected, the roundest, whitest ones they could find, and then carefully laid down together. She glanced behind. Joe had gone back to the party.

Helen's dwarf lilac had never really thrived in that spot. They'd always meant to move it. The branches with blossoms fanned out from a spindly trunk that had never grown past four feet or so. And Ruthie came to dislike its tight, selfish petals. She preferred the full-grown lilac bush, blowsy in its confidence.

She thought of Helen's droit-du-seigneur smile as she took Ruthie's life in her teeth and shook it. Mindy couldn't help being Mindy. Was it even worth it to despise her? She was just a sad thing, powering through life with the manic aggression of a person who felt unloved, even by her own mother. With that kind of need matched to that kind of money, casualties occurred offstage. Mindy's treachery was impersonal, because Ruthie had never been a person to her at all.

But Carole, disappearing with a blithe "see what they have to say," knowing the bad news was coming? Catha, whom she'd worked side by side with for five years? *Helen?*

She crossed to the shed. She dug into her pocket for her keys and unlocked the door. Moist heat rolled out, redolent with damp cardboard and earth. The shed was crammed to the roof with their off-season life. Boxes full of sweaters, quilts, blankets, financial records, bathrobes, slippers, knickknacks, books, extra dishes, the second-best pots and pans. Shoehorned in there somewhere were boxes they hadn't opened since they left Tribeca, another life. So many things that only made clutter, that caused closet doors not to close and drawers to stick, that stacked up in teetering piles in linen closets. Her life.

It should have made her feel sad. A life small enough to fit in a shed.

Instead it was as though she'd discovered a lost continent of rage.

The voice came from behind her. "Can I help?"

Lucas. Ignoring him, she wended her way through the maze, looking for the ax. There was a newly empty section where paintings had been shrink-wrapped and stacked against one wall.

"Mike's paintings are gone," she said.

He leaned against the doorframe, then looked at the dust and reconsidered. He brushed off his shoulder. "Adeline took them to the city. She was horrified that he stored them out here in all this humidity. No doubt she'll have dinner parties and hang them in the dining room."

"How entrepreneurial."

"Yeah. He's her new project. He doesn't seem to mind. Can I help you with that?" Lucas reached over and shifted a box. She wriggled through the space to get to the far wall.

He bent down. "What are these boxes marked PETER CLAY?"

"Some things he gave me when I left," she told him. "He chewed me out for leaving him, and then he felt guilty, so a few weeks later I got a big box of crap. Paint. A couple of canvases. I never used them."

"Why not?"

"I stopped painting."

Lucas swept his hair back and crouched down. When he looked up at her, he looked vulnerable, boyish. "There's so little of him left. The studio was basically destroyed on 9/11. The rest was scrutinized and handed off to the foundation. Adeline has cataloged every scrap."

"It's just paints and brushes."

"It's *his,* though. Can I see?"

Ruthie was unexpectedly touched by this. She thought only artists had a romantic relationship with materials. She flipped open a toolbox and found a box cutter. She cleanly sliced through the tape.

Lucas closed in eagerly as she pulled back the flaps. The smell of paint and solvent hit her. She was swept back into Peter's studio, cans of brushes, carts covered with paint spills, canvases turned to the wall, a cassette player splotched with paint. Everything had been smeared or stained with paint, even the coffeepot.

She remembered the kitchen chair with the red leatherette seat where he'd sat staring at the canvas on the wall—what had happened to that chair? Left outside on the street for someone to pick up, not knowing that it contained the ass imprint of an artist who had defined his generation. And the stacks of art magazines that in a frenzy Peter had once painted white and bound with cord, creating a massive white sculpture that the assistants often perched on to drink soda or coffee and bitch about him behind his back? Had that been cut up and destroyed? She had never thought about that before, that Peter's studio had been a hazmat site, most likely.

Lucas pawed through the box eagerly. "These are all his colors."

"Yeah." That was the point, the uselessness of the gift and maybe its malice; Ruthie did not paint like Peter.

"And a couple of small canvases," he said.

She nodded. "They're works of art in themselves, really. Hiro had the best frame shop in the city, maybe the country. Peter would only let him build his canvases personally. That might be the last of them. Hiro died a year after Peter."

She picked up the ax and swung it experimentally.

"Holy shit," Lucas said. "What are you doing?"

She slid through the boxes and marched to the tree. If she could hack at her own life she would, at every limb—job, house, husband. Or hack away at assumptions. That she would never make a fuss. That she would just go away.

She raised the ax. The trunk was barely two inches in diameter. She was no Paul Bunyan, but she could do this.

"Maybe you should calm down," Lucas said.

She swung at the tree. She felt the shudder of one clean, excellent cut. Again and again she swung until the trunk splintered. She tore it away from the stump, twisting until the living stalk snapped.

"Okay," Lucas said. "And now we're going to do what, exactly?"

She staggered with it to the car. She popped the trunk and wrestled it in. She yanked the door and fell into the front seat, scratched and dirty and bleeding. She toppled over the gearshift.

Her nose against the cushion, she breathed out and in. The leather smelled of old coffee, dry leaves, and something else, something elusive but desperate, the scent of years spent coaxing an engine past a hundred thousand miles.

My life is shit, Ruthie thought.

She was pathetic, a faded woman standing at a dinner party, hoping not to make an ass of herself, and making an ass of herself. Since Mike left she'd been living like a tiny gray mouse, compressing her bones to fit into the smallest crack, skulking along the baseboards. Sniffing out the crumbs. Chasing the cheese. Until she'd scurried right into the trap, and been broken. Snap!

Lucas stuck his head in the car. "What's with the tree?"

"It's a present." Maybe she *was* drunk. She couldn't tell.

He placed his hand on the door. "Come on, I'll drive and taxi back. This is much more interesting than the party."

"I have to deliver the tree." She clambered like a Great Dane over the gearshift, all snuffle and hindquarters.

Lucas slid into the front seat and pulled out. They drove in silence except for Ruthie's murmured directions to Helen's house.

The lovely shingled house sat quiet as a cat. Ruthie saw Helen moving across a window. She directed Lucas to pull over. She lurched out of the car and wrestled the lilac tree out of the trunk.

Helen stepped onto the porch, a welcoming expression on her face that slowly drained into puzzlement. "Ruthie?"

Panting, Ruthie threw the tree on the driveway. "Should I tell you where to stick this?"

Helen's mouth dropped open. She looked old and stricken.

Ruthie decided not to feel guilty (*One can choose this,* she was thinking) and slid back into the car.

Lucas laughed. "Badass!"

"Just go."

They drove with all the windows down, through the swollen summer evening, symphonic with cicada song. Ruthie felt her exhilaration ebb. The sight of Helen's face had flipped her mood to shame. She rested her head on the door. The wine was sloshing through her and she was starting to feel sick.

"Don't give up on me now, cowgirl." He pulled into the driveway. "Want to ask me in for a drink?"

"No. Take the car. You can leave it by the post office. I'll bike to it tomorrow."

"Your ex is an idiot. You're hot."

"Thanks."

"I'm serious. Look, every five years, she remakes herself and finds the man to match it. She had an expat period. Moved to London. Hated it. Too hard to crack, even for her. Got dumped by an earl. Decided to become a businesswoman and built up the foundation. Bought a lot of lady coats. Hooked up with the big finance whiz. Now she's fallen for Orient. Wants a simpler life. A simpler man goes with that, I guess. I overheard her talking to Michael. About buying your house."

She stared at the dashboard. Adeline wanted the house? Or was it just idle talk? The way some renters promised *This was amazing, we're definitely renting next year* and then they never saw them again?

"She tends to get what she wants." He looked ahead and flexed his fingers on the wheel. "Did he ever give you anything, a drawing, a print?"

"Mike?"

"No, my dad."

She shook her head. "We did not part friends."

"That's a big club you're in. Did you ever think, for everything you did for him, you deserved something? A drawing, something he'd toss off in a morning, could pay for, I don't know, a very nice life?"

"No, I never looked at it that way."

"Wouldn't it have been wild if you did find something? Something you'd overlooked? What if you'd just unpacked those boxes and found something you'd missed?"

Ruthie shrugged. "I'd already gone through the boxes twenty years ago."

"I bet you used to do a lot of his work."

"Well, I was his studio manager."

"Come on, I've talked to his old buddies, I know how much the studio assistants did. Famous artists run factories, right? Nothing new about that. The artist is the thinker, the conceptual idea behind the work that others execute. Look at Jeff Koons, he's a genius."

"Sure." She swung open the door but he kept on talking.

"It's just funny, it's like a movie. You've got everything you need right there in the shed. The shop that made the canvases—it's gone. The studio, gone. You've got the last of his materials. It's like a message from the grave, right? My old man and his ego. He wants his immortality and he's giving you the chance. One last painting. Don't you think it's sort of hilarious, how it could work?"

"Not hilarious. Ridiculous."

"Can you imagine, though? Even a small painting would be worth ten million, fifteen, minimum. I mean, dealing privately. At auction, even more."

A flowery scent still hung in the air. The car smelled funereal. She had an urgent need to get out.

"And here's the funniest part. I'm his son. I work at his foundation. I know the crazy collectors, the ones in Japan and Russia. China. The ones who care that they'd get something unique, something that hasn't changed hands ten times. The ones who like to buy things under the table."

"Lucas, you're joking, right?"

"You should see your face! Of course! But hey, come on, don't you ever think of committing the perfect crime?"

"No."

"Well, I do, all the time. It's just fun to think about."

Lucas turned. It was evening but the light was still hard and bright. It didn't matter; his beauty took the glare without revealing a flaw. "Everyone has a number, you know?"

"A number?"

"A number that buys you the life you want. Buys you out of trouble, or buys you love, or a career, or the best doctors, or the best tables in restaurants. Or a house." Lucas laughed. "My number is very large."

He was just talking. Spinning his bitter wheel. Peter's kid. Suddenly the resemblance wasn't just the color of the eyes.

You lack the killer instinct, fishgirl. That's why you'll never make it.

"Anyway, rhetorical questions have answers," Lucas said. "Do you know what my favorite rhetorical question is?"

He opened her palm and put a tube of paint in it; he'd taken it from the box. Cadmium yellow.

"Why not?"

24

"OH, MAN, I need an espresso," Lark said. She opened her eyes. "Good morning, you." She dived into Doe's neck and snuggled for a moment. Then she flipped over and reached for her phone.

Doe turned over and grabbed hers. Two nights together this week; they were a couple now. They flicked through notifications, texts. Doe had two photos in *Hamptons Magazine* and one on the gossip website *YSK*, the one that everyone read. She got $250. It was a good week.

"Oh, God, I'm in *seekrit-hamptons* again," Lark said, scrolling through her feed. "I look good, though. Whoa, you are busted!"

Doe's pulse speeded up. "What?"

Lark showed her the phone. It was a different Hamptons account, Doe's competition, called *hamptoncomesalive!* and Doe was standing close to Lucas in the background of a shot. Lucas had his hand on her ass.

Doe shrugged. "We go out sometimes."

"It's okay." Lark hesitated. "It's just, he's sort of a dick, don't you think?" She cocked her head and then lowered her chin and swept back her hair in a way that instantly conjured Lucas. "Hello, Beauty," she mimicked in Lucas's careless way.

Doe snorted.

"How about tonight is just us," Lark said.

Doe joined in, lowering her voice and her chin. "Wait. I like the way that sounds . . ."

"Just us," they said together and giggled.

"Yeah, he's a dick," Doe said.

"Honestly, this is awful, but I only dated him because he was Peter Clay's son. I mean, come on, I was an art major, why wouldn't I be intrigued? Daddy encouraged it, he was with Adeline then. I thought, *What's it like to hang out with the son of a genius?* Then he turned out to be such a tool."

Doe thought of Lucas on Sunday, crying. "Maybe he can't help it."

"Look, everybody can help it. That's what medication is for." Lark snuggled closer. "Speaking of therapy, you never talk about your parents. What's the deal?"

"Dad died when I was thirteen, so, issues." Actually he had been close to a one-night stand. Maybe a two-week stand? So. No issues except for not knowing quite who he was. Shari hadn't known him long. Or very well, apparently, because he turned out to be married. When she told him she was pregnant, he wrote her a check and advised her never to contact him again. She said he was either Dominican or Brazilian, and didn't seem to get that this would be a significant thing for Doe to want to know.

Doe had to scramble her thoughts together. "Mom: Miami version of prep."

"Lilly Pulitzer."

"Matching shifts, when I was a kid."

"Do you visit much?"

"Not as much as she'd like me to. She moved to Minnesota."

"Crazy."

"Right? Married a guy who owns forests, or something." Doe occasionally used this lie because nobody was from Minnesota.

"Let's see. She's on the board of the ballet and walks like a duck. Buys vintage Mary McFadden on eBay." Odd details were important to create the sense of a real person. Shari flashed into her head, but the details of her mother's sad bio were off limits. *Her father broke her arm when she was twelve. Ron paid for her boob job. Her big thrill is when Victoria's Secret is 35 percent off.*

"Mmm. My mom is in the fashion biz," Lark said. "They might like each other. She's awesome. She lives in Paris, though. Daddy hates her. He has a meme for everyone. She humiliated him by leaving him, so he calls her a drug addict just because he found Valium in her purse once. He can be ruthless that way."

"What's his meme for you?"

Lark's gaze moved off in a way that Doe could now track. "Dream daughter slash loser. We had the hugest stupid fight yesterday. He gave me a deadline to apply for jobs. In the summer! He's insane. I think it's this political thing, I have to have the right profile or something. He wants to run for president in four years, he says why not run, now anybody can do it. He's some sort of crazy libertarian, it's embarrassing. But that means I can't be a rich-girl slacker. Which I don't want to be, by the way. I want to architect my life. So we have the same goal. He can be so amazing, I'm lucky, of course. It's just . . ."

"Just what?"

"I don't know if I'm good at anything, actually." Lark tried to smile.

"You're good at caring," Doe said. "About what you do in the world. That's a start."

"That's a really nice thing to say."

The sun hit the soft pressed sheets and Lark's hair, and Doe wanted to snap the shutter and print the moment. Whatever this turned out to be, it would never be as good as right now.

Lark checked her phone. "Oh, crap, it's him. He's coming out tomorrow, and he wants to have dinner. Like I don't have a life. It's not an invitation, it's a *summons*. I told him I was having dinner with you last night, and he said to ask you, too. I'm sorry!"

Doe felt pieces shift. This was scary but good. The first step. She'd been invited into the family. It had been more than a month since the party, since the photo of Daniel and Adeline made the *New York Post*. Daniel had fired the caterers, blaming them for the shot.

She knew how the household ran now. She knew Marisol wasn't a housekeeper, she was a "household manager." She knew the garage was called the "vehicle barn." She knew the chef would make lunch if Lark told him she'd be home, and it was always a salad. She knew there were people around for security, people for laundry, people to drive the cars, and that Lark said it was a reduced staff because things were so relaxed at the beach. She knew that Lark had twenty-seven summer purses. She knew Lark would drop blouses on the floor and they would get picked up and dry-cleaned.

She knew a lot but she didn't know Daniel. If Lark told Daniel how they met, how Doe had lost her shoes, Daniel might forget about the caterers and wonder.

She never backed out of things, though. Never out of fear.

"Sure," Doe said.

From: Lucas Clay
To: Doe Callender

Wassup beautiful

From: Doe Callender
To: Lucas Clay

Zzz just waking up

From: Lucas
To: Doe

Sorry about the other day I was an asshole

From: Doe
To: Lucas

No argument here

From: Lucas
To: Doe

u know I'll make it up to you I'm good at that . . . just us. You like the sound of that

From: Doe
To: Lucas

Maybe, my weekend is crazy busy

From: Lucas
To: Doe

Yah mine too

. . .

Btw do u know Jem fm the farm stand

From: Doe
To: Lucas

sure, Ruthie's daughter you know that

From: Lucas
To: Doe

how old is she exactly

From: Doe
To: Lucas

15 i think

From: Lucas
To: Doe

looks older

From: Doe
To: Lucas

She's in high school dude

From: Lucas
To: Doe

My friend Hale was asking guess I'll tell him no

From: Doe
To: Lucas

wld be wise

it's a crime you know

From: Lucas
To: Doe

Ya soooooo unfair considering how tasteee

From: Doe
To: Lucas

Gross

From: Lucas
To: Doe

lol

25

RUTHIE WOKE UP the next morning with a headache so thunderous she knew it was payback. She was now the kind of person who disgraced herself at parties. This was humiliating, but there was something pleasurable about being that person, too.

It had the quality of a dream, the lilac tree, Helen's ghost face in the dusk, Lucas talking about painting a Peter Clay like it was a joke, a big joke, that's what it had been, she was sure.

She took three aspirin with a tall glass of water. She opened the refrigerator and hung on the door. Then she sank to the floor.

She heard footsteps behind her. "Mom?"

"Are you talking to me again?"

"Oh. I guess so. Why are you on the floor?"

"Just wondering if we have . . . a drink thing with caffeine."

Jem sank to the floor next to her. They leaned together in the refrigerator chill. "Are you okay?"

"Bad day yesterday. Bad worse worst terrible day. But I'm okay," Ruthie said. "Oh, shit, I lied. I'm not. I was mean to someone who was trying to be nice to me."

"Daddy?"

"No, not Daddy. Someone I used to know."

"Well, you know what you always told me when I was a kid."

"No."

"If you say 'I'm sorry' with sorry in your heart, you'll be okay."

"What a sanctimonious ass."

"What?"

"By the way, I quit yesterday. Or maybe I was fired. I'm still not sure."

"Quit the Belfry?"

"It was a you-can't-fire-me-I-quit scenario, I think."

"But . . . you love it there. And everyone loves you."

"Do you know what Mindy said? That I serve at the pleasure of the board. She used the word *pleasure*. Like she was fucking Queen Elizabeth. I mean, not literally fucking Queen Elizabeth. That's Philip's job. I wish I could stop cursing. Shit."

"But what about Carole? And Helen? And . . . everyone! They can't just fire you! It must be a mistake. They'll ask you back."

Remembering the lilac tree, Ruthie shook her head. "I think the die is cast."

"But it will be okay, right? I mean, what are you going to do?"

"It will be okay, sweetie." Ruthie wiped her nose on the hem of her T-shirt. "I just need some time. And coffee."

"I'll make you coffee."

"You are the best of the best of the best of daughters."

Jem sprang up. Ruthie shut the refrigerator but stayed on the floor, hugging her knees. Jem found a pod and stuck it in the coffee machine. "What does Daddy say?"

"I haven't told him yet. He's, uh. Kind of hard to track down these days."

"Yeah, I know." Jem banged down a coffee cup.

"What?" Ruthie leaned back against the fridge. Her head felt as though it was being jackhammered apart.

"Everything this summer is so weird. It's like this house is a portal and we all walked through. Like we're trying on being rich, and it just doesn't fit."

"I know," Ruthie said. She had gone back to the main house and left the watch on top of Carole's dresser. She couldn't see tossing it into Verity's box again. Yet it sat there, at the front of her brain, like an obstacle obstructing a clear view.

Next to her on the floor, Jem's phone dinged. Ruthie glanced at the text hovering on the screen. "What's the Mayflower thing?"

"What Mayflower thing?"

Ruthie pointed to the text. It was from Saffy.

You are going down. #mayflower

"What does that mean?" Ruthie asked as Jem snatched back the phone. "Are you guys comparing ancestors? Because Duttons didn't come over on the *Mayflower*. They probably waited until there were hospitals and distilleries."

"It's a stupid nothing thing."

Jem's mouth stretched in that way that happened when she was upset.

"What is it, sweetie?" Ruthie struggled to her feet.

Jem banged down a spoon. She turned away, her shoulders shaking.

"Sweetie?" Ruthie reached out to hold Jem while the smell of coffee invaded the kitchen with a promise of something normal to come if they could just get through this moment. And the next. And a few more after that.

Jem was in her arms, her cheek flushed and wet against her. "Okay," Ruthie said. "You've *got* to tell me whatever it is."

"They hate me, Mommy. I have no friends."

She rocked her, her sweet, sweet girl, murder in her heart.

"I mean, I get it, they're awful, I shouldn't want to be friends with them."

"Yeah."

"But why do I still?" Jem raised her face, teary and red.

"Because you're buying into their story, maybe. That they're the coolest. They're making a reality and you're in it. What about Annie? Isn't she your friend?"

"Yeah, she's been cool. And there's this new friend . . ."

"A boy?"

"Sort of."

"A sort of boy?" she asked, gentle, gentle.

"A summer person. Out of my league."

"Nothing's out of your league. Is he nice to you?"

"He makes me laugh." She shrugged. "It's not important. It's just a thing, a flirty thing, at work. He comes by sometimes. It's just that I miss my own room. It's like here . . . it's beautiful and everything, but I'm afraid to touch anything. It's not *home*."

"You're right," Ruthie said. "We've got to stick it out this summer. But after this year, no more moving."

"Really?"

"Just us in our house. All year long."

"You promise?"

Ruthie set her jaw against the pain in her head. Cue sunset, cue her shaking fist. As God was her witness. "Nobody's taking our home ever again."

26

WHEN MIKE AND RUTHIE had heard that Mike's great-aunt Laurel had left Mike her house on the bay in Orient, it was an occurrence so startling, so out of the blue, that it was like the scene in that old movie where a secretary sitting on the top of a double-decker bus—who was it, Jean Arthur? Irene Dunne?—suddenly had a fur coat land on her head, tossed from a Park Avenue penthouse. Giddy from their luck, blinded by the thwack of luxury goods, they didn't stop to think that they could not afford the life that had fallen on them.

It was the fall of 2001. In New York City, Mike and Ruthie had moved back into their Tribeca loft with their baby after crowding in with friends uptown. The head of the EPA had told them they were safe. The instructions? Clean with a bucket and a mop.

Ruthie and Mike had been art majors, painters; they knew about toxic materials. They wore face masks and bought HEPA filters, but Ruthie found the ash everywhere: caked into the ridges of the Dreft plastic top, in the joints of the stroller, in the cracks, in the seams, in the hinges, in the vents. Her neighbor hadn't evacuated and had sores that wouldn't heal and an excruciating and recurrent case of bronchitis. Ruthie heard the dry cough every-where, in the stores, on the streets, in the diner. They stood in the lobby, mail in their hands, and spoke in low tones of dioxin and asbestos, PCBs and heavy metals, the toxic properties of jet fuel, what happens to computers when they atomize; they did not dis-cuss the other organic material they were no doubt inhaling, all those lives in a cloud of dust.

Then anthrax hit the news. Their friends were renting cars and driving to Westchester and New Jersey on weekends with their babies strapped into car seats, house hunting with easy, preap-proved mortgages in hand and gas masks in the trunk. Ruthie lay in bed at night, feeling as though she now lived on a perilous, ashy moon.

Leave Manhattan? A year ago they would have laughed. But the house in Orient could be worth something, enough to buy something else, somewhere, one of the river towns in Westchester, maybe. Enough to get them out of one big room with Mike's paintings stacked along a wall and the crib in the corner and the look in Mike's eyes that Ruthie read as *trapped*.

They borrowed a car and headed east.

Ruthie had only met Laurel a handful of times on Laurel's in-frequent visits to the city, but that had sparked a kind of friend-ship. She'd liked Laurel's sense of rigor about things. Where Mike's father was soft and indistinct, Laurel was as bracing as a salty wave.

Laurel and Mike's father no longer spoke, a long-ago quarrel they wouldn't discuss, though Mike traced it to Laurel finally erupting at his father's refusal to allow her to bring her girlfriend to Thanksgiving. He didn't object because she was a lesbian, he insisted to Mike, it was that Laurel just wouldn't settle down. Laurel had called out this bullshit with the contempt it deserved, and their relationship, never close, was severed. "A relief," Laurel said tersely.

Mike was a terrible correspondent. Ruthie sent Laurel a Christ-mas card every year with a note enclosed, and had sent a photo of

Jem when she was born. Laurel responded with a silver rattle from Tiffany's and a copy of *Frog and Toad*.

The truth was that they rarely thought about Laurel until they got a call that she'd died. Heart attack, on the porch. A neighbor had found her, had said that from the road, she appeared to be looking approvingly at her dahlias.

They drove and drove on that gray December day on an empty road lined with bare trees, wet black branches creaking ominously in a rustling, steady wind. The tiny village seemed forlorn and time-warped, waiting for summer. On the main street, everything was closed. Houses with brown lawns looked unoccupied. One lone person walked a frisky dog. They hailed him (later they would know him as a neighbor, Clark Fund, an eccentric who made an almost-living as an auction picker) and asked for Laurel's house. "Ah, Laurel," he'd said. "So you're the nephew with the good wife."

The first view of the house was not auspicious. It was weathered gray siding, paint peeling on the trim, a lopsided house with a second-story addition jutting up and out, an elbow in the side, your uncle the comedian making sure you got the joke. That cold day they stood in the front yard, holding each other and the baby. The wind slapped their faces like a wet mitten, but it was fresh and tangy. The clouds scudded away, and the sun suddenly shone on their faces. When they walked, their footsteps stirred only mud, not ash. They rounded the corner of the house and caught their breath at the expanse of sea and bountiful sky.

"I don't care about the inside, we can fix it," Mike said. "Let's do it."

Ruthie would have set the words to music if someone hadn't gotten there first.

"It's perfect," she said. "As far as you can go without drowning."

. . .

THAT FIRST WINTER Ruthie and Mike had truly gotten to know the house, every rotted sill, every piece of wiring, every creak and every draft, and had known that years of struggle lay ahead. The taxes might ruin them. They lay in bed dismayed, clutching each other and dreaming of decent takeout. They had left a rent-stabilized loft in New York. They knew they could never afford to go back.

Ruthie was the one to figure it out, on the first perfect summer weekend. She sat on the porch at the market on Village Lane with a cup of coffee and watched as the renters arrived, toting bikes and kayaks and coolers. All that summer she investigated fees, snooped, pondered, bought Elena, the local realtor, a cup of coffee.

They had the bones. They had the cedar shingles, the oak floors, the fireplace. They had the view, the classic Orient view of bay and sky and thin golden ribbons of sand across the water. They had everything, but it was falling down. They bought steel-toed boots and went to work.

By the next summer they were able to rent out the house for weekly periods in July and August, enough to pay taxes for the year, plus hire an electrician for an overhaul of the wiring. No more glass fuses! They bundled up Jem and rented a studio apartment in Greenport.

Year after year the renters came, and as the North Fork adjusted to the spillover from the more chic Hamptons, as more potato fields were turned into wineries, as the fifties motels became retro rather than dingy, Ruthie had a vision. It wasn't enough to rent—they had to rent *big*. They had to, over time, make their house into the kind of place that could command a fee substantial enough not only to cover taxes but to do real improvements as well. They would build up to the big money—fifteen thousand for the summer, twenty thousand . . . the sky was the limit for the right kind of property. That would give them income, enough to live comfortably, have a savings account, save for Jem's college. It was the only way to lift them out of the bohemian poverty they lived in, two art majors scraping by. By then she was director of the Belfry, a job that didn't pay much but required all her time and energy. They were barely making it. A second mortgage plus summer rentals would make all the difference.

All they needed were the correct basics—the farmhouse sink, European appliances, closet systems—and they could fill in carefully with vintage items so that the place wouldn't skew too flea-market-y. They were artists; they knew what color and texture could do, how to cull from house sales and Craigslist. They found out about billionaires buying renovated twenty-million-dollar homes in the Hamptons who invariably hired a designer who decreed that everything must be completely redone, and that's when they pounced. They'd picked up Italian cabinets and double ovens for peanuts or for free. Mike entered the genial core of workers who renovated houses all over the North Fork, and made friends and did favors and called them in, and floors were sanded, kitchen counters were installed, closets expanded, bit by painful bit.

Now it was the house that people photographed, that was gestured to from passing sailboats, the house with the cornflower-blue French doors opening out to a slate patio. In summer, roses tumbled, bright pink and yellow against the seagrass, and it was all topped off with a briskly flapping American flag.

Everything had gone exactly as Ruthie had envisioned on that freezing day so long ago. Except for the ending.

The thing was, when he said he wanted to leave, she thought he only needed room to turn around and come back. And if an occasional rageful thought of how he had seemed to leave her so casually (just because of a lack of *happiness*, really?) came over her, she was determined to wait it out.

It wasn't just that the house was something they created together, sacrificed for. It was that it was indeed everything, need and want and desire and safety, all the connective tissue that held her together.

27

AFTER THICK SLICES of toast and honey and a cup of coffee, Ruthie felt able to face the world. She took her second cup outside and sat by the pool, sipping carefully and watching the ruffling of the waves out on the bay. The heat felt like a blanket she wouldn't throw off until October.

There were so few days in life that changed everything. It was always a surprise, the blow at the back of the knees that could come so fast you don't even hear the whistle of the bat through the air.

She knew she'd made a fool of herself. She knew she'd been hard on Joe. She knew it was unfair to hate Mike, that he hadn't cheated, but she couldn't stop the wide, wild anger beating through her like the wings of a raptor.

Mike's pickup jounced up the driveway. He got out and slammed the door. He saw her and stopped. He was wearing a new shirt, soft cotton that matched that perfect sky. She clutched her warm cup to her chest and kept her face turned away as he approached her.

"Is Jem ready?"

"She's getting dressed."

"Good, it will give us a chance to talk."

"I really don't think it's a good idea."

"It's better to just air it out, don't you think?"

If she were hoping that Mike would look ravaged, or even un-happy, she was disappointed. He looked nervous, sure, but also . . . she could smell it if she leaned over, if she got away from the coffee steam, she could sniff it out . . . he was *satisfied*. She had had moments of hating Mike over the past years, moments of temptation when she wanted to kick him, or stab him with a fork. But not this. This was a whole other level of temptation. Murder. Mayhem. Truck torching. She ran over the possibilities in her mind. After all she was a woman with an ax.

"So, there's a hole where the lilac tree was."

"Wow. That's terrible."

"There was broken glass on the porch. Roberta got some in her foot."

"So sorry to spoil the party."

"Look. We've stayed friends. Really, truly friends. I want us to stay friends through this. I think we can do it. We've *done* it."

"You're not my friend anymore. You're fired." Ruthie placed her cup carefully on the side table. "Speaking of which, so was I."

"What do you mean?"

"I mean, I quit. But I had to. It was clear that I was being set up by Mindy and Gloria. Even Helen. That's why I was looking for you." She didn't know why she was telling him. It wasn't just be-cause she wanted him to feel bad. It was that she needed so des-perately to tell someone who understood. Mike had been through years of Belfry Museum politics.

Mike slowly sank onto the chair next to her. "Helen, too? That's crazy. You should go to the full board."

"That never works. Boards hate fights like this. The director always loses."

"You could sue."

"Nobody sues. She's going to tie me up with a nondisclosure and dangle the severance to make me sign it. That's how it works."

"Wow, I'm so sorry. There has to be something we can do."

"Not your problem."

"Of course it is—"

"If you say *We're family*, this conversation is over."

"Ruthie." His voice was gentle. "I didn't know. This is awful."

"How could you know? That would imply that you'd answer my texts, or see me once in a while, instead of being so busy fucking our tenant."

"Okay. Okay. We need to talk about it. But can we just . . ."

She shot forward so fast he reared back. "No, we can't *just*!" she spit out. "There will be no qualifiers in this conversation. For once, we're going to say it plain, without your Connecticut WASP evasions."

He held up his hands, as if she were attacking him. "Can I remind you that we're not married?"

"But we're *family*, remember?"

"I didn't tell you because it was so new, and it happened so fast. Why upset you if I didn't have to?"

"Because it's *lying*!"

Mike shook his head. "I'm sorry my moral compass isn't as finely tuned as yours. It never was."

"Compasses aren't tuned, genius," she said, and saw him flinch. "Does Jem know?"

"No." Mike ran a hand through his hair. "Something is going on with her this summer. She's become so secretive . . . Adeline thinks—"

"Excuse me, do I care what Adeline thinks?"

"—that we should expose Jem to new things, open up her world a bit, get her away from Meret that way. That's why she invited her to Roberta's. She's a good person, Ruthie. She wants us all to be friends."

"Really? What a swell idea."

An exaggerated sigh.

"We're not telling Jem about you two," she said. "This could all dissolve after Labor Day."

"It won't."

"You sound sure of something that just began."

"It's been more than a month."

"Oh, come on. Did you start sleeping together the day she came?"

Under any other circumstances, the look on Mike's face would have been comical.

"I'm sorry. What can I say? It was the thunderbolt. Wasn't this inevitable for one of us?"

Inevitable? Sure. Maybe. She had braced herself for Mike's first girlfriend, his lovers. If he'd had one or two, she hadn't known.

"I'm in love," he said.

She dropped her head in her hands and laughed. Her head pounded, the headache back in force now.

"You're in love," she said. "The two of you. Wouldn't you say that there are some obvious differences between you?"

"She's less than ten years older. She's fifty-six."

Ruthie raised one eyebrow.

"She has money. Yes. I get it, Ruthie. She travels in circles in New York that I've never had access to. But she's just a girl who grew up on a farm. She came here from California and became a waitress. She happened to fall in love with an artist."

"Oh, my God. Is that what she said? 'I'm just a girl from a farm'? Are you kidding me? Is that how she presents her story? Peter Clay was *famous* when she met him. He was thirty years older than she was!"

"She loved him."

"So did his wife and child."

"You know they had a terrible marriage. You *told* me what it was like. Peter fell in love with her. He pursued her. She was young—"

"She was past thirty. She was an aging waitress in a SoHo restaurant who saw her chance. She took what she wanted. And now she's taking you."

Mike's face flushed. "She's not taking me. Nobody's being taken, nobody's going anywhere."

"Yes, she has a sudden whim for the simple life. She's trying it on with her handyman. She likes to remake herself every five years, and hey, perfect timing, you show up with a pickup truck and a hammer."

"Have you been talking to Lucas?"

"Why do you say that?"

"If I were you, I'd stay away from him. She's been bailing him out for years."

"And now she's bailing you! How sweet. What's going to happen when she goes back to New York? Are you going to put on a suit—she'll buy it, of course—and go with her to those charity events? Get photographed? Wait, I can see the headline now—the carpenter and the lady."

Another hit. Mike pressed his lips together and looked away. This was exhilarating. Ruthie had crossed over to a new realm of combat, where you actually *can* say whatever you want. Even in their worst arguments when they were married they were careful to stay away from the most bitter truths about each other. They never stuck in the blade and wiggled it.

But this? This felt *fine*.

"You were never mean like this," Mike said.

And didn't he count on that? Didn't everyone? "I'm just getting started."

"I can't see the future," Mike said. "Who can? I just know I've never felt like this before."

Ruthie's breath whistled out her nose.

"I'm sorry, but it's true," Mike said. "And if you're honest, you can admit that what we had was love, absolutely, but it never felt . . . *fated*. We were never swept away."

"And her money has nothing to do with it," she said. "That's hilarious. Poor you, brought up a Dutton, a legacy to Choate and Yale. You got every advantage a rich white boy gets. Except the inheritance. And now you've got it. Money and connections. Are you going to be an artist again, Mike? Hang out with Tom McGreevy? Be introduced to his dealer?" She looked at his face. "Oh, that's already happened, hasn't it? She's a fast mover." She laughed. "Well, I knew that already."

"Thanks for the confidence, sweetheart. Did you ever think that an art dealer might be interested in my work? You never thought I was good enough—"

"I did! I thought you were good enough!" She tossed her coffee on the lawn. "It was you who quit! You *always* quit when things get hard. Well, you've got your insulation back. Your privilege. Just check your balls at the door. Don't worry, she'll buy you a new pair!"

He rose angrily, and she followed him. "You'll sit at their tables. You'll tell your stories with a glass of wine in your hand and they'll laugh—"

"Stop it!"

"—and you'll get what you always wanted in the bargain. What you never really had."

"Don't fucking say it."

She spit the words out in his face. "A mommy."

His skin stretched tight on his face, his mouth a bloodless line. "I have never been so close to hitting you as I am right now."

"Go ahead! Make it worse! Let's just burn down the whole barn!"

In a sudden movement that made Mike rear back, she picked up the side table. Her coffee cup went skittering as she threw the table into the pool. They watched it sink.

"What the hell, Ruthie! This isn't you!" He came toward her with such ferocity she shrank back. "We were never an *us,*" he said. "I tried. You never made room for an us."

"What does that mean?"

Mike looked away, over at the glittering sea. "I've felt more at home in that house in the last month than I ever did."

"That's a terrible thing to say."

"It's a terrible thing to feel."

"Jesus, your self-pity is sickening!"

"Can we please not do this? We loved each other. Can't we hang on to that? I don't want to hurt you, you're pushing this—I loved you, but I was never *in* love with you. I was never in love with *anyone*," Mike said. "Until now. Now I know what fate is. I'm positive we can stay friends if we just face things. Things can be *better*. For all of us. For Jem."

Jem. She pictured Adeline and Jem walking through the revolving door at MoMA. Lunching in some small, exquisite French restaurant. It would be warm, and Adeline would look slender and fresh in her summer dress and sandals, with her perfect pedicured feet.

She pictured Jem being driven to Yale, because now they could afford the tuition, Adeline would pay, and thus it would be Mike and Adeline who drove her up. Ruthie would take the bus to New Haven and stay in a bad motel. On the walk to campus, she'd get mugged.

"I called an attorney," Mike said. "I think it's time we finalized this."

She grabbed the back of a chair. She felt the wood underneath her hands and she wanted to dig her nails in and come up with splinters to flick at him, sharp and flecked with her blood. "You think I was controlling, that I managed you? Well, you needed managing. You think Adeline Clay isn't managing you already? Introducing you to the right people, grooming you? Where did you get that shirt, anyway? You're her problem. She'll probably hire you a therapist. You'll be her fixer-upper."

"Mommy!"

She turned. Jem behind her, looking from one to the other. "Daddy? Are you seeing Adeline *Clay*?"

"Sweetie, we can talk about it on the way to work." Mike ran his hands through his hair. "Do you have your stuff?"

"What's happening?" Jem looked afraid. "What are you two talking about?"

Ruthie turned back to Mike. "She is not getting the house."

They glared at each other, enemies.

"Mommy!" Jem cried. "Why is the table in the pool?"

28

THE BELFRY NEWS was out, and the phone calls and emails began.

SAMANTHA WIGGINS: "WE started out hating Mindy and now it's spread to hating each other. This board used to be fun. Honestly? I think she's emotionally disturbed. Ruthie, I'll help you any way I can. Shall I see if I can talk to people?"

CRYSTAL SCANLON: "I can't believe this! Well, actually? I can. She's such a pill. But Ruthie, what can we do? Let's have lunch next week, I've got a household of guests."

EDITH HOLLIMAN: "I called Mindy about this as soon as I heard. She said that it's better for the Belfry, and it's better for you. The place has to move forward out of a box, or something. What does Carole think?"

STEPHANIE GREEN: "I can't believe this. It's a coup. I didn't know anything about it! I'm calling Mindy right now. Ugh. Nobody likes that woman except Gloria. And everyone hates Gloria."

WALKER HOLLAND: "CATHA gave a presentation to the exec committee on taking over the job permanently. She has some good ideas. The North Fork really is changing. There are new markets to tap. And Mindy is such a force."

TOM CRANDALL: "MINDY told us that we can't talk to you. It's against board policy. She's hired her father's attorney. She's always so thorough. I'm sorry, Ruthie. It was a great run. We'll just have to see where it goes."

PAM WOLFER: "I can't imagine the Belfry without you. Are you selling your house? Because my daughter is looking."

CLARK "QUADS" FUND: "They suck."

TOBIE PINCUS: "I told Catha that she was a traitor and a skunk. Right to her face. She started to cry and say how hard it was for her. The staff is furious. We hate her! Did you know she's been undermining you for at least a year? She knew there were board members who didn't think she was doing a good job, so she went after yours. Even after you protected her. I was there, I saw it. You had her back, she stuck a knife in yours. It's nice when things work out that way."

GUS ROMANY: "MUSEUM boards are brutal, baby. Get out while you can."

SAMANTHA WIGGINS: "I can't get in touch with Carole. Don't they have cellphones in France?"

From: Ruth Beamish
To: Carole Berlinger
Subject: need advice

Carole, the *merde* hit the fan at the meeting. I resigned. I found out that Catha has been campaigning for my job. I know you're exploring stone circles or something but can you write back? I need advice! And tranquilizers.

Thx, xo r

From: Catha Lugner
To: Ruth Beamish
Subject: this mess

Ruthie,

Crazy times, huh? Mindy said you were leaving and asked me to step up. I hope you can recognize that it's for the good of the institution that we both worked so hard for. I'm sure there will be exciting new things on the horizon for you! Midlife change is awesome. Let's stay friends during this transitional time! I sent you and Jem a basket from Locavoracious. Be on the lookout!

xo CSL

From: Catha
To: Ruthie
Subject: disappointed

There really was no need to throw the basket on my porch. The raccoons dragged all the food all over the lawn. I'm sorry you can't be an adult about this.

From: Ruthie
To: Catha
Re: disappointed

Fuck you, Iago.

From: Penny Kaplan
To: Ruth Beamish

I just heard. Holy shit!

. . . The Chinese ideogram for crisis is danger and opportunity you know. You could get a tattoo.

From: Elena Serrano
To: Ruth Beamish

I'm starting a petition for reinstatement. Come over for coffee.

29

PENNY ADDED A plop of whiskey to Ruthie's coffee. Ruthie had sat in the same chair at the kitchen table when she told them Mike was leaving her. Penny had leaned toward her in the very same way, her fists on the table. Ruthie had the same expectation, that Penny would excoriate her enemy and then map out a plan for a new life.

"That Mindy," Penny said. "She's a venomous . . . ah, meal-worm. And Catha. Didn't I tell you? A smug, self-aggrandizing cardboard lady."

"Cardboard lady?"

"Look, I think we can turn this around," Elena said. "I've been making calls. People are outraged. They know you made the Belfry what it is. You are a part of this community. We can get up a petition. You have a huge amount of support."

"Please don't," Ruthie said. "It won't do any good. And frankly, if we cause a fuss it could impact my severance. Mindy has a hotshot attorney from Manhattan. The nondisclosure is like I worked for deep ops."

"We can't let them get away with it!" Penny cried.

"Worse things happen every day, and you know it," Ruthie said.

"That's my point," Penny declared, waving her mug. "What's wrong with people? Is lying and betrayal not only okay now, but you actually get rewarded for it?"

"Yes!" Ruthie and Elena said together.

"I need to tell you something else," Ruthie said. "That. Mike," she got out. "Is sleeping. With Adeline Clay. Since Memorial Day weekend!"

"Wow," Penny said. "I mean, oh. Bastard."

She saw by their faces that they hadn't known, and she felt better. Elena and Penny dragged their chairs closer to surround her, and Elena held one hand and Penny held another, and she told them how she found out, and that she'd thrown a glass and chopped down a tree (muffled guffaw from Penny), and how she was a mouse with a collapsing skeleton, and that her life was shit.

Penny squeezed her hand. "You know this was inevitable."

"It was either you or him," Elena said. "Somebody was going to get a lover."

"You two seemed to be able to do it, but nobody can really do it," Penny said.

"You can't sleep with your ex on a regular basis without paying the piper," Elena said.

"Sleep with my ex?" Ruthie looked from Elena to Penny.

Penny's head bobbed backward in a gesture she knew well. "You and Mike aren't still sleeping together?"

"We just assumed . . ." Elena said.

"Or else how did it work?" Penny asked.

"We're friends," Ruthie said. "I mean, we were."

"But . . . neither one of you was ever with anyone else since the divorce," Penny said. "You saw each other all the time."

"And it's been three *years*," Elena said.

Penny and Elena exchanged glances.

Elena patted her knee. "Now, let's just sit here and look at this.

Mike is having a summer affair. A ridiculous summer affair with a ridiculous summer woman, so obviously it will end by Labor Day."

"Am I really this pathetic that I need to hear that?"

"You're not pathetic, sweetie," Penny said. "No matter how you look right now. Look, can I say this? Mike set this up. I love him, I do—though I'm really, really mad at him right now—but he's the one who insisted that you could be friends. He pursued that, doll. He was so guilty about breaking up his family and so terrified at losing Jem that he made the rules. He came up with the Wednesday-night dinner and the cookouts and the sitting together at school events."

"And he was the one who put off the divorce. He wanted to be an intact family without the commitment," Elena said.

Ruthie wiped her eyes with her sleeve. Elena handed her a napkin. "She wants to buy my house. I guess he needs a dowry. Ha. The thing is, we always had this agreement that if one person really, really wants to sell, we'd sell."

"Can you buy Mike out?" Elena asked.

"I don't have that kind of money."

"Nobody does," Penny said. "Well, I mean, not nobody. Just not us."

"Well, we'll be unemployed together," Ruthie said.

Penny shot a glance at Elena that clearly signaled that they did not feel comfortable being happy in front of her.

"You got a job!" Ruthie cried.

Penny nodded. "Woodhull Vineyard is opening a restaurant. A soft opening in the fall."

"Fantastic!"

"It hasn't been announced yet, it's still under wraps. It's a gorgeous space overlooking the vineyard."

"You're the chef?"

"I'm planning the menu."

"That's wonderful."

"With Roberta Verona. Do you know her? She's an amazing chef. Her name will be prominent, of course, I get that, but I'll get to run the kitchen."

Ruthie leaned back. "Are you kidding me?"

"No, isn't it great?"

"Roberta is Adeline's best friend."

"Really?"

"You didn't know?"

"No! Mike told me about the job, but—"

"I told you that Jem was offered a job in her kitchen."

"You never told me!"

"I thought I did. I mean, it just happened about a week ago."

Penny looked stricken. "I didn't know."

"Don't you see? That woman is taking over everything. She knows you two are our best friends! She's going after you, too!"

"She's not taking over," Elena said. "Penny got the job on her own. She didn't use Adeline."

"But Adeline *knew*! She set the whole thing up. Don't you see that?"

"We don't know that," Penny said. "Mike just said he heard about the new place, and I know David, the owner, so I just called him. And anyway, what difference does it make?"

"It makes every difference!" Ruthie felt the whiskey eat through her stomach lining, and she put down the empty cup. "You're in the friend loop now! Won't it be great next summer? Mike and Adeline will have a favorite table—of course it will be the best one—and you'll be sending out amuse-bouche and free glasses of champagne and chef's little tasting appetizer things! Except all vegany because she doesn't eat dairy!"

"Now you've gone too far. I don't cook for *vegans*!"

"This isn't a betrayal, sweetie," Elena said. "It's a job. And we need it."

Ruthie had always admired Elena's beautiful serene gaze. It had always soothed her. Now it infuriated her. She stood up, the chair clattering. "Why doesn't anybody *listen* to me anymore? Do I have a voice? Can you actually see me? Am I a ghost?"

"Let's cut to the chase. Do you want me to turn this job down?" Penny asked. Her voice was quiet.

"I didn't say that."

"You are saying it." Penny slammed her fist on the table and sent the cups rattling. "So just say it!"

Elena put her hand over her mug. She looked from Penny's white face to Ruthie, standing now and trembling, hanging on to the kitchen chair.

Penny pushed back her chair. "Say you want me to give up a fantastic opportunity so that *you* won't have to feel uncomfortable if your *ex*-husband and his girlfriend happen to stroll into my restaurant on a random Tuesday evening and I cook them food. Because that is what you are saying and I am hearing you say it."

"Why would I say it? It would mean that you'd have to actually listen to me instead of talking about yourself all the time."

"And you'd have to be not such a fucking victim!"

Ruthie strode to the door. Elena took two steps after her but stopped.

"When did you become such an asshole?" Penny shouted.

"Today!" Ruthie yelled. "Okay? Tell everyone. Ruthie is now an asshole! All she had to do was tell the truth!"

"Ruthie!" Elena spoke with the sternness of a schoolmarm. "You can't blame Penny."

"I am going to blame everyone in the world," Ruthie said, opening the door.

30

PENNY WAS HARD on people, she told herself. Penny held grudges. When she let you in, you felt lifted, because she didn't bestow her friendship easily, only her acquaintance. Maybe that was why when she let you in, she had to tell you everything in her life (which was admittedly entertaining), but often it didn't leave much room for anybody else. Ruthie was not the kind of person to elbow herself into getting attention, even from her best friend. Now they had bumped into the thing that maybe had wrecked them for good. They had shared their meanest thought about the other.

When had love become a thing that choked her instead of enfolding her?

Maybe all relationships, friendship, partner, parent and child, were held together by the things you did not say as much as the things you did. The unsaid was the keystone in the arch. Once you kicked it free, you had nothing that held you up.

Without Penny, she was a boat unmoored. A woman without a best friend.

She left the playhouse for the lawn. She needed plenty of pacing room. Earbuds in, she dialed her father's number in Tampa.

He would be surprised to hear from her. They had a regularly scheduled phone call on the first of the month, as if she were a bill on automatic payment.

"Ruthie! We just spoke! Anything wrong?"

"No, I just wanted to talk to you."

"Great! It's just that we're going out to dinner. New place in Hyde Park. Berte already put on her earrings, that means two minutes and we're out the door. That woman is a clock," he said fondly. "How's my little girl?"

"Fine."

"And my beautiful granddaughter?"

"She's good. She's been working hard at the farm stand. She likes it."

"Good. Never too soon to be responsible. Hang on." She heard him speak to Berte. "Go ahead out, cool down the car for us, darling." Of course his darling should cool down the car; Ruthie had been to Tampa in July, it was hellfire. Of course Berte was anxious to make their reservation, of course he would call her darling, of course the easy affection of their marriage would cut her to the heart every time. She pictured Berte in a tropical-print full skirt, red lipstick, dangling pretty sea-glass earrings, swishing out into the warm night to cool down the Buick.

Conversation with her father was always bumpy. On the mornings of their scheduled calls she drew up a mental list of items to talk about. She could sense his impatience now. His cocktail was waiting.

"How's that museum of yours?"

She hesitated. That was what she was calling for, to tell him what had happened, to ask for a loan, to ask for something for the first time in her life since she'd left for college. She had already planned it out, how she would structure the payments to pay him back, the amount she would ask for, the amount she would offer to Mike to buy him out. Her father, she was sure, had the money.

"One of these days we'll get up there to see it. Such a long drive, though."

"You could fly."

"Right. Berte is going to take that course, you know the one where they cure you of phobias? They use meditation now."

"Great idea."

Usually a variant of this sparkling dialogue continued for ten excruciating minutes, until they were allowed to hang up. There was so little in common between them. Love, of course. Love was a given, but if she wanted a place in his heart she had to get in line. That was just the way it was. She didn't need to go to therapy about it. She got it. He was a man who had been overtaken by an overwhelming force. True love. Berte had given him all the warmth he'd been missing, and she was all he needed and wanted.

Her father had always been called "such a sad sack" by her mother. He had been a creature of routine, and that didn't include smiling. By the time Ruthie woke up in the mornings he was gone, heading out to buy fish for his shop in Bayside, Queens. When he got home he walked to the cabinet, took a slug of Scotch, and went immediately to the shower to wash off the smell. Sometimes on weekends when Ruthie got in the car she could see blood on the floor. She never asked her father to drive her and her friends to the movies, for fear the car would smell like bluefish.

When she was nine he started leaving on Wednesday evenings to take lessons in Portuguese, so he could communicate with the fishermen, he said. He'd listen to tapes in the car. *Um dois três,* they would chant together. *Domingo, Segunda-feira, Terça-feira.* He fell in love with Brazil and spoke of its beaches and jungles to Ruthie as if it were a place in a book, something enchanted. He nagged her mother to make *moqueca* on Fridays instead of broiled swordfish. Finally he himself tied on an apron and made *feijoada,* pronouncing it correctly with a flourish. Her mother worried about a nervous breakdown and was on the phone with her friend Marie for hours, but Ruthie liked this new perky version of her dad. Until the day he moved out to live with Berte, a Brazilian widow. Apparently his fishermen didn't speak Portuguese after all. Berte had come into the fish store every Friday. They'd fallen in love over the fluke.

In less than a year they'd moved to Tampa. Ruthie was not allowed to speak his name in the house. She used to whisper *Lou Lou Lou* with her mouth smashed in her pillow. His calls were sporadic. A card on her birthday, urging her to visit. "Your father is *louco,*" her mother said, proud of her pun. She waited for Lou to realize his mistake, to come back and reclaim the fish store and his family, but he sent pictures of himself tarpon fishing instead.

All through her adolescence, Ruthie's yearly visits were painful, her Julys excruciating, when she arrived for four weeks. Berte had three teenage daughters, girls from a fairy tale, each more beautiful than the next. They all ran in and out of the sunny house with the terrazzo floor, dressed in tennis whites or bikinis, grabbing fruit from enormous colorful bowls. Lou now dressed in baggy short-sleeved shirts and shorts that showed his tanned knees, sandals that revealed his toes, the toes Ruthie had never seen, and a variety of caps that covered his bald spot. He had gone into real estate at the right time in the market. He laughed and smiled, he kissed Berte every morning, he owned a juicer. Full of citrus and mangoes, Ruthie would arrive back on the plane in a state of fruit-drugged anguish. Her mother would meet her at the baggage claim at LaGuardia and ask through tight lips (what an effort that must have been, to seem disinterested) how the trip was. Ruthie knew, even at twelve, even at thirteen, that a one-word answer was required.

Fine.

Because saying *This has saved him* would not go over well. Even at ten and twelve and fifteen she had known this, that her father was one of the charmed people in the world whom love had transformed. Angela was wrecked by love. Maybe she'd gotten over Lou, but she never got over being left.

Angela sold the fish store and got cheated in a collusion between lawyer and buyer so devious it still had the power to visit

Ruthie at 3 A.M. and send her blood pumping in anguish for her mother, so lost and alone she put her trust in two men who saw a way to make an easy buck. Angela took the money and they moved to a smaller apartment in another neighborhood. She took a bookkeeping course (she never got cheated again) and got a job for a furrier in Astoria. They moved again. Then again, to someplace smaller. It was a time of rent hikes, and they moved every year for much of Ruthie's childhood. She went to three different high schools.

Angela developed fears. She couldn't make a left turn in the car, she had to make a series of rights before getting to the destination. She couldn't go to movies because they were too loud. She couldn't buy fish, she couldn't travel, she couldn't attend Ruthie's school events because people expected to talk to you.

Then she began to go to church again. This is what Catholics did with heartbreak, threw themselves into rosaries and jealously guarded their special friendship with Father Peter or Father Anthony.

Ruthie drew. Ruthie did the grocery shopping. Ruthie painted. Ruthie got an after-school job. Ruthie made collages of fish out of parchment paper. Ruthie hung with the art kids and got into Cooper Union, a day she still remembered as one in which elation finally filled up every empty space. Tuition was free and she was about to take the E train to a new life. On high school graduation Angela gave her a check for ten thousand dollars. The amount of sacrifice it must have taken for her mother to save that much almost broke Ruthie enough to decide to give up her future and stay home (for that minute, anyway), but all they did was hug. "Don't embarrass me," Angela whispered in her ear.

In the middle of college her mother got sick. Angela's friends from church rose to help, bringing meals, rides to chemo and doctor visits. Lou called but did not come. Angela's sister, Nancy, arrived from California and slept on the couch for a week. Ruthie dropped out for a semester. Her mother bore it all with no complaints except for the food. A constant stream of casseroles showed up at their door. Ruthie, after all these years, still couldn't look at baked ziti without pain.

They didn't say much, in those last months. There were appointments and hospital stays and sudden fevers, but there were quiet days of sitting, Ruthie reading aloud or both of them staring at the TV. Everything was painful for her mother to watch except black-and-white movies and baseball. It was a good season for the Yankees. On one of those unbearably long afternoons they had been watching the ball fly across the green field and Ruthie had said, "I'll get us some lunch," and her mother had said, "Not yet," and taken her hand. They had watched an inning holding hands, Angela's dry and all bone. To be in the middle of that much terror and find that much love was a surprise that could shatter a heart.

"So what is it, kiddo? Berte just honked. Maybe we can talk tomorrow? Hang on, no, Vanessa is showing up with the grandkids at eight A.M. sharp. We're all heading to Disney World."

Ruthie swallowed. "Let's just talk next month," she said. "It's fine."

ACROSS THE BAY were dinner parties under shady trees, where the food was never fried and the wines were exquisite, where the women were slender and fresh as stalks of green grass and the men, bare feet in thousand-dollar driving shoes, wore watches worth as much as a house.

She'd always been a scrupulous rule follower of a person. She had always told the waiter if he left something off the bill. She had never cut in a line or gone through a red light, even at one in the morning. Have a headache? Ruthie has aspirin in her purse. A sweating glass? Ruthie will run for the coaster. Heartbreak? Ruthie will bring the wine and the tissues.

Now she was a door off its hinges, and she was ready for the gust of wind that would blow her free. She wanted the bang. The crash. Then a whole lot of open air rushing in.

Would it be a crime, exactly, to take a watch thrown away into a junk pile?

She could walk in the door of her own house and write a check to Mike and the house would be hers. With no rent, only taxes and upkeep, maybe she could cobble together a freelance life, make it through the years before Jem left for college.

Didn't she need it? Didn't she deserve it? Didn't Jem?

A sudden, lucid thought: She was thinking like a criminal. Because wasn't justification the second step, after desire?

31

LOGISTICS.

How does one broker an expensive watch? The best option would be privately, through some sort of watch dealer to the extravagantly rich. She would need an introduction. When she ran through a list of all the wealthiest people she knew, they were hardly the people she could ask—Mindy, Helen, Carole.

She was still mulling the question when she drove to the farm stand the next day to pick up Jem. Joe Bloom cruised the aisles.

She could ask Joe. Discreetly. If he didn't run at the sight of her. She collided with the fact that living in a small town had enormous disadvantages if you turned into the kind of person who humiliated herself at parties.

She owed him an apology. A graceful one. If she could somehow be the kind of person who could deliver a short apology, a crisp, heartfelt sentiment. She must not overexplain, she must not dribble, she must not abase herself.

She spied on him as he examined the eggplants and peppers. Maybe it was a sign of something beyond caponata; she knew he liked Italian food. Surrounded by local tomatoes, he would be in a tolerant mood.

She caught up as he stood palming two small cantaloupes. She came from behind, hoping to catch him by surprise; she needed the advantage. "You need either a handbasket or a brassiere."

"A handbasket," he said. "Isn't that what you go to hell in?"

She lifted one out of his hands and sniffed it, then the other. "These aren't ripe."

"Actually, I was looking for cherries. I got waylaid by a canta-loupe."

"You can't trust a melon."

"A most untrustworthy fruit."

"Those aren't local, either. Local is usually to the right."

Joe looked over. "Zucchini, cherries, and lavender."

"In California, they'd put it on a pizza."

"But we're New Yorkers, so we stick with mozzarella."

They were lobbing the ball back and forth, but there was no glee in it, only a desperate need to be genial. "Speaking of hell . . . um, the other night. All that. I didn't mean to be a rude bitch. Or yell at nice people. Which would include you. I'm sorry. I . . ."

"I get it. You just found out about your ex and Adeline. Totally normal behavior."

"I chopped down a tree."

He shrugged. "You did a little landscaping."

"Here's the thing." Hands clasped, shoulders up around her ears. "I'm not usually a maniac. I don't really get angry. I just get sort of circular. Thinking, oh God, this is probably my fault for not doing whatever, and then, I don't know, I talk myself out of anger because it rarely gets the right results, does it? So it just sort of dissipates instead of getting expelled. I mean, not ex-pelled in a school way, in a purgative way." She was dribbling. "Anyway, I'm sorry for making fun of you with the gorgeous Sancerre thing."

"You used to get angry," Joe said, and she remembered again

dumping wine on his lap. "Look, I think everybody understood. Adeline felt terrible."

"Yes, I'm sure her suffering is worse than mine. Dinner party disruptions can be so tiresome."

"She's used to getting her way, but that's not entirely her fault," Joe said in a gentle way that almost—but not quite—felt like a rebuke. "The world works for people like Adeline. They all get their way all the time. I would imagine it's difficult not to get used to that. Anyway, the point is, you don't owe anyone an apology. Just show me the cherries."

He ambled behind her as she snapped open a paper bag and began to pick through the cherries. Because she was still apologetic, she examined each one.

"What are you doing?"

"Looking for bruises."

"Let's live dangerously." He took a handful and dumped them in the bag. "Are we allowed to cheat?" He held one out to her, ready to slip it into her mouth.

"I have an in, so yeah," she said. "That's my daughter at the counter."

"She's beautiful," Joe said. "She looks like you."

Oh, shit, she thought, that tumbling sensation, as though she were falling, somersaulting into Joe. In the middle of all this muddle, here she was. Maybe pain could make you reckless. It was a new feeling; she'd never been reckless in her life. Except, maybe, years ago, with him.

The moment was there; all she had to do was seize it. Open her mouth, let him slide the fruit past her teeth. Let him yank the stem. Not drop her gaze. Do that, and then follow her body along. *It's hot. Shall we get a beer? Sure.*

She took the cherry and popped it into her mouth.

"Cheater. I knew it." He held out his hand, and she spit the pit in his palm.

"I feel so close to you right now," he said.

"It's those fleeting moments that mean so much."

"Maybe we should share a cigarette. Or go to dinner."

There was a pause while he just stood, and she just stood, and he cocked his head.

"Well?" he asked.

"What?"

"I just asked you to dinner."

"No, you didn't. You suggested it as a *possibility*."

He shook his head and looked up. "I forgot what a pain in the ass you were," he said to the sky.

"Actually, I lied," she said. "I *am* turning into a rude bitch. So you see, I can't have dinner like a normal person."

"How about a crazy person, then?" He took the bag of cherries. "What can I say? I'm a sucker for a woman who parses my sentences. Have dinner with me, Ruthie. You parser, you."

32

JEM'S PHONE

From: Lucas Clay
To: Jemma Dutton

It's so hot your beaches suck

From: Jemma Dutton
To: Lucas Clay

So go back to the Hamptons rich guy

From: Lucas
To: Jem

Too much traffic doesn't anybody have a pool

From: Jem
To: Lucas

I do but I'm working

From: Lucas
To: Jem

Invite me over after work for a dip

From: Jem
To: Lucas

My mom will be out, having dinner w an old friend I don't think she'd like it

From: Lucas
To: Jem

I'll be a good boy promise

Who are those girls by the tomatoes they keep checking me out

From: Jem
To: Lucas

Girls from school ignore them

From: Lucas
To: Jem

Introduce me we'll have a party

33

RUTHIE ARRIVED AT the restaurant in a state of internal clamor so loud it was a wonder Joe couldn't hear it. They sat at the smallest table at a noisy place in Greenport. Ruthie had to shrink into her chair so that her knees wouldn't brush his.

"Let's not talk about our ex-spouses," Joe suggested as they looked at their menus.

"Or the past," she said.

They sat, silent. Ruthie had felt like a new, more interesting person in Carole's fitted dress with a silver zipper down the front. She'd been sure it meant she'd be able to have brilliant, brittle conversation. She would skim through the evening on raw clams and fast talk.

"This is not a good start," he said.

"I'm sorry. I just think it's smart not to talk about the past, since you dumped me," she said.

Joe moved his fork, then his spoon. "*Dumped* is a terrible word. I thought I was too old for you."

Their affair had lasted less than a summer. Joe had left near the end of August for Italy, a long-planned trip. When he returned he was involved with an artist named Sami LaGuerre, a rococo beauty with hair to her waist who had been born Samantha Bernstein in Montclair, New Jersey, and had never looked back.

It was fair to say that he'd broken her heart.

"I didn't feel that comfortable with you, I guess," Ruthie admitted. "I mean, the kind of places you brought me, in your fancy suits. I was always scrounging for the right clothes. You seemed so sophisticated."

Joe grinned. "It was a pose, I promise you. We never really talked about our pasts, did we?"

No, they hadn't. They had never progressed to that level of intimacy. They had never told their stories.

"I grew up in Brooklyn. Before it was cool. My father was a Jewish public defender, my mother was a Puerto Rican social worker. Then I fell for art. The way you do. For what it was, sure, but also for what it can *do*."

"It took me a while to fall for what it can do," she said. "Peter sort of messed that up for me. I thought I was learning about genius but after a while I realized I was learning about commerce. Then I got into museum work. I saw that regional museums are this giant bulwark against, I don't know, non-culture? A place of ideas and beauty right smack in the middle of a town. Like a cathedral. But I mean the way it really was, with people crowding in and hay on the floor. Every day I walked into that building I thought, *Okay, one more for the good guys*. Things get more barbarous every day. We need some . . . exaltation. Connection." She looked down at her plate. "God, I'm sorry. That sounds so stupid."

"Do you know something? I think you've said 'I'm sorry' to me at least fifteen times in only three conversations."

"I'm sorry," she said, and they laughed. "It feels so stupid to have lost what I had to such idiots. Idiots with action plans."

Joe sighed. He pushed his wineglass around. "Museum boards can either do the good work or turn it into some sort of Ionesco farce."

"There you go again with the sophisticated references."

"You always get my references, so shut up."

"Let's talk about you. So, there you were, a boy from Brooklyn with his own gallery."

"I always felt outclassed. I used to read Louis Auchincloss novels in this pathetic attempt to pick up tips. Trying to learn Park Avenue syntax. I was an extremely careful person."

"I remember when you told me about Sami, you kept saying what a brilliant artist she was. I think that's why I dumped the wine on you."

"I deserved it. Yeah. I got a little tired of the posing, though. You know what my son's middle name is? Pocket. She wanted something elemental, she said."

"A pocket is elemental?"

"It's better than Ravine."

"Not really."

"We were not a good mix. We broke up, got back together for Henry's sake. Moved to LA for a few years. Moved back. Now Henry's in college."

"So why did you move out here?"

"To be near my dad. He lives in Southold. And I got interested in restaurants. Food, not art. I'm not really a chef, I just cook, so a fancy place was out. But, man, I can open an oyster. I'm thinking in winter I could do chili. Not sure. Big decision." Joe grinned. "I arranged my life so that the decisions are as simple as I can make them. You?"

"Oh, I make decisions as hard as I can." Ruthie laughed, but Joe didn't. "But at work, it's different. Was different. A hundred decisions a day."

"You look sad," Joe said.

She looked down at her wine. "I loved my job."

"This might be a *get off my lawn* thing to say, but the world is getting meaner," Joe said. "You could be the only person I know who bothers to apologize." He poured more wine. "Anyway, that sounded glib. I'm sorry about what happened. I'll help if I can."

Ruthie waited until the server had checked in and Joe had waved her away again. "You could do something for me, maybe. If I had something to sell—a luxury item, say—would you know the right way to go about it?"

"That's pretty vague, but probably."

"I'm not ready to do anything yet, I just wanted to know."

"Letting go of things can be great," Joe said. "Change is good."

She impatiently shook her head. "That's what the changers say. I mean, if you choose change, it's good. If it's thrust upon you, it sucks." She picked up her menu, suddenly annoyed. "Should we order?"

"You do look exactly the same as I remember, by the way," Joe said, picking up his menu. "Change looks good on you."

"You just contradicted yourself."

"What I mean to say is, you haven't changed. Not the *you* you."

"It's the dress."

"I didn't notice the dress. Except for the zipper. It's rather provocatively placed, if that sort of thing is in one's head."

"Oh fuck, don't flirt with me, my heart will just explode," Ruthie said. "Just buy me dinner and stay on that side of the table."

"It's a very small table."

She felt his hand on her knee.

"You're very handsy," she said.

"I had to do something. I made you mad about the change thing."

"I'm over it."

"It's because I threw my life up in the air to see where it would land, and I know what that's like. I left out the anguish part. And it's because I kept looking for you, planning how I'd ask you to dinner. You're very hard to run into."

"Why didn't you just call me?"

"When the last time you saw a woman you were such an asshole that she dumped half a bottle of wine on you, you tend to be skittish. I wanted it to be casual, so that rejection would be easier to take. I heard the words 'gorgeous Sancerre' come out of my mouth and I wanted to knock myself out with the bottle. When I saw you at the farm stand, I practically pounced. I had to grab you when I could."

"Under the table."

"There was always something with the way we talk," Joe said. "I always felt . . ."

"Randy?"

He grinned. "Understood. And now I have you in my grasp—"

"Literally—" His fingers on her leg, just resting.

"I am shamelessly flirting with you so that you will like me again," Joe said. "But I'm rusty. Help."

She wanted to put down her wineglass and run. That would be the sensible thing.

"Let's eat first," she suggested.

"First. That sounds hopeful," Joe said. "Or maybe it's the zipper."

34

DANIEL MANTIS FUSSED over Doe, insisting she sit to his right and ordering glasses of rosé champagne "for the beautiful girls" and a martini for himself.

Doe concentrated on Daniel so completely she could barely acknowledge Lark. His head was shaved close, his face tan and smooth, his beautiful white shirt open and pressed sharp. He wasn't a good-looking man, but he was a billionaire, so everyone and everything was available to him, and everything about him said that he knew it.

For the ultra-rich the world moved at superhero speed. Valets and maître d's and waiters and bartenders were there a second or two before you wanted them. Then they disappeared and came back again with whatever you asked for, plus things you didn't, treats from the chef and fresh napkins and forks. Disappearance, reappearance, disappearance, until you had everything you could possibly need except for a catheter. You still had to get up if you wanted to pee.

Daniel focused his gaze on the waiter as he recited the specials.

He clasped his hands together and leaned forward a bit. "Last summer I had the most exquisitely simple pasta," he said. "Olive oil, pecorino, fava beans. Can I have that?"

"I'm not sure if we have fava beans, sir. I'll check in the kitchen."

"Fantastic."

No fava beans, but Daniel bravely withstood the disappointment and ordered fish. He decided on four appetizers "so we can all have a taste, the crudo is amazing." They sent over six. It was something Doe had always wondered, why those who could afford it were the only ones who got stuff for free.

Doe was careful with the wine. She knew better than to get even the slightest bit tipsy. Lark, however, had finished her champagne in two swallows and started in on the white Daniel had ordered. The meal would cost double Doe's month's rent.

Doe kept her face on alert. She was alive to everything Daniel was saying, even if it was pass the salt. Not that he'd salt his food, that was for the middle class. She had to be Daniel-worthy, a wealthy Florida prep kid with style, not the sneaky low-rent paparazzo who'd grown up in a concrete block house with cockroaches in the kitchen, geckos on the wall, and a mother who was a masseuse who occasionally threw in a hand job if the rent was due. The mother who was sending her increasingly desperate texts because she wanted to move to the Hamptons and Doe needed to get her a job, "as a concierge, I think I'd be really good at it." She ate her sea bass and it tasted like nothing spiked with lemon.

"So when did you two meet?" Daniel asked.

"At the Memorial Day party," Lark said. She giggled. Under the influence of champagne and wine drunk too fast, she'd turned into a teenager, half sullen, half giddy.

"I gave Doe a dare." Then she laughed again. "Doe, a dare, a female dare!"

"It was such a great party," Doe said. "This fish is superb."

Once she'd been at a gallery dinner in Miami and someone had said that. She'd practiced saying it later, when she was alone. *This fish is superb.*

"A dare?" Daniel asked.

"To get you to take off the hoodie," Lark said. "I let her in the house to interrupt you."

"The house is so exquisite," Doe said. *Exquisite* was another word she used to slip into conversations when she felt outclassed.

"Thank you. I always say it's like heaven, if God had taste," Daniel said.

"I never heard you say that," Lark said. "It's a little self-serving, don't you think?"

Doe rushed in to fill the silence as Daniel shot Lark a cool look. "Anyway, I never got to you," she said. "But she took me to lunch anyway." She put on her brightest smile, hoping Daniel would be deflected. "Such a good cause, protecting the farms."

Daniel passed this off with a short chopping gesture. "Doomed. And yet another big check I wrote for my daughter whose career seems to be spending my money on plants."

"Oh, no, let's not go there," Lark said. "I refuse to have the career conversation now. Why can't I just enjoy my summer?"

"Because I gave you a deadline of September first last September first. Which means you had a year to find your path."

"I don't see why you get to give me deadlines."

"Because I've given you three years to plant flowers at that so-called farm of yours."

"It's not So-Called Farm, it's Larkspur Farm—"

"It's called fifty million dollars, that's what it's called."

"It's not like you gave me fifty million dollars, Daddy."

"I'm on the hook for it, and that's the same thing. You have an MFA. You had about fifteen lunches—with Aggie and Larry and Amy and everyone I could possibly line up—"

"I did the MoMA thing, I had a job at a gallery. It's not for me, okay? All I did was make copies and file things."

"You worked on that exhibition."

"Like I said, I made copies and filed things. Then I stood around in a little black dress at the opening." Lark ate a forkful of spinach. "That gallery was bullshit. They came up with busywork for me. It was obvious they just wanted me for decoration."

"You're going to be twenty-seven in September and you don't have a career."

"So who would hire such a loser old crone anyway, Daddy?"

"Forgive me for thinking my intelligent and talented daughter should have a career." Daniel swiveled his attention back to Doe. "Doe, tell me about your museum. How long have you worked there?"

"Two years," Doe said. "Technically I'm part of the membership department, but I also handle all the social media. That's my real interest."

"Do you enjoy that?"

"Visibility is a commodity, just like everything else. So, yes. I like to get coverage for things I believe in."

"Excellent. And what's your big ambition?"

"World domination, of course."

"Ambition, I love it. Did you hear that, Lark?"

"Sitting right here, Pop."

"Tell me about the Belfry. What's the collection like?"

"We don't have an art collection. We have historical artifacts. Like Benedict Arnold's buttons."

"Buttons?" Daniel's fork stayed in the air.

"A small historical collection. Kids love it. We also do contemporary art. There's a project space in the barn for special exhibitions."

"Contemporary art—that's Lark's big interest."

Lark rolled her eyes and took another gulp of wine.

Before the waiter could glide in, Doe refilled her own glass with wine she would not drink, just so she could place the bottle closer to Daniel. Lark would have to reach past him to get it. "Ruthie and Tobie have done some great exhibitions. When we get a review in the *Times,* Ruthie bakes a cake."

"Is it that much of an occasion?"

"They don't cover much regionally," Doe said. "So, yes. We also run educational programming, classes, lectures. During the year we bus in schoolkids from all over. Ruthie started this pilot program to get underserved schools through the doors."

"Sounds worthy, that's great. Giving back. I heard your director—Ruth, did you say?—might be leaving."

Doe frowned. "I don't know. I mean, Ruthie is fantastic." Had Mindy and Catha's plot gone this far, that gossip had flown all the way over Peconic Bay? And since when would someone like Daniel Mantis care about someplace like the Belfry? "Anyway, it's a terrific museum," she said.

Lark picked up her phone, but at Daniel's look she put it down on the banquette. "Orient's cool."

"I never heard of it before Adeline decided to discover it." Daniel chewed on a bite of fish. "A little less lemon next time, I think. Balance is everything. What's your endowment?"

Luckily Doe knew this. "A million and a half."

"Seat of the pants, is it?"

"Pretty much. But we do a lot."

"Can we order a bottle of red?" Lark asked. "Daddy, stop quizzing poor Doe."

Daniel signaled the waiter. "Art is a mind-opener, isn't it? We don't get enough arts education in this country. I'm thinking of starting a foundation."

"What?" Lark rose out of her sulk. "You never said anything." She put her fork down. Doe knew from experience that Lark only ate half her food.

She put her fork down, too. She knew the rules of this game. You always left food on your plate. And no one, ever, asked to bring something home. Not even dessert. Once out to dinner in Miami she'd asked for the rest of her crab cake meal to go, and the man she was with, an art dealer who taught her so much and then ghosted her texts, said, "No. This isn't the Cheesecake Factory." She never did it again.

"Why not, everyone's getting one. It's the newest accessory. That's a joke, Lark."

Daniel said this without looking at his daughter. He was looking at Doe. She felt suddenly buzzed and very awake.

"I think it's time I supported more local causes," he said.

Doe tried to hold his eye but couldn't. Was she imagining how intensely he was looking at her? She couldn't read this glance. She didn't know whether he was thinking about exposing her or thinking about fucking her. Either way she could be as doomed as a bag of kittens.

35

RUTHIE WOKE UP to the sound of crockery in the kitchen, always a sign that meant coffee was on the way. She hoped Joe hadn't turned into a tea drinker. Sunlight was pouring through the window and she was nestled in a soft bed and she was filled with something close to happiness if she didn't think too hard or too long.

"I just can't help believing!" Joe sang from the kitchen.

She was only a block away from her own house, and she felt as though she were in a secret clubhouse, hidden away in a dumpy rental. Jem was with Mike, and no one knew where she was.

They had danced in the living room last night. They had sipped ice-cold limoncello. Their kisses had tasted of lemon and sugar. They had wound up on the bed, tilting onto it together, hanging on hard because they didn't want to break the embrace. She touched her mouth. The night had felt like one continuous deep kiss.

Joe stood in the doorway, holding two mugs. "Don't start regretting it yet," he said.

"I wasn't."

"Liar. I have a radical suggestion. Let's tell the truth. Right from the start."

"Toss me a T-shirt. There's truth, and then there's truth at eight in the morning."

Joe put down the coffees and tossed her a T-shirt. She slipped it on. She ran past him while he chuckled. She thought this was over in life, wearing a man's T-shirt and examining his bathroom items while she used (this, a mark of their maturity) a new toothbrush he'd left for her on the sink.

When she came out, hair arranged, breath minted, and after a delighted dazed look at herself in the mirror—who was this woman having fun?—he was sitting up in bed, waiting with her mug, in boxers and another T-shirt just as faded and soft as the one she was wearing.

"I want you to know that I regret nothing," he said. "I'll even sing it. In French."

She took the coffee. Last night was hazy, not from wine, but from a certain rushed urgency to the proceedings. Dinner and then he invited her over for a nightcap, an invitation so ridiculously transparent that they giggled. The end of the evening had been inevitable since the moment he put his hand on her knee. Or when she sat down at the table. Or when she saw him again. The truth was simple. When she was with him she felt alive.

They sipped, watching each other. Ruthie spilled a little coffee on his shirt.

"I like this house. It's nicer inside," she said. "Outside it's a dump."

"Consider it a metaphor. I painted the floors and the walls before I moved in. The kitchen was chartreuse, and not in a good way."

"The thing is, you don't have much. It's very bachelor."

"Part of my reinvention."

He didn't even have a dresser. There was a nautical map on the wall and a single ceramic vessel with sharpened pencils on a table. A stack of books—cookbooks! How promising!—served as a night table for her coffee.

"No art," she said.

"We argued so long about the collection that one day I just said, Take it all. Halfway thinking she wouldn't. She did. A shocking thing happened. I didn't care. I ended up giving away mostly everything in the apartment. I know that sounds monkish but it's not that elevated. I didn't want it, it was from another life. The apartment with the vases and the plates and the books and the trays and the lamps . . . now I've got one set of sheets and towels, three pairs of pants, and seven T-shirts. When things get dirty I wash them."

"You have six T-shirts. I just stained one."

"When I knew my marriage was over, I talked to my dad about it. I was back here—my parents moved out to Southold when they retired, have I mentioned that? Anyway, my mom was dying. We were at the hospital and Mom was asleep. I said it was a tough decision, to leave—Henry was still in high school. And I asked him how he did it, how he always seemed to know what to do. And he thought for a minute. And then he said, 'I never made a decision in my life.'"

"What does that mean?"

"I never really got it. I was kind of pissed, actually, because it wasn't helpful. But last night . . . I got it."

Wasn't that just what she'd been contemplating? The whole unthinking *rush* of it? The lack of decision when she walked through the door? Could that still happen, in the middle of your life?

"I'm sorry to say this, but I have to go to work soon," he said.

"I'll find my dress."

"I will always remember that dress," Joe said. "It is the pinnacle of summer dresses."

Only it wasn't her dress, it belonged to Carole. Sooner or later he'd see her in her own wardrobe, the untailored, unsilked her.

He gently pulled the neck of the T-shirt down and kissed her shoulder. "Of course," he said, his mouth against her skin, "I don't have to leave immediately."

He leaned in, and she leaned back, resisting the pull, the kiss, the feeling that she was not at all able to control this. "Look," she said.

"Don't say that. Don't say *look* in that fashion."

"In what fashion?"

"In that *We're adults let's talk about this* fashion."

"But Joe—"

"And don't say *but Joe*."

"We don't want to get ahead of ourselves."

"Let's get ahead of ourselves," Joe said, scrambling to sit up straight and spilling more coffee on the sheets. The man was going to have laundry to do. "Let's flirtatiously text each other during our days, and then at the end of it let's have you come to my bar and let me pour you a chilled glass of Muscadet and lovingly shuck my best oysters and let me make you dinner and let us do all this over again, tonight and all summer, for God's fucking sake."

"Whoa."

"Whoa as in stop, or whoa as in, that sounded really great?"

"Whoa as in, I'm not in a good place right now."

"What would make it a good place?" Joe leaned back again.

"To have what I used to have," she blurted. She meant her house, her job, her peace, her place, so that she would feel grounded enough to try this. She saw immediately it had been the wrong thing to say.

"I guess that brings me to a question," Joe said, looking down into his mug. "Are you still in love with Michael? Do I have competition here?"

It was the name "Michael" that snagged her. She could hear it in Adeline's cool, cultured voice. It brought her back to what was waiting for her outside the door.

She heard how much he didn't want to ask that question. So

much banter between them and it had all fallen away last night. They had knelt, naked, and touched palms. They had not been afraid. It had been a night so filled with charged touch, with lust and tenderness, that it would make a poet stand up on a chair and cheer.

Her thoughts moved so fast. In the time it took for him to look down in his mug and look up again she knew she would have to give him up.

She knew this: He was the most honest man she'd ever known. Whatever story she came up with about the watch—a street purchase in the city, a family heirloom—it would be a lie. She would have to pile lie on lie in order to keep her house, and while she had talked herself into the fact that these lies harmed no one, she still had to tell them.

She could tell them, she was almost sure. But she could not tell them to Joe.

"I can't let go," she said, and saw his heart fall. He thought she meant Mike, of course, when she meant everything but Mike. To have Joe believe she loved her ex-husband was a lie, but at least she hadn't had to tell it.

Oh, Ruthie. You parser, you.

36

THE NEXT MORNING at Lark's, Doe took the side door of the house to the driveway, the family door. The one that looked like a window. She received a blast of panic when she saw Daniel standing in the driveway by the garage—oops, vehicle barn—drinking an espresso. Waiting. He knew she'd stayed over, of course, she had followed Lark up the stairs last night.

"Thank God," Lark had said when they were alone in the bedroom. "It's always easier when he knows things."

"So it's okay that I'm here?" Doe had hovered by the door, almost ready to go back down the stairs, even though wanting to be with Lark was lighting her up.

Lark had kicked off her mules, sending them crashing into the closet. "He approves of you." She leaned against the wall and closed her eyes. "That was awful."

Then she had folded herself up in the bed, tucking her knees under her chin, covering her head with her arms, her hands in tight fists.

Doe had kissed each finger until the hands uncurled.

Now Doe watched Daniel as he smiled and raised his cup. Did

he approve? Or did he want something? His gaze . . . she couldn't figure it out, the way he looked at her. Not the dry slithering gaze of Ron back in Florida, but not without assessment.

"Beautiful morning," he said. "You're up early."

Doe nodded. "Summers are busy."

"I admire industry. My daughter will stumble down at eleven," he said. "She's worthless. Don't give me that look, I know, I sound harsh. That's the trouble with honesty." Daniel leaned against Doe's car. "She doesn't try."

"Is that it? That she doesn't try? That's her problem?"

"You'll understand the whole continuum one day. Her mother is worthless, too, with her pretend job. Medicated and nuts and married to an asshole. I had to take over. Look, I financed Lark's business for three years and watched her drive it into the ground. Do you know what they called her in the press? 'Flower girl Lark Mantis.' Flower girl! My assistant showed me some Instagram feed, it's full of her just standing at parties. Now they call her Luminous Lark. Jesus. She has a hashtag. It's embarrassing."

Doe leaned against the car because her legs felt weak. This conversation was now straying into her territory. He was talking about *seekrit-hamptons*. She did what she usually did when forced into an uncomfortable conversation, repeated back what Daniel said. "She's embarrassing you."

"She's embarrassing herself, and she doesn't seem to care."

"She doesn't seem to."

"Stop repeating what I say, I'm on to that trick," Daniel said. "So what is this thing with you and my daughter? A fling or a thing? Okay, don't answer. I could see it last night, you two are in deep, even if you don't know it. Your generation with your fluid sexuality, you don't need my approval or not, she's an adult, you too, I get that. But I also think you might be good for her. I noticed the wine trick last night, by the way."

"I don't know what you mean."

"Certainly an improvement on Lucas. He encouraged her faults. So work with me here."

"Okay," Doe said. "You want me to help you. Am I right?"

"What's it like on the North Fork? Nobody stays here in the fall and winter."

"Yeah, the locals only come alive when you're here to crank the keys in our backs. When you leave we just slump over until Memorial Day."

"I don't feel bad about being wealthy, all right? What am I if I can't use those things for my kid? She went to Brown, she went to Yale. She's had every opportunity to rise. But every time I set up a meeting, she drifts away."

"She doesn't want to work for anybody," Doe said.

"What is she, a five-year-old who wants to be an astronaut? You've got to work for somebody," he said. "Even I work for somebody. I work for the deal. And who said she was good at being a boss? She was a terrible boss."

"I'm not so sure about that," Doe said.

Daniel squinted at her. "And you know this because?"

"The way she talks about the farm," Doe said. "She had their loyalty. They're still in touch with her, you know that? Not because they want something, either. They're still trying to make a go of it."

"I know, she talked me into giving them seed money to take it over," Daniel said. "Seed money for a farm." He snorted.

"She needed a financial manager," Doe said. "She needed someone who knows how to run things. What she's good at is being a figurehead. That's not nothing."

"That is nothing."

She waved her phone at him. "She's Insta-famous. Those pictures your assistant showed you? She's in all those photos not just because she's photogenic. She's an influencer. People look to her for trends. They're not just looking *at* her. That dress she wore last night will sell out at Net-a-Porter by the end of the day. They weren't taking a picture of *you* outside the restaurant. It was her."

"That's not an achievement."

"Are you kidding me? It's a profession!"

"It's a con, I promise you."

"I'm just saying, she could be a change agent."

"I'm not even sure what that is. Why do I feel there's something wrong with it?"

"Because you're old."

His eyes went flat. That was it, that was his weakness. She'd found it, and it turned out to be something so boring! Irrelevancy! The fear of every white man in his sixties with money and power. He almost disappointed her.

"I'm just saying she needs a platform," she mumbled.

"Oh, Jesus, you kids. She doesn't need a platform, she needs a job." Daniel looked at her carefully. "You seem to have a lot of confidence. What did your father do? Where did you go to school?"

"Reed."

"You grew up out there?"

"Florida. Miami."

"Nobody grows up in Florida. Or if they do, they stay there."

"Are you interviewing me now?"

"Where are your people from?"

"My *people*? I have a cousin in Boca, if that's what you mean."

"You look mixed, that's all. Miami is a cosmopolitan city. South American? Don't look at me that way, I'm just asking. Come on, help me out here. You've got an exotic look. It's a compliment, okay?"

"Is that what it is?"

"No judgment here," Daniel said. "Where you're from has nothing to do with anything. America is about the now. The past is just a path. That's all." He drained his cup. "And I need another espresso." He looked down at his bare feet. "Tell you what. I'll drive you to work if you'll hold the espresso cups."

"My car is here."

"Don't worry about your car. I want to see it."

"You want to see the Belfry."

He dinged her nose, lightly, with an index finger. "I asked you to stop repeating everything I say."

She wanted to smack his hand away. He knew it, and only grinned. "You can tell me about platforms." He turned and walked away, knowing she'd wait.

Fuck this, she thought. *I don't have to wait.*

She waited. He reemerged with two espresso cups. She climbed into his car, a hybrid Porsche (selling at somewhere near one hundred grand, she looked it up, "Daddy brings all the toy cars to the Hamptons," Lark had said), and balanced the two cups. He would shift, hold out his hand for the cup, as though she were a waitress. Doe retaliated by kicking off her flats and crossing her legs. Her goal was to make him look. He did. So maybe it was sex, then. She did not want to sleep with Lark's father. There would have been a time when she would have done it, but that time had passed. She liked to think she was getting smarter.

"If I drive up to the Belfry with you in this car people will talk," she said.

"And do you care?"

"No." Not true. She'd have to go through a tedious debrief with Catha.

"Good girl."

She hated his condescension but she wanted his approval, a condition she often found herself in with older men. At Sag Harbor she directed him to the ferry that would take them to Shelter Island, then drove across the island to the ferry that would take them to the North Fork.

"This is a stupid system," he said. "Incredibly inefficient."

"Two different ferry companies."

"So you wait on a line, take a ferry for five minutes, drive across an island, wait again, another five minutes across the water. It takes an hour to get to a place when it should take ten minutes. Insane."

"That's the point. Keeps it the way it is."

"Yeah, well, even hellholes on the planet know about bridges."

He drove through Greenport, looking at everything.

"What a dump," he said.

"We actually like not living in a Madison Avenue facsimile."

"Hey, I'm not criticizing. I like the country. It has so much room for development." He grinned at her eye-roll. "No, seriously, this place has what I like. Vineyards. Nice views. When it comes to water, you just need the view, maybe a dock if you've got a boat, right? Nobody goes in the ocean in East Hampton. We just look at it. We're packed with women who don't want to get their hair wet."

"That's so sexist."

"Darling, all men are sexist. Women, too."

"Sure. But women being sexist about men is just complaining. Men being sexist about women gets them places."

"Everybody has an equal shot in this country."

"Do you really believe that? Didn't your father finance your first business?"

"Father's money, a loan from a bank, what's the difference? I made the rest." They were driving out of Greenport now, heading toward East Marion. "This is a town? Obviously this place isn't maximized."

"I'm telling you, most people don't want maximized here."

"Everybody wants to make money. You think these people don't want their houses to appreciate? They all want to retire to the Carolinas, send their kids to good schools."

They hit the causeway. "This is a decent view," he said. "You need a hotel here."

She pointed to the Belfry ahead, visible from the main road, and he slowed down. "Excellent visibility," he said. "And up on a rise, like a church. Is it walkable from the village?"

"Easy walk."

When he pulled into the parking lot, he unbuckled his seatbelt but didn't move. He looked at the building for a while. "Not bad," he said. "Good bones. Farm vernacular. I like that. Is that the barn? Potential for sure. Dodge's show was great, not enough people came."

Wait. She hadn't told him about Dodge's show.

"Now that the median price is shooting up, the town is changing. Dodge's show, that one with May Werlin, shows like that—they need an audience. What's the most expensive house for sale here?"

"I have no idea."

"Ten million. You know Nate Billows? He just bought it. Hedge fund guy. It's just starting."

Things fell into place. "You knew all the answers about the Belfry last night," Doe said. "You just wanted me to say them in front of Lark."

"Did you know Ruth Beamish quit a few days ago?"

"No," Doe said, startled. She didn't think it could happen that fast. "Why do you?"

The front door of the museum flew open. Catha stalked out.

"Who's that?"

"Catha Lugner. Deputy director."

"You like her?"

"Do I have to?"

Visibly upset, Catha jumped into her car and started the engine. She hit the gas and reversed without looking, straight into Daniel's rear bumper.

"What the *fuck*!" Daniel twisted the rearview mirror. "I think I bit my tongue!"

"I'm fine, thanks," Doe said, shouldering open the door.

Catha stumbled out of her car. "Oh my God oh my God!" she wailed. "Shit!"

Doe slammed the car door. "Catha? What was that?"

Catha rubbed her cheek. "I don't know! I didn't see you! Shit! You're in a red zone, you know!" Tears began spilling from her eyes. "I deserve this. I did terrible things! I deserve what I get."

"Chill, we're not hurt," Doe said. "What terrible things?"

Catha glanced over. "Wait, that's not your car. Who is that?"

"Daniel Mantis. What did you mean, terrible things?"

Color drained from her face. "Are you serious?" she whispered. "What are *you* doing with Daniel Mantis?" Catha tucked her hair behind her ears several times. "Why didn't you tell me?" she whispered.

Daniel exited the car. He strolled back to the rear bumper and inspected it. "Just a scratch," he said.

"Mr. Mantis, I'm so sorry," Catha said. Her lips stretched over her teeth, trying and failing to swap warmth for panic. "I don't know what to say. I had a moment of . . . inattention. My foot just . . . slipped. Naturally I'll pay for any damage."

"Twenty-five thousand should do it," Daniel said.

"I . . ."

"Relax, I'm kidding," he said. "You were in quite a hurry."

"But this is actually great, I mean, not the car, but to meet you. I'm Catha Shand-Lugner. Acting director."

"What?" Doe asked.

Mindy's SUV drove in. She craned her neck, saw Daniel, and almost crashed into a tree.

"You gals could use some driving lessons," Daniel remarked.

Mindy scrambled out of the car, all fluster and activated antiperspirant. "Daniel! You're here! You're naughty, not giving us notice!"

Daniel knew Mindy?

Doe watched the dance. Daniel in his shorts and sneakers, hands in his pockets, back on his heels, accepting the courtship. Mindy, groping for lines of flattery she could employ, and settling on seeing his "fabulous" house in *Architectural Digest*. They were listing toward him as though on the deck of a boat. They were so obvious, so bad at this. Would he like some coffee? Or juice? Mindy suggested. "Are you a juicer?" she asked in that way she had, injecting a jolly archness to her tone that only smelled like the left-out girl in middle school, desperate to be liked.

Poor Mindy. Doe could almost feel sorry for her, if she didn't also know what a complete bitch she was.

"Do you have mangoes?" Daniel asked. Turning just a fraction, he winked at Doe.

"I don't know," Catha said.

"We could send someone out," Mindy said. "Doe?"

"Never mind. I'd love a tour, though," Daniel said.

"I'd be glad to do it," Mindy said. "I was an art history major at Smith."

"Good for you."

Daniel turned companionably toward the entrance. Mindy gave a little skip to keep up with him.

Doe's phone buzzed, and she almost didn't check it.

But it was Lark.

> Just waking up and missing u

> U Doe

> I go to the U of Doe

She felt the warm pleasant music of Lark's morning, the slow waking, the texting, the sliding downstairs in a silk wrapper and bare feet, where chef James would be slicing a peach for her smoothie. Or a mango, if she wanted one. No doubt some specialty food store somewhere on the Hamptons would deliver one piece of fruit. She pictured it, perfect and plump, nestled in a little wooden box. For a princess with a taste for it.

HE FOUND HER later, after the tour, after the glass of springwater, after the chat. He loomed over her desk.

"I'll have your car driven over."

"Thanks."

He crouched down. Now they were eye level. Close enough where she saw how soft and pampered his skin was, with the plump tight look of injections. She pressed her knees together to stop herself from leaning back.

"These people are idiots," he said.

"I know."

"The historic collection is a joke. Buttons. They should be auctioned, raise some money. They belong in a museum."

"This is a museum."

"Lark could be a change agent, isn't that what you said?"

"Yes. But I didn't mean this. She wouldn't want this. Did you meet with Mindy before this? Did you push Ruthie out?"

"I had coffee with Mindy a few weeks ago. Weird smell. I know her parents a little. She said Ruthie was on her way out. I said, I have a very talented daughter. That was about the sum of it."

"Sure, if you don't factor in your money. You pushed her out!"

"Please. If a board president wants you out, start packing. And I've met your Ruthie, she's hardly destitute. Hey," he said, peering at her, "don't be scared, little girl. You have a role here. But let's keep this idea from Lark, shall we? Just for now."

"I can't lie to Lark."

"Sure you can." He looked around, down at his feet. "I hate this carpet," he said. He jackknifed to his feet, smiling. "All I have to do is change it."

"The carpet?"

"Everything."

37

Jem's Phone

Draft Folder

From: Jemma Dutton
To: Olivia Freeman
Subject: apocalypse now and then

When opossums sense danger, their nervous systems cause them to pass out and emit a foul odor.

Do you remember how hard we laughed at opossum farts?

I'm sitting here with laptop, thinking, I wish it was then right now. Or I wish it was last week, or yesterday right before I said yes.

It was really hot yesterday. And the farm was super busy. This guy Lucas was texting me. The one I told you about. The god. Annie calls him Mr Sex McManPants. He sort of invited himself over for a swim. Mom was going out, Dad was picking me up for an overnight at nine, so why not a quick dip? And I got nervous, like, was this a date? That would be weird and skeevy. He's got to be, like, twenty-two? So I asked Annie along.

And then the weirdest thing happened. Meret and Saffy came to the farm stand and saw me talking to him and they were all, we're best friends, right? They had already checked out his Instagram and they were totally on board. Like nothing had ever happened! And the next thing it was like, Hey, let's all go and cool off.

So at first I'm all chill, because I think, ok, nothing to see here, we're all just going to swim, and Meret has gotten over her thing, so everything will be normalish again.

So everybody is there, and Meret is just all over Lucas, I mean, rolling this cold water bottle around her chest, come *on*. I stay so far away from them I might as well have been in your backyard in whatever state you live in now. And Meret is kind of being a jerk (what do you mean, kind of? you are saying) and says things to Annie like "I like that suit, on you it works." And I'm starting to think, This blows, why did I do this.

Meret says, So what's the big house like, and I say, It's nice, and she's all, So, let's see it. I say, We can't, we have the pool house to pee or change or whatever and there's a fridge and everything. And Lucas says, But there's no beer. Annie says, I don't think we should, and then it's like me and Annie against them, and Meret makes it seem that way, so what could I do. Annie sees this is not ending well and takes off. Because she is not an idiot.

So I get the key. We go inside. We'd all put our clothes on after the swim, except for Lucas, but Meret is just wearing her bikini. Lucas drinks a beer, and Meret finds a bottle of wine and opens it. And you really have to wonder what he's doing with high school kids, but nobody is thinking that, because he's so beautiful and we're all trying to act older.

I'm the one trailing after everyone and saying things like "We should really go" and "Be careful with that." I don't want to be that person, but I am. But hey, you know what, it feels like whenever I'm with Meret I don't want to be the person I'm being.

Meret just keeps opening beers for Lucas, which was totally annoying. She pretends to get drunk. I know she's not because I watch her. She's always like this, she'll say she's dying for a cheeseburger and you go to the diner and order it and then watch her watch you eat yours while she eats a fry and says she's so full. She doesn't get drunk, she takes a few sips and the next day says, "OhmygodIwassodrunk." And then tells you how everyone else humiliated themselves.

She says, I have to pee, and she goes upstairs, and Lucas says he wants to see the house and goes up and after a few minutes of them not coming back down I'm like, I'm going up there no matter what. They're picking up stuff on Carole's dresser and looking at it and talking. Meret is wearing one of Carole's hats. I tell her to put it back and Meret calls me a prison guard and rolls her eyes, and Lucas laughs, and now I'm really, really not having a good time.

When we go downstairs again Meret starts a pillow fight with Saffy. So naturally they break a wineglass. And everybody laughs like crazy, that laugh that is all "Oh no, we're so bad, isn't it cool."

So finally that does it, I finally grow a pair and kick everybody out. Even Lucas because I'm so pissed. Then I spend the next hour getting the stain out of the rug and finding the wineglass pieces and basically dusting and cleaning and scrubbing and then I have to ride all over town to find a garbage can to toss the wine bottle and the broken glass. It was the worst day of my life forever.

I don't know, all this takes up so much space in my brain. Meanwhile my dad is so checked out. He's in love, have I mentioned that? In loooooove. He says it doesn't change a thing except now he's really happy. It seems to me it changes everything.

Lucas texts me and says he's sorry about the glass and it was fun to see me without a cash register in front of me. Wtf. The farm stand doesn't even use cash registers.

I'm still mad so I text back *whatever*.

And he gets it. He texts back that he really meant the apology. He says: *I hate emojis. But if I had to design one right now it would be an exploding star of sorry.*

And so I forgive him, because it really was all Meret's fault mostly. And because an exploding star of sorry is so cool. You know what, Ollie? He's sorta sad. I know what that emoji means because I feel that way literally all the time. That star is in my pocket every day.

xojem

38

THE WATCH WAS GONE.

She'd left it on Carole's dresser.

Hadn't she?

She raced through the big house. Then the playhouse. Under furniture, on the tops of tables, under sofas. Nowhere. It had tumbled into the black hole of missing things, single earrings, stones out of rings, buttons, socks.

It couldn't be just . . . gone.

She sat in Jem's room, surrounded by pink toile. For the first time she realized that it was made up of *Alice in Wonderland* imagery. Poor Alice, trying to hit a croquet ball with a flamingo. Poor Alice, down the rabbit hole, and having to make sense out of nonsense. She'd never liked *Alice in Wonderland* as a child. It had made her feel queasy to think of a world without rules.

What kind of an idiot criminal loses the loot? Had she left it on the dresser, or had she worn it again and just *thought* she put it on the dresser?

She heard Jem's step and a moment later she swung in, a little rushed, a little distracted. "Sweetie, have you seen a watch lying around?"

"You don't wear a watch."

"I mean, just, a watch. Have you been in Carole's house?"

"Why would I go in Carole's house?"

"I'm just asking. I'm missing something. I left it there."

Jem had her head in the closet. "Where?"

"On Carole's dresser. I think."

"I haven't seen a watch."

"Are you sure?"

"Is this an interrogation?" She tossed a sweater on the bed, light and soft, in a shade of blue that was close to the color of her eyes.

"That's pretty," Ruthie said. She crossed to pick it up. She read the label. Isabel Marant. "Where did you get this?"

"More questions!" Jem's mood had shifted to defensive. "Adeline bought it for me a while ago. That time we went to East Hampton for lunch with Roberta. I was cold. She went next door and bought me a sweater."

"She bought you a designer sweater because you were cold?"

"It was no big deal!"

"It's got to be two hundred, three hundred dollars. It's a pretty big deal!"

"Not to her. It's like a Gap sweater to her. What was I supposed to do, say no?"

"We haven't really talked much about her," Ruthie said. "I mean, you and me. I guess you've talked to Daddy."

"Yeah. We had a chat."

"What did he say?"

"That he hoped that I didn't think that you two were getting back together. Which I didn't, duh. And he said we have to give you room to adjust and everything? But that it will all work out in the end. Daddy says since you lost your job, you need time, but if Adeline bought the house it would solve things. Like, you'd have money. And there would still be the house in the family."

"In the family?"

"That's what he said."

"Adeline's not family."

"Well." Jem slipped her arms into the sweater. "That's what he said."

Bastille
Day

39

THE AIR WAS full of water and Ruthie was drowning. Humid day had followed humid day. Floorboards swelled. Dogs panted. The water settled into Ruthie's bones. She felt a tug like a current, sweeping her toward Joe, and it took all her will to resist it. She yearned for him. She could feel the word, *yearn*, like the plucking of a string.

A hurricane with an alarming tendency to wobble moved up the coast. Landfall was uncertain. Weather broadcasters had been blown sideways in the Carolinas, shouting of approaching doom.

People decided they needed bread and milk, even if they didn't eat bread, and the country store was crowded. Everyone really just wanted to talk about the storm arriving and storms from the past. Sandy, of course. Irene, Floyd, the letdown that was Charley. There was no panic. These were Long Islanders. It was just a storm.

Ruthie bought her bread and her milk and left the market as quickly as she could. She was now in that peculiar place of being a source of gossip. She knew the gossip wasn't unkind, that it was sympathetic, neighbors and friends angry or worried about what had happened, but since nobody knew what had happened, speculation reigned. She knew that a petition had gone around to reinstate her. She knew many had signed it, but she also knew that Mindy had come out swinging, making phone calls with one message: "It's better for Ruthie and better for the museum if she goes," a form of professional assassination that was not fully recognized as the slime it was. Some people wondered if she was ill, or had embezzled. She had disappeared so fast. With her severance and nondisclosure agreement in hand, she could say little to defend herself. Instead of a lump sum, severance was being paid monthly. Mindy controlled the strings. If she said anything to defend herself, or told the truth, she knew Mindy would cut them.

Mike and Adeline Clay were now a public couple. She had seen them eating ice cream cones at the pie shop, she had driven by them as they walked hand in hand, her own hand twitching to yank the wheel. Everyone knew, and it was either grace or caution that stopped them from bringing it up. Maybe she had started to look as feral as she felt.

ROBERTA VERONA'S ANNUAL Bastille Day dinner party was legendary, and this year Jem and Mike were invited to be houseguests along with Adeline and Lucas. They would each have their own room, Mike told Ruthie politely and pointedly. Adeline and Lucas in the main house, Jem and Mike in the guesthouse out back. Jem wanted to go.

Ruthie knew she was boxed in. Glamorous event, exquisite food, shiny people, Jem's first grown-up dinner party. Jem was invited to come early and help with the cooking. Ruthie Googled the dinner, reading articles about past years in food and lifestyle magazines, the guests who came every year (artists, writers, chefs, a famous political comedian), the sprinkling of the new (musician, journalist, surfer). These were the kinds of things that kids of the privileged received, access to great talents and remarkable achievements, a sort of insider trading that is not about money, but minds. How could she say no when this was something she would give Jem if she could, these bright jewels, this glimpse of a life that could be hers?

"Can she go?" Mike asked.

Ah, now she knew what divorce really was. Sharing decisions with a person you would run down on the street.

RUTHIE WAS AT the beach at Pete's Neck watching the whitecaps when she saw Carole's name pop up on the phone. Her desperate voicemails had finally gotten through. *Carole, Mindy basically fired me but I quit. Carole, have you talked to any members of the board? Carole, Mindy's attorney is drafting a severance agreement and I don't know if I should hire a lawyer. Do you know anyone who can take it on pro bono? Never mind about the attorney, Mindy's lawyer gave me a deadline, so I signed it. It's only for six months.*

"Ruthie, it's Carole, can you hear me?"

"Yes! I'm so glad you called! I've been—"

"Thank God I got you! I need you to do me a huge, huge favor."

Carole had disappeared into the Neolithic wilds of the Hebrides and ignored her for days. Now she needed help.

If it were another friend Ruthie would communicate her disappointment, her hurt, but this was Carole, and Carole was a reference for her next job.

"Sure." Her voice sounded like a chirp.

"We're going to this event tonight. *Le quatorze juillet* and all that. This is what I get for insisting on packing for Lewis, the man is hopeless at it, if it were up to him he'd bring one suit. Anyway, I'm laying out his outfit and I just noticed that his watch isn't in the case. I've looked everywhere."

Ruthie felt a drop of rain hit her forehead. She jerked away as if it were burning oil, her hand to her chest. "His watch."

"He bought it after his first major deal, it's hugely expensive, he only wears it on big occasions—and I can't find it! I have the *case,* just not the watch. It's a vintage Patek Philippe. I don't even want to tell you what he paid for it."

You don't have to.

"I've gone over and over this. I remember packing, and everything was just all over the bedroom, you know? Dash and Verity were fighting, and Verity had on my Louboutins and Dash had on Lewis's Charvet tie, and I had a fit. Maybe I was busy yelling and the watch fell on the carpet and somebody kicked it or something? Would you look? If I lost that watch I'd never forgive myself and Lewis would never forgive me. Could you please, please look? Like, right this second?"

"I'm not at the house, but of course I will," Ruthie said.

"Lifesaver! And what do you think about what's going on at the museum? I just talked to Helen. Daniel Mantis is involved! Apparently he wrote a fifty-thousand-dollar check!"

Ruthie pressed the phone so hard against her head that it might have impressed itself upon her skull. "Daniel Mantis."

"Apparently Mindy and Catha roped him in. It's too bad it didn't happen on your watch, but, really, it's a great thing for the museum. Apparently his daughter is completely charming, too. Very artsy. I can't wait to meet him."

Daniel Mantis.

Daniel had lifted her wrist, had noticed the watch.

"Could you call me whether you find the watch or not, okay? Please please? I'm just sick about this. *À bientôt.*"

Ruthie hung up. She looked up at the scudding clouds, the lowering sky. "What the *fuck!*" she screamed.

When Carole returned, she would meet Daniel. Sooner or later the watch story would come up somehow, somewhere. Two watch-loving moguls, Daniel and Lewis! The tale of the missing rare vintage Patek Philippe with the minute repeater! And Daniel would remember her, arm outstretched to point to a Rothko.

The story would be spread through Orient and the Hamptons and move westward to Manhattan. People wouldn't believe that she didn't know it was real, wouldn't quite believe that a casual offer to borrow a blouse meant she could strap Lewis's watch on her wrist and strut around town. She would look like a fool and a cheat. And maybe they wouldn't believe that it had simply gone missing. She was either careless or stupid or a thief.

She was all of those things.

She was tainted forever. She would know the meaning of the word *ruined*. She would know the meaning of the word *shunned*.

40

THE BAY ON her left was dark blue with a flashing knife of silver, a sharp blade of pure light. She parked the car in front of the house and got out.

As if the day could possibly get any worse. Mike had texted her, asking her to come over. *Just hear what we have to say. It's about Jem.*

It was the *we*. Now Adeline and Mike were the *we*.

It was afternoon and a light drizzle fell, occasionally intensifying into a pattering rain. Adeline crossed in front of the window. Mike walked toward her, and Ruthie stopped. Adeline said something. He said something.

Adeline spoke again, and while she was speaking he reached over with one hand and put it on top of her head, lightly, and rubbed. She leaned into the touch.

Ruthie felt her throat close.

If someone had been walking by—Clark, say, or her other neighbor Martine—on some other random day, when she and Mike still lived in that house, what would they have seen? Two people in the same room. One in an old sweater, catching up on

her reading, or listening to a podcast while she organized something. Another passing by on his way to the kitchen to check on
dinner.

Perhaps they would exchange a word. But would you see a
touch that tender?

She walked across the yard. It gave the appearance of having
hosted an unhurried day. One trail bike was propped against the
tree. Another lay on the grass, as though dropped so that its owner
could go on as swiftly as possible to another pleasant activity.
Adeline had lined up glass canning jars filled with dahlias on the
front porch. The Adirondack chair that was usually on the patio
had been dragged to a corner of the yard in the shade. A book sat
on its arm. Fighting years of habit, Ruthie did not pick it up to
save it from the damp.

Adeline walked out on the front porch. She stood, her hands in
her pockets, and nodded a hello.

"I'm glad you're here," she said.

Adeline turned and Ruthie got a look at her muscled shoulders
in a gray tank top. She was wearing a pair of loose khaki trousers
and rubber flip-flops. Ruthie would have looked as though she
was ready to strip paint in the outfit, but Adeline looked gorgeous, with a lariat of chunky crystal wrapped around her neck,
the ends swinging with the motion of her walk.

Mike was waiting inside. A leather duffel sat by the door along
with a canvas tote. Adeline noticed her gaze. "We want to get out
before the storm. We'll pick up Jem in half an hour. Would you
care for a glass of water? Iced tea? It's so hot."

Ruthie shook her head so hard she felt something crack in her
neck. "So you want to buy my house?"

Adeline cocked her head. "It's not an impulse, I promise you.
It's a solution."

"And I'm supposed to just roll over."

"Of course not." Adeline shook her head, blond hair skimming
her cheeks. "It's your house, yours and Michael's. I made an offer
to buy it, but it's your choice. Both of yours. It's really simple."

"Of course it's not simple," Ruthie snapped. She felt the edge of her patience like a jagged piece of glass. "Can we have a real conversation instead of sanctimonious *bullshit*?"

Mike glanced quickly, worriedly at Adeline. They were afraid of what she would do. She was a lunatic who chopped down a tree. Maybe she still had the ax. There was a luscious power to that, to being a person who would do anything.

"Also, please stop buying Jem expensive gifts."

"The sweater? She was cold," Mike said.

"How much was the sweater?" Ruthie asked. "I'll pay you back."

"It was a gift," Adeline said.

"It's too expensive. She doesn't wear things like that."

Adeline sighed. "I'm sorry if I overstepped. I really don't think there's any need to hate me for it."

"I don't hate you," Ruthie said. "I just see you clearly."

"For Christ's sake," Mike said. "Ruthie, calm down. I assume you talked to Jem."

"I am perfectly calm, and I always talk to Jem, I'm her mother. Apparently I have to be handled. I have to be given *room*. I can't have my house, but at least I get a room to change my mind in."

Adeline poured a glass of water from a pitcher filled with lemon slices. She pushed it toward Ruthie as if it were medicinal.

"Let's just get to it," she said. "Ruthie, I'm sorry you're upset. But you need to know something. We're engaged."

"You're engaged." Ruthie repeated the words, trying them on to see if there was any sanity in them. "I don't know if you know this, but Mike is still married."

Adeline shrugged. "A detail. You've been separated for three years. Divorce will be easy."

"Yeah, that's what everyone says. Divorce is so easy."

Adeline walked over to stand next to Mike. "This is very new for everyone. We should all talk about when to tell Jem."

"You've known each other for a month!"

"Seven weeks, and we're adults," Adeline said. "When you

know, you know. We've been talking about things, and we came up with a solution that seems good for everyone. I love the house and I want to buy it." She put up a hand. "Just hear me out. This might change things for you. When Michael and I are married, this could be a family house for Jem. If I buy it, there would be enough money for you to buy another house, anywhere you like, but in Orient, of course, if that's where you want to stay. If you need help, a little extra, we can talk about that."

Adeline was speaking in a totally reasonable tone of voice. Mike was gazing at her as though she was wise and good.

"What are you saying?" Ruthie asked. There was something underneath this, something she wasn't getting.

"That you'd get the asking price, and you'd get it all," Mike said. "It would be part of the settlement."

"Of course I'll have the place in the city during the winter," Adeline went on, "but we'll spend more time here, weekends and some holidays and so on. After the renovations."

"Renovations."

"There are improvements that can be made. Things I would want. I always think ten years ahead. We want this to be a family house, for Jem to return to as an adult. Possibly with her own family, grandchildren . . ."

"Stop." Ruthie almost strangled on the word. "Stop talking about *my grandchildren* or I swear to God you'll have to hide the fucking knives."

Silence descended. Adeline took a sip of water.

"I'm not your enemy," she said. "I just happened to fall in love with your ex-husband. It happens every day. If you want to play the victim that's your choice."

"I'm not playing." Ruthie turned to Mike. "This is it, this is what you want? This woman? You let *her* tell me this, that you're getting married? Don't you see it? Don't you see how controlling she is? Don't you see how she's taking everything away? Don't you see she's *buying us*?"

Mike slammed both hands on the countertop. "She's *saving*

us!" he shouted. "She's saving me. That's what love *does,* it saves you!"

"Because she's rich?"

"No. Because she's *kind*."

"Michael," Adeline said.

Mike turned his back and walked to the window. He stared out, his back implacable.

"The offer is made," Adeline said. "All you have to do is take your time and think it through. You just lost your job. It's going to take a while to get on your feet. If you sold the house to me, you'd buy time."

"How great for you. You can buy anything, even time. You bought my husband. But you can't buy me."

"It's a house, Ruthie. It's not you."

"Or my child."

Adeline flushed. "All right," she said. "There are other houses. But I'm not going away. We're going to be family, whether you like it or not."

Ruthie stood in the middle of the living room, her room, her view, her home. Her memories, one after another, like a pocketful of stones.

Her gaze traveled out to the yard, to the storage shed. She wondered, for the first time in her life, if derangement came about not because you didn't know what you were doing, but because you knew exactly what you were doing, and you didn't care.

41

From: Catha Lugner
To: Doe Callender (bcc) +15 more
Subject: mandatory all-staff meeting

There will be an all-staff meeting tomorrow in the main conference
room at 10am. Thank you in advance for your enthusiastic attendance! Let's impact the future! CSL

"Hey."

Doe looked up. Annie stood hesitantly in the doorway. There
were splashes of red on her thighs and cheeks from sunburn. She
hadn't seen much of Annie this summer. Lark had taken over her
nights. Sometimes she'd pass Annie on her bike, riding home from
the farm stand. Last summer they'd shucked corn together, paper
bags between their knees. Last summer she'd been welcome at the
family table.

"Hey, dude. Enter."

Annie came in with a show of reluctance. Her hair was red and curly and barely tamed in a ponytail. Pretty green eyes, freckles, the shoulder-hunch of the bullied.

"How's life?" Doe asked.

"Sucks to be me, basically," Annie said. "Used to it, though."

Doe nodded. "I had a crap fifteenth summer, too."

"Why?"

Doe searched for the way to wrap the truth in a lie. "My mom. She decided to let me down on a regular basis. I was supposed to go to . . ." *an art program in Savannah* "Europe that summer, everything was all arranged, and she . . ." *cashed in my tuition and spent it on cocaine* "decided I needed tutoring instead, so I had to stay home, and . . ." *she got this new boyfriend who hit on me* "my best friend decided to let me know that she'd been waiting for me to go to tell me she was fucking my boyfriend." Truth at last! If Doe ended up at a truth, it made her feel better.

"Wow," Annie said. "Harsh."

"How about you?"

"I had a fight with my mom."

"Yeah. I remember those days. You'll make up, your mom is cool."

"She sucks."

"Okay," Doe said, silently agreeing. "What else with you? How's the job?"

"Job is okay, I like making money. But, I don't know, I'm becoming friends with Jem again, kinda. Proximity friendship. We used to be friends in elementary school, along with this girl Olivia? But then, you know, high school. There's this girl, Meret?"

"You told me. The queen of Teenworld, right?"

"Ha, exactly. Jem was all friends with her, and now Meret is like doing the thing she does where she makes fun of her and everybody laughs. I swam with them one day, and Meret was totally being an asshole to Jem, and Jem was just taking it. And there's all this groupchat drama about how Jem is going to lose her virginity this summer, only they call it 'mayflower' like some inside joke. The thing is . . ."

Doe knew better than to ask what the thing was, because the answer would be *Nothing* or *It's stupid,* and Annie would change the subject. She just put on an *I'm curious but it's cool if you don't share* kind of face.

"I feel bad for Jem. She dropped off all the threads, so I don't think she knows how bad it is. Meret gets people to do things. It's like hypnosis or something."

"Probably more like fear. I mean," Doe added, when Annie looked confused, "they're afraid she'll burn them."

"Yeah. Exactly. Jem isn't like Meret. There's this guy, this older guy, who comes to Lawlors and buys one thing—just one thing, like a peach—and he waits until Jem is free. It's so creepy. I'm just afraid I guess."

"What's the guy's name?"

"Lucas somebody. We call him Mr. McManPants. I'm guessing he's just playing with her. Except. I think he texts her, too. Meret knows because she's psychic, or maybe she just guesses. She's super jealous. It's all, you know, material for her to punish Jem. She used to call me Rags in elementary school because she said I looked like Raggedy Ann? So I even called myself Rags, just because I wanted to own it, right?"

"That's why you're cool," Doe said. She felt something winding inside her, tightening with every turn.

"Anyway we're in high school, so we've all forgotten all that crap, but not Meret. She still calls me Rags! Especially if she sees me with a boy or something. Not that I'm ever *with* a boy. Then she pretends that we're super-good friends and that's why she has a pet name for me. That's the kind of asshole she is." Annie picked at the table. "Anyway. It's just a pain to even be a *bystander* to all this stupid mean shit."

"That's the best summary of life I've ever heard," Doe said.

42

JEM'S PHONE

From: Jemma Dutton
To: Lucas Clay

Excited but nervous about Roberta's party hope she doesn't
cancel because of storm

. . .

can't wait are we all driving together

From: Lucas Clay
To: Jemma Dutton

Not going after all sounds boring I've got a party on SI

From: Jem
To: Lucas

You said you were going

From: Lucas

To: Jem

Don't you be boring too

43

Hey I have a surprise for you

Guess where I am

where are you text me back angelpie xxo

"What's that?" Lucas lifted her phone from Doe's hand. It was one of the habits she wanted to kill him for. She lunged for it.

"You bitch!" Lucas tossed the phone back at her. "I think you scratched me."

Why was she here? She knew they were done. Lark was in the city for "maintenance," which meant hair and skin. A hurricane might be coming, or at least a bad storm. Hurricanes terrified her.

As a child Shari had always thrown hurricane parties, and Doe associated high winds with adults too drunk to put up the shutters and take in patio furniture. Once a chair had blown right through their window, shattering the glass and sending the adults scream-ing and stumbling away, some of them laughing in hiccuping shrieks. A giant of a man had stepped on Doe's hand with a big callused bare foot. The pain was commensurate with the gross-out quality of the injury. The curved yellow toenail had caused her to wail uncontrollably. Shari had stuck her hand in the ice bucket.

So when Lucas had texted her, saying Adeline was away and the house was his, she was tempted. She wouldn't be alone.

Anxiously, she looked out at the wind-whipped bay. It was like a living thing, malevolent and liable to rear up and swamp her at any moment. She didn't want to get trapped here. She had listened to Lucas robotically, idiotically, to ride out the storm. He had promised good wine; he had promised a binge watch of whatever she chose. He'd planned to be at a party on Shelter Island, but his friend Hale had been too "chickenshit" to pick him up by boat. The outdoor party had been canceled, anyway. It was typical of Lucas to tell her all this, letting her know that she was second or third choice. Yet she was here.

Lucas lay back on his elbows on the bed. "You are so mysterious with that phone." He raised his eyebrows.

"We're all mysterious with our phones," Doe said. "That's where our secrets are kept."

Lucas laughed. "Word."

"What would I find on yours?" Doe asked. "I bet your passcode is one-two-three-four or your birthday. Would I find out things you don't want Adeline to know?"

"I don't give a shit about Adeline."

"If you hate her so much, why do you stay here?"

"Bad luck. I thought she'd be living with Mantis and I'd be crashing there on weekends. Instead she sticks me in bofuck Long Island." He flipped through his texts.

"You know what I've noticed about you?" Doe asked, leaning against the dresser. "You blame Adeline for everything."

"Everything is her fault. She gives me a job with no responsibility."

"Please note she *gave you* a job. Let me guess, there might be opportunities for advancement in the Peter Clay Foundation for you."

"No thanks. I quit this week. I had enough."

"It can't be that hard to get another job."

"Excuse me, who died and appointed you my career coun-selor?" Lucas scowled. "I'm his son, and she gave me a crap sal-ary."

"You seem to be doing fine."

"Well, I'm not. It's ridiculous that I'm short of cash all the time."

"So be an actor. I mean, actually commit to it. You basically just post selfies on Instagram."

"I'm developing contacts, okay? You should see my followers." Malice glinted in his eyes. "What about you? You girls all have pretend jobs. Then you get engaged and show the ring at the of-fice, and within the first year you quit because you're trying to get pregnant and it's just too stressful. Please."

She laughed, not because he was wrong—he had just described some of Lark's friends—but because she wanted an end to the hostilities. He was on edge today. There was an undercurrent be-tween them that had never been there before.

"Though I can't see you doing that," he said. "You're not like the girls I know. You live here year-round, which is weird. What's your story?"

"You're not interested in anyone's story."

"Maybe if you were nicer to me you could be part of mine."

"Even though I'm a year-rounder?" She kept her voice light. She must have been crazy to come here. She was no longer the least bit attracted to him. She missed Lark.

"Adeline's got one, why shouldn't I?"

Doe didn't ask who. She knew Lucas would tell her.

"Your boss's husband," he said.

"Catha?"

"No, the other one. With the hunky carpenter."

"Mike Dutton?"

"That's the one. Bingo. Lots of blue-collar banging going on in this house."

"Ruthie's not my boss anymore, she quit."

Lucas raised up a bit, interested. "She did?"

"She was kind of forced out."

"Yeah, well, downsizing sucks, I hear."

"It's not downsizing. That's just a word to you, isn't it. Jesus."

"It happens to *be* a word. You know Ruthie pretty well?"

"She was my boss, so, kind of but, you know, not friends."

"Losing her job was pretty bad, huh."

"Yes, Lucas, when people lose their jobs it's bad."

He flipped over and leaned his head on his hand to scrutinize her. "What are you, a Marxist?"

"I'm a human with feelings," Doe said. She stared back at him, stretched out like a lion on the veldt of a bedspread, tawny and lazy, blinking at her in his beauty, but able to take her head off. "What about Jem?"

"The hot daughter?"

She gripped the phone. "You know, you might want to consider what happens when you fuck a fifteen-year-old."

"I'm just having fun. I like blondes with legs. Don't worry, I like tiny little brunette girls, too. Girls I can put in my pocket."

He patted the bed, but she ignored him. "Maybe you should rethink the flirting."

"You're cute when you're jealous. Okay, okay, I'll have the fat girl check out my corn from now on."

"Annie isn't fat."

"All right, the girl with such a pretty face can take my money."

"I'm just skeeved out at a twenty-three-year-old hitting on a kid."

"Relax. I didn't fuck her. She had a pool party and I went. What's it to you?" He raised himself up and then flipped off the bed. A pillow fell on the floor and he whipped it sideways to toss it back on the bed with a hard stroke. It knocked over a water glass. Lucas ignored it and walked toward the door. "You know what's nice about high school girls? They don't give you any shit.

Come on, let's find the champagne. This is supposed to be fun, remember?"

Doe saw a watch on the dresser, casually thrown facedown. The back was transparent and she saw the workings, the tiny, tiny wheels and gears whirring so perfectly. It was the most beautiful object she'd ever seen. Doe reached for it. Something about it was familiar, like she'd seen it before. Yet she was sure it hadn't been on Lucas's wrist.

She felt her phone buzz.

> From: Annie Doyle
> To: Doe Callender
>
> Hey, your mother's here? Shari? She's looking 4 u
>
> She's going to check at the museum is it open? I told her to wait here, the storm and all
>
> From: Doe Callender
> To: Annie Doyle
>
> DON'T LET HER GO TO MUSEUM TELL HER TO STAY I'LL BE RIGHT THERE
>
> . . .
>
> please

"Are you going to pay attention to me or your fucking phone?" Lucas asked, turning back to glare at her.

Doe looked up, trying to swallow. She'd forgotten where she was, and that he was here. The rain had intensified, she could hear it pounding on the roof. The bay was dark pewter, ruffled with white.

"I have to go."

"You can't go!"

"I have to take care of something." Where was her purse?

He put his hand on her wrist. "What is this shit? You're not leaving me alone in this storm!"

His grip was too tight, making her panic. "Let go!" She pushed him and he hadn't expected it and stumbled back, hitting a chair. She tried to get past him and he grabbed her elbow and yanked her hard so that she fell backward on the bed.

Not a good position for a woman. She felt something new in the air, like a burning wire.

He snatched her purse from the floor and swung it by the strap. "Come and get it," he said in a singsong voice.

He was between her and the door, the only exit. She reached out for her purse and he lifted it higher, cackling in a high laugh she'd never heard before.

She wasn't going to deal with this shit. She came up fast, the top of her head connecting with his chin. He howled and stepped back, dropping the purse.

"Bitch!" He felt his chin, his eyes wet and aggrieved. He grabbed her by the arms, and it pinched her skin.

She didn't like being restrained. It reminded her of an old boyfriend and that made fear settle in her belly. Impulse overcame caution and she jerked her arm, flipping his wrist so he had to let go, and hit him in the face.

Her ring cut him, and he touched the blood. "What the fuck," he said. He reached out to steady himself on the wall, and left a tiny smear of blood. "That's my *face*."

He took a step toward her. "Don't even fucking think about it," she said.

All she heard was their breathing. In out, in out. Everything was so clear, the water glass on its side, the pool of water, the pillow, her purse, his bare feet, his fists.

He turned and walked out, and her breath left her all at once. She felt everything drain out of her and she was trembling but she needed to find her shoes and pick up her purse.

The watch had fallen on the carpet. She considered kicking it under the dresser, but he would find it. He deserved to lose something so beautiful. Something he carelessly tossed on a dresser. She put it in her pocket, found her things, and left while he was examining the cut in the bathroom mirror and calmly saying she'd better get out or he'd fucking kill her.

44

RUTHIE RODE OUT the storm alone, huddled on the couch, clutching a blanket. Barely sleeping, alternating panic with rage that battered as hard as rain. She had never hated anyone before. She understood why it was called a "towering" rage. It made you bigger, stronger, as gigantic as a building, willing to crush whatever lay between you and your enemy.

Adeline had taken something from her that wasn't a house, wasn't a man. It was the past. *I was never in love with you,* Mike had said.

The first time he'd said it was only months after they met. Holding hands on Franklin Street, leaning into each other, and him turning to her and kissing her, saying, *Watch out, I think I'm in love with you.*

Watch out? A warning she'd ignored.

Did men have to do that, reframe the past into a lie, so they wouldn't feel guilty moving on? They had the strength to break things, but not the strength to carry them.

They'd met in the mid-nineties. She was at a party at a loft downtown. She was wearing a baby-doll dress, hugely popular at the time, with tights and boots. She'd bought the dress at the Sat-urday flea market on lower Broadway. Her hair was pinned on top of her head. She was having a miserable time. Everyone at the party seemed to know one another, and she'd long before lost the friend she'd come with.

There was an artist who dressed Barbie dolls as all the Bond girls, then took color-saturated photographs of them against tiny fabricated settings. There were painters. Matthew Barney was ex-pected at any moment. Everyone was gathered around a sculptor who was supposed to become the next big thing, but Ruthie no longer remembered his name, because he'd never become the next big thing. Matthew Barney had become the next big thing.

Ruthie had clutched her beer and swerved through the crowd. She was working for Peter and going to grad school at night, and she was always exhausted. She wasn't over Joe. She half hoped he was there with Sami so that she could ignore him. She wanted to go home and polish off some cookies in her pajamas. She left, clomping in her heavy boots down the stairs, worn and sloping to the middle. Five flights down, hoping for a cab, her black coat flapping open.

At the bottom of the stairs, a man was pushing through the battered metal door. His coat was wet, and so was his hair, subdu-ing the dark blond. When he looked up at her, she felt the impact of it in her stomach.

She smiled as she went by. She opened the door and the wind blew the wet snow in her face. She felt the tug of attraction to the stranger, but she also felt the tug of Pepperidge Farm.

She heard footsteps behind her as he hit the stairs. He went up two stairs and stopped. For a moment there was just silence. Him on the stairs, her at the open door. A taxi went by slowly, still within hailing distance if she ran out and shouted for it.

She turned.

Their eyes, as they say, met. That first look, that spark, and there is nothing better in life. Just for that moment, though. It can go all kinds of ways from there.

Mike tilted his head. "Goodbye, road not taken," he said, so softly it was like the drift of snow against her neck.

Ruthie, in her day, had been a sassy, accomplished flirt. She lifted one eyebrow, a skill she was passionately proud of. "So," she said, "take me."

She can still, if she wanted to, remember the impact of the slow, delighted widening of his smile, and how he gave her a second, more serious look, and how she saw that he appreciated his good fortune. Someone so handsome, she'd thought, wouldn't be hers to keep, but she'd give it a whirl.

Mike had told her later that he'd lusted for her as she opened the door and watched how she didn't flinch from the cold. How the snow had melted in her hair, how the snap in her eyes had sent a jolt of joy through him. She'd fallen for him that night, the next morning, waited for his call, waited for their casual dates, agonized over how long it would take before they spent Sundays together, and then, at last, when they were, in fact, a couple, when he had met her father (agonizing), when she had met his parents (difficult), she had a roaring fight with Peter, took a curatorial position in Philadelphia, and moved.

Mike took over her illegal loft sublet. They settled into long-distance coupledom. Marriage was never mentioned. A boat that solid shouldn't be rocked. Ruthie got a better curatorial position in Massachusetts and moved again. More weekends, more vacations together, but Mike was a New York artist and he would never move, he said. They spent a lot of time plotting his career, talking about trends, galleries and museum shows and submitting work. They didn't have the tedium of competition. She had no regrets about giving up her own work. She'd been surprised at how little it mattered. Bringing art to people turned out to be more important to her than making it.

Then she got pregnant with Jem. Diaphragm failure, what were the odds? Ruthie had been sure that it would be the end of the relationship. Oh, she knew Mike would say the right things, but she could not see him taking her to doctor appointments, pouring her glasses of milk. He was a kind man, but it was clear to her that he liked the people he loved to fend for themselves. She knew her need of him would signal the slow seepage of doubt into what they had. She couldn't imagine him with a baby on his shoulder. Though, to be fair, she couldn't imagine herself with one, either. *Mom. Dad.* She would say the words in her head, and she might as well have been saying *orangutan* or *Republican*.

It had taken him a week to absorb the news and suggest they get married. Ruthie looked at Mike, at his ardent face, and especially at his worry that she would turn him down, and felt a page in her life turn. It filled her with joy. Mike asked her in concern if she had to throw up.

Within a month, she had left her job and moved back to New York, picking up a part-time job at the Whitney. They bought a bouquet at the Korean deli and went down to City Hall. Their friends threw them a party. She wore the baby-doll dress, so perfect for her widening waist.

Their families didn't come. Lou and Berte called with apologies, they were about to be grandparents any minute. Mike's parents said they would fly down, but it had snowed heavily the day before and the roads to Logan, they said, were too treacherous to drive. Ruthie wanted to erase the twist that happened to Mike's mouth whenever his parents came up in conversation. Mike had gone to Yale, but he'd worked his way through and come out with substantial debt. For a wedding present, his parents gave them a family heirloom, a silver bowl with a dent in it. After his parents died in a car crash—it turned out Richard Dutton was indeed a bad driver in snow, especially after a pitcher of martinis—Ruthie sold it on eBay.

Married. With child. Stroller in the hallway, crib at the foot of the bed. Balancing blue-wrapped packages of laundry while mincing through slush. Mike out at openings while she stayed home and nursed. Mike looking trapped, Mike looking haunted. Until the September morning he was making himself coffee when an airplane flew so low overhead that he ducked.

Orient had saved them. It had given them a common enemy, mold and rot. It had given them something to talk about and something to fight for and the sweet exhaustion of finishing a project. They had become *the Duttons:* such a great couple, him so friendly, her so fun, and that beautiful Jem. Look, they are planting hydrangeas, they are strolling to town, they are laughing on the porch.

Now he was truly gone. There were letters from an attorney, there were details she would not answer but would have to, and soon. They would do the civilized things. They would not criticize each other to their daughter. They would *co-parent.*

She would do those things; she had already done them for three years. Now there was the other woman. There was blood in the water. Another woman could take her place in her bed, but not in her kitchen. Not with her child.

Adeline was used to getting her way. Adeline had a ten-year plan. She would live in the home Ruthie had created out of mildew and mice and mud, and she would invite their friends to dinner parties, and her money would make things right, make things perfect. She would erase the life Ruthie had strived to create by doing it better than Ruthie ever could.

Unless.

45

IT WAS A fast-moving storm and by the time the sun rose it had moved out, leaving the lawn littered with branches and leaves, as though the world were broken.

The causeway was flooded. Orient was cut off.

She drove to the house. A substantial limb lay on the front lawn, blocking the driveway. She pushed her way through the hedge. The storm had left an oppressive damp heat behind. There was cleanup to do, but the house had stood through the storm, just as it had stood through hurricanes and nor'easters for two centuries. Love for it welled up inside her, tears stinging her eyes. At that moment she loved it more than a human. *Way to go, house.*

She walked around to check on the patio. Lucas stood at the edge, his back to her, one hand gesticulating as he yelled into the phone. He was barefoot, dressed in shorts and a yellow button-down, shirttail flapping in the still-brisk breeze.

"I don't care, dude. I'm good for it, I promise you. I'm not going anywhere. I'm trapped! I'm lucky to have cell service out here. I can get it in exactly one fucking spot, and let me tell you, the view is getting boring."

Lucas turned and saw her, and shrugged, making a comical face. He said "Later" into the phone and put it in his shirt pocket.

She noticed a cut near his eye, which had a bruise darkening into purple. "You okay?"

He winced and touched his face. "I drank a bottle of wine and passed out. But first I walked into a wall. You wouldn't have a power saw on you, would you?"

"The causeway has been breached. There's nowhere to go, anyway."

"Terrific. This place is motherfucking hell. Aren't you sick of being trapped yet?"

"As a matter of fact, yes."

It was like being in an unfamiliar house, in the darkness, and suddenly coming upon another person, and feeling your heart beat fast with alarm. But it was only you, the glint of you in a dark mirror.

She held up her keys and shook them. "Shall we take a look inside those boxes again?" she asked, and Lucas smiled.

Sneak Zucchini onto Your Neighbor's Porch Day

46

"I WONDER WHY they call August the dog days of summer," Shari said. "It's not like dogs are hotter than we are."

Doe heard the sentence as noise. She didn't bother to answer. Much of Shari's conversation consisted of asking questions without answers. The woman needed to discover Google.

"Look, if you're not going to talk to me, then forget it," Shari said.

Doe took out one earbud. "What?"

"Do you want breakfast or anything, I said."

"No." Doe put the earbud back in. It had been like this since Shari moved in three weeks ago. Her mother would say something, Doe would take out one earbud, say "What?," respond to whatever it was, and put the earbud back in. You'd think Shari would get tired of talking. But not her mother, who would no doubt chat her way through the apocalypse.

Weeks of texts at work like *Is this a good interview skirt?* and *I think the guy at the gas station likes me* and *What is there to do here* and *So, when am I going to meet your girlfriend.*

It was August, and there were no jobs, because everyone had

been hired and in September would be laid off. As usual Shari expected things to go her way when they clearly would not. She continued to pretend she was looking, but Doe had her doubts that putting on heels and a skirt while making phone calls was a workable strategy. Shari's dreams of a job as a concierge were ridiculous. She had no experience, first of all, and she hardly had the personality. You had to be unflappable and discreet, two qualities no one would ever associate with her mother. Yet every time Doe pointed this out, Shari accused her of not believing in her mother.

She needed to get Shari back to Florida. Shari said she didn't have money for a deposit on a place, and she was afraid to live in the same city as Ron. It hadn't occurred to Shari before Ron broke her nose that a man with a mysterious access to cash and a tendency to buy ten flat-screen TVs at a time was not a good bet for a boyfriend.

Doe felt somewhat responsible, that was the trouble. Shari had met Ron through her. He'd been the big tipper at the pool, the guy who sat with his laptop every Tuesday and said he was in real estate (which was somewhat true, it turned out), the guy who said he'd grown up with Johnny Depp (which was totally not true), the guy who gave her a gift certificate to Joe's Stone Crabs for her birthday, the guy who gave her a ride home one day and said "Who's that?" when he saw Shari.

Doe should have known but she didn't. Her boyfriend the bartender was Ron's partner. He had the swipe machine in his pocket, and when she brought the credit cards he turned his back and did his thing while she looked around at the tables, making sure everybody had their mai tais and mojitos. While the bartender swiped, Ron was picking up the numbers on his laptop. Within a few hours Ron had sold the numbers to someone else.

At least when she got fired the manager said he wouldn't call the police on her, but she had to go. She never saw the boyfriend again, but Ron was home with Shari when she got there.

Shari told her Ron had confessed everything and said that he was going straight. Shari said Ron was going into commercial real estate full-time with his friend Trevor, who owned a motel and a strip mall. Ron just needed a stake, that's why he got into the whole identity theft business. Ron felt terrible about what had happened to Doe. Ron had asked Shari to move in with him. Shari felt this was a good idea.

"I'm going to make waffles," Shari said now at the window. "Oh, goodness, look at Kimmie, she's got a whole basket of zucchini! Do you know about sneaking zucchini on porches today?"

"Yes," Doe said. "It's stupid."

"I think it's fun. Everybody's sick of zucchini by August, right? Do you want to go to the softball game with me? Zukes against Cukes! Kimmie invited me." Shari had charmed Kim and Tim, who were suddenly friendlier, or maybe it was because Doe was finally paying full summer rent.

Doe heard the clunk of the freezer door, the sprocketlike ping of the toaster rack sinking. Plates rattled.

Two years ago she'd been happy to get this place. A separate room for a bedroom was a step up from crashing with boyfriends or squeezing into studio apartments. She'd boxed up the lighthouse paintings and the sunsets and the ceramic seagulls. She'd pinned up some of her photographs and bought a gray cotton coverlet at Target and tucked it into the cushions of the couch. She couldn't take up the green carpet or change the tiles, but she'd done enough to make it hers.

The kitchen at Lark and Daniel's house was three times as big as her apartment, with marble counters and open shelves with stacks and stacks of white plates and bowls and sparkling glass. Custom cabinets hid the microwave and the toaster and the espresso machine. Lark's toaster even sounded different from Doe's merry Sunbeam, the one that disgorged toast with a ping and a pop that sent the toast jumping for joy at its release, half burnt. At Lark's house the toast rose in a stately fashion, perfectly browned. But nobody ate toast at Lark's house. Nobody ate potato chips or cheese. For breakfast there were bowls of sliced pa-

paya and blueberries, egg white omelets with greens, and broiled salmon for Daniel. Perfect lattes and espressos in exquisite breakable cups appeared within sixty seconds of your arriving in the morning room, where breakfast was served.

Since she'd left Shari's house her goal had been to get just a little bit ahead, each time she moved. A little more secure, a little more safe. This summer in the Mantis house she'd learned what ultimate safety really meant. Not safety from big things like death or accidents or cancer—that happened to everybody—but safety from the small things that could pile up and crush you. Blown fuses, cracked engine blocks, broken appliances, rent hikes. You never had to remember to buy toilet paper or coffee or even gas for the car. Mail was invitations in thick creamy envelopes and stacks of magazines. You never saw a bill. The shampoo bottles were always full, and the soap—scented, thick, the color of honey—never diminished to a latherless disk. You were safe from the tedium of washing a shower curtain. It was a lovely way to live. It left *time*—time for exercise, for massages, for haircuts, for cocktails, for concerts, for dinner parties with fantastic food where people had interesting things to say.

When Lark's face rose up in her brain—it seemed to rise from the ground and shoot up through her body, the feel of her skin, her neck, her breasts, her breath, her laugh—she felt happy. Which was ridiculous. Happiness blinded you just when you needed to pay attention.

Doe had always expected the end to come on Labor Day. Lark would return to her life. They would say that they'd keep in touch. Maybe they would text a few times. Doe would have no right to complain, because she'd known the ending from the beginning.

But Lark was staying. Lark would be taking over the museum in September. Lark would be her boss. They had laughed about it, but Doe had a feeling she knew the pitfalls better than Lark.

She had told Daniel that Lark could do anything, and then she had to follow through. No one knew the part she'd played. Doe had talked up the Belfry to Lark, complained about Catha's cluelessness (this was not a fabrication), said how the North Fork needed a cultural landmark and someone with the taste to create it.

"Daddy mentioned this, too," Lark had said. "He made me have coffee with that Mindy woman who smells like paste. He wants to stick me out here in the boonies where I can't embarrass him. The North Fork? Come on."

"You're so right," Doe said. "But."

"Don't give me a but," Lark said, frowning. "Me, living there? Run a *regional* museum? It's demeaning."

Lark did not seem to realize that she'd just insulted Doe. But that was okay. "Look, the North Fork is changing so fast," Doe said. "All those pockets of hip are going to merge into a thing. Something real. And you could lead the way. Quoted in every article as it all starts to happen. You'd be the influencer about more than what sandals you're wearing, or what party you go to. Be a real agent of change. From there you can do anything."

"But year-round? Not to mention that I don't know how to run a museum."

"That's what consultants are for. What you're good at is sensing the next new thing. And you wouldn't have to spend the winter here, you could fundraise in New York. Your second does the boring work of running it while you have the vision and represent the brand. And I'll do all your social media."

"Stop, you." Lark laughed, but then she looked thoughtful.

That was when Doe knew it would all happen, just the way Daniel wanted. But would it be the right thing for the Belfry, or the town?

If Doe told her the truth, she'd have to explain what a museum like the Belfry really was, family day and kids' programs and Alzheimer's painting classes. A regional museum wasn't MoMA. You actually had to love all that shit. You had to pay attention to people. "Community" couldn't be in quotes. You had to care. Like Ruthie had.

Doe hadn't fully realized that the atmosphere at work had

been nudged and fostered by Ruthie, that vibrations of good cheer could keep a workplace humming. Catha was clearly over her head and had turned into a snappish boss who spent most of her time racing out to coffee meetings with board members. Now a new boss was arriving who had even less experience running a museum. Mindy was so inflated with pride in her catch that it was amazing she didn't expel it in a giant fart of self-congratulation. She didn't stop to wonder if Lark was the right fit, or why Daniel Mantis would be interested in buying his daughter a job.

Catha had made all this noise about how she was going to "partner" with Lark, but nobody was buying it and Doe knew it was wishful thinking. The staff was shell-shocked and furious. They could feel layoffs in the air, and Doe didn't think they were wrong.

Things were a mess, and she was sorry for Ruthie, but she couldn't save anyone. She had learned that early.

Daniel had a superstar realtor on deck to find a house. Daniel was secretly lobbying for limited helicopter service from Manhattan. There was a closed airfield about two miles out of town, and Daniel was talking to the right people, whoever they were. Daniel was looking into buying the house next to the Belfry, and the one on the north side, just in case expansion was in the plan. Cap Hunter, who was eighty-five and a longtime resident, was tempted, but the Beechams, in the big white house behind the screen of trees, were not.

To kick it all off, to show the town just how much serious glamour lay ahead, Lark and Daniel had moved Lark's twenty-seventh birthday party to the Belfry. Lark was consumed with the plans, the complexities of which had been going on for six months at least. Only the venue had changed. They did not think it strange at all that a new director would rent out the museum to throw herself a party. The staff was horrified, but it was clear that they didn't count, and the board was busy panting to be invited.

Lark had used an event planner but hadn't listened to him much, preferring to pick the music, the flatware, the plates, the food, the flowers, everything herself. Doe had no idea what this must have cost, but she no longer wondered about things like that. The dress code, Lark had decreed, was "empyrean." Doe was certain that mostly everyone had to look it up; she knew she had to, in the bathroom, right after she'd told Lark what a fabulous idea it was.

For Lark's birthday gift, Daniel had commissioned the artist Dodge to fabricate oversized inflatables of Lark's favorite animals—lambs, kingfishers, cats—in silver and white, her favorite colors. It was supposed to be kitschy but tasteful. Dodge had also designed a bouncy castle for grown-ups, which would be tethered to the lawn.

Doe and Lark had driven to Dodge's studio in Brooklyn to see the work a few days ago. The artist had totally ignored instructions and his crew had fabricated surreal hybrid creatures built out of parts of raptors, hyenas, and wolves in bright primary colors. Flashing teeth and snarling faces. The face of one creature—part wolf, part raptor—Doe immediately recognized as Daniel's. It was shocking and demented and silly, and Doe loved it. She'd stood back, watching Lark's face. A woman who cared enough to spend weeks deciding on what shade of apricot was pale enough but still a color would certainly combust over acid-green hyenas and a mutant animal who looked like her dad.

Lark's eyes had widened and she was silent for a long moment. Then she'd hooted with laughter and hurtled herself inside the pink bouncy castle—modeled, Doe learned much later, on the Camp 7 detainment area at Guantánamo Bay—to jump as high as she could, the castle leaning crazily to one side while Dodge laughed and told her to stop it, it wasn't stabilized yet. Lark had bounced on her knees, laughing so hard she'd even snorted. "I'm inside a giant vagina!" she'd screamed.

Dodge had flashed his handsome grin, but Doe could see the relief underneath it. You really didn't want to screw with the daughter of Daniel Mantis. But if you surprised her . . . it was magic. While he explained the process of transport, installation,

inflation, weather regulations, electrical needs, she watched Lark
bounce on her knees, delight on her face. Doe had been intensely
jealous of Dodge at that moment, and that had been something
she'd been chewing on for days, that flare of sadness at wondering
if she would ever be able to provoke that much delight in her girlfriend. There was no birthday gift she could bring Lark that was
special enough. Doe was close to terrified. She had four hundred
dollars in her checking account, money she saved for emergencies
and escape. Even if she drained it, what could she afford that
would be special enough for Lark?

Keeping up with Lark was exhausting. Doe had to invest in
pedicures and waxings and invent fictions like she never used a
wallet (too much of a tell) and she liked cheap keychains because
she was always losing her keys. She'd carried the Marni purse too
often and had to retire it. She told Lark that her perfect idea of a
summer dress was one with pockets.

Conversations were like picking your way through potholes
in heels. Any moment she could wrench an ankle and get flung
into the cement. Lark's friends talked about travel and museums
and restaurants and SoulCycle and paddleboarding. Doe didn't
get it, really—they all went to the same places and mostly had
the same things to say—but she still had to fake her way through
with smiles and comments that didn't mean anything. She pre-
tended to know things, like where Lyford Cay was (Anguilla)
and whether Sorrento would be perfect for a destination wedding. She agreed with the consensus that the Seychelles had been
"totally ruined." One night she studied streets and shops in
Paris, memorizing names and places she had never been and listening to pronunciations, just so she could toss off *Saint-Ouen*
without stumbling.

People would feel sorrier for liars if they knew how much *work*
it took.

"You should eat something," Shari said.

"What?"

There was coffee, so she went to the table. Mr. Coffee had pro-duced a brew. Her waffle smiled at her with a blueberry-dotted grin and banana coins for eyes. Shari peered over her mug, hoping for a reaction. Doe grabbed the mug and poured in milk. The milk was cold and cooled the coffee, which tasted burnt.

"So you have this fancy girlfriend, who I haven't met, okay, but don't you think she'd have some contacts over there in the Hamptons?" Shari asked.

"So go back to Florida. You have contacts. Of the non-criminal variety, I hope." Doe took another sip. "Or maybe it's time for Phoenix."

Phoenix had once been a joke between them. Shari's sister Belinda lived there, a woman so odious Shari kept her name written on a piece of paper in her freezer. *Things are bad*, they used to say, *but at least it's not time for Phoenix.*

Shari pushed her plate away. She was quiet for a few minutes.

"You blame me for that girl," she said.

The girl had been sitting at the kitchen table when Doe had come over to see Shari one afternoon back in Florida. She wore an oversized Miami Dolphins T-shirt and did not look up when Doe said hello. By now Doe was a gallery girl in a tight black dress and Shari and Ron had been together for two years. Shari hadn't looked as happy during the last six months or so but kept saying she was, because any relationship took work, said Dr. Phil.

Ron muscled Doe just a little bit into the living room and said the girl couldn't speak English, that she was a cousin of a friend, she just needed a place to hang for a day. Doe said it had nothing to do with her.

Doe knew a few words of Spanish. After they'd eaten and Ron had left, Doe asked the girl in Spanish if she could help. The girl said nothing, just gave a slight, terrified shake of her head.

Doe canceled her evening plans. She sat in her car and followed Ron when he came back and picked up the girl. He drove to Trevor's motel. A woman was waiting, a woman whom Doe knew without knowing her, a woman she'd cross the street to avoid, or, back when she'd waitressed, would make sure to bring her what she wanted quickly and efficiently. The woman took the girl by the elbow and led her inside.

Shari had wrapped up leftovers for Doe and the bag was sitting on the seat next to her, fried shrimp and plantains. She threw them out on the street. The smell was making her sick.

Doe figured that if she waited too long, she'd start thinking of reasons not to, so she drove west to the turnpike and north to the Pompano rest stop, because they still had phones there. She placed a call to 911, spoke briefly, and drove away.

She lived like a cat for the next two days, spooking at every sound, until Shari finally called at midnight. She drove to the house, which was dark. No one answered her knock and it wasn't until she saw the glow of a cigarette out back that she found her mother.

Shari sat smoking. "He said he didn't know," Shari said.

Doe stood, barely breathing. "You believe that?"

"He was hoodwinked by that guy Trevor. Running a prostitution ring out of the motel."

"It was sex slavery, Mom."

"It wasn't him, it was Trevor. He's going to beat it, he said. He's got a lawyer. Did you do it? Did you make the call?"

"Does he think I did?"

Now she could see Shari's face, puffed and bruised, all along the left side. Her nostril was caked with dark blood. Doe sank to her knees. "Mom—"

"He thought I did it. He was mad, said I should have told him what I thought. He could have steered me straight."

"Where is he?"

"I don't know. My life's blown apart."

"He was trafficking in underaged girls, Ma!"

"That girl. Elena, Maria, whatever her name is. Don't look at me, it wasn't her real name anyway. She got hurt."

"How?"

"I don't know. She's in the hospital. The police came and she ran, and I guess she got hit by a car? Run get me some aspirin, baby doll, will you? My head hurts."

"Your head hurts because your boyfriend beat you up!"

"He thought I turned him in. It was all Trevor, the motel was just an investment for Ron, he was never there. I never liked Trevor's eyes. Stop looking at me like that. Like I'm stupid."

"You're not stupid," Doe said. "That's the trouble. Then you'd have an excuse for this shit." She went to get aspirin and ice.

That night she drove back to her apartment in North Miami and packed. Ron would know that she did it. Somehow she hadn't bargained on him being that smart. She was afraid of him but she was more afraid of Trevor and that woman.

She sold her car to her roommate. She talked her surfer boyfriend into leaving that night. He'd been talking about Montauk all June, about how easy it was to get jobs. It was so hot in Miami. They left as the sun was coming up.

Doe put sugar in the coffee, but it didn't help. "I don't blame you for the girl," she said. "I blame you for staying with Ron."

"I left him!"

"You gave him another chance."

"I believed him. That was enough to go on. Everybody deserves a second chance. I didn't give him a third, okay?"

Doe put her earbud back in.

"Do you remember that time I came to your class? Kindergarten, I think. That teacher with the frosted lipstick."

Miss Karen.

Shari leaned over and yanked out one of Doe's earbuds. In one ear, Drake. In the other, Shari. "You met me at the principal's office and led me to the classroom. You were so proud of me. I wore that dress you liked, and you said, 'I hoped you were going to wear that.' I read that book you liked, *Outside Over There.* I sat on a chair, with all of you on the floor, and you sat right at my feet. You kept your hand on my foot the whole time I read."

"I don't remember."

"All I'm saying is? You really, really loved me once, okay?"

Doe sipped her coffee. "I remember a picnic," she said. "I was maybe ten? You were still with Steve then. I got a nosebleed. We didn't have any tissues, so you stuck a tampon up my nostril to stop the blood. I started to cry. You and Steve just about pissed yourselves laughing. You made me walk all the way to the car with a tampon up my nose. Past all my friends."

"You always remember things wrong."

"You were the one operating on a six-pack that day."

Shari picked up Doe's plate and scraped the happy face and the waffle into the trash. She poured herself more coffee and stood at the window, looking out into the yard. Doe picked up her earbud and put it back in. She muted the volume.

"You got it wrong. You weren't ten, you were eleven. It was after Shane. Here's what you forget about that day. That's when I was drinking, really drinking. And Steve was an asshole. Admitted. But when I was alone I wanted to kill myself. I took you to the park that day because Steve the asshole told me I was unfair when I told you Shane was your fault, he said that could really fuck up a kid. So he wasn't an asshole all the time, okay? I made your favorite sandwiches. Tuna with crushed potato chips. So, okay, we got a little drunk."

Shari gave a wave to Shannon and Shawn, standing on the lawn cradling two zucchinis the size of newborns.

"That's the thing you should focus on, the picnic," she said. "You dwell on the negative constantly, that's your problem. I don't know what you're afraid of."

"What?" Doe asked.

47

RUTHIE WASN'T A sailor, but you couldn't live in Orient without knowing one. Once she had asked her neighbor Josh about the worst trouble he'd ever been in at sea, and he described a squall that had blown up so quickly it had overtaken him in minutes. "In weather, everything is hard," he'd said. "Sometimes you have to work to separate water from air. You've got to be comfortable with losing the horizon."

Classic sailor understatement. Turning "storm" into "weather." Would that work for her? Could she turn "crazy" into "temporary derangement"?

She'd lost her horizon line. It had been like this since Lucas had come to dinner at the playhouse that very night (typical of him to invite her to dinner and then assume she would cook it) and they'd mapped out the only way it could work. A picture painted at the same time she'd worked in Peter's studio, a portrait: one of the Dowagers, Lucas had said.

Ruthie remembered the painting in Daniel's house. The Dowager Series was Peter's winking nod to misogyny, as though Peter had been in on the joke. Of course he had, but the ultimate joke was that he actually *was* a misogynist. He delighted in punishing women; Ruthie was well versed in his methods, as were all his female assistants.

She transported the brushes, paints, and canvas to the pool house. Told Jem she was looking for work and turning back to painting as a stress reliever. She bought canvas and painted again, terrible paintings since she was just repeating what she used to do. When she wasn't painting, she was on the computer, scrolling for work. Applying to jobs within a two-hour commute. Calling old friends to nose around and find out what was coming up. Maybe she could freelance. There was a job in New Mexico, a job in Texas. She wasn't ready to apply yet. She was hanging on to her turf.

Lucas had thought twenty million would be under the radar as a sale target. She would take what she would need and no more, enough to write the check to Mike and then buy another watch for Carole. Any more than what she needed would be too much. She was already having trouble sleeping at night. She dropped into dreamless, deep naps in the middle of the day.

There was an "Important Watches" auction coming up in November, including one with the same make and model as the one she'd lost. She would have to confess, but at least she'd be able to hand Carole a watch.

She kept her own painting on the easel in case Jem walked in. Peter's was kept in the closet.

First the primer, an individual mix, a little glue mixed in. Painting the blue background had been easy; she'd mixed it a thousand times. A wash of color, laid on with a thin brush. A critic had called the blue "severe clear," a kind of blue sky that pilots knew. The blue sky they'd seen on 9/11. Clarity and depth all at once, what infinity must be like. Now it was just known as Clay blue. Just as everybody knew an Yves Klein blue, they knew a Clay blue.

It was his secret sauce, his glop, he called it, a precise mixture of paint and medium. She painted for him when he had the shakes, when he'd had a bad night, when he didn't feel like painting. She went from mastering the color to capturing the line.

He had his own line. Almost illustrative, so irony was there, as well as freedom. He laid down a grid and projected the photo. In his portraits the skin color of white people had been compared to a newly born piglet, though the critic who coined this had most likely never seen a piglet unless on a plate.

When the Upper East Side ladies, with their Altoid breath and their beautiful shoes, came to have their Polaroids taken, the assistants would fetch espressos and springwater, and often disappear if the vibe sometimes changed to seduction. Many would tumble, hoping his brush would be kinder to them than he was. It never was.

As Ruthie painted, she told herself it didn't matter. Artists used projections, used assistants, and nobody cared, they just wanted the work. It was still Peter's eye, his mockery, his line, his color, his wit. She could easily have painted this twenty years ago.

She found several photos of a younger Adeline online, scanned and studied them. He had painted her only once, but there was also a beautiful suite of drawings that had made up a small, gorgeous exhibition at MoMA a few years ago.

Adeline's face was the same, her penchant for turning a quarter to the left, tilting her chin for a photograph in that way that beautiful women know their best angle. It wouldn't be a nude, the canvas was too small, so it would just expose bare shoulders. Besides, if she had to paint Adeline's nipples she *would* go crazy. Ruthie stared so long into the serene gaze of her nemesis that she began to feel as though she knew the woman Adeline had been, knew what the expression in her eyes meant. *I found my chance and I am taking it, even if it farts in bed.*

She had three canvases, one with the word C U N T scrawled on it. She saved that one for last. She practiced on the first two. The first was not good. The second, close. Loose, precise. Good but not quite there. She covered the last canvas with primer, whiting out the word. Making invisible how he'd made her feel, how he'd whittled down her confidence. While she worked she remembered things she'd wanted to forget. Once he'd admonished her to be sure and always "wash down there" before she was with a man, because he'd been with a woman the night before who had "stunk like an after-birth." He'd told her that her breasts were too small, he'd told her that she would have been prettier if her eyes weren't brown. He'd told her that he hoped she knew how to give a decent blow job.

The female assistants had talked about him over beers, but the guys had laughed at them, called them pussies. That word was allowed because Peter said it all the time. The girls knew this job would get them places, and so they'd just gone back to work.

How strange, twenty years later, her hands would shake when she thought of it.

She pictured Peter shouting into the phone on the other side of the studio. She listened to *Eat a Peach* and *Dark Side of the Moon*. She thought of him saying that she was only a magpie.

The magpie is back, motherfucker.

So why did she come here, down the alley, toward the pier, finding the tiny place with the whitewashed sign OYSTERS. The night they'd spent together still thrummed inside her. Sometimes it filled her up with such urgency she'd dash outside and keep running until she came back to herself and saw she was standing on the beach, or on the road.

Inside she could see him at work, shucking with a sharp knife, wearing a blue rubber glove. Placing the oysters on shaved ice, the lemon just so. Smiling at the customer, saying something as he delivered the platter and the beers.

She watched without the nerve to go in.

If she hadn't had so much to hide now, she would push through the door and ask him. *How did you learn how to do this, whittle the complex down to simple?*

Outside the picnic tables were full. It was a roaring Friday happy hour, a perfect summer evening. Giddy people, drinking beer, eating cold oysters, looking forward to picnics and pools, beaches and cocktails.

He saw her through the window and stopped, then lifted his hand in a half wave. He leaned over to speak to the waitress, and walked outside.

"Did you come for that Muscadet? I promise not to call it gorgeous."

"I came to apologize for my atrocious behavior."

"Okay."

"And my cowardice. Ducking your calls."

"Only two."

"What did you want to tell me?"

He shook his head, smiling. "Doesn't matter now."

"How did you do it? How did you throw your life up in the air to see where it landed?"

Joe thought about this. What she loved about him was his attention to questions. "I really do believe we can choose to be happy," he said. "I made a list."

This was a disappointing answer, somehow. "Oysters make you happy?"

"They're a simple food. They filter out a ton of crap."

"That's a useful skill."

"Exactly."

The server popped her head out. "Joe?"

He half turned to her, then back to Ruthie. He reached for her hand, and her pulse jumped. He only pointed to a mark on her third finger. "You're painting again."

"Not seriously." She rubbed at the paint. She couldn't get it off. She heard a helicopter buzz overhead, flying out toward Plum Island so it could loop back to East Hampton. The noise was loud and she moved her lips. "I'm sorry," she said.

"Me too," he said.

Then he walked back into the restaurant, and she walked away.

THERE IS NO *difference between my canvas and the air.*
    I would paint on water if I could.

Women are mired in the body, it's why they can't be artists. All they see is themselves.

Men sit astride the world. Women are afraid they'll fall off.

Peter in her head again.

Every time I paint a woman I am painting myself. How can I hate myself?

Name a truly great woman artist. You see? You can't. Joan Mitchell? Are you fucking kidding? She's crap.

Women can't paint other women. They can't see them clearly enough.

Copying his stroke, pushing the brush.

Photos of Mike and Adeline had cropped up in the last three weeks. Adeline had said that she was in Orient to get away, but apparently this did not include eating at Nick & Toni's in East Hampton, attending the Artists & Writers Celebrity Softball Game or the Parrish Art Museum brunch in Water Mill, and being photographed with "artist Michael Dutton."

The third canvas, she knew, would be perfect.

Labor
Day

48

THE FIRST LEAF had crunched underfoot, and the summer was fall, falling away. Everyone was talking about Lark's event at the Belfry. The party had its own hashtag. It would be covered by the *Times*. Dodge had done a special installation. Daniel Mantis was running yachts back and forth from Sag Harbor to Greenport for the Hamptons people. He'd hired cars and even a famous eighty-two-foot ketch. There was a rumor that all the museum members would be invited. This turned out to be untrue.

Ruthie carried the painting, wrapped in brown paper and in a canvas tote, to the car. She placed it in the backseat, suddenly worried about rear-end collisions. The car felt as inflammatory as a Pinto. The word *collision* was so close to *collusion,* she thought, and wondered if she was in the middle of a nervous breakdown.

She drove to Southold in the beginnings of holiday weekend traffic. They couldn't meet in Orient, and Lucas had chosen a café with a large, busy parking lot. She pulled up next to him in a spot underneath some trees. He got out of his Jeep and they both slid into the backseat, as if they were teenagers ready for action.

Ruthie unwrapped the painting and handed it over.

Lucas sat for a moment and then burst out with a laugh that sounded like a cartoon bird.

"Adeline! Oh, my fucking God, you painted Adeline!"

Ruthie bit her lip, then her thumbnail. "It made sense, right? She was his model in the beginning."

"It's delicious," Lucas said. "She looks awful. So old! Wait. Why would he paint her like this? He was in love with her. This could be a mistake. We should have discussed this."

"I needed a model, okay? And there's lots of photos of her on the Internet. And he painted everyone that way. Look, I thought about this. The timing could be soon after they met. Maybe he did the painting before they were in love—she was his model, re-member? He never showed it to her, he always worked from Pola-roids. And so maybe he left it in the Sag Harbor studio, where your mother found it? It makes sense."

"Okay," Lucas said. "Sure. Genius. That's the story, that's the narrative." He held the painting at arm's length, as much as he could in the backseat of a car. "You caught her. It's what she'd look like if she hadn't had all the work done, right? If she just got progressively uglier, like most women in their fifties."

"Did you just really say that?"

"You know what I mean. The ones who don't care." Lucas laughed that strange laugh again. "This isn't just going to be easy, it's going to be fun. Let's get this sucker in my trunk." He looked at his phone.

"Wait." As soon as the painting left her hands, she would be committed. "Maybe we need to think about this again."

"Jesus, will you take a Klonopin? I'm his son, they're not going to question anything, all right?"

They had gone over this. "How can you be sure they won't sell it?" she asked. "Someday it could find its way into a museum. They could do some kind of tests I don't know about." And they would see the word written under the paint, which wouldn't dis-qualify it, but it certainly would gain it attention. That pleased her, that years and years from now, after she was gone from the world, that word could float through in damning pentimento.

"You're paranoid," Lucas said. "This is getting boring." He looked at the painting again. "Holy fuck," he said again. "You did it."

The signs of decay on that beautiful face, just as disturbing and awful as Peter meant them to be. Recognizably Adeline, those eyes of glass.

"Maybe I made her more grotesque than he would have," Ruthie said.

"Nah. You caught her sad pathetic soul."

She took the painting and slid it back into the brown paper. She taped it carefully and slid it into the bag.

His leg was jumping. "Come on." He took the tote out of her hands.

Such a small painting, Ruthie thought. *Not so important in the scheme of things.* Ten million in a bag. Lucas was right about provenance. He could get away with it. She wouldn't end up in a tiny apartment, scrounging money for rent and waving goodbye to her daughter as she jetted off to France with Adeline. She wouldn't lose her place in the world.

"The thing is . . ." he started.

Ruthie felt something happen along her hairline, sweat springing up. *The thing is* was never a good way to start a conversation. *The thing is, I've been unhappy for a long time,* said Mike. *The thing is, I met someone. In Italy,* Joe said. *The thing is, your father is a bastard crap person.*

". . . the Russian guy fell through."

"What?"

"Am I in charge of geopolitics right now? Oligarchs aren't who they used to be." Lucas opened the car door.

She grabbed on to a strap of the tote. "You said you were knee-deep in oligarchs! Those were your exact words!"

"No worries. I've got someone else. It's better because the deal will be, like, instant. I've already prepped him."

"Who is it?"

"Better you don't know, right? I'll probably have a cashier's check by Monday."

"The banks are closed on Monday."

"Jesus, you're a buzzkill. Tuesday." He yanked the strap from her grasp, slid out, and stuck his head back in. "I'll let you know." After he shut the door Ruthie watched him check himself out in the reflection. Life for Lucas was a series of poses.

She tried to swallow. She had an urgent need to pee.

She slid out of the car. Lucas was behind the wheel of his own car, checking his phone. She bolted like a rabbit toward the café.

The place was crowded. It had only opened last year, and they roasted their own ethically sourced beans and had barnwood on the walls and scattered couches and armchairs, so it was a hit. Ruthie ignored the coffee line and launched herself at the bathroom door. She peed and then washed her hands, out, out damned spot, even though her hands were paint-free, but wasn't that the point for Lady Macbeth anyway? She remembered being pregnant with Jem, that low-level nausea in the first months, that bitter taste in her mouth that never went away. This was like that. As though she were carrying something inside her, something that in the end would undo her and leave her stranded, gasping and bewildered.

After this, after it was done, after she had herself back, she'd get her best friend back, she'd get on her knees (well, maybe not that, but she'd bring wine) and deeply apologize to Penny for being such an asshole. She'd been thrown off something moving very fast and she was dizzy and totally sick and she was sorry she lashed out. She would apologize to Jem for neglecting her and maybe even to Helen for throwing a tree at her. Ruthie met her frantic eyes in the mirror. It was almost over. She just had to hang on to something real instead of the edge of a sink. And get a coffee.

She stood on line behind a couple. The fortyish woman had skin tan and smooth as a teenager's. Her legs looked as though they'd been rubbed with oil. She wore heeled white sandals, her toes painted a cyanotic lilac. "All the choices," she said to the man. "It makes me need a hug or something. Someone to say There, there, you can't go wrong with just ordering a coffee. There's no bad choices here."

The man gave a distracted smile and ordered a soy latte. Ruthie realized that the two weren't together. The woman continued talking, this time to the barista. So she was one of those people, the ones who held up lines, who never could find their wallet or their receipt, who asked for directions and then didn't listen to the answer. GPS and Apple Pay had not eliminated them from social discourse. Not yet.

Thank God. Ruthie loved this kind of person. She liked people who would willingly share, since she had been married for years to someone who guarded his feelings like a leopard snarling over a carcass. So when the woman turned and smiled at her, Ruthie was happy to smile, too, to have a pleasant exchange in a spinning world.

"Stupid to drink hot coffee in this heat, right?" the woman asked. Now that she had turned, Ruthie noticed her breasts, because she had to. Two perfect mounds, as if someone had modeled them from wet sand.

"Well, we're in air-conditioning all the time anyway," Ruthie said, and gave her order to the barista. The woman's dress was familiar, a seersucker shift with lime-green lines. She was petite and pretty, honey-brown eyes that also seemed familiar. Pink lip gloss that looked like the kind with a flavor. Compared with the distracted women around them in rumpled linen, she was as cheerful as a Skittle.

"I'm from Florida, so this heat is nothing," the woman said. "You know, I thought there would be more opportunity here. It's kinda dead, right? I mean, not this weekend, it's pretty crowded, but, you know, September."

"You're on the wrong fork," Ruthie said. "You should try the Hamptons."

"Stuck on the wrong fork," the woman said. "Story of my life."

The bell on the door jingled, and Doe walked in. When she saw them, Ruthie saw something flicker on her face. Annoyance and something like fear.

Doe strode forward. "Mom, what are you doing here?"

"Dora!" The woman's face lit up. "You know, having coffee? Oops, I'm wearing your dress. Busted!"

Doe's mother? Ruthie recognized Doe's expression, the hurried way she turned to her. She recognized it because she'd known it herself as a teenager, if she ran into a classmate while she was with her mother. Shame.

Angela, who never met a purse she wouldn't clutch, never met a restaurant bill she wouldn't declaim as ridiculous. Ruthie wished she could touch Doe on the arm and say, *One day you will miss her. You will miss being that loved.*

"Ruthie, hi. I didn't see you—"

"You know each other?" Doe's mother interrupted. "How funny is that? Wow, this is such a small town, right?"

"Shari, this is Ruth Beamish. My boss. I mean, my ex-boss."

Ruthie had never seen Doe anything less than perfectly composed. Even around two dozen clamoring, squirming kids, she'd pass out the art materials efficiently and answer questions politely. She rarely smiled, and never looked flustered, and now she was doing both.

"Ooh, the good boss, right? I came up from Florida to live with Dora," Shari said to Ruthie. "I mean, Doe. I'm trying to get a foothold. A foothold in Southold, ha. Doe loves it here so much, I thought, you know. I'm a masseuse—I mean bodywork, not just massage? I realign your body and your chakras. I have a card, but it has my Florida number on it . . ."

"Mom, don't pass out your business card—"

"Anyways, I'm kinda stuck on Doe's couch." She nudged Doe, who recoiled.

Ruthie saw Lucas push through the door. He tilted down his sunglasses when he saw them.

"Well, good morning, beauties. Ruthie, I haven't seen you in weeks." With one glance he ignored Shari, instantly assessing her as someone he didn't need to consider. He bent to kiss Doe on the cheek, but she stepped back. Lucas covered by stroking her arm.

"I'm Doe's mom," Shari said.

Ruthie watched as Lucas took Shari in, from toenails to breasts to lip gloss. "I should have known. Beautiful girls always come from beautiful mothers."

"Well, aren't you adorable and handsome," Shari said. "Let's sit together and have coffee! I'm so glad I got to meet Dora's friends. She hasn't invited me anywhere. Like she's hiding me. So this is so fun!"

"Yeah," Lucas said, with a glance at Doe. "It's delicious."

49

JEM'S PHONE

Draft Folder

From: Jemma Dutton
To: Olivia Freeman
Subject: snakebite

If you get a snakebite, keep wound above the heart. Raise arm or leg, etc. Cut into wound with knife and suck out blood and venom. Then spit it out and rinse with Gatorade.

We totally made that one up because we really, really wanted to suck out venom.

Here's what happened last week:

He asked for a "real date." He said when he has the house to himself. He kissed me.

Ollie, I know something now. You can actually fall for somebody you're really not sure you even like. You wait for his lame texts. You wonder if you like his smell. Something about him kind of turns you off, but you still like him touching you. It's sick.

Meret knows he goes for a coffee at eleven at Aldos, so she waits there or happens to be walking by. Yeah. How do I know this, because I was with him yesterday and that is why. She is flirting w him, she knows about my crush. She's a witch, she just knows things. Annie tells me that on groupchat she's calling me a slut and they're betting on my losing it to him. Yeah. I'm a ho. Ha. Ho Ha. So yesterday Meret says to me, with Lucas right there—*puts on concerned face* "Aren't you dreading the first day of school, Jem? I mean, especially you." When I ask her why she just laughs and says Lucas doesn't want to hear about high school stuff.

Annie fills me in. Meret made up T-shirts with #MAYFLOWER on them and everybody is going to wear them first day of school. Even the stupid boys.

Lucas told me he might be hanging out into September. Hale invited him, he has a house on Shelter Island. Lucas quit his job, so he says he needs "recovery time." And he said why should he leave, when there's a girl like me to hang with?

So I have a stupid plan. It only requires losing my virginity, ha ha.

Okay not ha ha, I'm totally serious. Kind of.

The thing is, I have to pull a Crazy Ivan. Remember when Wash does it in *Firefly*? I've got to spin really hard and fast and go straight at it. It's the only way to beat the bad guys.

If Lucas and I hook up, I could ask him to drive me to school the first day in his white Jeep. Because you can ask something that little and they have to do it, right? I could kiss him with the top down. I could just sit there in the parking lot, kissing Lucas.

Even if they do the mayflower thing, it won't matter. I'll just seem all older and above it. Meret will completely cave and find another victim.

Do you think it's creepy that my dad might marry Lucas's stepmom? Because it's not like we grew up together. And it's not like Adeline is his mother. His mother died when he was I think sixteen? Which explains maybe why deep down he's sad.

He hates his stepmother, you can tell. I don't know why. Adeline found a house she wants to buy in Orient and she's going to renovate it for next summer. There's a wing for me, she said. A *wing*.

That just makes me feel all confused, honestly. And I can't talk about it with Mom because Mom gets crazy eyes when Adeline comes up.

It's like Mom is mad all the time, or sometimes she's just sitting there at the kitchen table, staring. This summer we broke this huge rule and I'm allowed to wear earbuds and watch something on my phone while we eat dinner. She started painting again, I guess that's good even if the paintings aren't? Dad is super preoccupied with Adeline. I get how Dad is happy, because love, obv, but being with Adeline is like a vacation from real life all the time. Nothing is hard. You just pay for things and get them. You can read the paper about some new play and just go, "We should see this in previews." We used to go to the theater in New York like maybe once a year, and that was a huge deal.

Turns out she has a *plane*, Ol. Like, when she goes to California or something? She goes in her own plane.

Maybe you'd hate that. Maybe you'd say, she should be arrested for that Spinosaurus-sized carbon footprint.

I just can't stop myself. I check my phone like fifty times a minute. He hasn't texted me in three days. And it's Labor Day weekend and it feels like my very last chance. He might stand me up, he did it once before, when we were supposed to go to Roberta's in Sagaponack and he said he was going to a party instead because she was boring. Turned out he was right because the dinner party got canceled because of this big storm and because Roberta wasn't feeling well, so all I did was sit in another rich person's guesthouse and watch TV on my phone.

Is he ghosting me?

Should I text him?

What if he doesn't answer?

It's like stepping off the edge of the world and never landing.

> From: Jemma Dutton
> To: Lucas Clay
>
> I'm off work at 1 we could maybe get ice cream or something
> LOL
>
> Ignore that LOL so lame
>
> . . .
>
> you didn't tell me what time Saturday

50

DOE FROWNED AT her phone.

Door you're not answering

. . .

Sorry this phone keeps calling you Door

. . .

maybe if I came to the party it would be a good chance to meet her

You said there could be something in send a product

. . .

Said a panic

. . .

autocorrect is killing me softly

You know, the town

"Sagaponack," Doe said to the phone. And texted *not now see u at home.*

She heard the shower turn off. Lark was up early. It would be a busy day. Lark would be at the museum installing Dodge's inflatables, but Doe really had no reason to go and would be in the way. She didn't want to go home and bump into Shari, and she didn't like staying here without Lark.

Lark emerged from the shower in a towel. "Hey, sleepyhead." She bent over and kissed her, lingering so that Doe slipped her arms around her neck. Lark pulled away.

"Don't you dare distract me, I am a professional person today. Meeting Dodge and the crew at the Belfry." She stopped to look at her face in the mirror and ran her fingers along her cheekbones. "I need my game face. Do I look as scared as I feel?"

"I didn't think you were scared of anything."

Lark turned. "Hey, I do have a sense of my limitations. Rare, but it happens."

"High five on your voyage of self-discovery," Doe said with a straight face.

"Brat." Lark grinned. "But, really? Sure, I'm stressed, but I'm pumped. It's my first real curatorial gig. I get to run a crew!"

"Is Tobie helping you?"

"No, I want to do it myself. Prove I have the chops. Besides, it doesn't seem fair if I'm laying her off. I've got a whole list of curators to interview in New York."

"Wait a second." Doe struggled to sit up. "Are you firing the whole staff?"

"I don't know what I'm doing yet," Lark said. "I mean, maybe people will just want to leave if they aren't comfortable with the new direction."

"But . . . they do good work."

"I know." Lark sighed. "I feel bad about it. But really, what's more important is the new direction, so. And you're the one who told me I'd just have to hire the right people."

"What about Catha?"

"Daddy thinks she's useless. If I hire the right curator and a development person, he doesn't think we need her. Plus he's lining up this really amazing consultant." Lark adjusted the towel. "Okay, right now I feel like you're thinking I'll fail."

"Of course not. I think you can do anything."

"Because I really think I can do this." Lark hugged herself for a moment, and the bright hope in her face made Doe wish she really believed in her the way she wanted to. It didn't matter, though. She was here to protect Lark. Lark would have the title, and Doe would make it look authentic to the world.

Lark disappeared into the dressing room. "I've been checking the weather incessantly. Chance of t-storms after midnight, so we'll be fine." She stuck her head out of the door. "Guess who I forgot to invite to the party? Lucas!"

"Accidentally on purpose?"

"Maybe." She ducked back inside. "Anyway it's weird because of course he knows about it, he lives in Orient, plus Daddy invited Adeline." Lark came out in a pair of shorts and a lemon-colored lace bra. "I just remembered last night because Daddy told me Lucas was coming over this morning for a breakfast meeting. So I quick sent him a text saying, Hey, you didn't RSVP. You know, pretending it got lost. And so he texts back, I'll be there, pretending that I didn't forget. Modern manners, right?"

"A breakfast meeting?"

"Can you imagine, he hates going anywhere before noon." Lark pulled a tissue-thin T-shirt over her head. "He brought over a painting. Apparently he made this amazing discovery. A lost painting by his father. From, like, the nineties, his best period."

Doe sat up. "What? How?"

"I don't know, he cleaned out his mother's storage unit? Found it." Lark twisted her wet hair into a bun on top of her head while she hunted for pins. "Pretty big news. I mean, it will be, once it gets out. Lucas is totally into it while trying to act all *Oh, this old thing.* And get this—it's a portrait of Adeline. Looking horrific, I must say. Naturally Daddy is thrilled. No way he won't buy it, it's a steal. He told me Lucas is asking ten million but Daddy is going to offer eight. Even if something's a steal, you don't meet the price if you don't have to. He says. He still thirsts for revenge on Adeline. He has it on approval right now. So listen to this. Daddy wants me to hang it at the Belfry for the party! Right in that front gallery so that everyone can see it. I mean, it's a lawn party so nobody will be inside except for staff and caterers. But we'll light it so it will practically glow. If Adeline comes she'll have a fit. Not that I want that, but Daddy does. So what can I do."

"Say no?" Doe suggested, but Lark had disappeared into the closet again.

She came out in a pair of sandals, frowned, and kicked them off. "Daddy is delusional if he thinks that Adeline will come tonight." She ducked into the closet again and came out wearing fawn-colored boots. "I think this is the end of our families meeting, like, ever again. I liked Adeline fine, but what a relief. No more Lucas for me. Hale Channing swears he stole a pair of Buccellati cuff links from him."

Doe swung her legs out of bed. Her brain was buzzing. "His mother's storage unit? How come he didn't find it before?"

"No idea. Gotta run, angel." Lark pressed herself against her face and nuzzled her like a sweet pony. "Do you know what, you," she murmured. "I think this director thing is going to work out. And we'll be together every day. I've never, ever been so happy."

And then she was gone in a moment, before Doe's skin had even cooled. The way she did. The way she would do for good one day.

Lucas had crammed everything in the trunk of his car, hadn't he? Thrown it all away? Unless he'd lied to her? But she'd seen it, she'd seen the empty storage unit, she'd seen him close out the account.

Lucas discovered a painting worth ten million? It didn't make sense. What would Shari say?

If an asshole sells you a story, why be surprised if it smells?

51

RUTHIE HAD NO choice but to pass the Belfry; it was on the main road, right before the causeway. She tried not to look, but how could she not, when there was a giant inflatable hyena bobbing in the breeze on the front lawn? She pulled over.

Off in the distance she could see Dodge directing his crew. Various piles of plasticky material were laid out on the lawn. She could see Lark Mantis, in shorts and a T-shirt and boots (Boots? It was ninety-two degrees), pointing and suggesting, placing the inflatable sculptures. Ruthie had heard about them, of course. In the back courtyard a bouncy castle looked like a giant, cheerful prison.

Lark was crowding the sculptures. She wasn't allowing for the right sight lines. Ruthie watched as Dodge walked over, talked to her with one hand on her shoulder. She could tell from here that he was frustrated.

She was about to drive away when she glimpsed a vivid flash of familiar blue.

She slid out of the car. She walked up the lawn unnoticed. She climbed over the knee-high wall.

One small painting in the gallery, blazing clear blue.

It seemed impossible, but there it was.

Lucas. That bastard. That spoiled, careless idiot.

What *the fuck* was he thinking?

She walked back to her car, feeling weightless and doomed, a passenger in a plane in a long stall.

52

DOE ENDED UP driving into the village of East Hampton. She bought an iced coffee and sipped it, window-shopping down Newtown Lane. So many thin white people. So many pairs of white jeans, so many straw hats.

She saw Lucas ahead, jingling his keys, looking at his phone. He hadn't seen her. She had time to reverse direction but she didn't. She counted off a couple of slow breaths.

"Look who's here," he said. "You meeting your mom for a little lunch? Is there a Hooters I don't know about?"

"Just killing time before Lark's party. Sorry she forgot to invite you. I hope you weren't too humiliated."

"I heard about you two. Like it will last." He reached for her wrist and pushed up the long sleeve of her linen shirt, and she stepped back.

"Relax, I just wanted to see if you were wearing a watch." He studied her over his sunglasses. "Because I'm missing mine. It disappeared after the storm."

Doe shrugged. "Did you check under the dresser?"

"I saw you looking at it."

"Are you sure it wasn't Hale's? I hear he's missing some cuff links. Maybe it's a set."

"Fuck you, I got it for my graduation."

"Right. Do you know, the entire time we hung out, all you did was complain about not having enough money? Do you remember that date we had back in July? After the Montauk party?"

She couldn't see his eyes behind his sunglasses. He stepped back and raised both hands in a *what the hell* gesture. "Am I supposed to remember every stupid date we had? Please, I'd like to forget I ever asked you out."

"When you cleaned out your mother's storage unit," she said. "That was me in the passenger seat, remember?"

"So?" Had he forgotten, or he just didn't care?

"Lark told me that you discovered a painting. A major find, she said."

"Amazing, right?"

"Lark said you found the painting in the storage unit. Such a big surprise, she said. For me, too. I remember you throwing everything out."

"Not . . ." She sensed him searching, his mind adjusting. "She had another unit I didn't know about. They called me."

"Same place?"

He nodded and pushed his sunglasses tight against the bridge of his nose.

"Funny," she said.

"What."

"That you didn't know."

"Not really," he said, using the bored voice that meant he was about to lie. "My mother was a drunk. She didn't exactly fill me in on what she was doing."

"So there were two separate—"

Suddenly he grabbed both her elbows, hard, startling her. He smiled, as though they were playing. A man looked over and he dropped her arms.

"Don't fuck with me," he said.

Doe wasn't afraid. They were right on Newtown Lane. "Remember what happened the last time you grabbed me like that?"

"Yeah. I almost got a scar. So I'm in the mood for payback. Are you hearing me, *Dora*?"

"I hear you," Doe said. "Asshole."

"At least now I know why you were so lousy in bed. A dyke."

She leaned closer. "I'm the only person who really sees you. So why don't you back off?"

"You're out of your league, Beauty," he said, and moved away with his great assurance, already lost in the happy crowd.

53

JEM'S PHONE

From: Jemma Dutton
To: Dad

Didn't you and A get invited to that big party at the Belfry

From: Dad
To: Jemma Dutton

Yup, why?

From: Jem
To: Dad

Well r u going

From: Dad
To: Jem

No. Why?

From: Jem
To: Dad

I was thinking you could take me party of the summer etc

From: Dad
To: Jem

Sorry sweetie Adeline doesn't want to go.

From: Jem
To: Dad

But why

From: Dad
To: Jem

Plus I don't think Mom would like it.

From: Jem
To: Dad

I would ask her if it's ok

From: Dad
To: Jem

A is not on great terms with Daniel Mantis.

From: Jem
To: Dad

But they're good friends right? Saw it in Us Weekly

From: Dad
To: Jem

Yeah right. C'mon sweetie you know what I'm saying.

From: Jem
To: Dad

I really really really want to go tho

. . .

really really could you ask A please Daddy? I could Instagram it
and Meret would see it and diet

. . .

Autocorrect fail I mean die lol but diet too

. . .

please

From: Dad
To: Jem

I'll ask. This one is her call. Talk to your mom.

54

LUCAS DID NOT answer the texts or his phone. His car was not at the house. Asshole. Coward.

Ruthie had lived in Orient long enough to know who to ask. Information was traded and gossiped and shared, and it took her about fifteen minutes and a walk through town to learn that Daniel Mantis was the buyer of the painting and that was why it was at the Belfry.

Mantis was high-profile. He bought, sold, sent pieces to auction. He loved publicity. She would be reading about it in the *Times* next week.

She had to think, she thought frantically, but it was just a pulse, a beating throb of panic.

PANIC, CALAMITY, STRESS, didn't matter, you still had to pack your suitcases and get out of the rental.

"How's it going, Jemmie?" she asked outside the closed door. She knocked. Knocked again.

She gently eased the door open a crack, expecting the bark of *Changing!* or the more exasperated *What?*

She sensed the minefield from the door. Jem sat on her bed, earbuds in, texting, disarray around her, clothes tossed on the bed, the floor, drawers half open, sneakers scattered. She hadn't seen Ruthie, hadn't heard the door.

None of this was unusual, but. A tide of feeling swamped Ruthie. She felt as though she'd broken through the surface of the sea and blinked away the blur. She saw Jem, maybe for the first time that summer. She saw the tightness and the misery. She saw the long legs and the blue eyes and the hair, but she saw a lost little girl. She saw someone hurt and scrabbling for a handhold.

While she'd been scrabbling herself. Both of them reaching for handholds, when she should have been the one to say, *Here. Reach here. Hold on.*

All those silent dinners when she let Jem watch a video on her phone, earbuds in, while she sat eating, trying to force food down, thinking her burning thoughts, of the painting, of her house, of Mike and Adeline, of getting it all back, when the center of her life was right at the table with her.

That last year before Mike moved out, he turned into an insomniac. There was one step on the way downstairs—never up, why was that?—that resounded with the crack of a rifle. Deep in dreams, she would hear it and awaken, and Mike would be already gone, downstairs to pace, to stare out a window. She thought he just couldn't sleep. Instead, he was planning a life without her.

Why hadn't she ever followed him? Why had she woken, heard the crack of the family breaking, and not fought for them?

Was she missing the crack of the breaking right now?

She crossed the room to touch Jem's hair. Jem flinched, but maybe that was only out of surprise. Maybe she could reach her, right now. Not ignore the crack, the life gone and the life she could make.

"Everything okay?"

Jem took out an earbud. "What?"

"I'm just seeing if you want help packing."

"No, I'm good."

"Are you . . ."

"Am I what."

"Okay."

"Yeah. Do you have to be here right now?"

Ignore the insult, keep going. "The thing is . . ."

Exasperated and showy toss of phone onto pillow. "So there's a thing?"

"You seem upset."

"I'm not upset, okay? I'm fine."

She waited.

"I really want to go to the Belfry party."

"Oh."

"At first I thought Daddy and Adeline and Lucas were going and I could go with them. But Daddy and Adeline aren't going."

"Lucas is going?"

"Yeah. I can't go by myself. I asked Daddy and he said he wouldn't take me. They were invited and everything." Jem flopped back. "It just sucks because I said I was going. I don't know, it's even more ammunition for Meret against me. She'll say I lied. I don't want to be a liar on top of everything."

Ruthie's heart was bursting. Slamming. Something was happening to her and maybe it was a heart attack but she didn't think so.

"Mom?"

Leverage. Lucas had something on her, but didn't he have more to lose? Wasn't she, right now, the most dangerous person? A woman with nothing to lose?

She'd confront him there. Surrounded by his crowd, he wouldn't want a scene. She'd make him come up with a story. She'd threaten to expose him. He hadn't officially sold it yet. Until money changed hands, until the check was cashed, he could take it back. Right there, at the party, he could tell Daniel that he'd changed his mind. If he refused she'd threaten to tell Daniel she had examined the painting and had doubts about it. Daniel would take her seriously. She had worked for Peter Clay.

Could she do that? Threaten and blackmail Lucas?

Why not? She'd done worse.

All she wanted was to wake up tomorrow and feel clean. She'd fix the eggs and toast and be able to look into her daughter's eyes for the first time this summer. How can you be present in your life if you're not really looking at the ones you love?

She realized that Jem was waiting.

She swallowed. "I'll take you."

"You?"

"Yes. I think I still have some pull over there."

"You're sure?"

Ruthie felt something clean wash through her at the hopeful look on Jem's face. "I can't think of anything I'd rather do," she said. Ah, a truth! She would take back the lies, one at a time.

55

DOE STOOD ON the back lawn of the Belfry, looking out at the party. It was an incredible success, exactly as Lark had envisioned.

Lark had instructed everyone to dress in an "almost color," and the lawn was awash in pale floaty dresses and beautiful shirts, blue lanterns hanging from the trees. The inflatables—pool toys and giant animals bobbing from compressed air—dotted the lawn and were tethered with bright ropes. The bouncy castle was ignored except for those who had consumed a few too many signature cocktails. There was vegan food and black cod and sushi, there was prosecco mixed with Aperol, and party favors were pareos from Calypso, tied with ribbons and stacked, ready to be handed out as people left for their cars.

It was nothing like a Belfry event, nothing at all. Ruthie never could have committed this much money to one party. She saw board members, but none of the usual local crowd. The question of whether these new glittery people would ever become a base of support for the museum was not considered. Doe could see Mindy in the crowd, beaming with the excitement of having a *New York*

Times photographer at the Belfry. Gloria was by her side, the only person dressed in glaring white.

The girl nobody could take their eyes off wore a long dress with embroidered flowers that seemed to only whisper the color apricot. Her hair was loose and golden, her feet in the creamy laced flat sandals that everyone was wearing this summer because Lark had been photographed in them. Doe had been the one to take the shot and post it.

Daniel was there, in off-white pants and a pale-blue shirt, standing with his Hamptons girlfriend, the TV journalist. Doe scanned the crowd and saw Catha at the food table with the scowling husband nobody liked, she couldn't remember his name, who was filling his plate with the lobster mac and cheese—weird, because she thought he was kosher. Nobody else was eating.

Arms slipped around her from behind. "Why are you hiding?" Lark asked in her ear.

"I don't recognize anyone. And you gave me the night off, remember?"

"Daddy hired the photographers so that you wouldn't have to work. He can be sweet, you know. In the last two days I think he invited everyone he ever ran into in his life. As usual, it's his party. Help me face it. You look positively gorg, by the way."

Doe had allowed Lark to buy her the dress. They'd searched and searched in the shops of East Hampton until Lark was satisfied. She pronounced the color exquisite—somewhere between iced butter and crème fraîche, she said. It fit Doe perfectly, having been altered by Lark's tailor. A fifties look, very Audrey in *Sabrina,* a tight bodice and a full skirt with hidden pockets in the folds. Lark had the tailor add them, remembering that Doe had said a dress with pockets was her ideal.

Doe allowed herself to be tugged. They walked out onto the lawn, arms around each other's waists, and waded into the crowd of posing people having the last fun of summer. So many photo ops for her Instagram. Not tonight. She would not take out her phone, not once, no matter who showed up.

"Oh my God, Alec Baldwin is here," Lark said.

"Lark!" Daniel beckoned.

"Oh, shit, the summons," Lark said. "Let's get it over with."

Catha had joined Mindy and Gloria, leaving Awful Husband to go back for seconds. Mindy had a look of concentration on her face that probably had to do with holding her stomach in.

Doe enjoyed the start of surprise on Catha's face when she saw her, arms linked with Lark. Mindy looked displeased, and Gloria, teeth clenched with the effort of being amusing, didn't notice anything at all.

This was enjoyable, more than enjoyable, an actual high, having board members focus on her as more than an afterthought, having them wonder why her arm was through Lark's, why Daniel knew her so well.

"Look around at this party," Daniel said. "Amazing. You can see that Lark is a visionary. I think she's going to do incredible things."

"Incredible," Mindy echoed. "The Belfry is transformed! It's like a breath of fresh air!"

If there was a cliché floating by, Mindy would always spear it and serve it up on a platter.

In her pocket, in an organza bag with a silver ribbon, she had the perfect present. She was waiting until the end to give it to Lark. How funny it was that she'd had it all along. *My father's watch,* she would say. *Sorry I don't have the box.*

56

RUTHIE AND JEM lurked at the edges of the party. They had un-derdressed. Beautiful young women and men drifted by in silky fabrics the color of moonlight on water, or a heat wave white-blue sky. Ruthie piled up the metaphors in her head as Jem seethed next to her, because Ruthie had forgotten the whole "dress code empyrean" thing, and Jem was wearing her Isabel Marant blue sweater. Ruthie herself was in a black tank and black capris, which unfortunately and exactly matched the wait staff uniforms. Three men had already handed her an empty glass. If it happened again she'd either throw it against a wall or bring it to the kitchen.

No one talked to them except Dodge, cheerful about the ex-alted response to his crazy menagerie and on his way to another party on Shelter Island. Ruthie glimpsed Daniel Mantis chatting with Mindy and Catha and stayed on the other side of the party, back under the trees. She hoped they would never know she was here. Tobie had gotten her in, saying no problem, she was going to get fired anyway.

Here they were, but where was Lucas?

The Peter Clay—her Peter Clay—was dramatically lit, visible in the closed museum. She watched the valets, lounging now. Everyone had arrived, even latecomers, and there was already a trickle of people leaving.

Jem scanned the crowd but did not move. Ruthie wondered why she had wanted so badly to come. She had suggested that Jem take a selfie she could Instagram at least, but Jem had vehemently snapped "Not yet" at the suggestion.

It must be a boy. Why else would Jem be here, taut and expectant, scanning the guests? Was it that boy who made her laugh? The one she had never mentioned again? Maybe one of the servers? Ruthie wanted to snatch Jem's phone, where all the answers lay. If only parents could get over this ethical thing and spy like a government.

Ruthie remembered that—to be fifteen, to be so intent on desire that you could believe with all your heart that just being seen by the object of your crush would be enough. Enough for everything else to fall away.

Just as she had felt, seeing Joe at Daniel Mantis's party at the beginning of summer.

She wasn't fifteen. It was no longer possible to be engulfed in desire, to be luminous with it, to use it as a beacon to draw your lover.

"Who is it?" Ruthie finally asked, unable to keep quiet. "Who are you looking for?"

"Nobody," Jem said. "God."

"You're looking for God?"

"Mom, stop."

Suddenly Lucas was there, fuming behind the wheel as the valet took too long to run up to his car. The valet opened the door and a blond woman in a flowered print dress got out.

"Somebody else didn't get the memo," Ruthie said, nudging Jem. Then she recognized the perfect pair of breasts, the tan. Doe's mother . . . Sherry? Shari. It didn't seem like Lucas to be kind enough to escort a mom to a party. She remembered back at the coffee shop, she'd left Lucas alone with Shari and sped to her car. Lucas had offered to buy Shari a muffin . . .

Jem focused intently on the pair. "Is that his date? She's old!" She had the incredulous tones of a teenager unable to believe that a middle-aged woman had the right to exist and wear stilettos.

"Not a date, I don't think," Ruthie said.

Lucas caught sight of them but quickly turned. Shari gave a pleased wave. Unlike Lucas, she seemed delighted to be at the party. Lucas stalked past, turning his head away and pretending not to see them.

"Let's go now, Mom? Please?"

"You said you didn't—"

"I know but can we please go now?"

"Just wait here for a minute, I have to talk to someone. Then we'll go. Promise!"

Ruthie hurtled across the grass, heading toward Lucas, who was now standing alone with a glass of champagne, surveying the crowd. A few yards away Shari was transfixed by a drunk man straddling an inflatable raptor.

She yanked Lucas behind a bobbing hyena. "Don't start," he said. "Just be cool, for once."

"We have to stop this now."

"Stop?" Lucas closed his eyes for a moment. "You need to stop. What are you doing here?"

"I saw the painting, you little shit! What's it doing at the Belfry?"

"Daniel has it on approval, he thought it would be a great idea to showcase it, so I said sure."

"You idiot!" she spat, and Lucas's eyes darkened. "Daniel Mantis? Don't you realize the kind of scrutiny this puts you—us—under? It's one thing to get it out of the country, but this is the stupidest way possible to sell it! Didn't you think of that?"

"Don't call me an idiot," Lucas said.

"You *are* an idiot! You pulled me into this—"

"Oh, please."

"Okay, it was my decision, I'm not blaming you for that. But I'm blaming you for this . . . recklessness. It will be in the *Times,* every curator in the country will want to see it!"

"Exactly! You're the idiot. You can't see how perfect it is. That horrible painting of Adeline, and Daniel owns it? It's going to be glorious. She'll see it everywhere!"

Ruthie stared at him, aghast. "This is some sort of freakish revenge thing for you? Is that it?"

"And what is it for you?"

Was it revenge? She had never thought of it that way. It had felt like necessity. Then again, she hadn't been thinking clearly. Of course it was revenge.

She was wrong. It drained out of her, all that stupid wasted effort of shaking her fists at a world where only beauty and money mattered. She didn't have to live in that world, even if it was right next door.

Ruthie let out a breath, a long exhalation. "I don't think I could hate anyone as much as you do."

"Says the woman with the ax."

"You have to cancel the sale. Tonight."

"I'm not going to do that."

"You are. You're going to go over there right now and tell Daniel that you changed your mind, that the painting has too much sentimental value."

"You're insane."

"I've got news for you. You don't own that painting. I do. It's just canvas and paint and a stretcher, and they all belong to me. Remember the word under the paint?"

"I know, that's the funny part."

"Don't you think if it's ever x-rayed they're going to wonder why it was underneath a portrait of his lover?"

"No. It's obvious. My old man was a shit!" Lucas drained his champagne. "Okay, so you're pissed. I recognize that. But is it worth going to jail for? If you confess, I'll just say you sold me the painting. Who wouldn't believe it? Poor Ruthie, out for revenge. You're the one with the motive."

"You are despicable."

"Who the fuck do you think you are? Do you really think Daniel will believe you and not me? You're a nobody. You're a middle-aged woman without a job or a husband. Who's going to give a fuck?"

She walked away, over the lawn, back toward the Belfry. His words didn't touch her. She was too busy thinking. She had miscalculated. He wasn't afraid of what she could do.

Big mistake.

"Where have you been?" Jem pulled at her arm. "Can we go now?"

"Look, they're bringing out the cake. Get us a couple of slices, okay?" Ruthie looked over at the museum. If she didn't do this now, tonight, she'd never get the chance again. "We'll take them and leave. I'll be right back, promise!"

Jem's protest floated away in the gathering dusk as Ruthie hurried across the blue lawn. The valets were busy now. People were walking to their cars, some of the women shaking out their sarongs and throwing them around their bare shoulders. The temperature was dropping.

She stopped. Through the window she saw Joe Bloom cross the room and examine the painting, Daniel Mantis behind him.

Daniel gestured; Joe nodded. He moved from one spot to another, looking, looking. Up close and far away. The way a curator looks. He picked up the painting and examined the back.

It was then that Ruthie remembered what she should have remembered a month ago, that she had told Joe that Peter had sent her a box of supplies from the studio. She had asked him about selling a luxury item. How could she have forgotten that?

He had picked up her hand. He had seen blue on her finger.

She couldn't swallow, couldn't breathe.

Joe walked back to Daniel in the middle of the room. They spoke while Ruthie tried to limn each tiny movement of two men standing in a room, talking.

What was she doing, standing here in the dark with her mouth open.

Just continuing on her criminally stupid path. It had to stop.

57

IT WAS LATE, and the party was dying. Dying not out of inertia, but from the sweet exhaustion of a good time at the end of summer. The valets were running now because after lingering long at the party everyone was suddenly in a hurry, the fringes of their gifted pareos fluttering in a quickening breeze.

Daniel had left, the celebrities had gone, the board ladies had followed, and the last string of duty had been cut. Lark and Doe slipped away across the lawn to be alone. They lay on benches and looked up into the shadows of the trees. The blue-bulbed lanterns had been lit, and they swayed with every gust, flashing through the dark green like shots of phosphorescence in a watery world.

Their hands occasionally brushed each other's as they reached for their champagne flutes in tandem and sipped. The champagne was ice-cold and filled with the same radiant fizz as the stars in the night sky over their heads. Doe felt herself floating in a deeply pleasurable state of intoxication, where tomorrow was far in the distance and summer was spinning on.

Lark tipped her head back. "I'm delirious," she said. "Usually I get drunk at a party, or bored, or I feel useless. But tonight I feel as though everything in my life that's wrong has been solved. Like I'm a kid again, and my nanny says tomorrow is a new day."

"It's a teachable moment," Doe said.

"Failure is how we learn."

"Good job!"

They giggled.

Lark sat up to face Doe. Her smile was slow. She touched Doe's eyebrow, the one with the scar she said she got playing lacrosse, only it was from tripping over a pool chair to get to Shane. Blood in her eyes, blood in the water as she fought her way to him.

"It's all because of you," she said. "You encouraged me. This feels so right. You said I could shape the job to my life, and you were right. You said I can do anything. Do you know what a gift that is?"

"Well. Not everything. You're not a farmer."

"You wench," Lark said. "Thanks for bringing up my worst failure."

"It's not a failure," Doe said. "You learned things that you're going to use."

"I like how I am when I'm with you," Lark said. "It's like . . . having someone believe in you. That's totally a new thing for me."

"What are you talking about, ethereal it-girl Lark Mantis?"

"I don't want to be a hashtag. That stupid *seekrit-hamptons* account made me into some sort of icon of vacuousness."

"Hey, it made you into a brand."

"Please. It made me into a joke."

"No, it—"

"Daddy's right, it's time I got serious."

"Okay, let's get serious. It's time for your present." Doe sat up.

"Oh, you didn't have to. But, hooray!"

Doe reached into the pocket of her dress and pulled out the present. "It's the thing I love the most," she said. "It belonged to my father."

Lark unwrapped it carefully from the tissue paper, smoothing the silver satin ribbon. She withdrew the watch and held it up.

"For the girl who has more than everything," Doe said.

"Oh, honey. Are you sure? This is amazing. It's a Patek Philippe!" Lark turned it over in her hand. "Vintage?"

"Vintage."

"It's gorgeous. But . . . I can't accept your father's watch."

"You have to. It's the best thing I have to give."

"No, the best thing is that you wanted to."

Doe leaned over and fastened the watch on Lark's wrist. "You see? Perfect." Doe was taking a chance, but she wasn't worried. Even if Lucas were to see it, he wouldn't say anything. He wouldn't dare.

"I love it so much." Lark took the ribbon and wound it around Doe's ring finger. "Will you marry me?"

Doe looked down at her finger, at the silver ribbon twisted around it, two girls playing fairy tale. "Only if your father gives us a maid as a wedding present. You're a slob."

A shadow passed over Lark's face. As though Doe had hurt her? Doe saw it happen, how the shadow grew and overtook the mood. "What is it?"

"Is it so funny, to think that I'm serious about you?"

Doe felt the precipice, ahead in the dark. There seemed to be some sort of call-and-response needed here, something not in her skill set.

Even as Doe's brain was trying to move fast enough to solve this, the moment was flying by, and she was losing ground with every passing second. Soon whatever she said wouldn't be enough. Doe was usually so adept at reading currents of emotion, of want and need, and tucking herself into them. How had she missed this?

Lucas walked across the lawn, heading toward them. The woman next to him stumbled in the grass—ridiculous shoes, Doe had no patience for women who wore stilettos to a lawn party—and she saw it was Shari.

"Shit." She jumped up, knocking over the champagne, and heard the tinkle of breaking glass. Lark started, but Doe was already moving, ignoring the sharp pain in the sole of her foot, heading off Lucas if she could. The prick. She should have seen it coming.

Shari's mouth opened in an O of exaggerated happiness that didn't fool Doe one bit.

"I found her alone at your place," Lucas said. "I stopped by to see if you needed a lift."

Shari's uneasy smile widened. "Lucas got pissed that I took so long to get ready. But we're here!"

"Doe, you're bleeding," Lark said, coming up. She leaned down. "We need a bandage or something."

"Oh, angel!" Shari cried when she saw the blood. Lark looked up sharply, alert to the intimacy in Shari's voice.

Doe looked down. Lark was on one knee, risking the magnificent embroidery of her dress. She felt the warmth of Lark's hand on her foot and saw the stain on the hem of Lark's dress, bright red. She felt nausea overtake her like a wave, and she had to close her eyes, which made her dizzy. The beautiful dress was ruined. But what did it matter, since Lark could replace it? What did anything matter, really?

"Lark, this is my mother, Shari Callender," she said. "Mom, this is my friend Lark Mantis."

Lark unfolded to her full five feet eleven inches. She and Lucas stood almost shoulder to shoulder, twin American gods, the stiff breeze ruffling their blond hair and fluttering their silks. Never had Doe felt shorter. Darker. Runtier. Brought up on diet soda and factory chicken and bottled salad dressing.

What did it matter.

Shari was talking, Lark was nodding, Lucas looked around for a waiter. Lark signaled and a tray appeared. Shari accepted the champagne by thanking the server profusely, as if he'd delivered a cash bonus, took a long sip, and belched out a "Delicious!" Doe felt herself shrink smaller still. Shari was loving every second of the fancy party while being utterly clueless about what was happening in front of her eyes. In Shari World, you smiled at the servers, you drained a glass of champagne and said "Ooooo," and if someone gave you cake that was delicious you ate every bite and then pressed your fork into the crumbs and licked them off the tines. You cleaned your plate, swayed to music, called a big house a mansion. *Look,* Lucas's smirk said, *you come from people who know nothing.*

There is nothing wrong with those things, she wanted to say.

Lark's manners held throughout as Shari chattered about arriving from Hollywood, not the fun one, the one in Florida, about looking for work, about what a hard worker Doe was, how she was always crazy for art—had her friends ever seen her artwork, her photographs?—and Lark found cake and seats at a table. Lucas tried to drift away but Lark firmly and pointedly noted what a gentleman he was to keep Shari company while she had a word with Doe.

Doe allowed herself to be steered (limping now, her foot hurting like a mother, ha) toward the museum, into the gallery where Adeline regarded them with brittle amusement, an Adeline with wrinkles and sags and a thick line of dark plum along her soft jaw. She waited for Lark to start. She'd seen her happy, sad, sleepy, pissed, nonchalant, drunk, tender, eager, lustful, breezy, sullen, asleep and awake and in the shower, but she had never seen her like this.

"Tell me you have two mothers," Lark said.

"What?"

Lark shoved her. "Tell me."

"I don't!"

"So there's no Katherine Callender from Minneapolis? There's only Shari from Hollywood-not-the-fun-one? No Katherine, who studied ballet and never got over it? No mining money? No family ranch in Upper Michigan? No Mary McFadden originals collection?"

"No."

Lark shoved her again and Doe went stumbling back and almost fell.

"Okay! I'm Dora Callender from Florida," Doe said. Never had she been so far from tears. "I didn't go to Reed. I went to Miami Dade College and worked my way through. My mother is a train wreck. I have one sister who lives in Pensacola, who used to be a speed addict. My little brother drowned when he was four because I left him alone while I ate cereal and watched TV. We all have different fathers. I don't know mine, he left before I was born. He was either Brazilian or Dominican because my mother is an idiot who thinks anyone who speaks Spanish is either Cuban or something else. I made myself up, okay?"

Lark shook her head.

"Okay, I'm sorry my mother crashed your party. Lucas is a dick. He wanted to embarrass me. I can get her out of here—"

"You think I'm angry because of your mother? I don't even know her! You are such an asshole!" Lark turned away. Doe saw her reflection in the glass of the window, a ghost Lark that wavered and threatened to dissolve. "Don't you realize you just blew it all apart! You were the only good thing in my life and you ruined it!"

"I'm the only good thing in your life? Jesus, Lark! You have everything you want, everything you need. You live in a twenty-million-dollar house!"

"Thirty million."

"And you just had this job handed to you by your father. You think you got it because of your experience? Because you *interviewed well*?"

Lark jerked her head away. Doe watched her chest rise and fall.

"You don't get it, Doe. You don't get that wealth is a neutral. It doesn't *bestow* anything on you except nice stuff and staff and yes, opportunities. You have to look for goodness just like everybody else. It's not easier or harder. Maybe it's harder, okay? Maybe we don't have the tools to really see things, because no one is real with us. But I thought you were real! I thought we were *true*." Was Lark drunk? Her voice wobbled, and she scraped a hand hard across her mouth, as if to wipe away a kiss.

"You wouldn't have given me more than two seconds if you knew who I really was," Doe said.

"You're right," Lark said. "You know, I can spot a climber. I knew that's what you were. That was okay. I saw that you were turned on to all of it—my father and the house. I didn't mind, because I get it, it's a lot to take in, take on. But you don't just exaggerate, you fabricate a whole story. The *details* of what you told me! It was a fantastic construction, let me tell you. You are really a player and I got played. I fell for all of it. I never fall for it."

"You fall for everything!" Doe cried. "It's what I like about you!"

"Shut up," Lark said. She struggled to take off the watch, then tossed it to Doe, who almost dropped it. "Take your fake watch and get out of my life."

"Go ahead, then," Doe said. "Add this to the list. Just another thing you throw away. A shoe with a scuff mark. A bloodstained six-thousand-dollar dress. A shirt that is just the wrong shade of pink after all. A little too close to that tacky breast cancer ribbon color—"

"Fuck you."

"Lark. We can't just *stop*!"

"I can stop if I hate somebody's *shoes,*" Lark said. She looked weary. "Go. You're fucking bleeding on the gallery floor. And by the way? You're fired."

58

YOU CAN'T STEAL *a painting if it's yours. You can't steal a paint-ing if it's yours. It's not a forgery if you don't sell it. It's not a forgery if you don't sell it.*

Over and over, she told herself this.

She walked into the service door of the museum. She knew this place as well as her own home. She knew that Vivian was always the last to go, after the caterers had packed up, after every car had left, one last check and then set the alarm, but before that, with caterers in and out of the side door to the kitchen, dressed like a server, she could walk right in.

She could just see a corner of the kitchen, where servers were moving fast, packing up glasses. Dodge's crew was scarfing down the leftovers.

Empty flat pizza boxes were piled by the door near open plas-tic containers of used glasses. She grabbed an empty box from on top of the pile and walked out into the hallway, then toward the front gallery.

Lark and Doe had left. She'd seen them in here talking, their heads close together. Then Lark had run out the service door

straight toward the parking lot. Ruthie had watched her peel out
of the parking lot fast and screech a right turn to the west.

The gallery lights were out. She couldn't hear the party at all.
Outside the dark window there were only a few groups of people
on the lawn in the fading light. The trees danced with a sudden
gust of wind and a woman pressed her skirt down against her
thighs, laughing.

She could see the painting, bluish and spooky. Adeline's green
eyes looking at her.

She put down the box and crossed to the painting. She lifted it
off the wall.

It's not stealing if you made it.

Carefully she placed the painting in the box, as though it were
a real Peter Clay and not a worthless Ruth Beamish. She would
text Lucas that it was gone and instruct him to tell Daniel and
Lark that he'd changed his mind. What could he do but comply?

She walked out, through the same door, heading for where
she'd parked, in the spaces saved for employees. She placed the
box on the roof while she reached for her keys.

"I've been looking for you."

Ruthie jumped and dropped her keys as Joe stepped forward.
She might as well have been wearing the black mask of a cartoon
criminal, a striped shirt, stubble on her cheeks. Caught.

"I saw you on the lawn with Lucas before," Joe said. "I thought
you left. Did you see the painting?"

She nodded.

"What do you think?"

"I think . . . it's . . ." Her voice trailed away.

"Classic Clay, right?" He strolled closer. "Quite a find. Do you
remember the show at MoMA, those exquisite drawings of her?
This seems to nullify them. Why would he paint her like this?"

"He painted all women like this."

"Not all. Just the commissioned work."

"I could never understand why Peter did the things he did."

"Daniel called Adeline and told her about it. She was surprised. She didn't remember the painting. She asked me to check it out. Strange how it popped up."

"What do you mean?" Ruthie bent down to pick up her keys, allowing her hair to conceal her face. "Paintings have a way of doing that, don't they? Popping up?"

Joe shoved his hands in his pockets. "I was trying to remember. Maybe you can. The year Peter got divorced."

"I don't know, maybe '96? Why?"

"I was his dealer then. It was a complicated couple of years."

"I left the studio before that."

"I remember when you left, yeah. Because I wished you were still there. We had to do a complete inventory of everything, drawings, sketches, paintings. The settlement's value was based on all the unsold paintings in both studios, Sag Harbor and New York. This wasn't in the inventory. I'd remember this."

Ruthie leaned against the car and crossed her arms. She tried to look interested, as though she was following the action in an anecdote about people she didn't know.

"Why would Simone conceal it?" Joe asked.

"I don't know."

"They split everything down the middle during the divorce. Which means, I think, that since this was painted before the divorce, technically half of it belongs to Peter's estate and half to Simone's."

"Adeline owns half the painting." *How could they have been so stupid?* They were the most inept criminals in criminality. "So it's not Lucas's to sell, then," Ruthie said.

"I'm not a lawyer, but no. There's no paperwork, so he can't prove it was a gift to her from Peter. And logically, why would it be? In any case Lucas is morally obligated to inform his stepmother and offer it to her first. That's what I told Daniel. He wasn't happy. Or maybe the word *morally* confused him. The thing is . . ."

"The thing is?"

"What do you think? You know his work as well as I do."

"What do you mean?"

"The painting. Something. That's why I wanted to ask you." He shrugged. "Lucas—do you know him well?"

"Not really."

"Me neither. But I did know Simone. She was not an easy person, and God knows at the end she hated Peter with every cell of her body, but . . . she was honest. A no-bullshit person. She either concealed the painting—which I can't quite believe—or forgot she had it, it was overlooked, which is beyond comprehension. Lucas said the storage unit was rented when she moved from Sag Harbor. So at that point, she knew she had it. So why throw it in a storage unit? She was out of money a few years later. She left Lucas almost nothing."

Ruthie leaned against the car to conceal the fact that her legs were shaking. "Are you saying it could be a fake? That Lucas might know it's a fake?"

"I'm not saying anything. I just wouldn't say that he's automatically trustworthy. I know Adeline has had trouble with him. And this . . . could hurt her."

"You want to protect her."

"I'm used to protecting the Clay family. I did it for years. I still do consulting work for the foundation. When you're someone's dealer, you're their best friend and their confidant and their attack dog. So, habit."

His gaze moved, absently, to the leaves fluttering.

She needed to say something. She needed to say, *This has nothing to do with me.* She needed to lie. She needed to take the painting and run.

A low, distant rumble of thunder. "It's going to storm," he said.

59

"I'M NOT HAVING as much fun as I thought I would," Shari said.

Doe sat in the grass. It was dusk now, the sun behind the trees, a few fireflies flitting, turning off and turning on. The party was just about over. "Yeah. Time to go."

"Lucas dumped me here and took off with a blonde. I mean, I'm not mad, I get it, I'm not his date or anything, but he didn't introduce me to anyone and the *way* he took off was kind of rude. I know he's a friend of yours, so. Sorry."

"He's not a friend." Doe collapsed backward and looked up at the sky, an inverted bowl of murk, like diner gravy spilling down onto her head.

Starting over again would be exhausting.

"How's your foot?"

"Fine."

"I hope you put cream on it or something. Listen, I knew your girlfriend was rich, but this is ridiculous. There's, like, crab puffs and caviar."

"She's not my girlfriend."

"And Lucas isn't your friend. So why are you here?"

"Mom, do me a favor. Don't talk."

"I wore the wrong thing, didn't I."

"It doesn't matter. I'll drive us home." Doe looked up through the trees for the moon, but couldn't find it. Clouds covered the sky. The leaves were making a scratchy sound, as if the edges were already dry. A sudden strong gust fluttered the edge of her dress. Weather blowing in from the sea.

"The girl was pretty," Shari said. "The blonde. I mean the one Lucas was with. She looked really young, though."

Doe had seen Jem, wall-flowering on the edges of the party. She sat up. "What was she wearing? The blonde?"

"I don't know, a blue top? It was a pretty color. Everybody else here is so boring. No color at all."

"Did you see where they went?"

Shari waved a hand. "That way. Toward that bouncy castle."

Doe sprang up. "She's fifteen, Mom."

"Fifteen?"

"Ruthie's daughter."

"That nice Ruthie?" Shari stood up, too.

Doe looked toward the castle. A blast of wind lifted it off the ground at least a foot. The ropes shuddered. She remembered back in his studio, Dodge saying something about wind, about what the regulations were. He had the safest crew in New York, he said. Yeah, but they actually had to be there. Lark was supposed to keep an eye on things, direct them. She was the curator, she was the one to keep them on schedule. And she was gone. They were scheduled to dismantle everything fifteen minutes ago.

A seagull cried, one of those annoying sharp yelps.

Did seagulls cry at night? Or was it a scream?

60

THE TREES SHOOK like hula dancers. Down the lawn, a napkin flew into the air. The inflatable animals were whipping side to side. One of the enormous pool toys barrel-rolled free and a woman shrieked in happy fright.

"The sculptures," Ruthie said. "They have to be deflated. This wind is gusting."

"Where's Lark?" Joe asked.

"Gone. And the crew is eating cake."

Then a blur of someone running hard across the lawn. Doe? She vaulted inside the bouncy castle.

"I'll get the crew," Joe said, and turned and ran.

Behind her, the slap of running footsteps. Time slowed down as Shari ran toward her, carrying her pink heels in both hands. Calamity approaching, slowed down to the pace of a royal procession, Ruthie trying to read Shari's face, her open mouth, ready to speak.

"Ruthie!" She stopped in front of her and put a hand on her arm. She was panting, almost doubled over. "Jem . . . the bouncy castle! We think she's in there with Lucas. Mom-to-mom, you should maybe check."

"With Lucas?"

Now her mind speeded up in a flutter of images. Jem, expectant, every muscle quivering, staring at the entrance to the party. *He makes me laugh. Lucas is going to be there. Is that his date?*

Things went white.

She took off, running flat out. She felt a raindrop, she felt the sudden, surprising strength of a wind gust. The bouncy castle strained at its ropes, and one side lifted completely off the ground.

The events of the night now seemed inevitable, like the end of a play. She would pay. She would pay. The knowledge seared her with each thudding footstep, the grass slick under her feet. Ruthie now clearly heard someone screaming. *Jem.*

"Holy fuck!" someone yelled.

Another gust and the house rose, tilting, the wind now underneath it, lifting it, the last three ropes straining.

There was no breath in her lungs to shout. There was too much distance between her and the bright-pink inflatable prison, and panic and running had squeezed her lungs tight. The unfolding nightmare of this.

The house was now a good five feet in the air, and Lucas slid out, hitting the ground with a shout of aggrieved pain. She saw Jem's face, white and scared, holding on at the opening as the house bounced.

Ruthie skidded to a halt underneath. Jem looked down into her face. Their eyes locked. Ruthie shook her head hard. She held up both hands to say stop. The castle was too high, she needed to wait for the gust to die.

Behind her daughter, Doe's hands were on Jem's shoulders, her mouth by her ear. Someone, one of the crew, threw himself at the rope and tried to grab it as it whipped out of reach. Joe was next to him, straining to catch it.

The wind flattened for a moment, the house tilting closer to the ground.

Ruthie screamed a scream that could wake up a slumbering world. "Jump!"

Doe let go of her shoulders and Jem leaped out, in the air for less time than Ruthie could even cry or pray, and then she was on the ground, landing on her feet, legs bent, even sticking the landing for a moment, her daughter, her baby, her beauty, her treasure, her heart, her love, her life, miraculously summoning up three years of gymnastic training before she got bored and too tall, then tilting onto the ground and Ruthie was there almost in time to catch her. Holding her so tightly, sobbing into her hair, saying *It's okay it's okay it's okay.*

And then the divots came loose and the house took off in a great galumphing heave, ropes swinging like Tarzan. Up, up in the sky, fifteen feet, twenty feet, and a wisp of twirling fabric drifted out of the opening, pirouetting like a tiny dancer as it fell so softly on the lawn. Jem's bra.

And Doe was still inside.

Everyone looking up into the darkening sky, breaths held. People shouting *holy shit,* people screaming. The castle tilted past a tree, its branches scraping the bottom, past the museum grounds, riding another gust.

Joe and the crew frozen on the lawn, looking up, and Shari screaming.

And they all saw it then, something incredible, a blur of almost color, a dress made of light, a cloud, an angel, a girl falling through the sky.

61

YOU WOULD EXPECT Shari to be the type of person who would shatter. You'd expect hysteria, you'd expect appeals to Jesus.

She was calm. She spoke urgently but politely to the paramedics. She sat in the chair in the emergency room, bent double, her face against her knees. Ruthie kept her hand flat on Shari's back. When she sat up again her face was pale. Ruthie recognized a mother who had tightened every string, screwed every bolt, to hold herself together because she was coming apart.

"One day I was upset about something," she said to Ruthie. One tear trailed down her cheek. "What was it, I don't know, probably money, it was always money. And I said out loud, *What's going to happen to us, Dora?* She was, I don't know, maybe four, maybe five? And she piped up from the floor where she was playing. *We're all going to die, Mommy.* She was always a no-bullshit kid."

"I know," Ruthie said. But she didn't know. The truth was she'd never gotten to know Doe very well.

None of them had seen Doe land. Within minutes they heard the sirens, even after everyone seemed to be running in circles.

The paramedics arrived so fast no one at the party had time to find her. She had landed in Laura and Sam Beecham's pool, right on top of one of the enormous inflatables that had blown into their yard. Earlier in the evening and with great irritation (it had almost hit their dog), Sam had wrestled it into the pool and tied it to the ladder. Sam was an orthopedist. He was the first one to reach Doe. He had called 911.

"Can you call her girlfriend? She'd want to know. Lark Mantis." Shari's jaw wobbled, and her teeth began to chatter. "Doe has been staying over there in East Hampton all summer. They'll want to know, right?"

Ruthie had already tried to call Mike, but he wasn't answering. She didn't have Adeline's cell number in her phone. Finally she did the only thing she could think of. She texted Joe.

> At hospital no news yet. Jem is ok. Not even a sprain. Can you tell Adeline and Mike what happened? Mike not answering. Also Doe's girlfriend is Lark Mantis. Can you alert them? Thx

The text came back immediately, he would do it, he would come to the hospital if she needed him, how was Jem, could he do anything.

She stared down at the text. He was the last person she could ask to help carry her through this night. When she'd run to the car to drive Shari to the hospital, the painting had been gone from the car roof. Who else but Joe would have taken it?

The story would unravel. The forgery, the theft, Lucas. Tomorrow would happen. The sun always does come up. She would realize that the fear and panic she'd lived with through most of August had been nothing.

But that was tomorrow. Tonight Jem had leaped into thin air and survived. Now she sat next to her, her knees up under her chin, her face pale, her jaw working. Something was wrong with Jem. If Shari was holding herself still, Jem was frozen, except for her jaw. Everything in life had funneled down to this, sitting in a plastic chair in a hospital waiting room as minutes passed, each one ticking closer to a reality no one wanted to face.

She could feel time move in her pocket. When she had caught Jem after the jump and held her while Doe had flown away, while everyone had screamed and shouted, while she had gasped and shuddered, she'd put one hand down on the grass and she had found Lewis Berlinger's watch, right there, as though waiting for her.

How it got there she didn't know, and she never would. She would take it as the miracle it truly was. She must have been mistaken, in her distraction. She must have worn it to work earlier in the summer. The band had always been loose, it had slipped off her wrist. Finding it again . . . it shouldn't have happened to her, something that lucky, not to that frantic, pathetic creature focused on something so stupid. A house. A house instead of a child.

The automatic doors opened and Mike and Adeline rushed in. When Jem saw her father she started to cry. He ran and she stood and hurtled herself in his arms.

She had never seen Mike look so helpless.

"It's all my fault, Daddy!" Jem's face looked like her baby face, as though it had compressed into a tight ball of misery, mouth open, cheeks red and slick.

"No, dear," Adeline said. "It is not your fault."

The authority in Adeline's voice! It filled the room, the air, their bodies!

Ruthie wanted to kneel at this woman's feet and thank her, because Adeline had spoken and stopped Jem's tears.

She put her hand on the top of Jem's head, cupping it. "It is everyone's fault *but* yours," Adeline added. "You hear me?"

The inner doors to the ER swished open and a woman strode out, dressed in scrubs and clogs. The authority said *doctor* and the gaze was on them. They knew, and they stood. Ruthie grabbed Shari's hand, and her hand was squeezed so tight she felt her bones come together.

"Mrs. Callender?" The doctor reached out and put her hand

on Shari's shoulder, and the humanity of the gesture telegraphed the worst news so clearly that Shari, for the first time that night, cried out. Her knees started to go and the doctor hurriedly said, "She's okay," even as she helped ease her backward into the chair.

62

THE RIDE HOME felt so long. It was four in the morning. Gray light. Sunday morning, and the rain had stopped, and the world was slumbering. A season was turning.

"It wasn't your fault," Ruthie said. "Adeline is right."

"Doe jumped in to save me," Jem said. "She saw what was happening and she jumped in."

Ruthie knew what every parent knew. She was in the perfect place to have this conversation: the car. It was the place teenagers told their secrets, because it was the place they did not have to meet their parents' eyes.

"What was happening?" she asked. "I mean, before."

Jem jerked her head and looked out the window. "I liked Lucas," she said.

"So he was the boy."

"Yeah. I know he was too old, okay?"

Ruthie's hands tightened on the wheel. She was grateful for the past tense, but she would kill him anyway. She had a whole list of crimes on her sorry docket, why not add one more?

"Were you . . . seeing him?"

"No! He came to the farm stand to see me. And I saw him a few times. Not a date or anything! Just, like, walks around Greenport. He'd buy me ice cream or whatever. We texted a lot. Tonight I just wanted . . . I thought . . . I don't know what I thought. But I started it. I said, Let's go into the castle before they take it down. I just wanted to be alone with him. We went in together and we just sort of fell, the way you do in a bouncy castle. He said it was like a waterbed. And so we kissed and stuff."

And stuff. What a wide load of possibility in that. Ruthie thought of the bra, revolving in the wind.

"He doesn't care about me," Jem said. "He didn't even try to help. He pushed past me, Mom. He jumped out. And then when Doe fell, did you see? He just took off. He didn't check to see if I was okay or if she was okay. He just left! How could he do that, Mommy? How could somebody do that?"

Should she drop off Jem, drive directly to Adeline's, and kill him now?

She thought of the wild turkeys in Orient. Those prehistoric creatures, noble and hulky. They took their own time. They meandered across the road with majesty and purpose, with elastic, nodding necks. They did not scurry, they did not hesitate, no matter how many cars honked. They owned their own road. Squirrels were common roadkill. Deer. Turkeys? Never.

The secret was to let the monster bearing down on you know that you had a path and you were sticking to it. The secret was to take your time.

She parked the car by the playhouse. The pool glinted an unreal blue.

Jem got out, hugging herself. There was a slight chill in the air, the first chill of fall. Ruthie's phone buzzed. It was Joe.

Doe?

She's ok. Staying overnight at hospital.

She waited, her fingers in the air.

Thank you.

She stared hard at the ellipses on the phone that told her he was typing. They weren't even a mile apart. Holding their phones and not knowing what to say. The dots disappeared—he erased something. Appeared again.

I'm so glad. Btw I delivered your pizza.

. . .

Sleep tight.

She didn't know what that meant but it seemed he was telling her to go to sleep. Which was good, because now they were so exhausted that they could barely walk. They changed into pajamas. They were reckless and did not floss.

"Will you sleep in my bed?" Jem asked. Blue smudges under her eyes.

Ruthie drew up Carole's fine cotton blanket. In the dimness she saw the streak of tears on Jem's face, steady, silver, dripping down cheek, rolling off chin, down her neck.

"I had sex with him, Mommy," she said.

The softness of Carole's blanket. The exquisite comfort of the sheet under her hand as she smoothed it over Jem. Ruthie was wide awake now.

"Okay," she said.

"I just wanted to connect with somebody," Jem said. "I wanted a boyfriend. I know that's stupid."

"Not stupid. Did he force you?"

"No. I wanted to."

Ruthie let out her breath slowly, so Jem wouldn't hear it.

"I figured okay, this is my time. Then years from now, even if I'm being a total idiot, even if I regret it, even if he's way too old, it will just become part of my story, like what hospital I was born in or what age I was when I got my ears pierced."

"Uh-huh."

"I sort of let him think I wasn't a virgin."

"Mmm."

"But it was so *wrong*!" Jem began to sob.

Ruthie got out of bed for the tissue box. It took effort not to rend it asunder. She got back in bed and handed Jem a tissue.

"Did you ask him to stop?"

"No. It wasn't like that."

"I'm sorry, I have to ask this, did you use—"

"Yeah. He had one. But I don't think he . . . um, finished. I just didn't think there would be so much *pushing* involved. To you know, get it done, I guess? I just waited for it to be over. All of a sudden I wasn't into it at all. And that was the worst. And that's when I noticed the castle really tilting. I could feel the wind underneath it. He didn't notice at first, because . . . you know. And I got panicky and he told me to be quiet." Jem put her hands over her face. "He told me to be quiet! Like I didn't matter!"

The story came out in shuddered bursts now. Ruthie handed her one tissue after another. "Then he realized what was happening and he got scared. We felt it lift. And the next thing I knew he was pulling up his pants and running for the door. He kept slipping and falling, it was almost funny. Only it wasn't. I think that's when Doe crawled in. She smacked him really hard. Right in the face."

Score one for Doe. She owed her Jem's life, and now this. Flowers weren't enough, a basket from Locavoracious, nothing was enough except a trunk full of gold.

"And he just jumped out and left us! I was hanging on so hard, and Doe told me I had to time a jump and I would have to let go. I said I couldn't and she said I could. I looked down and saw you yelling *jump,* and Doe yelled *now,* and I jumped. And then she blew away. I was on the ground and she was in the air. And he . . . was running for his *car.*"

Ruthie held her, rocking her, but Jem sat up straight.

"You have to promise not to tell Daddy."

"I can't promise that, honey."

"Mom, just listen. It will break up him and Adeline. You know it will."

Of course it would.

"It just feels like . . . with everything . . . somebody should be happy. If I was the reason they broke up, that would be just sort of awful, you know?"

"But you aren't the reason, Lucas is," Ruthie said.

Jem gave her a look through her tears that clearly said *Give me a break*.

"But if they do get married, you're going to have to see him, at least sometimes. You'll be sort of . . . family."

A look came over Jem's face then that gave Ruthie a different picture of her daughter. The strong person she would become. No. Already was. "Not family."

"I don't know, sweetie."

"Please, Mom!"

"Let me sleep on it. It's time for bed now. It's time for sleep. We can talk more in the morning."

Murmuring, she drew up the covers again. In the moonlight she placed her head close on the same pillow. She whispered in Jem's hair. *Not your fault, baby, not your fault, Doe is fine, everything will be okay.* Still whispering, she felt the moment Jem slid into sleep. She lifted on one elbow to watch her. The moon was so bright.

Despite all of it, this terrible, terrible night, she felt the bright presence of hope.

Pool toys and fortunate landings and the light of the moon. Miracles abounding.

63

EVERYTHING HURT, AND all they gave her was extra-strong ibu-profen. A torn ligament in her knee, two bruised ribs from hitting a branch on the way down (which, apparently, was lucky because it broke the fall). She had landed like a circus performer, the doc-tor said approvingly. Feet first. Doe had no memory of hitting the pool or what came after until the ambulance. The last thing she remembered was running across the lawn, jumping in the castle, punching Lucas, telling Jem to jump, and then . . . liftoff.

Somewhere along the way she'd lost Lucas's watch. She had put it in her pocket and now it was gone.

Nothing lost that was hers. Nothing broken.

Lark had not come. She had not called, or texted.

Doe swung her legs over the bed. "You need rest," the nurses all said, and then they woke you up every fifteen fucking minutes to check your whatevers. Now it was the next day. Shari had gone for coffee and breakfast. The relief of her absence was something, anyway. She had a crashing headache but it wasn't from injuries, it was from Shari, talking, making plans. Doe would be released as soon as the doctor came. The doctor would be here soon they kept saying. That was two hours ago.

The bouncy castle was front-page news. It was THE BIG BOUNCE in the *New York Post* and MANTIS BASH CRASH in the *Daily News*. She wouldn't want to be Lark at the breakfast table this morning. It was only a matter of time before they blamed her lack of experience for the disaster.

Doe was fighting a great tug, that embarrassing, savage need of every dumpee to have the last conversation. Even though you knew the last one had already taken place. *One more,* you cried. There was always more to say and even more to take back.

She kept replaying Lark's line in her head, that the privileged had to look for goodness just like everybody else. Wasn't that just like Lark, to think that everybody looked for goodness? Doe never had. She had looked for the opposite. So she could be ready.

She would never have the last conversation. She would not be able to explain, to sum up what made her so broken, to explain what it's like when you're wired to feel every innocence that was lost.

She'd have to learn to be a better person. Was that something you could learn? Was Shari finally right about something other than laundry? Could she forget the tampon in her nose, and remember the tuna sandwich?

The last thing Shari had said to her was "Phoenix." With no job and no money, they had nowhere else to go but to her aunt. Shari was going to wait until it was later and then call the odious Belinda. It would be hell, but for a girl who had always cultivated options, Doe had run out.

Doe mapped the route on her phone. Turned out there were a thousand ways to get to Phoenix, basically. Despite Shari's pleas for "scenic stops," Kansas City barbecue or New Orleans or the St. Louis arch, Doe was headed for a straight line down superhighways. When you blow town, you blow town.

"I read somewhere that the next thing that's going to go is

water," Shari had said. "And isn't it like a desert there already? I'm sure Phoenix knows what it's doing, though."

"Yeah," Doe said.

"They have museums there. I looked it up. And fancy hotels. With concierges. Spas! We'll get killer jobs. We won't have to stay with Belinda long."

Doe lay back down again, weighted by her mother's buoyancy. She had been raised by a child.

The luck of the exile: You get to choose where to go. Well, not if you're leaving Syria. But if you're a pretty girl with a good brain, a dependable car, and $422.15 in your bank account, sure. She'd heard on a podcast that most Americans couldn't find $400 if they had an emergency. She was $22.15 ahead of the game.

Jem and Ruthie had come earlier (waking her up—after this experience she would sleep for days) and she had endured Ruthie's weepy thanks and Jem's tears. Ruthie had kissed her on the forehead and said she was her friend for life. Which was a first, for Doe.

Then Ruthie had left to find Shari, who was out in the hallway somewhere, and Jem had looked at her miserably and Doe had felt worse, because they had an asshole in common.

Jem picked at the hole in her jeans. "Everyone keeps telling me it's not my fault."

Doe sighed. "You didn't make the wind. You weren't the crew. You weren't the curator who forgot the instructions and didn't tell the crew to take the things down. And you weren't the guy who fooled around with a fifteen-year-old. First time?"

A deep blush began on Jem's cheeks and spread to her neck. "Yeah."

"Shit, that sucks." Doe adjusted her position, which hurt, so she relied on eye contact to signal interest.

Jem looked at her hands. "Annie says you're nice."

"I like Annie."

"I do, too. I sort of trashed her. I mean, we used to be friends."

"Yeah. She still likes you, though. She hates that girl Meret."

"Yeah."

"It's funny how people you don't even like sort of make you do things," Doe said. "I remember that from high school. Don't worry, it wears off."

Jem snapped off a thread and wound it around her finger until it was white.

"Hey," Doe said. "Every single person on the planet has been an idiot about sex, okay?"

"Even you?"

"Oh, dude. Especially me." Doe waited. She wanted to still Jem's hands and rub some circulation back in that finger, but she knew better.

"There was this thing he said," Jem said.

"Uh-huh."

Jem twisted in the chair. "I said something about how weird it would be if his stepmom and my dad got married. And he said he thought that would be so cool, because hey, easy access for him. It was so . . . awful the way he said it."

"Pig," Doe said.

"I got pissed. So I said, Wow, how romantic. What the eff. And he said I was cute, because I wouldn't say fuck. So already I'm thinking, How can I want to get with this person if I don't even like him?"

"Well, that happens sometimes," Doe said.

Jem twisted even more in the chair, winding her ankles around the legs. There was more.

"What else did he say?" Doe asked.

Jem dropped her head. "So he said, Are you a little girl after all, the little girl who can't even say fuck, even when she wants it so bad?" Tears squeezed out of Jem's eyes, and Doe watched them drip. "I hated him, and I did it anyway! I'm so stupid!"

Doe placed her hands under the covers and squeezed. The problem was that the world was full of men like this.

"Thank you for hitting him really hard," Jem said.

"My pleasure."

Jem's face was now gross with tears and snot, so Doe groped for the box with the flimsy one-ply tissues that didn't do shit. Did that make sense in a hospital, a building full of tears? She slid the box across the bed toward Jem.

"Let me guess. He called you Beauty."

Jem looked at her over the tissue.

"He said, Let's be alone, just us. I like the sound of that. Just us."

"How do you . . . oh." Jem twisted the tissue. "Oh."

"I told you I was an idiot. Look, I don't want to make you feel bad. I did a lot of things at fifteen that were worse than this. The thing is, you've got a gift you didn't even ask for. You're beautiful. You've got to be careful with that. Anybody will want to get with you, but you've got to think it through."

Listen to her, giving advice. Easy enough, especially with her acres of hindsight.

"Someday," Doe said, "you're going to be sitting in some dorm room, talking about your first time, and you're going to say 'Bouncy castle,' and everybody's going to scream. I'm telling you, you're going to kill it with that story, for the rest of your life."

Jem smiled a little. "But it will never be funny, because you almost died."

The sweetness of this girl! Doe remembered watching Teletubbies while Shane got out the kitchen door. How long had he been out there? How long did it take before she looked around and saw his bowl of Lucky Charms abandoned? The milk stained pink. Not long. Maybe two minutes. Three. Long enough. Seconds and minutes counted, and who knew that better than her?

"Hey, we're a team," Doe said. "We survived Howl's Moving Castle, dude."

"Are you really okay, though?" Jem asked.

I don't know, Doe wanted to say, and she felt like crying.

Shari pushed open the door, followed by Ruthie. "We have doughnuts!" She saw Jem, slapped down the bag, and hugged her. "Honey! You were so brave! There you were, holding on for dear life, and I'm thinking, *Jump, jump,* but you waited for the exact right time! And you jumped! So brave!"

"Not really," Jem said. "Doe was the brave one. She's the one who said *Go!* And she's the one who got hurt."

"You know what I say, there's a crack in everything," Shari said. "That's what glue is for."

Doe dropped her face in her hands and groaned. "One time my mom picked me up at school in seventh grade," she said.

"Not that story!" Shari cried. "Doe!"

". . . and all the car windows were down, and Shania Twain was blasting, and she was wearing a bikini top and orange pants, and she got out of the car and waved and yelled my name and everyone saw."

"She yelled your *name*?" Jem repeated, in horror.

Shari shook her head, placing the doughnuts on the bed tray, pushing a cup of coffee toward Doe. Smiling as big as a river.

"Believe me, compared with that? This is nothing," Doe said. Taking the coffee, smiling into the cup.

64

THE BREEZE OFF the water brought a green, loamy smell Ruthie's way. She pictured peeling emotion off her nerves like bark off a tree, leaving her a pale column of oak. Like one of those mortals who got changed into a tree. She'd like to be a tree.

She felt calm.

First, Adeline.

Mike was with Jem, helping her pack. She had a little time.

Adeline opened the door. She didn't look glowy and perfect. She looked like an aging beautiful woman with troubles, surrounded by cartons and suitcases. She said hello in a distracted way. "Come in, I'm sorry, I promise this will all be organized in some fashion. I know you and Jem are moving back in this week."

"Don't worry about it."

Ruthie stopped short. The painting was on the floor, leaning against a wall.

"Joe Bloom brought it over this morning," Adeline said, waving at it. "Apparently Lucas found it in a storage unit."

"I know, I saw it at the Belfry last night."

"Well, Daniel can't buy it." Adeline gave it a quick glance. "I hate it."

"Well, it's not . . . flattering."

"It's not that. It's a stupid thing. Embarrassing to admit, really. I think you'll understand because you knew Peter so well. How he was with women."

"Well, sure."

"The thing is, if he turned his attention to you, he sort of . . . enshrined you. And you felt you were . . . special among women. If you were vulnerable to that, he had you. And I was vulnerable. Now I know, of course, how dumb I was. I loved him. But this . . . that he could paint me this way. Well. I deserve it. It's my fault for wanting to be first among women." She looked at the painting. "Jeez."

"We all want to be first," Ruthie said.

Adeline wrung her hands. Ruthie had never seen anyone do that before, and now she understood the term, watching Adeline's slender, well-kept hands squeezing, rotating, squeezing.

"Lucas had sex with Jem last night," Ruthie said.

Adeline gasped. "What? When?"

"In the bouncy castle."

"Oh, my God. How is she?"

"She's okay. She's shook up, of course."

"He didn't—"

"No. Completely consensual. If there's such a thing with a fifteen-year-old. Which there isn't."

Adeline sat down slowly. "No, there isn't, is there." Her hands were still, and she stared at them, clasped in her lap in a prayer position. "What are we going to do?"

"We have to talk to him."

"I'll get him."

"Maybe first we should—" Ruthie started, but Adeline was already moving fast, her bare feet thudding against the hardwood.

She rapped on his door. "Lucas. Lucas."

"I'm not awake."

"Come out here. Now. It's important."

"Christ, you're kidding me."

"Now!" Adeline returned to the kitchen. They said nothing, just stood and waited in silence. In a few moments they heard the bedroom door open.

Lucas entered the room in a pair of shorts and no shirt, his hair messy. "Ruthie," he said. "What are you doing here? Is there coffee?"

"Apparently you had sex with Jem last night," Adeline said.

Lucas said nothing, but his gaze went from Adeline to Ruthie. "Is that what she says?"

"So it's true. Terrific. This is just what I need. Lucas!"

"Let's forget about the fact that I was almost *killed* last night!" Lucas crossed to the cupboard and took out a cup. "That bouncy castle thing blew like fifty feet in the air!"

"And you jumped out and left Jem in it," Ruthie said. "And Doe."

"I told them I'd go first," Lucas said. "It seemed safer."

"Oh, please," Ruthie said.

"I was going to hold it down!"

"Lucas! Let's get back to the sex part," Adeline said.

"He's been pursuing Jem all summer," Ruthie said. "Or maybe I should say *grooming* her."

Lucas slammed down the cup. "Oh, here we go."

"She's fifteen!" Adeline cried.

"I didn't know that."

"Of course you did," Adeline said. "Don't lie to me!"

"I didn't *at first*. So there's an age difference. Look at you and your handyman!" Lucas smirked. "At least I kept it in the family."

Ruthie breathed out her nose. She was going to stay calm because it was the way to win. "If we want to get technical, it's rape," Ruthie said.

Adeline closed her eyes.

"So what are you going to do, call the police, Ruthie?" Lucas asked. "I'd think twice about that if I were you."

"I have thought about it," Ruthie said. "A lot. Believe me."

Suddenly he lunged over the counter. "You fucking bitch!"

Adeline moved faster than Ruthie imagined she could. She placed herself between them and shoved Lucas back. He knocked into the table and a cup turned over, spilling coffee before rolling off and smashing on the floor.

"What the fuck!" Lucas yelled. "Don't push me!"

He sounded like a child. Adeline took a step toward him, her palm out. "This will not happen. You will not threaten, you will not raise your voice, you will shut up and listen to me."

"I don't listen to you," Lucas said, but he looked unnerved as he leaned against the counter and crossed his arms.

"The law says there's no such thing as consent at Jem's age," Ruthie said. "Just so you know."

"This is ridiculous," Lucas said. "I just want you to know, Ruthie, she pursued me, okay?"

"Yes, I'm sure you're completely innocent, as usual," Adeline said, rubbing her forehead. "And in another minute, you'll tell me you're the victim."

"Here we go again." Lucas went to a thermos on the counter. He got another mug and poured himself coffee. "All the things that are wrong with me, right? Maybe you should have given one fucking shit about how I was raised. How I was shafted. He tied me to you, knowing that we hated each other." He held his cup in two hands and sipped.

"I don't hate you, Lucas," Adeline said. "I never hated you. I tried. You got a bad deal, and you made it worse." She rubbed her mouth. "How am I going to tell Michael?" she asked, but she wasn't asking them.

"It all comes back to you, doesn't it. Who cares." Lucas threw his coffee in the sink. "This is slop. I'm going out."

"You are not going out until we talk about this!"

"I'm sick of being blamed!" He stomped into his room, pulled on a shirt, grabbed his keys, slammed the door.

Adeline lowered herself into a chair. "My fault," she said. "I should have seen something. I didn't see a thing. They weren't together in this house, I promise you."

"It was only the one time. And I didn't see it, either," Ruthie said. "I think the fault is mine."

Adeline pressed her fingers against her eyes. "When are you going to tell Michael? Should we tell him together?"

Ruthie took Lucas's cup and rinsed it. It was one of her favorites, the one she saved for her tea. She'd never drink out of it again. She dried her hands and sat across from Adeline.

"I'm not going to tell him."

"What?"

She folded the dish towel and pushed it away. "Do you remember your first time?"

"What?"

"Was it lovely? Was it meaningful? Was it your true love? Do you cherish the memory?"

Adeline laughed. "Hardly. It was the guy my parents hired to paint the house. A college student. He wore white overalls with no shirt underneath. I was dazzled. He went back to school and never called me again. We did it in his truck. I was sixteen."

"Mine was my high school boyfriend," Ruthie said. "I held him off for months and then we did it at a party. It lasted about a minute. He broke up with me a week later."

"Girls." Adeline shook her head. "What we get through."

"It's just part of our story," Ruthie said. "Look, I'm trying to figure out the right thing. I'm trying to see around corners. My daughter lost her virginity to a twenty-three-year-old. How she'll deal with that over time is something I can't see. There are so many traumas we absorb and then we just get on with it. We didn't tell our fathers about how we lost our virginity, did we? Or our mothers? I don't want to paper over this, but I know that if Mike knew, he'd never be able to look at Lucas again."

"I know," Adeline said. "I'm not sure I can, either."

"Or even hear his name. Ever. And that would be the end for you both."

Adeline opened her mouth, but then closed it. "But I can't keep a secret from him."

"I know, it feels terrible. For me, too. Mike and I are still partners when it comes to Jem. She doesn't want him to know, she's adamant. I can't believe I'm saying this, but I think I agree."

"Why would you do that for us?"

"I'm doing it for Jem," Ruthie said. She felt impatient. Adeline was staring at her hands. *Keep up,* she wanted to say. But then she'd had hours to think about this, to plan. "Having her father know would bring it home in a fresh way. Seeing Mike would be painful and embarrassing for her, and for a long time. If the two of us can keep this secret, I think we have a shot at keeping things okay for Jem. But Lucas can't ever be in the same room with her again."

There was a pause. "I can do that," Adeline said.

"Send him away."

"I can do that, too." Adeline nodded. "It's time. We've come to the end of the road."

"And buy this house."

Adeline lifted her head, startled. "What does that have to do with Lucas?"

"It has to do with Jem. I think it will be good for her to still have this place to come to."

"I have an accepted bid on another house."

"Oh."

"But I can still get out of it. Ruthie, are you sure? I mean about all of it."

"Very sure."

"All right, then. That's what we'll do." Adeline looked at her hard. "Why are you doing this? You're protecting Jem, but you're protecting me, too. I thought you hated me."

"I just want the best outcome," Ruthie said.

Adeline only grimaced. "I don't know what that is, in the middle of all this mess."

She thought of Mike and Adeline glimpsed through a window,

his hand on her head. "I don't want to sound like a complete cheeseball," Ruthie said. "But it's when love wins."

Adeline's gaze traveled back to the painting. "Joe told me to buy the painting from Lucas. But not actually buy it, give him an advance on his inheritance. Personally I never want to see it again. I know he wants to move to LA."

"That's good."

Ruthie heard the kitchen door shut, and Mike and Joe walked in.

Mike immediately saw the sign of distress on Adeline's face. "Roberta?"

"No, I haven't heard anything." She turned to Ruthie and Joe. "I'm waiting for a call. Roberta . . . hasn't been well. She's been in the city for tests." Adeline's eyes filled with tears. "It's just that . . . she's my *person,* you know?"

Penny, Ruthie thought. "I know."

The cellphone on the table rang, and Adeline jumped. She grabbed it and walked quickly out of the room. Mike started after her.

Joe inclined his head toward Ruthie. "I think we should go."

As they moved to the front door Ruthie saw Mike reach Adeline. He put his hands on her shoulders. He bent his head close to hers. Adeline leaned back against him and gripped his hand while she pressed the phone tightly to her ear.

They walked out, quietly shutting the door, out onto the lawn.

Ruthie opened her mouth to speak, but Joe started talking.

"Adeline will never show the painting," he said. He looked over her head, over at a bush, anywhere but at her face. "Some paintings have bad karma. This one was designed to hurt someone."

Shamed. She was shamed. He knew she'd painted it and he despised her for it.

Except she had this need to *confess.*

"This is best for everyone," Joe said. "Sometimes the right thing happens if we let it."

He was talking fast, filling up the silence, because he didn't want her to confess. If she did, she would implicate him as well. That was clear. She would have to take a reprieve she didn't deserve. Just like Lucas.

It would always be between her and Joe. Any future, closed.

She had already done that, the first time she'd laid down a brushstroke of blue.

"People mourn the end of summer, but I'm happy," Joe said, his tone shifting. "Business slows down but the oysters just get better. What about you? Fall plans?"

"I have no idea," she said. "It's all up in the air."

Up in the air. Ruthie stopped, aghast. The words echoed, the way they do when you say the worst thing at the worst possible time. If there was sympathy between the two of you, you acknowledged it. Ruefully, the near-miss of the accident still fresh, you smiled, maybe you even laughed. Someone would maybe say, "Too soon?" And the remark became part of your history together, the anecdote you started and the other person finished. *Remember that time . . .*

"Goodbye, Ruthie," Joe said.

65

DOE STOPPED FOR sandwiches for dinner. They would pack tonight, and take the early ferry tomorrow. They would drive
through Connecticut, they would drive through New York, they
would cross the Hudson, they would find New Jersey. They would
drive through states they'd never been to, Pennsylvania, Indiana,
Illinois, unfashionable states where a farmhouse with a porch
didn't cost a million dollars. She would have to hear Shari cry
with joy at every charming town, every vista, "Maybe we should
live *here*!"

A miracle, people were saying about her landing. Who would
have thought you'd land in a pool, on top of an oversized inflatable pool toy?

Unlike some other unlucky person, a kid, for example, who
wanted to show his sister that he could swim, and didn't have an
inflatable mutant to land on. Why would one drown, and not the
other? There was no answer to that question, and yet you still had
to go on living.

When she pulled up there was a Porsche in her driveway and
Daniel was sitting on her lawn, cross-legged. His hoodie was up.

She got out slowly. It saved time if you were willing for a scene to play out. She sat next to him, grunting with pain as she lowered herself down. He didn't even open his eyes. What an arrogant bastard. She tried not to wonder what Daniel wanted, because what was the good of that.

At last she heard him exhale, and he swept off the hood. She expected him to ask how she was, but of course he didn't.

"I've been on the phone with lawyers all morning," he said. "Lark is dealing with the Belfry board. Dodge is threatening to sue us for negligence and for harming his reputation."

"And then there's me," Doe said.

"I'm prepared to make you an offer," he said.

Well, of course. How could it be that she had gone through almost an entire day without realizing this moment would happen? How could it be that the girl who looked for the big chance had missed the one staring her in the face and blowing a horn?

"It's predicated on a couple of things," he said. "First, our friendship. That's why I'm here, talking to you—you're hard to find, by the way—instead of my lawyers."

"Yeah, thanks for all the feels," Doe said. "I'm doing fine. Contusions, a ligament tear, every muscle hurts. No worries."

"Second, you were present at the studio visit in which Dodge explained the weather parameters of the sculptures—"

"I was there as a friend only," Doe said.

"—and witnesses report that instead of trying to secure the castle or locate the crew you climbed inside it. Lastly, Lark, before leaving for the night, told you, as an employee of the museum, to alert the crew to take down the sculptures immediately."

"She didn't!"

"The settlement is one point five million," Daniel said. "Considering that your MRI was clear and you have a couple of bruised ribs, I find that generous."

Doe said nothing.

"You did not graduate nor attend Reed College," Daniel said. "That's about the extent of my investigation into your background, but I'm sure there's more. You, Doe, are a girl on the make, and girls on the make always have things to hide."

Was that what she was, a girl on the make? Quite the little operator?

In the movies, the girl walks away from the money. The decent girl.

"All medical expenses will be covered in addition, of course," Daniel said.

The question pressed against her teeth, it came from someplace that was almost like a howl. *Is Lark a part of this?*

Shari popped out of the house, the wind whipping her hair. She held up a plastic bin full of toiletries. All those shampoos and conditioners and body oils and shower gels she had brought into the house, crowding the bathtub ledges. *Fortune favors the moisturized!* In another life, Shari and Lark would have bonded over lemongrass.

Shari didn't recognize Daniel, sitting in his hoodie, looking like a neighbor. You couldn't spot summer-weight cashmere from that far away.

"What should I do with these?" she shouted.

"Toss them!"

"Are you crazy? It's L'Oréal! We should start packing the car!"

Daniel gave her a sharp glance. "You're moving?"

Shari laughed as the breeze blew back her hair. She leaned forward against the wind, frozen in position.

"Look at me, I'm a mime!" she yelled.

Doe laughed.

It felt strange.

It didn't mean that anything lightened—not leaving, not being trapped in a car for two days with her mother, not heading to odious Belinda—but it was good to remember that Shari could make her laugh occasionally.

The screen door banged behind Shari. The sound drove her crazy. Doe was used to the door, she always stopped and caught it with the sole of her foot and eased it closed, an action that was by now involuntary. Shari let it bang. It was one of a thousand irritants that made up her mother.

One of the thousand irritants that made up love.

"How's Lark?" she asked.

"She's fine. She'll deal with this and move on."

"She's a mess," Doe said. "Her first big curatorial gig, her first big event at the museum, and it goes so far wrong you can't even imagine. I was just at the market, everyone is talking about her. A hyena ended up on Sally Jameson's roof. A wolf in the electrical wires. Someone almost died. That would be me. Criminal negligence, I think you'd call it."

Doe stood—she tried not to grunt, but she did, the movement catching her breath—and continued, "So I'm supposed to say that I'm the one who was negligent, and I guess I can't sue myself, so, good solution. This is what you do, right? You goad her and push her, she fails, you cover it up."

"Your point?"

"I don't have one, really. I'm just sad about it."

"Take the deal, Doe."

Doe hesitated.

"Well? It goes off the table as soon as I get in the car."

The Porsche door opened. Lark got out. How had Doe missed her? The sight of her made her weak in the knees. No internal injuries. What a laugh.

"Get back in the car!" Daniel roared as she walked up.

"Oh, Daddy, be quiet." Lark stood in front of Doe. She looked at her a long time, and reached to touch the bruise on her chin. "I'm glad you're okay."

"I'm not okay," Doe said.

"They said nothing was broken—"

"That's not what I mean."

"You really hurt me," Lark said.

"I'm sorry."

"That's the first time you said that, you know? It shouldn't have been so hard to say."

"Whole *songs* have been written about how hard that is to say."

"Shut up," Lark said, crying. "You look so awful."

Behind Lark, Doe could see Shari on the lawn, holding a suitcase, standing still, as though by not moving she could make it happen.

Or Doe could make it happen, maybe.

She carefully put her arms around Lark. She leaned in. She smelled . . . nothing. No lavender, no grapefruit, no essential oil of anything except Lark's real scent, the scent she had come to know in the dark, in the places she'd been the most real with another person. Lark had not perfumed herself this morning. By the smell of her hair, she hadn't even showered.

She felt Lark's arms encircle her. She touched a sore place, and Doe tried not to wince.

"Did I ruin it?" Doe asked, whispering.

"Do I really fall for everything? Because it kind of devalues what I'm falling for, here. If you follow it to its logical concl—"

"Shut up," Doe said, and kissed her.

"Okay, I think we need to reevaluate our next step," Daniel said, and Shari clapped her hands in applause while Daniel winced, and so, a new dysfunctional family was born.

66

ON TUESDAY THE machinery of the world began to turn again. School bells rang, buses flatulated their way along the roads. Ruthie walked through the rooms of her own house.

There were tiny differences: a vase moved a few inches, a spatula in the wrong drawer. Some very nice French wine had been left in the laundry room. A new vinegar in the pantry. Crackers still in a wicker basket from Locavoracious. A puzzling abundance of tissue boxes. A tiny splat of blood on the wall in the guest room, perhaps a residue of a squashed mosquito. An echo of other lives. In no other year had Ruthie felt the imprint of summer tenants. This year she did.

RUTHIE WALKED THE Manhattan streets like a native, even though she knew she would be taken as a tourist. She looked like what she was, a suburban mom visiting the city for the day, searching for a restaurant picked by a more sophisticated friend.

Daydreaming, she got on the subway at Penn Station but forgot to get off at 42nd to transfer to the shuttle, so she decided she had time to exit at 59th and cut across the park to the East Side. She hadn't reckoned on the heat slowing her steps. The sun still blazed in early September. A new skyscraper—a needle poking the sky—was under construction. She'd read about these new buildings in Midtown, how the penthouses would be ninety-plus stories up, looking down on clouds. How the buildings had to be calibrated to offset a human's normal instinct for danger, the elevators at precise speeds to forestall unsettling g-forces, gigantic dampers that acted as shock absorbers so that the sway could be controlled. It wasn't that the buildings were unsafe, it was that humans did not feel safe in them without unseen assurances settling their equilibrium.

Life did not offer the same assurances. There were no cosmic engineers. Equilibrium was a matter of trust as well as balance.

She was going to be late, or sweaty. She had to choose one. She chose sweat. When she reached Madison every article of clothing was damp, from her underwear to her shoes. She couldn't find the restaurant and placed a finger on her phone to unlock it, but her finger was too wet to register her identity.

She realized she was in fact standing in front of the restaurant. She pushed open the door, ready for anything—iced tea, salad, consequence, jail.

She spotted Carole along the wall, looking cool and polished. She bent to kiss her cheeks, one, other, back in for another.

They commiserated about the heat while they perused their menus.

"Isn't this marvelous?" Carole said. "I want everything. I'm so dying for a real American meal. Can you believe I've gone a whole summer without a lobster roll? I'm tempted by the cheeseburger."

After they ordered—Ruthie got the lobster roll, Carole ordered a salad—Carole leaned over the table. "So how are you, really? I heard about what happened at the Belfry. So distressing!"

"Yes," Ruthie said. "Someone could have been killed."

Carole shuddered. "Thank God. Can you imagine how awful? The publicity has been bad enough."

"How was Paris?" Ruthie asked.

"Glorious. Isn't it always? And we went to the Île de Ré in August. You must go someday. These French children have such beautiful manners in restaurants. You just want to start the whole parenting thing all over. Now Dash wants to go to the Lycée Français. I say, do you know how many hoops I had to go through to get you into Dalton? No bread, please," she said sweetly to the server, who was hovering over them with tongs. "Oh, God, we're off the track. I'm here to find out about you. How's the job search?"

"Picking up. It was slow in the summer."

"You know you have me as a reference. I'll sing your praises. You were the best director the Belfry ever had."

"So why did I lose my job, Carole?"

"Those people are so awful. I sat in those meetings, and I wanted to just run out of the room."

"So why didn't you, Carole?"

"Helen is so upset. Now she thinks Mindy is crazy. She canceled her end-of-year party, you know. The invitations had already gone out!"

"No, I didn't know. I wasn't invited. So why didn't you stop her?"

"Oh, who can stop Helen?"

"No, Mindy. Catha, too. You knew she was after my job."

The lobster roll arrived in an explosion of chive. Ruthie stared down at it, a glossy pink lump. She could not imagine eating it. She took a sip of her iced tea. Carole picked a sliced roasted pepper out of her salad.

"I hate roasted peppers," she said. "Why do they put them on salads without telling you?" She scraped them onto her bread plate.

Ruthie pushed a box across the table.

"It's a texture problem," Carole said. "Slimy." Then she noticed the box. "What's this? Did you get me a present? And I didn't bring you back anything from Paris! You know how the city closes down in August!"

"It's not a present," Ruthie said. "And it comes with a story."

Carole opened the box and took out the watch. "Oh, my God! You found it! Why didn't you *tell* me? I looked everywhere in the city this weekend. Lewis is ready to divorce me."

"I found it in Verity's dress-up box," Ruthie said.

Carole sat back. "That's amazing. That little thief! I should have known! But when?"

"Right before Spork. I wore it with the pink shirt and the white pants."

Carole went very still. "You wore Lewis's watch?"

"I didn't know it was Lewis's watch. I thought it was a knock-off. Along with all the other junk in Verity's box."

"But I called you . . ."

"By then I had misplaced it."

Carole's face! Such confusion! "But . . . I looked in every pocket, every purse, every *shoe*! I almost ripped open the linings of our suitcases! I've never been so desperate!"

Ruthie gripped her hands under the table and told her the story. How panicked she was, how she just wanted time to find it. That she was sorry.

"So between the time I called and today, it's . . . over a month? And you let me think it was missing?" Carole's tone was icy.

"I kept thinking I'd find it. I was a little crazy. I'd lost my job, I was going to lose my house . . ."

"Lose your house? Why?"

"Because I'd lost my job," she said.

Carole looked confused. "But why would you lose your house?"

"Because that's what happens, sometimes. I just sold it to Adeline Clay."

"Adeline Clay is going to live in Orient?"

"I'm just here to give you the watch and profoundly apologize for all the worry I caused you."

Carole pushed the plate away with its stripes of red pepper. "Ruthie, I don't know what to say. It's an *all's well that ends well* situation, I guess." She put the watch back in the box and tucked it in her purse. "So where do you think you'll move? Back to the city?"

The seconds ticked on while Ruthie stared at Carole. The bright, birdlike interest, the frown at the continuing presence of a roasted pepper in her salad, the mask of affability.

"Can we go back to the question?" Ruthie asked. "About why you didn't stop Mindy? About why you didn't warn me that Catha was after my job?"

"I told you she wasn't your friend!"

"That was a little vague, don't you think? Do you think if I'd known that she was actively trashing my reputation behind my back to everyone who held my future in their hands, I might have done something differently?"

"Well, I don't know. Isn't it a moot point?"

"And then why *reward* her for lying? The committee then handed her my job. She'd still have it, if Lark hadn't come along."

Carole smiled, a tight, patronizing smile Ruthie had never seen before. "This is turning from an apology into an interrogation."

"Imagine this, though," Ruthie said. "Imagine if everybody who was distressed at what Mindy was doing said it out loud, instead of behind her back."

"Well, that wouldn't change her."

"I'm not talking about changing her. I'm talking about *the right thing to do.*"

"I was in the Hebrides! I did everything I could!"

"You didn't answer my emails for weeks."

"They told me I shouldn't contact you until the paper was signed. Listen, I'm all about transparency. It was hard for me."

"All along, you could have done one thing. One thing simpler than all the rest. You could have told the truth about how you felt. Publicly. You could have stood up and said *This is happening and it's wrong.*"

"I don't know why I'm getting the brunt of your anger, Ruthie," Carole said. "All this rehashing is so pointless. And I wasn't even going to mention that Baccarat wineglass that's missing at the house. Margarita told me about it."

"I'm not angry anymore," Ruthie said. "Truly I'm not. I'm just trying to understand how it all happened. Now the Belfry is being run by someone who will change it utterly. I don't think Lark Mantis cares about schoolchildren and family day." Ruthie folded her napkin. "But that's not my concern. My concern is finding another job and a place to live." She pushed back her chair.

"I'm truly sorry about the watch," she said. "But now I'm going to do what you did back in July. I'm going to leave you sitting alone. And stick you with the bill."

67

From: Jemma Dutton
To: Olivia Freeman
Subject: prepare yourself

Hi it's me.

This is an apology. The biggest sorry in the world.

I was awful to you. I sucked. I ruined it.

All this summer I've been writing to you. Because bff. Best friend forever means forever. You were the one who always listened, all those years of my "you knows" and my "I can't explain it buts."

I don't know if you'll read all of them. The emails I'll send after this one. If you want to write back that would be so great. If you don't, if you don't even feel like reading them, that's ok. I mean, I get it. Writing them was worse than social studies essays. Reading them won't be any better.

First day of school. I was kind of famous because of what happened. Everybody coming up and asking me, Whoa, what was it like? So only a few kids wore #mayflower shirts. (if you read the emails, you'll get all this.) I sat with Annie at lunch, and kids kept coming over and sitting with us and dragging chairs over until we were so crowded we started throwing pretzels at each other and that's when they made us stop. It was cool.

Mom and Dad will be moving. Not together, no. No chance of that! Which means I will be moving, too. Yeah, that's the big news and if you want to know why you'll have to read the emails.

I fell in love this summer. Or thought I did. He was too old for me and he lied to me and treated me like shit and even stole a watch I think—I mean, it disappeared and he was there when it did and now that I know him better I think it was him—and I had to lie about it and in the end he was the biggest coward you ever saw.

I almost blew away this summer, Ollie. There's something about almost blowing away that makes you see everything different. Like, I'm not scared of moving to the city or whatever we have to do. I kind of want to. You did it. Let me know how it was, and this time really tell me.

I ran out of friends this summer. I got a few back today. I'm hoping maybe I have another one and that's you.

So. Start with Memorial Day. Labor Day requires a conversation. I'm pressing Send on the summer. Here I go.

xojem

68

THE DUSK WAS softer than soft. A wisp of color in the sky. Lamps lit. The light was blue. Bluer than blue. Across the dark water was a tiny spray of lights.

She left the Jitney and turned down Village Lane. At the wharf she stopped and looked back. Lamps were lit in half the houses. Once they had been owned by farmers and sea captains. Orient had been a prosperous town with a busy harbor. Now it was a town that was often half full.

It was too warm for fall, but it was fall. The summer renters were gone. The summer people would be back to sail on weekends, to enjoy summer's last gasp, but this night the breeze smelled like dry leaves.

Since the castle flew in the air the calls and texts had come in. *How is Jem. How are you. What can I do. Can I drop off dinner for you. We are making halibut on the grill come on over.* And from Penny: *We would like to see you both.*

They were having dinner tonight.

Landscapes spoke to people. Something that went past the heart and lodged deeper. This place spoke to her. It would hurt her to leave it. But people left places all the time if they had to. Then you opened a drawer and found a key to a lock to a door that was no longer yours.

She turned down the road to her house and wondered how many more times she would turn this way, her feet on a familiar road. It would be a number, fifty or one hundred, or more, but one of the times she turned it would be the last.

69

JEM'S PHONE

To: Jemma Dutton
From: Olivia Freeman
Re: madsummer

Too much to absorb in one binge-reading episode sitting at work (meet Iowa City's premier ice cream scooper!) and will reply in detail but just to say for now: Are you insane? Bffs. That last f means forever, bitch.

Independence
Day

70

IT HAD BEEN a winter of crazy weather, sudden spells of warmth, swift and violent storms. Ruthie and Jem had been insulated in the city, where even big snows melted in days and in a blizzard you could still find takeout. There was none of the cabin fever of Orient, because city streets were made for walking.

They'd moved over Thanksgiving break. Ruthie had packed alone, throwing away as much as she could, whittling down clothes, boots, coats, books, vases, casseroles, candles. Her goal was fifteen boxes. Adeline had bought the furniture, too, the dishes and the pots and the blankets, and she would use Ruthie's things until her designer descended and it was all given away.

The things you find! Pine needles under the bookcase from some ancient Christmas. Christmas! Jem in footies and braids, snow on the gray bay, kisses and carols, smoked salmon and champagne on Christmas Eve. A slow waltz in the kitchen to "Silver Bells" while they ignored the dishes. Oh, the things that hit the heart so hard. Jem's height markings inside the closet. A peridot earring lost, a surprise birthday present from Mike in a lean year. In Jem's room she found a cheap best friend necklace, one half of a jagged heart. Ruthie sat down and cried, not knowing for what.

In the city at first they'd covered their ears for jackhammers, lost their MetroCards, took the express when they should have taken the local. The Upper West Side was a new land.

The first month she brought Jem to school, riding the subway together, holding hands underneath the flaps of their coats. She'd leave her three blocks away, exchange a silent *you'll be okay* gaze, and then sit with her coffee until she could move again. It was worse than dropping a three-year-old Jem at preschool.

Ruthie had found a sublet, a Columbia professor who was going on sabbatical who had one bedroom and an office. The apartment was light-filled, and he didn't mind if she brought in a bed for Jem. It was tight for both of them—one bathroom!—but it was all she could afford.

The Whitney had committed to a retrospective for Gus Romany, and that meant Gus mattered again. It turned out that Gus had been right, the new work was the best of his career. Ruthie had indeed picked up the fucking phone and gone over to his studio and told him so. He didn't need her to tell him; the Whitney was already sniffing around. Apparently Joe had seen the work earlier in the summer and passed on his thoughts. Gus had stopped by Ruthie's house the day before Thanksgiving and in the middle of the boxes and the bubble wrap had told her the news, cackling with happiness, and said by fucking God she was going to help curate the show.

He insisted to the Whitney that she was the right person, and surprisingly, they'd agreed. He needed her eye, he'd said. The money wasn't much, but it was almost enough, and she no longer had to worry about being able to afford things like the dentist for Jem. Those things were now taken care of.

Jem had slid into the best high school in District Three, the one parents pull every string to get their kid into, and now, thanks to Adeline, Jem had as many strings as she needed. Within a few weeks she came home with news of electives and clubs and this cool girl who sat with her at lunch. She'd become a self-importantly busy person, slothful in the mornings and energized at night, needing Ruthie desperately and condescending to her, yelling about bathroom time and finishing all the sesame noodles without asking. Things were back to normal.

Ruthie found her new routines. Takeout on Friday nights, researching and writing, taking Sundays off for solitary walks while Jem did her crushing load of homework. There were friends she could call, for a dinner, a drink, and she would do it someday soon. What surprised her the most about her quiet winter and spring was how often she thought of her mother. It was like discovering a new vein of grief. Maybe it was because mourning a marriage was like mourning a parent—you miss the person you wished you had, as well as the one you did.

Jem would spend the summer in Orient. Ruthie had rented a car for the drive, and the backseat was crammed with Jem's bags and boxes, plus supplies for the pantry she didn't think she could get out on the North Fork, spices, Iberian ham, and a selection of cheeses from Murray's. In less than a year, Jem had become a New Yorker.

As soon as they turned off onto the two-lane road, they were officially back on the North Fork. The road went up and down, the wooden signs announcing pies and tomatoes and cherries. When at Southold the road narrowed and they saw the Sound, just a flat gray on this overcast day, Jem grabbed her arm. They hadn't been out to the North Fork since they'd moved to the city.

The Orient house had been renovated, Adeline pushing an architect to complete a two-phase plan so the first phase—the kitchen, Mike's new studio, the home gym—would be ready for the summer. Next year the whole house would be jacked up in case of another hurricane storm surge, and the deck expanded. The house, Ruthie knew, would no longer look the same.

"When we get to Orient, can we stop at the store for a salted oatmeal cookie?" Jem asked. She lowered the window and stuck her head out like a dog, sniffing. She'd cut off her long hair and wore it cropped very short.

"Of course." Ruthie knew she would cry when she dropped off Jem for the summer, but like any mother, she would do it after driving away. She would head to Penny and Elena's for coffee, and she would leave after lunch, against the traffic. She could not spend a night in Orient.

Mike and Adeline had married in the spring, a quiet wedding after Roberta's funeral. It was strange not to have to worry about the big things now, about college expenses and launching Jem into the world. Vacations were now taken care of—there were already plans to take Jem to Italy next year. Ruthie would be left behind, but that was okay, that was fine, all her pleasure now was watching her daughter explore the world. Penny had called her Mildred Pierce without the melodrama.

They passed the Belfry, now a construction site. The old sign was gone. Instead a new sign had been erected: THE MANTIS FOUNDATION.

It had taken almost a year, but Daniel had dismantled the board, Lark had fired the staff, and she was at work on the renovation for the private museum that would bear his name. Access would be limited to "scholars," which meant no family days, no after-school art classes, no local artists' organization, no school outreach. The historical collection had been donated to the Southold Historical Society.

Mindy, having facilitated the changeover, had clearly done it for a seat on a more prestigious board, but Daniel had squeezed her out. Her house in Southold was on the market. Ruthie heard that she and Carl were looking in Quogue. Catha was now selling real estate in Mattituck.

New executive director Lark Mantis had been profiled in the current issue of *Vogue,* along with her partner, Doe Callender, for the article "They Call It New Hampton: A Power Art Couple Defines Cool on the North Fork."

They stopped for the best salted oatmeal cookie in the world.

That was the same. Ruthie paused on the porch of the market, just to inhale. Orient smelled like nowhere else in the world in the summer: salt, sea, lavender, pine, rugosa, lilies.

Jem jumped back in the car and they drove to the house. Ruthie pulled up, took a breath, and told herself she could do this.

The hydrangeas were gone. She had expected that, Penny had warned her. *"I heard Adeline hired Anna Wintour's garden designer, so don't freak the fuck out."* The scraggly bushes had been replaced with boxwood. The lawn was now a meadow with clover and clouds of Russian sage. The white stones were gone; a pathway of trimmed grass made a desire path to the front porch. Pink roses tumbled in profusion with small fireworks of white allium.

Mike stood outside, waiting. He'd taken to wearing tortoise-shell glasses, and they made him look younger. Or maybe that was because Adeline had introduced him to her dermatologist.

"How was the drive?" he asked her as he helped Jem lift her duffel from the trunk.

"Not too bad. We left before the birds."

"Let me." He hauled a tote bag out and put it on the grass. "Come in for a coffee?"

"No, thanks, Penny and Elena are cooking a second breakfast."

"Then come by for a drink later?"

With the invitation was a plea—*please make this easier.*

"Not today," she said. "I'm heading back this afternoon. But sometime."

"Mom!" Jem hurled herself into Ruthie's arms. Soft cheek, resounding kiss, a squeeze that left her without breath. "I'll miss you! And I'm coming to the city for lots of weekends."

Ruthie knew she wouldn't. The rhythm of summer would overtake her.

Adeline emerged and came toward them. She leaned in to kiss Ruthie on the cheek. "We'll take good care of her," Adeline said.

"Can Annie come over for dinner?" Jem asked.

"Of course!" Adeline said. "We're making all your favorite things."

This had been what she'd feared, just this. And what was it, anyway? Just three people, one of whom was trying too hard.

Watch as the three start toward the house, Jem's arm around Mike's waist. Watch as you see through the (new, larger) front window as Jem moves through the house, exclaiming. Watch as Mike points at something, no doubt the expanded kitchen. A better stove for Jem to cook on, a bigger fridge, new counters. Everything new and better.

You get back in the car.

You drive away. You cry.

Your enemies are not your enemies forever. Time passes. Things change. They suffer losses deeper than yours. And you realize they are as befuddled as you at the way life goes. Once, they acted badly, they took what they wanted without care. They are just like you, though. At three in the morning, they wander to a window. They stand watching the night sky, and they are afraid.

RUTHIE PULLED INTO Penny and Elena's driveway. They were outside on the porch, and with them was Joe Bloom.

Okay. She could do this, too.

She took her time gathering her bag, her sunglasses, her phone, the cheese she'd brought from the city, the wine. She slammed the car door shut with her hip, and they looked up. They were waiting for her, smiling, rising. She climbed the few steps onto the porch and just dropped everything, except the wine, thank God. She hugged Penny and Elena and then, impulsively, stretched to kiss Joe, who had been stooping to pick up her sunglasses. They knocked heads, then laughed a little.

"Joe came by to get signatures for the Stop the Helipad petition," Elena said.

"Joe, stay for brunch," Penny ordered. "I have a frittata in the oven and we have the most delicious cherries. Ruthie, sit, keep Joe company while we get the food."

"I should be going," Joe said. "I didn't mean to barge in."

"Oh, stay," Elena said.

"I'll help Penny," Ruthie said. She almost ran after Penny into the kitchen.

Penny got out a tray and utensils. She slid the frittata onto a platter. She placed the napkins next to the forks.

"Why aren't you talking to me?" Ruthie asked.

"I'm talking to you, I'm just gathering words," Penny said. She turned around and slapped a knife on the tray. "What the fuck is wrong with you?"

"What?"

Penny made a downward swipe with a spatula, as if she were cutting Ruthie in two. "Enough, okay? I don't know what you're punishing yourself for, but stop it."

"Punishing myself?"

"You spent two seasons in New York in which you did nothing but eat takeout and wait for Jem to get home from school."

"I was working!"

"You connected with no one. You saw no theater. You did not go to one concert. You got the same takeout from the same Chinese restaurant every Friday night, and that might be the worst thing of all. There are *restaurants* in New York, you know. There are *neighborhoods*. You're turning into your mother."

Ruthie felt the breath knocked out of her. "That's a terrible thing to say."

"Yeah, well, if you're afraid to make left turns, you know what? You only go around in a circle."

"I make left turns! I got here, didn't I!"

"It's a metaphor, you idiot! And what's all this bullshit about you can't stay in Orient? Do you think you'll crumble if you see Adeline and Mike? Do you think when you pass the Belfry you'll burst into tears? Guess what? Sometimes you have it good for a while, and then it goes. Poof. It's called life."

"I know that!"

"And what about Joe?" Penny waved her spatula at the window. "Look at that terrific man. He pines for you."

"What? How do you know that?"

"Because I have eyes. He came here to see you, and you ran away."

"He's here collecting signatures."

"He already got our signatures, he's been here stalling until you got here. Because all winter and spring the weight of him *not* asking about you was just as comical as him asking. Wake the fuck up, dude. It's *criminal* watching you fuck up again."

"What am I supposed to do?"

"Forgive yourself, for fuck's sake!" Penny pointed the spatula at her. "Nothing's going to crash down on your head, okay? Nobody is going to fly away. I mean, sure, those things could happen, but stop *expecting* them to. You have to *abide,* dude, and the fact that you don't get that reference doesn't make me love you any less. Now go out the door and be a person. Joe made that call to the Whitney, he talked you up, you might start by thanking him."

"Joe got me the job?"

"No, asshole, you got yourself the job. He made a call. I would have done it if I could have, you needed help. Now take this and go outside, because that man is on one cheek right now. He'll leave if you're not nice to him."

She shoved Ruthie out the door with a bowl of cherries in her hands. She stopped, her head whirling. She felt as if she'd just been diced into ribbons by a spatula.

"Sit," Elena said.

Ruthie sat.

"Elena, I need your help!" Penny yodeled from the kitchen. "I can't find the good napkins!"

"She's a chef, and she acts like she's never seen a kitchen," Elena said, and went inside.

Silence. Then, "So," Joe said.

"Thank you for making the call to the Whitney, to whoever," Ruthie said.

"It was an easy call."

"Well, thank you. And thank you for . . . what you did. About the painting."

"I did it for you."

"For me?"

"I thought you knew. That day we stood outside the house. I told you that."

"No, you didn't. You said, sometimes the right thing happens."

"I gave you a significant look."

"That was significant?"

"I was trying to be cryptic!"

"You were trying to tell me not to talk about it. This way you had deniability."

Joe let out an exasperated breath. "No, I was trying to protect you without your having to confess. I talked Adeline into taking the picture because it was the right thing to happen, the only thing that made sense for everybody. Whatever made you do it, it's clear you regretted it before it went too far, so . . ."

"Did it make sense for everybody?"

"The painting was never bought, technically, so there's no record of a payment. It's been cataloged and sits in a rack. One more Peter Clay in the world, who cares. Lucas is out in LA, getting kicked off one reality show after another. Somebody torments him by posting his picture with the hashtag #chickenshit."

Ruthie laughed. "Really?" *Doe,* she thought.

"One day the real money will come in and it will be enough to really get him in trouble. That's his problem. Adeline is married to someone she considers the love of her life. And if you have a broken heart, I'm sorry. You . . . well, I don't know how you are, because you never called, but here you are."

"Here I am," Ruthie said. Here she was. In a moment he would go. She read his reluctance and confusion. She knew him that well, because she no longer knew him as Joseph Bloom, who was too good for her, too old for her, too rich for her. He was Joe. She had known his whispers and his kiss. She had known his touch and his heart, and she had treated him badly. It was time to turn left and face him. Even though it would split open her heart.

A helicopter buzzed overhead, heading out toward the point. Penny emerged from the house with a platter. She flapped a dish towel at the helicopter, as if it were a wasp. "Fuck you, fuckers!" she yelled at the sky.

"Daniel Mantis is putting a lot of influence behind the helipad," Joe said. "Limited service, he's saying. He's gaining some support. After all, we're fighting an antiquated train service and an expressway that's a parking lot. There are a few big-money people who want it to happen. The village will stop it, though."

"Yes, we'll stop it," Elena said, slicing into the frittata. "For now. Something else will come along. Everything passes, everything changes. Even Orient. The sea is going to get us one day. We'll be an island. Maybe we'll float away, all of us lesbians and lefties and arty folks. What can you do."

"Make ourselves fast," Joe said. "We belong to the mainland. They need us."

The breeze had nudged the clouds away from the sun. Ruthie lifted her face to feel it. The noise in the sky faded. She realized that her hands were fists, tightly curled, and she opened them so that her sticky palms were cooled by the wind. Today the breeze was gentle. It wouldn't knock anything down or carry anything away.

"What shall we do with this beautiful day?" Elena asked.

"I'll be opening oysters," Joe said. He looked at his watch. "Actually, I should go."

"Maybe we'll come by later," Penny said. She shot a furious look at Ruthie.

"For a glass of gorgeous wine," Ruthie said.

She smiled at Joe. A second ticked by, then another, before he smiled back.

The classic love story ends with a wedding, but it begins with a look across a distance that seems unbridgeable. Ruthie's story wasn't a love story, though, so this wasn't a beginning, or an end. It could be too late, no matter what Penny thought. No matter what she herself thought, or Joe thought, or how deeply they would fall. Whatever was going to happen could fall apart or melt away. It could be frost on a windowpane, dew on the grass. But stop, look, how beautiful is that.

Acknowledgments

DEEPEST THANKS ARE owed to the inhabitants of Orient, who were, to a person, somewhat dismayed to hear I was setting a novel in their singular and bewitching village. I did not include your suggestions of mosquito plagues and tick-borne diseases as plot points, and I apologize for that. I am certain that anyone who stumbles on your hamlet will be met with the same generous welcome and good cheer that I received. Thank you to all who answered my questions and opened your doors to me, especially Jeanne Markel and Chris Wedge.

Orient is a real place, but the village portrayed in this book is part imagination. They do not celebrate Sneak Zucchini onto Your Neighbor's Porch Day, and the Belfry Museum resides only in my imagination, as do its board members. Instead, Orient is blessed with the excellent Oysterponds Historical Society Museum, which bears no resemblance to the Belfry whatsoever, and you will spend a delightful morning there if you visit it. A special thank-you to the stupendously talented baker and owner of the Orient Country Store, Miriam Foster, for the afternoon iced teas and perhaps the only factual element in the novel, the greatest salted oatmeal cookie in the world.

I've been an observer of museum culture in a spousal role for many years. It has been a marvelous place for a writer to perch. I thank every friend, acquaintance, and dinner partner who leaned over and told me a bit of gossip. Ninety-nine percent of the board members I've known or heard about have been exemplary examples of commitment and principle. This makes for great museums, but dull novels.

Heartfelt thanks and a deep bow to friends and fellow writers who read the manuscript at various stages and gave me excellent editorial advice and a kick in the pants: Deborah Heiligman, Rebecca Stead, Susan Scofield, and Donna Tauscher.

My agent, the brilliant Molly Friedrich, was instrumental in shaping this book by telling me what was wrong with it and ordering me to finish it. There are not enough pink peonies in the world to thank her for her fearlessness, acuity, and humor. Thank you to the shining star that is Lucy Carson and the team at The Friedrich Agency. You deserve more cookies than my husband can bake.

I could not ask for a better dream team than what I have at Random House Books. Gina Centrello, Susan Kamil, Andy Ward, and Maria Braeckel, you make my heart sing. Every writer wants an editor with a mind like a scalpel and a heart like a bear. Andrea Walker is that editor.

I owe my dearest ones, Neil Watson and Cleo Watson, the deepest thanks of all, for making my house such a joyful one.

ABOUT THE AUTHOR

Judy Blundell is a *New York Times* bestselling writer for children. Her novel *What I Saw and How I Lied* won the 2008 National Book Award for Young People's Literature. She lives on Long Island with her husband and daughter.

judyblundellbooks.com
Facebook.com/judyblundellbooks
Instagram: @judyblundellbooks

ABOUT THE TYPE

This book was set in Sabon, a typeface designed by the well-known German typographer Jan Tschichold (1902–74). Sabon's design is based upon the original letter forms of sixteenth-century French type designer Claude Garamond and was created specifically to be used for three sources: foundry type for hand composition, Linotype, and Monotype. Tschichold named his typeface for the famous Frankfurt typefounder Jacques Sabon (c. 1520–80).